DAUNTLESS

SONS OF TEMPLAR MC #5

ANNE MALCOM

DAUNTLESS
The Sons of Templar MC #5
By Anne Malcom
Copyright 2016 Anne Malcom

No part of this publication may be reproduced, distributed or transmitted in any form or by any means, including photocopying, recording, or other electronic or mechanical methods, without the prior written permission of the publisher, except in the case of brief quotations embodied in critical reviews and certain other noncommercial uses permitted by copyright law.

This is a work of fiction. Names, characters, businesses, places, events, and incidents are either the product of the author's imagination or used in a fictitious manner. Any resemblance to actual persons, living or dead, or actual events, is purely coincidental.

Edited by: Hot Tree Editing
Cover Design: Kari at Cover to Cover Designs
Cover Image Copyright 2016
Formatted by Max Effect

AUTHOR'S NOTE

Lucky's story is one that I have wanted to tell since we met him in Making the Cut. I knew I couldn't write it until the time was right. His character is so much more than the joker we've met in previous books, there is darkness in him that has never seen the light of day. Until now. This is still a love story, but it's darker than I've ever gone. Bex is a complicated character with heartbreaking demons that might be triggers for some people.

This book depicts addiction, rape, child abuse and violence. It's different than previous books in the Sons of Templar series but I love every page of Bex and Lucky's story, even the parts that broke my heart to write.

I hope you fall in love too.

Anne
xxx

DEDICATION

To everyone who believes in fairytales.
And everyone who doesn't.
May you realize that happy ever afters don't exist
in real life, but sometimes we're lucky enough
to find something much better.

Love.

PROLOGUE

God, grant me the serenity
to accept the things I cannot change,
the courage to change the things I can,
and the wisdom to know the difference.

Everyone measures time differently; the most common, of course, is hours, minutes, years, days. People count the days until weekend, until their next holiday, the moment they can sink onto a sofa after a long day. That's what life is, a big yawning expanse of time, and we find different ways to measure it along the way. Pass it. Find ways to distract ourselves from the grim reality of mortality.

I say we. I mean *they*. It's tempting to include myself in the proverbial we, to give myself at least the illusion of belonging. But I don't have time for illusions. For euphemisms.

They measured time like that. I didn't. Ever since I was old enough to grasp the concept, I understood I was different. My mind never thought in those terms, searching for a yardstick to measure my existence. I was too busy trying to *survive*. I lived in the present, the moment. I had to. The luxury of daydreams or plans for the future meant getting lost in my own head. Being more vulnerable than I already was.

That's my long-winded way of saying I had a less-than-stellar childhood, where I had to be on the ball if I wanted to stay alive. If that's what it was back then.

In this yawning tunnel of the present I've found myself in for most of my life, there was a time when I did venture tentatively into the future. Made plans. Dreams.

Then it was all shot to shit.

I couldn't tell you, not even an estimate, on the amount of time I'd been in the damp concrete matchbox with a prison-style bed and steel bucket serving as the only décor. The rusty handcuff on my wrist served as my only accessory. I mean *only*; nothing else covered my body. The rough cotton sheet scratched my bruised skin when I huddled under it for warmth.

Hours. Days. Weeks. Months, even. It was possible. I couldn't say. I also couldn't say how long it had been since I'd eaten, showered.

I was measuring time differently now.

The next hit.

There was no such thing as the passing of the sand in the hourglass. The rising or setting of the sun. Only the yawning chasm of loneliness and despair between now and my next fix.

It had been a while, I knew. Too long. A thin layer of sweat covered my body, despite the chill in the air. My heart thumped in my chest, the beats seeming to hasten with every passing second. I had been deprived of my medicine, my escape, once before, and I knew it wouldn't be too long until I was hunched over that bucket, sick from not getting what I needed.

Dying. Convinced I was, anyway.

I sat on my hands, the only way to stop from picking at my skin. My eyes were glued on the steel door in the corner of the room. Not so I could devise an escape plan, but willing it to open, for my next fix to be on the other side. That was the only escape I needed.

A murky memory surfaced as I distractedly hummed a long-forgotten lullaby.

"You're stronger than this," he told me, his voice serious and soft.

"Than what?" I half hissed, aware that my voice was far from soft.

He stepped forward, cupping my chin in his hand, choosing to ignore the way my body stiffened at the contact. "Than letting some demon have control over your body, like your skin is merely a vehicle, an empty vessel," he said, eyes blazing.

I blinked, his words jabbing me like tiny spears. Anger bubbled up from the cauldron it had been simmering in. Not because he was wrong—because he was right. *That was the problem. For someone who seemed so obtuse, he knew far too much. Saw far too much.*

"You have no fucking clue what you're talking about," I snapped.

With a tilt of his head and a hardening of those hazel eyes, he saw. Saw it all. "I know what it's like to have the monkey on your back, to feel the need not to fill the void in your soul but disguise it." His hand tightened on my chin. "I may not know everything, as much as I'd like to think I do. But I at least know that. I also know what beauty is. True beauty. Mostly 'cause I'm staring straight at it. I know there's nothing I can ultimately do to make sure that beauty don't get tainted with ugly. That's up to you. What I can do is remind you that you're more. *More than you think you are. A fuck of a lot more," he declared.*

I blinked at him. His words struck a chord deep within me. Maybe it was because no matter how hard I tried to deny it, I felt something for him. Maybe it was because it was unnerving to see him so serious, not a glint of joking in his hazel eyes. Whatever it was, in that second, that moment, I believed him.

The screeching of the metal door on rusty hinges jerked me out of my daydream. *Lucky too*, I thought for a second. Maybe unluckily.

Lucky.

I wished I could stay in that intangible place in my mind, get lost in that memory. Because now, after hurtling out of it, my entire body showed what a failure I was. How weak I had been.

"Junkie ready for her medicine?" a rough voice asked.

I scrambled as close as I could to the figure in the door, not caring about my nudity. I had in the beginning.

Before.

Before I gave in, I had cared about a lot of things. What they were going to do with my body. What my future held. The fate of my friends. My only family. *Him.*

That was then. Now I didn't care about the horrors my vacant body endured while my mind numbed me from the pain of the present, took away the filth that lived under my skin. Didn't care about the pain, which there was a lot of. It was creeping back now as the numbness receded. The steel of the cuffs had scraped a lot of the skin on my wrists away. It wasn't pretty.

Though I guessed from the way I smelled, and with the matting of blood, dirt, and grease, that I wasn't going to be winning any beauty contests.

A hand reached down to squeeze my breast roughly. I flinched at the pain, intensified by the fact my body was in the first stages of withdrawal. I was unable to move far past my position on the floor, and my flinch caused my head to collide with the edge of my bed.

There was a cruel laugh from above me.

"Don't pretend you don't love it, whore. I know better than anyone how much you enjoy me, how much you want it," the voice sneered.

I glanced up, anger bubbling from deep inside me. Somehow, I managed to muster a glare filled with contempt and venom, despite my body and soul crying out for what he held in his brutish hand.

"Fuck you," I hissed in a barely audible croak. My voice was raw from screaming, although I thought I had endured it silently—the torture, the abuse of my body. Obviously not.

He grinned and I felt sick to my stomach at the sight of it. Of him. His muscled body dwarfed my small form curled on the floor. Even if I had been standing, he would have towered over me. He was built, though not all muscle; his stomach protruded over the belt of his slacks. His hair was combed over and thick with grease. His beady dull blue eyes held me captive. Not a hint of humanity lingered beyond them as they roved over my battered and filthy body.

"I'll do that soon. You'll be begging for it," he mused, then held his meaty arm out in front of me.

My eyes bulged at the object. Despite wanting to be as far away from the sick fuck as possible, my body betrayed me, lurching forward to snatch the precious package from his hands.

I wasn't quick enough, and he yanked it out of my grasp. It wasn't hard; my entire body was shaking and I barely had the energy to hold my weight. I knew it was because of malnourishment, of the abuse I had endured, but none of that mattered.

"Not so fast," he cooed, making a clicking noise with his mouth. "You get this"—he swung the package—"only when you agree."

I stared at his hand. "Agree to what?"

He nodded. "Agree to anything we say. We *own* you now. As long as you agree, then we'll take care of you. We'll give you your medicine, as much as you want, for as long as you perform for us," he explained.

I didn't watch his facial expressions. I couldn't. My gaze was fixed on the one thing that would help, that would make the shame, the filth, everything go away.

"We'll take the handcuffs off," he continued. "Maybe even let you shower, if you're a good girl. As long as you keep your customers satisfied, keep Carlos satisfied." He grasped my chin roughly and yanked my shaking body off the ground. Beady eyes met mine. "Keep *me* satisfied," he drawled, his putrid breath making me gag.

My violated body knew the meaning of those words. They'd kept me there for however long, strung out and abusing me when the need came to them, which was often. I knew there was an endgame.

This was it.

"I agree," I said without hesitation, holding out my shaking hand.

He smiled, revealing yellowing teeth. "That wasn't hard, was it? Why did you give us so much resistance before?" He clucked his teeth once more.

Had I resisted? All I remembered was giving in. Finally taking the escape they offered after they'd beaten me. Starved me. Until I surrendered. How long ago was that? It felt like forever. Like nothing had existed before this. Like I'd always been there.

Something dangled in front of my face.

I snatched the package and frantically tore open the bag. My entire body was convulsing, and it took me a frustratingly long time to get it where it needed to be. To get out of this room. To escape the filth covering every inch of me. The filth that was me.

I finally got it—the escape, the relief. Everything melted away once more and my mind was freed from the shackles of my body. Gloriously, I barely registered the brutal way my body was pushed onto the rickety bed. The stinking weight that settled on top of me, the intrusion that pushed into me, dirtying my insides once more.

I wasn't there. I was somewhere else. Beyond caring. Beyond anything.

I didn't even jump at the dull bang that seemed to echo in my head. At the sudden emptiness above me as the body was yanked away.

My vacant eyes danced to the source of the noise, the reason for the various male curses and fury that even I could feel.

Then I watched, with a vague sort of detachment, as a familiar man in a leather vest savagely beat the creature who had just moments before been raping me. The rational part somewhere deep inside me both cheered and reared away from this.

He's killing him.

That was good. No, that was great. But *he*, the man who smiled at almost anything and always had a joke on his lips, was killing him. Because of me. That was a mark on his soul I would be responsible for.

I wanted to say something. To tell him to stop. But I couldn't. I was paralyzed.

I felt myself being covered with something, rough leather that smelled of tobacco and oil. The voices above me moved in slow motion, muffled as if my ears were stuffed with cotton wool I couldn't get out.

The room swayed.

Or maybe it was me who swayed because I was no longer on the bed. I was floating like a cloud, watching the man with the hazel eyes kick something on the floor. Shapes moved around him, trying to pull him away, I guessed.

My cloud moved. I shifted my gaze. I wasn't floating. I was in someone's arms. Strong arms. Scarred arms. The rippled patches on them seemed like they were moving. I held my finger to them and trailed it lightly along the moving scars, hypnotized. Everything else in the room was forgotten.

But not the man with the hazel eyes. He still existed. Somewhere.

ONE

"I am the architect of my own destruction."
-Prince of Persia

TEN MONTHS EARLIER

It started with a pill. Harmless, really. Everyone was doing it. 'A party favor' was what one of the girls called it. Never one to turn down anything to do with a party, I took it. It was surprising I hadn't indulged sooner. Maybe it was because before, I had deluded myself into thinking there was a way I could escape. Get clean. Transcend the life I was born to. At that moment, that time when that little pill was offered, I had been educated on how fucking wrong I was.

So I took it.

And it was awesome. Everything was better, more colorful, more complex. It was as if that little pill took the film off my eyes which had been there since birth and I could see the world. Really see it, in all its beautiful color.

I had been searching for an escape, but I'd been doing it in the wrong places. Trying to trick myself into thinking I could escape by becoming better, by becoming a doctor, learning how to clean the dirt off my soul.

I was wrong. Escape didn't come with college education and a medical certificate.

Escape came in the form of that little pill. I forgot. I forgot all of it. That I sold my body for a living. That filth was flowing through my blood. That the woman I considered a mother was fading before my eyes.

It was all gone. So easy.

I was easy. Weak. Took the simple way out. When the devil held out his hand and invited me into hell with that little pill, I took it without hesitation. And I descended into the fiery depths before I knew better.

I read somewhere that it apparently takes a few hundred injections and a year to make an addict. So written by an addict. What a wonderful romantic thought to have.

So then, by those standards, I was not an addict. The thought comforted me.

Tightening the elastic at my elbow and positioning the needle right at the vein that protruded after I did so, I paused. Not for long. Too long would be to bathe in the bitter sticky bath of shame that submerged me in these moments. I was always tainted by this feeling, knowing that the only person who gave a shit about me didn't see the filth. But in those short moments between expectation and exhilaration, the need and the fix, that was when my body crawled with shame.

What would Faith say if she saw me now?

What would Lily say?

What would that little girl who was curled up in a lumpy bed, broken and violated, say? The little girl who had had her innocence wrenched from her tiny body before she had time to realize it was something to be stolen?

They'd all rear away from this stranger in disgust. I'd do the same if such a thing were possible. But I couldn't run from myself. Couldn't escape nightmares when they existed when I was awake. I could only choose the things to make it bearable to stumble through the life I'd been given.

I chose the easiest escape. What was another mark on an already stained soul?

FOUR MONTHS LATER

I was flying high. Not exactly high; that's what the pills did. Shot me into space until I was floating and plucking stars from the air. Heroin was different. Gave me a happiness that had been unfamiliar until that first hit. It wasn't just happiness, but contentment. Life, for the first time since forever, was okay. I was okay. It wasn't gray anymore; it was color, it was fresh. My job wasn't dirty, or shameful. It was fine. It was good.

And the grief melted away. It still existed, but it wasn't draining me. It was part of me. It was okay.

Since the moment we buried Lily's mom—*my* mom—I had relied on the prospect of my next hit to get me through. Through the pain that not only sliced my soul, but the utter devastation that lay beyond my best friend's beautiful eyes. I couldn't surrender to that pain; I'd learned that early in life. I also had to be strong, put on that mask I'd become so skilled at hiding behind. I had to do it for my friend. My sister. The only person in the world who didn't see the filth.

I hid behind the drugs while her grief hid the drugs from her. I used them as a way to feel nothing in order to take care of my best friend as well as I could. Which wasn't exactly well. And I took it to escape my own demons.

When it got down to it, I just took them to make it easier.

So, as I strutted my barely clad ass onto the dimly lit stage, I was high. Soaring.

That meant the world was fuzzy around the edges, and everything seemed like it was underwater. I was wading through at exceptional speed. I could feel the music inside me, as if the beat originated within me. I let my vacant mind move my vacant body to the music, aimlessly looking over the crowd that was focused on me. I didn't see them. I never did. I learned quickly not to look at the mostly disgusting men leering at my naked body.

Drugs helped.

But I glanced at Lily's portion of the bar, just to make sure my girl was okay. Because even though I may be flying high, forgetting all the bad that took up ninety percent of my world, I wouldn't forget the good. The ten percent. My girl. And if anyone fucked with her, they were dead.

I was trying to help the best way I knew how. The only way I knew how. Dragging her around to parties where she knew no one and could embrace the anonymity. Be someone other than herself. Hide from the pain. Escape with the help of a cocktail or five.

I was a fucking terrible friend.

Bringing my socially anxious best friend to the strip club where I worked, which was full of disgusting assholes who would eat her alive.

Yeah, a bad friend. The worst.

Just add another stroke to the lines staining my soul.

My step stuttered slightly when my gaze landed on her. And on the *hawt-as-balls* biker who had his hand firmly around her neck. Then moved quickly to two more bikers, their eyes on me. I didn't have time to focus on them more because I was flying. Flying meant thought was hard to capture, like that fucking snitch in those *Harry Potter* movies. I gave up on the golden fucker and did the thing, the only thing I was good for.

I embraced the dirt.

••••

"Fuck, babe, I've seen a lot of strippers in my time. *A lot*," a deep voice exclaimed from beside me. "But you transcended mere stripperdom and became a celestial being. An angel sent down from heaven, designed by God to pursue a career in exotic dancing."

I rolled my eyes, sucking down the last of my drink and pushing off the bar where I had been leaning. This was the part I hated. I could shake my ass, show my tits, and objectify myself on stage without blinking an eye. Even before the drugs, I was fine with that. Fine with the lap dances where I had to get up close and personal with a wide variety of perverts with body odor issues or drunken frat boys, provided I had some form of mood-altering substance flowing through my bloodstream. Before, I'd had wine. Now I had better.

But this part blew.

Carlos insisted that, after our performances, we 'mingle' with the customers. We weren't at some fucking corporate mixer. There was no need to *mingle*. Unless, of course, you were soliciting; then the mingling was necessary. I would rather chew off my own arm than do that, as Carlos well knew. It didn't stop him from aggressively insisting I 'get to know' my customers, as if communing with the dregs of society, AKA patrons of a strip club, would convince me to let them pay to fuck me.

I had one small shred of self-respect, of dignity, left. I clutched it in a death grip and I wasn't ready to let it go, even though I'd let poison into my veins. A girl's got to have her hard limits.

Prostitution was a hard limit. Pretty much my only one.

"I can die happy, then, knowing that I've pleased you," I retorted sarcastically.

I may have to mingle, but I didn't have to be polite. I was also cranky because my palms itched and a cloud descended over my mind as I came down. I needed another fix.

"I'll have to return the favor, firefly," the voice said, a hint of promise tingling his playful tone.

I finally jerked my head from the perusal of my glass to face what was a no doubt middle-aged man with a beer gut and receding hairline. His voice may have been manly, but I knew I wouldn't be so lucky to meet the man I'd imagine having such a deep rumbling voice. Such men didn't frequent establishments like this.

"What? You gonna get up on stage and provide me with a strip show?" I asked seriously as I turned.

When my eyes drank in the owner of that voice, I found my sarcastic question being rendered to a hopeful plead. The man in front of me was most definitely not middle-aged, and from what I could see from the tight black tee clinging to his flat stomach, there was no beer gut in sight. I'd wager a six-pack lay under there. Ditto with the hair prediction, though he didn't have any hair at all; his head was shaved to the scalp, and man, did he work the ever-loving shit out of a bald head.

There was another bulky guy standing next to him, but my eyes were like steel drawn to a magnet.

I moved my gaze down to his muscled arms, which were covered in ink, impossible to decipher in the dingy light. His leather vest had my slow mind realizing he most likely belonged to the biker gang Lily seemed to be tangled up in. I'd seen him earlier, with Lily and the man who'd dragged her out of here. Asher, the man who'd taken her virginity three years ago, who she'd pushed away when she found out her mom was dying of cancer. Selfless as always, she sacrificed her happiness and one seriously hot biker for her mom. The thought punctured through my weary mind.

I was happy that it seemed he'd come back to give her the happiness she deserved. I wasn't the best person to yank her out of this pit of grief we were both treading water in. Fuck, I was yanking her further down. It made me sick, that thought, but I didn't know how else to help. I didn't know how to bring the light back in because my life had been devoid of light the day I was born.

I shook away the self-deprecating thoughts to focus on the hot guy in front of me. Well, two. The other big one with ribbons of scars on his arms was nothing to sneeze at either. But it was the bald one who captured my attention, which was a feat in itself as my mind was becoming jerky and unhinged as it sobered.

"You ask me nice, I'll don a feather boa and do my best," he deadpanned. "Though, I don't think I'll be getting the same reaction as the little firefly here," he teased lightly.

I met his eyes and, even through my residual haze of blurriness, arousal settled in my stomach. Yeah, this guy was hot. His features were sharp and pronounced, masculine. He was Hispanic, I guessed, from his latte-colored skin. His hazel eyes were soft around the edges and focused on me. They were also familiar.

"I know you," I said, searching the recesses of my mind.

He put his hand on his impressive chest. "Well, consider me touched. The little firefly remembers our brief but passion-filled meeting three years ago." Again his tone was teasing, but something lay underneath it. A heat. An intensity. Or maybe that was just me. It was easy to imagine things when I was coming down. Hard to pick apart what was real and what my high mind had plucked from unreality.

"Though we weren't properly introduced, apart from you threatening to throw a Molotov cocktail at me," he continued, winking. "I do like a girl with spirit. Lucky." He held out his hand.

I stared down at it, unmoving. I did remember that particular conversation. It had not been an idle threat either. Three years back, I'd had to pick Lily—*Lily*, of all people—up from the biker compound of the notorious Sons of Templar MC. This guy had been there, and had the gall to flirt with me while a red-eyed Lily had been standing in her clothes from the night before, holding her shoes, and obvious sorrow and shame, in her hands. On that day, she looked more like me than herself, and I hated that. I despised everything that turned her into that. Including this guy.

The same went for Asher, the man who'd painted that look on her face, until I realized how much he cared about her.

"Yeah, well, that promise still holds true if any of you decide to fuck with Lily," I told him icily, suddenly feeling stone-cold sober.

His easy grin instantly dissipated. His hand left the shake position and he crossed both arms across his chest. "That ain't gonna happen. You've got my word on that. That girl won't be seeing more hurt. I'll personally mix that particular cocktail if my brother fucks it up again," he promised seriously.

I regarded him for a long moment. For whatever reason, I believed the hot biker with the questionable sense of humor. "Good," I said finally, nodding. "I've got work to do, and you two probably have a couple of steroid shots to take." I gave their muscles a pointed look. I was saying this mainly to be a bitch, as their muscles didn't look like overinflated balloons like the bouncers here. No, they were much more enticing. Hence the reason for me needing to get out of Dodge. I might try and lick one, and that would be embarrassing.

"Oh I like her. She's got fire." He nudged the staunch and emotionless man beside him. He didn't take his eyes off me. "Dibs," he said suddenly.

Oh no, he didn't.

I put a hand on my barely clad hip. "Did you just say 'dibs' after talking about me like I wasn't here?" I asked slowly.

He nodded, unperturbed. "You see, our club has a history of beautiful, spunky women blowing through. I've missed out." He held up four fingers. "Four times. I'm not missin' out this time. I've got a feelin' all those times were meant to be so I could meet you." His gaze flickered to his emotionless friend. "I don't want this fucker snapping you up, so *dibs*," he said, his eyes latching back onto mine.

I narrowed my gaze at him. "You can't 'dibs' a human being," I snapped.

He grinned at me. "Think I just did, darlin'."

Glancing to the mute giant who had his scarred arms crossed and his unnerving blue eyes on me, I swallowed the unease that came with that stare. "I get this now." I gestured between the two of him. "You're obviously his caretaker or something. I'd suggest you get him back to his padded room before that crazy takes him somewhere it shouldn't."

I went to turn on my heel, deciding to indulge in one last hit to get me through the rest of the night and forget the slight pang at the bottom of my stomach I got from this guy. I didn't need that. Not right now.

Not ever.

He grasped my elbow, not tight enough to be painful but enough to stop me and pull me slightly closer to his body. "Wow, not so fast, firefly," he murmured. "We've barely gotten to know each other. I think it's only proper we exchange names after exchanging threats." He raised an attractive brow. "Phone numbers would also be a good start."

I raised my own brow back at him. "Cocky, aren't we?"

He shook his head. "Nah, I'm Lucky, but we'll get to that part," he said, grinning.

"That's one thing you won't be getting tonight, *Lucky*," I clarified, irritated at his demeanor. It confused the shit out of me. He was a biker, hot as balls, and looked scary as hell. That was until he grinned like a maniac and joked like a goof. I was also irritated at the fact I found this extremely attractive. I didn't do jokers. Bikers, yes. Scary, yes. Funny? No. I also got the inkling that this was a good guy. I stayed away from those at all costs.

"I already have been. Got to talk to the most beautiful lady in the room, and got to see the firefly has bite, as well as a great ass," he countered.

I was robbed of my sharp retort by a huge presence. "No touching," Tyson barked at Lucky.

Any other moment I would be loath to have this steroid-ridden oaf in my presence, but right then he was a godsend. It didn't matter that he never came and enforced that particular rule of the club. He usually encouraged all sorts of touching as long as money was exchanged.

Money he got a cut out of.

Lucky glanced his way, his grin gone entirely and the scary look that his appearance promised in its place. He didn't let go of my arm, commencing in a stare-off with Tyson.

I rolled my eyes, yanking my elbow out of Lucky's grasp. "No problem here, dude," I addressed Tyson. "I was just leaving."

I didn't look back after I turned on my heel and walked into the crowd. As much as I wanted to.

That was it. Our first proper meeting after three years when I'd stormed into his clubhouse to retrieve my best friend who had incidentally lost her V-card to his brother. It wasn't love at first sight then, and it sure as shit wasn't love at first sight now. But I found as I was walking away, my mind already on what the syringe in my handbag held, that I couldn't completely forgot the hazel eyes and the easy smile.

•••

I expected he would lose interest. He seemed like he either needed Ritalin or was taking too much. Like an overexcited puppy that wouldn't stop wagging its fucking tail.

Except puppies were cute.

Lucky—yes, that's really his name, or the only one he'd give me—was not cute. Not in any sense of the word. He may have been slightly goofy with the sense of humor of a seven-year-old, but he was hot. Hot in a way that had him invading my drug-addled dreams. Filtered through my foggy waking mind. His muscled caramel skin exposed to me and his sinewy arms wrapped around me. It was not good. Not because I found him hot, but because I actually found him something else. He didn't just arouse me on a carnal level; there was something else, a connection that seemed too fantastical and real all at the same time.

It was dangerous. I didn't need real connections. I needed that like I needed a root canal.

The fact he'd been at the club at least three times a week for three weeks and counting was pissing me off.

Pissing me off in the way I'd come to look forward to our banter when I 'mingled.' The way I was disappointed when he didn't turn up. Despite whatever high I was riding that night, only he made me feel different. Better. But when he didn't turn up, when I was convinced he'd finally realized what I was, it was worse. Much worse than any low a narcotic offered.

His presence was something my addict mind craved. So fucked-up.

"You changed your mind about me taking you away from all this and giving us a nice quiet life in the country?" his deep voice asked, silky and smooth across the rough ridges of my mind.

I took a breath and turned from the bar, hoping to hide the way my eyes were just a little too bright. I was an expert at hiding the effects of the junk. It was the effects of *him* that I was trying to conceal. I didn't want to show him that his presence did something to me. That would be bad for both of us.

"Hell frozen over yet?" I asked, trying not to drink him in too obviously.

As always, he was wearing his cut and faded blue jeans. A white Henley showed off the ridges of muscle underneath the fabric. I itched to see it freed from its polyester cage and run my hands, or mouth, along it.

"I'm workin' on it. Got a hundred air conditioners going full blast as we speak. Man downstairs will not be happy with the electric bill, but you're worth battlin' the Devil for," he replied, jerking me out of my daydream.

I gave him a look. "Those lines work, ever?" They were totally working.

He grinned. "Sixty percent of the time, they work every time."

"You know those are about eighty percent urine, right?" I nodded to the nuts he was stuffing in his mouth.

Lucky stopped chewing, his eyes bulging. "You're shittin' me," he said through a half-full mouth.

I shook my head, the corner of my mouth quirking despite the ice queen routine I was trying to perfect. "I'm sure you've been to a few bars in your time. I figured you'd know by now that you'd ingest as many bodily fluids from licking a toilet seat as you would from snacking on those." I paused, tilting my head and running my eyes over his cut. "Though, as a biker in a club that owns its very own strip club, I'm sure you see your fair share of bodily fluids," I added sweetly. Someone who looked like him would get the attention from the girls who worked at their club. I knew a few of them, and they all swore it was the best gig they'd had in the biz; the money was good, they were treated well, and the hotties from the Sons of Templar MC frequented the place.

Much better than the rat-infested shithole I worked at where we got paid shitty, treated even shittier, and the clientele looked like they had girls tied up in their basements.

Which was why it baffled me that Lucky was even there. It pissed me off too.

Lucky grinned at me. "I only exchange bodily fluids with people I've taken to dinner first."

Somehow, he made that line actually send tingles down my already-sensitive skin.

"Why are you here?" I snapped, my withdrawals making me twitchy, cranky. Okay, cranky was an understatement. I felt like I wanted to murder this attractive idiot with a rusty fork. Or kiss him. I wasn't sure which.

He quirked his brow. "I really like the chicken wings."

Despite the snake in my belly and the ants on my skin, I smiled, slightly. "You enjoy salmonella, then," I retorted.

He stepped forward, not close enough to touch me but close enough that I could see his face illuminated in the dingy light. "I enjoy the company and the conversation. Salmonella helps me keep my delightful figure." He rubbed his flat belly over the top of his tee. I followed its journey and could actually see the outline of his six-pack.

I swallowed the cocktail of emotions that came with his proximity, chasing away the worst of the itch. It wasn't gone, not completely—it never would be—but his tobacco scent was like a salve. "You come to a strip club for conversation?" I repeated, finding sarcasm as a shield to stop my voice from shaking. "That's like going to a hooker for a hug."

"Well, I do need a hug," he teased.

My skin went cold. "I'm not a hooker. Even if I was, you couldn't afford me. Or be able to handle me," I purred, my voice velvet and steel at the same time.

His eyes flared with intensity. "Oh baby, I could handle you," he rasped.

I swallowed, the pure sex in his tone like a physical caress. "No, buddy, you can't. Your muscles aren't big enough to contain me," I croaked finally.

Something moved behind his eyes, like he was seeing something I didn't even realize I'd exposed. Then they flickered back to the teasing glint. "Well, that's just mean. I work very hard on these." He stroked his arm. "You know, that's going to do shocking things to my self-esteem."

I let out an unladylike snort. "Yeah, I'm sure it's in the gutter. You'll survive. How about you go and engage in some riveting conversation with Nat." I nodded to my friend and coworker who had professed her utter jealousy that I had my very own 'pet biker.' She could have him. He was more trouble than I needed and I was more than he could handle. I cloaked my face before regarding him again. "I've got to get to work."

Before I could turn away from him and the complicated emotions he seemed to arouse in me, he stepped even closer, so his body brushed mine. All humor flickered out of his face. It was unnerving, the quick transition, and also hot as fuck.

"I want to see you," he half growled.

I swallowed. "You will." I nodded to the stage. "You and everyone else."

I tried to turn again and that time he snatched my hand in his, maneuvering it so the meatheads at the corner of the room couldn't see the gesture, his muscly body working like a shield.

"I don't want to see what everyone else sees," he murmured, his voice rough. "I want you to give me something. Give me *you*."

I was paralyzed, only for a split second but long enough for his words to filter through the utter fucking chaos of my mind and settle somewhere. I ripped my hand out of his grasp.

My eyes met his. "There's nothing to give," I whispered, and before I could inspect the way his face changed at my words, I turned on my heel and walked away. As soon as I left his presence the itch came back, more ferocious than ever, more intense and unbearable than before.

TWO

"Numbing the pain for a while will only make it worse when you finally feel it."
-Albus Dumbledore

I had to get myself sorted. In the far reaches of my mind that weren't captured by the villain in the syringe, I knew it was getting bad. The need, the thirst, the necessity of that rush. Of what I felt when I got it. What I didn't feel.

I was a slave to it.

But I wasn't dirty when I was high. I wasn't filled with sorrow. I wasn't broken.

I was *nothing.*

Nothing was hard to give up. Even when I was starting to realize I was becoming a slave to it.

I couldn't become a slave to it. Not when the horrors of my childhood already had me in chains.

So I sat on the sofa, rocking slightly, trying to figure a way out. To find out how to free myself.

"Bex?"

I jerked at the soft voice.

"You okay?" Lily asked.

My gaze darted up to my best friend, who was regarding me with concern. I noticed she looked better. She was eating more, which meant she was slowly putting on the weight she'd lost through the horrors of the past few years. Three of them. Caring for her sick mother.

Her dying mother.

Trying to care for me when I was intent on hitting the self-destruct button that had always been just out of reach, until it wasn't.

Her eyes still danced with grief but she seemed stronger somehow, more sure of herself. Her golden hair shone with health and tumbled down her back, no longer lank and lifeless. The dark circles were disappearing from underneath her eyes, and the pallor that had worried me was now disappearing. I knew it had a lot to do with Asher, the hot biker who seemed to believe she invented the Harley Davidson. He did what I couldn't, pulling her out of the abyss when I only yanked her back in.

I owed him a lot. I was also weary. For the three and a half years we'd know each other, it had been my job to protect Lily. She was shy. More than that, she suffered from social anxiety, stuff that made her vulnerable to the shitty world. That's how I'd met her, on her first day at college, on the verge of a panic attack. She looked so tiny, a fucking child, and something drew me to that. Some carnal part of me recognizing that vulnerability painted on her pretty face, that same vulnerability that was stolen from me when I was a kid. Something clicked, made me determined to make sure that wasn't stolen from her like it was stolen from me. I couldn't control it then, but I sure as shit could control it now. Since that day, it was my job to protect her. Asher had taken over that job. He was much better at it than me.

Me? I offered her a bottle and escape the only way I knew how, by partying.

He offered her more. Much more.

"I'm totally fine, Lilmeister," I lied, smiling brightly at her. I'd gotten good at this, at the act. Hiding the way I got twitchy if it'd been too long between hits. How I was spending all of my spare money on it. I was an expert.

An addict.

No. I didn't let my mind focus on that word. I wasn't that. *No.*

"You sure?" she asked, her gaze running over me.

I kept my grin in place. "Sure, babe. I'm just contemplating my outfit for tonight. I'm feeling inspired by Rihanna's S&M. Whips and chains excite me." I winked at her.

She stared at me with furrowed brows for a moment longer, then shook her head. She was used to such phrases from me. I *was* the vulgar, stripper best friend after all. Plucky and able to handle almost anything. I had to play my part. She couldn't see the crumbling filth beneath the façade I'd constructed with black clothes and an expert hand at winged eyeliner.

"You need anything at the supermarket?" she asked, rifling through her bag the way we all did, making sure everything of import was in there.

"Caviar, Dom, the usual," I replied, reclining back on the sofa.

She shook her blonde head once more, in a way that made her look older than me, like she was the slightly amused mother looking at her immature child. Then again, she had a lifetime of being that person, the responsible one. Her mom had been a free spirit, an artist. A wonderful woman and a magnificent mother, but not the best at remembering to pay the electric bill and keep the cupboards stocked. That had been Lily's job. She might need protecting but she took care of people. Of me. Of her mom. Until the moment her mom died.

It hit me then, the last time I spoke to her. Hit without warning, so I couldn't chase it away.

"Love."

My head jerked up from its resting place on the corner of the bed. Sleep released me from its grasp as soon as I saw Faith's eyes. She'd been sleeping more now. Closer to the end. Our lives were getting darker and darker as her light grew dimmer and dimmer.

Lily dragged herself away to work. She didn't want to. I knew she was terrified that Faith would slip away while she was slinging cocktails. That's what I was afraid of.

Faith leaving her.

Leaving me.

I rubbed my eyes. "Love?" I repeated, confused.

"Love isn't knowing every inch of the other person. Looking at the darkest corners and getting to know their skeletons. It's finding their truth, the core of who they are, the part of you that they recognize in themselves. Some people recognize that truth after spending a day 'getting to know' someone. Others a year. A special few, a moment."

I blinked at her, the journey into lucidity jarring. "I'm not looking for a Prince Charming or a 'love at first sight' deal, Faith. You know that's not me." I tried to smile and wink at the woman I loved more than anyone on the planet, the one who was little more than a skeleton in front of me.

In a very deliberate and devastatingly slow move, Faith moved her gray and bruised hand to cover mine. With a surprising amount of strength, she squeezed it, her eyes glittering. "I'm not talking about a Prince Charming," she rasped. "I'm talking about Rebecca. About you finding her truth and seeing how utterly beautiful and unique her truth is." She paused, sucking in a labored breath. "But Prince Charming? I doubt he could handle you. Nor would he deserve you. You'll get someone much better than him. And you'll get him."

The certainty in her voice unnerved me. Had me wondering whether the fact she was flirting with death gave her some glimpse into the future.

"Faith," I whispered. But I couldn't say more because the grip on my hand loosened and that lucid gaze disappeared.

It was the last time I saw myself through her eyes, got a glimpse of my truth before I buried it in dirt and darkness.

I swallowed the chunk of coal at my throat as grief crept through the itchiness of my mind.

"I'll get right on that," she said with a small grin.

A grin!

I was so going to mouth-kiss that biker for making it possible for my best bud to smile again.

I'd also totally disembowel him if he took that smile away.

My own plucky smile left the moment Lily closed the door, my relaxed demeanor changing immediately as I darted off the sofa into my room. My shaking hands unveiled the expertly hidden package, and I wasted no time in finding my escape. My way to be clean. It didn't escape me that my pursuit of washing off the filth gave me even more grime in the long run. Dirtied my soul. Like I said, future isn't really my game. I live in the now.

And in the now, flying on the cushion that circled around me the moment I injected myself, I was clean. I was nothing.

•••

An unperceivable amount of time later, a knocking jerked me out of my reverie. I was already coming out anyway. This stuff was shit. The high didn't last enough, but I couldn't afford any better.

Jesus, I wasn't even good enough for the 'good' drugs.

Tragic.

I slowly pushed my jellylike limbs to the floor, my movements lethargic.

The knocking at the door turned to pounding. I stumbled into the living room, rolling my eyes.

"Okay, okay, jeez. Keep your motorcycle panties on," I muttered as I reached the door. I was assuming it was Lily's biker man, there to throw around some alpha over the fact his woman did something that he could do for her. Like breathing and such.

I didn't expect to be shoved savagely aside by a huge angry form entering the room, slamming the door. Asher may have given a new meaning to the term 'caveman' but he would never be so brutal, even with someone like me. None of the men in his club would. I had come to understand that, although they were rough bikers who could be scary as fuck, their attitude towards women, even junkie strippers, was respectful.

Despite this current situation, my mind wandered to the man who'd been visiting the club for the last few weeks. The one who didn't seem to go away, despite seeing what I was. Not all of it, no one would ever see that, but it should have been enough to scare him away.

"What's this I hear about you givin' Carlos shit?" an angry voice hissed.

I moved my gaze lazily up past the muscled chest and to the contorted face of my kind-of-boyfriend. Kind of because I didn't 'do' boyfriends, and he was a dick. I hadn't seen him in a couple weeks, and I hadn't missed him. "Hello to you to, Dylan," I replied smartly.

His hands tightened on my forearms to the point of dull pain. Had I been stone-cold sober, I reasoned that pain might've edged on unbearable. However, I was still high, so it had a numbing quality, an unimportance.

His eyebrows narrowed and his eyes turned to slits. "Don't give me your mouthy shit. You've done enough of that," he clipped.

I regarded him, not feeling much fear at the fury in his tone, his lack of hesitation at getting physical. He was not cute when his face was scrunched up in fury. Another part of me, a shameful part, felt kind of turned on with this fury, this lack of respect I was getting.

Fucked-up, I knew. That was me. Fucked-up to the core.

I reached out to his grip on my forearms, gently stroking the white knuckles.

"How about we don't talk at all, then," I murmured.

Even as I said the words they tasted bitter. As I touched his arms I wanted to flinch away in disgust. At him.

At myself.

His gaze flickered, the anger rippling like a channel changing on the TV as he pushed me roughly into the wall. "Yeah. We'll get there. I'll get that pussy. First, that pussy is gonna make us some money," he said. No, *ordered.*

I straightened and jutted my chin up, glaring at him. "Excuse me?" I replied sharply. I might've been fucked-up enough to be turned on in the face of his anger, but even *I* wouldn't stand for being talked to like that. I was still clutching that last crumbled piece of self-respect.

"Don't act surprised. You know what I'm talking about. You're going to fully immerse yourself in the business."

Anger crawled up my throat as I laughed coldly. "You're seriously trying to be my *pimp*?" I asked in disbelief. I knew he was connected to Carlos through shady business deals but I didn't think he'd be that far into the prostitution side of the business. I tried my best to not find out what he did with his life. I wasn't interested in getting to know him. He was only around in order for me to turn myself into a stranger.

My gaze flickered over his flannel shirt and faded jeans. "You need to get yourself a tracksuit and some gold jewelry if that's the goal," I informed him smartly. My eyes narrowed. "And a new fucking girlfriend. 'Cause that right there is never going to fucking happen. I've told Carlos numerous times to go and fuck himself on that score, albeit more diplomatically because he signs my paychecks. You, on the other hand, do not, so go fuck yourself. I sure as shit won't be doing it anymore," I hissed, wrenching myself from his grip and moving to the door so I could open it.

His palm went above the knob I was clasping, making moving it impossible.

"You're assuming you have a choice," he murmured in my ear, his body pressing into me from behind. "I'm sick of you acting like you've got some kind of code. Like you're *better*. Newsflash, babe, you're not better. You're a fuckin' stripper. White trash. A good one at that, with a nice ass and nice tits." He paused so he could cup them roughly. "But still trash," he added in my ear. "That body is worth something, and it's going to be used to not only milk my cock but to earn me some fuckin' coin." The unmistakable feeling of his hard-on pressed against my ass.

I swallowed bile and struggled against the stab of pain at his words. The truth in them.

Trash. I was that.

But I wasn't his. I wasn't anyone's.

"I said it before, and I'll say it again. Obviously your tiny brain needs repetition because the only head that seems to be working right is the one between your legs," I hissed through gritted teeth. "Go. Fuck. Yourself," I uttered slowly, trying to exert strength in my tone since he had exerted strength over my body.

I was whirled so I faced him, so his front pressed to mine, so his face could dip close to me and I could feel his breath on my nose. "You need to learn a fuckin' lesson. Learn your place."

I stared at him, not feeling an ounce of fear. Dylan was an asshole; I'd known that from the start. That's what attracted me to him. He was a lowlife, which was perfect for me. Someone who was already filth so I didn't taint them.

But he was an asshole that would not assert his assholey power over me. I quickly brought my knee up to connect with his crotch, reveling in the grunt of pain and crumpling of his body once I made contact.

I may have been small, and still slightly strung out, but I wasn't weak. I took care of myself. That's why I started towards my purse, the one that held my gun. I didn't get there, seeing as my head was yanked back roughly and pain exploded in my skull.

"A woman does not put her fucking hands on me," he bellowed in my ear.

I struggled against his hold, trying to move my feet so I could kick his shin, but I failed.

"A fucking man does not put his hands on me, or pimp me out, asshole," I hissed.

I was pushed forward savagely, barely able to put my hands out to stop myself from colliding with our coffee table. Strung out or not, that shit would've hurt. Potentially killed. I may not have been happy with who I was, but that didn't mean I was too keen on leaving this world.

I scurried back, eyes on Dylan. He stalked forward like a predator, a look I was familiar with. One I knew meant very ill for me. One that promised violence.

He kept his promise.

It was when his hands circled my neck after beating me that I realized his glare could also have promised murder.

A cold fear settled in my body, followed by a grim sort of resignation. Did I really imagine any other end with my life? It was a miracle I'd made it that far. As much as I wasn't surprised, there was no way I wanted a lowlife to be the one who ended it.

I wanted to live.

But like always, fate didn't like to give me a choice in what shitstorm descended on my life.

Then Lily burst in. *Lily,* of all people. And she saved me. Fought for me.

"Get off her," she hissed, blood trickling down her forehead. This was after she shot the gun I had been scrambling for what felt like hours ago. Dylan must have hit her too, vague images of a struggle between them entering my mind.

I didn't take much of it in, too groggy from all the hits to properly watch it unfold. My head felt heavy, black spots dancing across my vision as I sucked air back in that had been stolen from me.

Then Lily was in front of me, her eyes wet with tears. Tears and fear. Tears and demons. That was me. *Me.* I put those there.

"Are you okay?" she whispered, her hand still firmly clutching my gun.

I wasn't. It wasn't the physical pain; I could take that, had worse. It was that my friend, my gentle and delicate friend, was clutching a gun as tightly as her hand could. That her forehead was dripping with blood.

Because of me.

I managed to tear my gaze away from that blood because I had to. That's when I saw that Dylan was on the ground and Asher and Lucky were standing by the door, guns pointed at him, their faces hard with fury. Lucky no longer looked like the easygoing man who'd been lighting up the dingy place where I took my clothes off for money. No, this man was dangerous. A killer. His hazel eyes fastened on me, dancing with something I couldn't understand. It was concern, I think, although I couldn't be sure because no man had ever looked at me like that before. I'd had a multitude of looks from the opposite sex, but not one mirrored his right then.

I pushed myself up, ignoring the pain that came with the movement. "I'm fine. Fucker hits like a girl," I said, hiding behind the bravado that had done me well so far.

Her worried eyes were not convinced.

"That bitch a whore for the Sons now?" Dylan grunted, as if he weren't standing in front of two very angry bikers who happened to be pointing guns at him.

His arrogance was breathtaking.

"You've got no power here. This one's mine. You're both as likely to shoot me as that little mouse over there." He jerked his head at Lily.

The gunshot that echoed through our tiny living room made my entire body twitch. I registered Lily covering my body with hers. Little Lily shielding me. As if I was worth protecting.

Our heads both turned to where Dylan had crumpled to the floor.

I registered the blood seeping from him and then glanced at Lucky.

"My finger slipped." He shrugged as he addressed the room. He was going for nonchalance, but there was no hiding the fury flickering underneath his gaze.

"You'll pay for that, you don't fuckin' shoot me without—"

Dylan was cut off by a swift blow to the head.

I felt a grim sort of satisfaction at the fact Dylan was bleeding. I also felt the shame of not being able to do it myself. My blood boiled and I was overcome by an unbearable urge to crawl over and reclaim my gun in order to put a bullet in his skull. But I couldn't move. Pain that had been distant before was now becoming more urgent. I was sobering and it sucked.

"You need a hospital, sweet thing?" Lucky murmured as he knelt down in front of me. His hand lightly, imperceptibly, trailed across my throbbing jaw. Asher had snatched Lily from my side, or Lucky had pushed her away, I wasn't sure which.

I flinched back and pushed myself off the ground so my back rested against the wall. Lucky's gentle touch was almost as bad as Dylan's angry and ruthless punch. No, it was worse. I had experience with anger, knew what to do with it. This I didn't. I didn't deserve it.

The anger on his face, the fury, that was familiar. Was okay. What wasn't okay was the tender concern mingled with that.

"No, I'm fine. A couple of bruises," I declared, trying to let strength leak into my raspy voice.

He raised a brow and didn't say a word. Instead he gathered me, as gently as anything, into his arms and took me to the sofa.

I was grateful for the fact he deposited me quickly on the sofa. I couldn't have his hands on me. They were clean. Good. That just made me felt even dirtier.

I only got a short respite as he ran his hands over my body, taking stock of my injuries. His face was marble, his mouth set in a tight line. No amusement was dancing in those hazel eyes. I had taken it away.

I tried to jerk away from his touch. "I'm fine," I declared.

His eyes met mine. They blazed. "You're a lot of things. Fine in the sense of being a fuckin' knockout. That milky skin being tainted with violence from some fucker is *not fine*," he replied tightly.

I couldn't think of that right now—what those words meant, that anger. I tore my gaze away from those hazel eyes and regarded my best friend. Asher was crouched in front of her, speaking gently with a worried face.

He would protect her. Protect her from me.

My blood boiled at the fact that I was responsible for this. For all of it.

Her gaze moved from Asher to the back of Lucky's head. "Lucky, you just shot someone." Her voice was dazed and almost dreamlike.

I gritted my teeth at the fact it could be because she was suffering from a concussion. Because of me.

"Sure did, squirt," Lucky replied, not taking his eyes off me.

"Give me your gun," I ordered, moving my eyes back to his. I held out a hand that I was ashamed to see was shaking. "I'll kill that motherfucker myself for totally ruining my ability to wear a tank top for the next month, and for hurting my best friend," I gritted out, trying to move. I wasn't joking. Though I didn't add he wasn't the sole reason I couldn't wear a tank top. The track marks on my arm did that all on their own.

"Killing someone requires effort. You need to rest. Let us unbattered men do the killing," Lucky demanded.

Rest. Letting the men take care of their work in the shadows while the bruised women basked in the light.

Problem was I was already in the shadows. Born in them.

My gaze flickered around the room. At Asher crouched over a bleeding Lily. At Dylan bleeding all over my favorite rug. At Lucky. All teasing was gone from his eyes and I saw it then, what he really was. The dangerous man who lurked underneath.

Dangerous not in the literal sense of the word, but dangerous to me and my emotional health. Because lying battered and broken on a sofa, half high and with the man I used to screw bleeding on the carpet in front of me, I wanted him. I wanted to drown in those eyes. Swim in the danger and drown in the something else they offered.

I so needed to get myself sorted. Away from the junk and away from those fucking eyes that offered me a fantasy.

••••

"Come in," I said distractedly. The door which had just been knocked on opened and closed. "You're gonna have to do my pedicures for the foreseeable future, babe. Bending and cracked ribs don't go together, but I'm not having chipped nails in addition to being a tie-dyed human of bruises," I said to Lily, who I assumed had come into my room. It didn't matter that she'd only just left an hour ago after patching me up in my bedroom while the bikers 'dealt' with Dylan.

Whatever that meant.

There had been talk of bullets to the brain, which I wouldn't have objected to, since he hurt Lily in the process of fucking me up, but she'd vetoed that option. Which was probably good, as I didn't need to owe anyone. I owed Lily enough already; I didn't want to owe her attractive boyfriend and his buddies for offing someone for me. I didn't want to be the reason why they had a black mark on their souls. Though I guessed their souls weren't exactly squeaky clean. Murder had come to them as natural as breathing.

I tried to convince myself the reason they were doing anything in the first place was because Dylan had hurt Lily, Asher's 'old lady.' They took that shit serious. But that couldn't explain away Lucky's fury, his confusing tenderness with me, him trying to make me go to their biker clubhouse and hide from the world.

Let the muscled men in leather cuts protect me.

What a joke.

I didn't need protecting from the outside world. Despite my bruises, I could take care of that. It was *me* that I was in danger from. Being close to Lucky was only one of the reasons I'd fought being sequestered in biker heaven. The second was to do with my little habit. Now that Lily wasn't spending all of her time at the hospital with her dying mother and getting back to a life she deserved, it was getting hard to hide. If she wasn't distracted by Asher, I guessed it might be impossible.

But bikers, with their shrewd eyes and badass skills, they'd notice. Especially one pair of hazel eyes that melted into me and seemed to see more than I showed the world.

"Doin' a thing like painting nails might fuck with my street cred, but I'll do it if I get to touch those delicious feet," a raspy voice answered. One that was way too deep to be Lily's. Plus her voice didn't cause my body to prickle with expectation. I didn't swing that way.

I jerked my head up from my nails and most likely fucked them up. "What are you doing here?" I snapped at Lucky. He was standing, his face light, though he held his jaw hard. His body seemed to take up all the space in my small room. "Plus, delicious feet? Ew. Do you have some kind of foot fetish? They've got 900 numbers for that," I added.

His eyes flickered down my bare legs. I was wearing a long tee and no pants, lying on top of my comforter. I was lucky that it was meant for men and the sleeves fell just past my elbows. It's the only kind of tee I wore, since it hid the red dots in the crook of my elbows when they weren't covered in makeup like they were for work.

Despite the fact it was more clothes than I wore on stage and he'd seen it all, I felt exposed. Maybe it was because my face was bare of makeup, the only decoration being the spattering of bruises. There was no hiding it with a curtain of my midnight-black hair, as it was piled messily atop my head. And due to the fact I was a pale as a ghost, the bruising stood out so much it was comical. It wasn't attractive, but I'd take it. Plus, when I was on stage, slathered in a mask—and, more often than not, high as a kite—I was somewhere else. I journeyed beyond a dimly lit room and leering gazes, kind of had to to survive.

But this was my little sanctuary. Sure, it was messy, with clothes strewn on the floor and makeup littering my dresser, but it was *mine*. The one place in the world the mask could come off. Well, not completely off; I still had to cling to a shred of it in order to face myself in the mirror. That had a little to do with the junk hidden in a lipstick canister and a lot to do with the little girl who still haunted me with her lost innocence.

"A fetish insinuates a habit," Lucky said, eyes moving down to my toes. Then they moved back up to my face and hardened. "I don't have any obsessions with other feet. Or other women." He paused. "Well, not for long, anyway. It's one in particular who fascinates me." He let that hang between us before his eyes went to my bedside table, where various bottles were littered. "Now, what color are we thinking?" He picked up a forest green, squinting and putting it back down. "I think purple would be best. Plus, it goes with this." He leaned forward to touch a tendril of my dip-dyed hair, which had escaped from my bun. My heart thundered at him touching my hair. My freakin' *hair*. I flinched back and his body stiffened.

"Not gonna hurt you, Becky," he murmured. "I'd never do that.

Despite how fuckin' pissed I am that you're too fuckin' stubborn to accept help and come to the clubhouse with me. If I wasn't worried about how those nails will embed themselves in my cheek, I'd be putting you over my shoulder and dragging you there myself... but I like my beautiful face untainted."

I narrowed my eyes at him. "Yeah, well it will stay that way if you don't try and forcibly take me to your compound. I don't do well in captivity."

Something moved behind his eyes. "Yeah. You're wild, baby. In a good way. No way in hell I'd try to rein in the spirit dancing behind those eyes. It's what drew me in, part of why I like you so fuckin' much. Caging that, it'd be a crime to humanity."

I swallowed at his words. At the fact I felt like a fucking teenager and wanted to dance around the room at hearing he liked me. *Me.*

He doesn't know you, not really, the voice inside my head told me. *If he did, no way in hell he'd call you beautiful. Not when he knew the real you. The drug addict fuckup. The tarnished little girl.*

The thought was like ice water on my psyche. I sat up and moved to stand on the other side of the bed, putting furniture between us. "You don't like me," I hissed. "You're just not used to someone not liking *you*. You think I'm something to be conquered and cast aside once you've satisfied your ego that you can claim any girl you like."

Lucky's face hardened. "You're right. I do want to conquer you." His voice dripped with erotic promise. "But I don't suspect it will be easy. Suspect it'll be worth it, and I sure as fuck won't want to cast you aside after the fact."

I straightened, trying to ignore the way my entire body responded to the pure sex in his voice. I'd just been beaten up by my very ex loser boyfriend, and now I was getting turned on by the biker who'd been borderline stalking me for two weeks? I was so fucked-up.

I met his eyes and hoped my bitch stare was firmly in place. "Whatever. Dreams are free. Which is all you'll ever get in regards to me. You're not getting what you want, for once. Try not to cry into your pillow tonight. Or do. I don't care either way. Just leave me alone," I ordered, my voice cold. It may have been an order outwardly, but it was also a plea. A prayer.

ANNE MALCOM

Lucky rounded the bed and stalked towards me. I backed up but had nowhere to go once my hip hit my dresser. He boxed me in. "You think I'm leavin' you alone?" he asked, his voice little more than a whisper. He brought his hand up to my bruised cheek. I held his eyes and refused to flinch away. "After that fucker did *this* to you?"

I jutted my chin out. "I can take care of myself."

Lucky nodded. "Yeah, I reckon you can. Reckon that's been your life. Looking out for yourself. Fighting to protect yourself. Can see it behind your emerald eyes. The glint of a warrior who's seen too fuckin' much. Fought against too much." He paused. "You don't know what it's like to have someone step up and do that for you. It's a fuckin' shame. But I'm also happy to be the first man to do that."

His words hypnotized me, gave me a glimpse at a life I might be able to have in a parallel universe. One similar to what Lily had with Asher. What normal people had.

Normal. Normal was clean.

Clean I was not.

The window to the world shuttered.

I wasn't normal. Wasn't innocent or unpolluted like Lily. I would never have that life.

Lucky's mouth was inches from mine. It took all my strength not to cross that small gap and just get a taste of what that life could be like. But even I wasn't that much of a masochist. Instead of pressing my lips to his, I placed both of my hands on his hard chest and pushed. My strength was laughable and I never would've been able to do something like that if Lucky decided to exert his considerable strength over me, but he didn't. As soon as he realized my intention, he stepped back, though he frowned as he did.

"You're not going to be the first man to 'protect me' from the big bad world." I used air quotes to go with the sarcasm in my tone. "This isn't the macho hot biker show where you have all-consuming powers to shield some whimpering female from the horrors of reality," I said, eyeing him. I put my finger to my chest. "This female is already well acquainted with those horrors. They're the fucking backdrop of my childhood. Demons are my goddamn lullaby. So thanks for the offer, but there's nothing left for you to protect me from. I've already lived through it all."

Seeing Lucky's face so blank and harsh, devoid of the humor that I'd come to understand was his nature, was more than a little unnerving. The fury of earlier today was downright eerie, and more than a little hot. But this, the way his body turned to granite at my little speech, it was something else. Like he was physically *feeling* the meaning behind my words.

The reaction was confusing. Impossible. We barely knew each other. He couldn't look at me like he knew every secret I clutched to my chest.

His eyes held me captive, paralyzing me even though all I wanted to do was leave this room, escape his shrewd gaze and the electricity between us. Escape my own feelings for him. I wanted to run and find a fix to take it all away. But his draw was even more hypnotizing than the needle.

"Yeah, you do need protectin', firefly," he said quietly. His gaze flickered on my body. "The ones with the hardest exteriors always got the sweetest softness on the inside." He stepped forward, not enough to get our bodies close but so I could smell him, feel his presence envelop me. "I'm gonna find it. Taste it. And own it."

I swallowed the stupid fucking butterflies crawling from my belly to my throat at his words. "Who speaks like that?" I snapped. "Seriously? Give me a list of people who thinks that's acceptable conversation to share with someone you've only met a few times."

His brow quirked. "Babe, I've seen you naked. I think it's more than an appropriate way to talk."

I pursed my lips at the stark reminder of reality. Reality was sorely needed in this little conversation. "*Everyone's* seen me naked. Everyone who pays the cover and frequents nasty strip clubs. They got deep pockets they can see me *real close*," I said, my voice a taunt. I was doing it to remind him of what I was, to make him realize that I wasn't whatever warped image of me he had in his mind.

The teasing glint left Lucky's eyes. His emotional transitions were giving me whiplash. "That shit's stopping."

I folded my arms and restrained the wince that came with this movement. "What are you talking about?"

"You takin' your clothes off for lowlifes in this fuckin' dive. The place owned by a bad motherfucker who tried to pimp you out. You're quittin'."

A red film covered my eyes and I went deathly calm. "I thought we'd already ridden this merry-go-round. If I remember correctly, I pushed you the fuck off, considering you have no power over me," I hissed. "So at what point in this conversation did you descend into your little fantasy world? Or did you always reside somewhere that isn't the here and now?" I paused. "That makes a lot of sense."

Lucky's eyes darkened. "Jesus, Becky, you can hardly fuckin' move. That hot little body is covered in evidence of just how bad that shit is for you. At how far away it is from where you should be. What you deserve. You ain't goin' back there."

I found my feet and stormed past him, taking a wide berth so he didn't get any ideas. I opened the door and leaned against it while staring back at him. "You're wrong. This"—I gestured to my face—"is *exactly* what I deserve." I ignored the way he visibly flinched at my tone. "Now this is the part of the conversation when you run along back to your biker buddies. Find a whore to boss around, rebuild your Harley, write the next great American novel. I don't give a shit. The main part is you *getting the fuck out* of my apartment and forgetting whatever has you thinking I'm some possession you can do with as you like and order around. That is not me. I'm never going to be that girl." My voice was ice.

Lucky stood in the center of my room, digesting my words. As he did so, I took a mental snapshot of him standing there, in the middle of my chaotic, messy life. The beautiful tattooed biker who was a contradiction. Funny as hell, carefree and kind, but ruthless and violent at the drop of a hat. And tender. And irritating as shit. Someone I'd never have.

Maybe I'd use it as motivation to get off the shit and finally get my life together. Something had to. Today my life hadn't exactly flashed before my eyes, but death had come knocking and I realized what a fucking sad story I'd have to tell the reaper if I'd answered. I didn't want sad. I didn't want some tragic end, to become another damaged junkie who'd lost their battle with their demons.

No.

I wanted to fight.

And I wanted to win.

I just had no idea how I was going to do that. A start would be to forget the biker who made me want to fight and surrender all at the same time.

He moved, not taking his eyes off me. My perusal of him, or maybe my distraction at the demons clawing at my back, had me unable to react as he stalked across the room and clasped the back of my neck. His eyes glittered with hunger that I only got a glimpse of before he pulled me in to press his lips to mine. I probably should have struggled, pursed my lips and turned to stone. I sure as shit shouldn't have opened to him the moment his lips crashed down on mine. But I was never one for doing things I should, and I definitely indulged in everything that was bad for me.

And that kiss, the way it set my body alight, the way he tasted as his tongue plundered my mouth, it was bad for me. The worst. Because it was good. Too fucking good.

In the blink of an eye—or maybe an hour later, who knew—he yanked back, resting his forehead on mine for a split second. Our gazes locked and I scrambled to shutter my eyes, to regain my mental shield. But it was too late; his hazel eyes saw to the core of me.

Not a good thing.

Because my core was not soft and beautiful. It was shriveled and rotten.

His jaw hardened and he stepped away from me. I shouldn't have been surprised. If he actually got a glimpse at the wasteland behind my eyes, I'd never see him again. I hated how much the thought of that hurt. I was momentarily pissed at myself for creating such a connection to someone I barely knew.

He scrutinized me a moment longer, then moved farther away. The absence of his body was similar to withdrawal. My skin itched without him. One kiss and I was hooked.

I quickly scuttled to the side of the room. I didn't need another addiction.

"Come here, Becky," he commanded, his voice a low growl.

I found my feet obeying his command without hesitation and I came to a stop in front of him. He grasped my hips, gently pulling me to him.

"I'll go," he murmured. "Whores don't seem to interest me anymore, and my bike's already a work of art. I'm sure I've got a few great novels in me, considerin' I'm a goddamn genius." His eyes twinkled, then turned serious. "I'll do none of those things. I'll only do the one thing that you suggest, which I don't want to do, and that's leave." He paused. "Forgetting about you is not an option, firefly. You're under my skin." He leaned forward to land a soft kiss on my bruised face. My eyes fluttered closed, feeling a cocktail of pain and pleasure from the gesture. When I opened my eyes, he was gone.

And I was well and truly fucked.

Because he was under my skin too.

Amongst the filth and the demons that had been there since I was a kid.

That was the last place someone like him needed to be.

THREE

"Drugs take you to hell, disguised as heaven."
-Donald Lyn Frost

You'd think I'd be a little hesitant at opening the door to someone banging on it, considering what happened the last time.

You'd think wrong.

And it wasn't just that I was riding a glorious little high my boy Silas had hooked me up with. Broken ribs and a battered face hurt, a *lot*, so I was able to get some heavy-grade painkillers. Yeah, the beating hurt, but now I had a socially acceptable reason to pop pills.

You know, because heroin wasn't enough.

But a girl needed something. Especially since I wouldn't have the cash for much more until I was on the mend. Carlos hadn't been happy when I'd called to tell him the situation. Not about Dylan beating me up, no, about me not being able to work a pole with four cracked ribs.

"You're letting me down, Rebecca. I'm disappointed," he clucked over the phone.

I scowled at the air. "Oh yes, I'm letting you down," I replied sweetly. "By not saying yes to prostitution after the first punch? Do you really think I'd play nice if you got Dylan to convince me with his fists, you chauvinistic prick?"

There was a long silence on the phone. Don't ask me why I'd even called him, considering he was the reason I was a lovely shade of purple. Maybe so I could finally yell at him.

"I'm going to choose to ignore that little outburst considering your situation," Carlos said finally. "I had no knowledge of Dylan's actions, and I'll see to it that our business relationship is severed."

I restrained a snort. *Yeah, right.* Dylan was a Tucker, and the Tuckers were a notorious wannabe mob family who thought they ran everything in this town. Carlos was so tangled up with them it wasn't funny.

"And I'll go and dye my hair, join a sorority, and wear pink," I retorted sarcastically.

Another pause. "You should be careful talking to your employer like that," he warned. "A girl like you doesn't have a lot of options considering your only assets are what you can sell and your little... habit." His voice was smug.

Of course he knew. Carlos was a weasel, but he knew everything that was going on at his club. "So I'll place you on unpaid leave while you think about your options. Your many, *many* options," he taunted.

There was an audible click as he hung up.

"Fuck," I hissed through my teeth. I threw my phone down with a force that sent barbs of pain through my midsection.

The fucker was right. I had no option but to go back to him. No one to fall back on but myself. And I was doing a pretty crappy job right now. But if I wanted to stay fed—and, more importantly, stay high—it was my only option. Lily would, of course, offer to sell her kidney for me if that was what it came to, but no way in hell was I letting that happen.

So, after slamming the phone down, I answered the door. I wasn't afraid of what I'd find on the other side. Fear was useless and not something I'd felt since that night all those years ago. I wasn't scared of opening the door.

Though I was confused.

I frowned at the skinny redhead in front of me. He looked like a pizza boy, tall, lanky, splotched in freckles, and looking like he had barely gone through puberty. "Wow, Dominos is really edging up their uniforms," I exclaimed, taking in his leather vest, jeans and boots. "I dig it. But you seem to have forgotten your pizza. And I didn't order one."

I tried to close the door and was not surprised when his skinny arm stopped me. There was astounding strength behind it.

"Lucky sent me," he declared, his voice way deeper than I expected. "I'm here to look out for you. I'm Skid."

I tilted my head. "Yeah, I didn't order a pizza and I certainly didn't order a *Skid* to look out for me," I replied. "What is with you bikers and the names? Seriously dude, Skid? What's wrong with freaking Scott? Or Bob? Just once I'd like to meet a biker with a normal name and normal bone structure," I babbled. Despite his teenage geek appearance, he managed to work it, almost like he should've been strutting down a runway or something.

He regarded me expressionless, though the corner of his mouth did a little twitch. "Sorry, ma'am, but I was informed you'd throw some 'spitfire-type sass'"—he finger-quoted a certain biker—"and I was instructed to tell you that I'm authorized to knock you unconscious and then transport you to the clubhouse." He quirked a brow. "Please don't make me knock you unconscious."

I stared at him. "I really can't tell if you're joking," I said, raising my own brow. "But I'm not joking when I say if you call me ma'am again, I'll throat-punch you."

He didn't grin but his mouth twitched. "I've also been told to get rid of any stains on the carpet."

I grinned, opening the door wider. "Well, why didn't you just say so, Skippy?" I asked. "I happen to *hate* cleaning, and you've just worn me down. No threats of unconsciousness needed." I stood back and let him in. The back of his leather cut had the 'prospect' rocker. Figured considering I heard they got all the crappy jobs.

I was guessing I was the crappiest job of them all.

With the help of my painkillers, I forgot that readily enough. "We're going to have to do something about that name, though. I just can't call you Skid." I scrunched up my nose, folding my arms. "You're gonna have to tell me your real name. I promise I won't tell." I crossed my fingers over my chest.

He stopped his perusal of the bloodstain in the middle of our rug—thanks, Dylan—and stared at me. "You aren't to be standing," he said instead of answering me.

I frowned at him. "What now?"

"That's another instruction. 'Make sure she doesn't move that sweet ass anywhere but the john.'" He used finger quotes but I didn't need them.

"I'm so killing him," I muttered.

ANNE MALCOM

Skid kept staring at me.

"You'll take me bodily to the sofa if I won't move, won't you?" I surmised.

He nodded gravely. "There was talk of zip-ties if you weren't cooperative."

I supposed I should have been angry. Furious, most likely. But nothing seemed to bother me with the magic painkillers. So I stomped to the sofa.

"You gonna tell me your name?" I asked while I watched him inspect the blood.

"It's Skid."

I grinned. "So we're gonna play it that way. Okay, Karl."

No response.

"Not Karl? That's cool, I've got Google and buttloads of time," I informed him.

Apparently I did. And now that I had a babysitter who was going to be watching me, I had to make sure I used that time wisely. Namely not shooting up in the bathroom.

ONE WEEK LATER

You need to stop, the voice pleaded. *No.* It was small and childlike, an echo of the plea from that horrible night eleven years ago. Only that time I wasn't fighting against a monster in the night, but myself.

And I was losing.

I tried. My fucking hardest. After Lucky left that night, with nothing but a gangly biker and healing bruises to remember him by, I'd tried to gather up the mess I called a life and give sobriety a crack.

I lasted about two days. Then the itch, the horrible shaking, the sickening yearning got the best of me. I welcomed the filth back with a relief. Found solace in the nothing.

It didn't matter that my finances were becoming dangerously depleted since I couldn't work looking like a bruised peach. Only one thing mattered.

The needle.

The nothingness.

There was no escape from it. So my body healed from the beating Dylan gave me while my mind became more damaged from the battering of my demons. I dodged Lucky; that was one addiction I had to kick, no matter how tough the withdrawals were. The universe seemed to be on my side for once because he and Asher were away on some biker mission and I was safe. Safe from the illusion of safety he offered.

Safe to continue the habit that offered the comfort of danger. Because Asher wasn't around to offer Lily the life raft she still needed, despite the fact she was treading water now, it was my turn to help her stay afloat. Though I feared dragging her out to some club and plying her with booze was dragging her deeper. I had no choice to come out to drown my sorrows, or at least drunken them, in order to gain the courage to go back to work tomorrow.

Yep, work. Back to the place where my boss had sent the guy I was sleeping with to rough me up in order to convince me to solicit.

I'd guess most people would say such a move was insane. Or at least people who had the luxury of choice.

I did not.

So in order to live with my choice, I came here. And dragged Lily with me.

Because I was such a great friend.

It was the shame that came with that realization that had me slipping into the bathroom to find solace in nothingness, so I could face my friend. So I could face myself.

I wasn't under the illusion that I was doing this for anyone but myself. Fuck, I couldn't get any more fucking selfish than leaving my vulnerable best friend in some greasy club while shooting up in the bathroom.

I almost retched from my disgust in myself.

As always, I shook myself, as if physical movement would chase those thoughts away, and plunged the needle into my arm. The pain of the needle was almost nonexistent now, the moment that blissed nirvana entered my bloodstream pain a rather arbitrary concept.

Everything fell away. The chattering of girls outside the bathroom stall I was crouched in, the thumping of the bass in the club. The filth. That was the most important thing. The filth fell away. No, maybe it didn't. It was tattooed onto my skin, onto my soul. It would never leave. But it was hidden. It was gloriously cloaked like everything else was in these precious moments.

I closed my eyes and leaned back, cherishing the moment. The future didn't exist. It was only the now.

Then, as the darkness dragged me deeper than I'd ever been, I had a horrible premonition that the now was all I was getting, all that was left.

Then there wasn't even that.

Then there was nothing.

•••

Almost overdosing in a dirty bathroom stall of some terrible club was a turning point for me. My bottom.

No, actually waking up in hospital after I'd almost died was a turning point.

The first thing that assaulted me when I woke was the smell. Unpleasant was not the word. It seemed to seep into my bones, that sterile, ammonia smell. Taunting me with its cleanliness, making my own filth that much more visible. Inescapable. Because the first thing I'd wanted to do was find a needle, a pill, a fucking cocktail to blur that dirt, make myself care just a little less about it.

Unfortunately they didn't offer narcotics or stiff drinks to junkies recovering from overdoses in hospital rooms.

Then it was the pain. Every cell in my body hurt, every strand of hair a weight on my pounding head. It was not pleasant. But that was all Club Med compared to a distraught and pale-faced Lily sobbing at my bedside when she'd come in.

I saw it then. The consequences of my actions. Of what my death would have done to the only person in the world who loved me. My only family. I saw how fucking selfish I'd been, looking for escape like a coward and then laying all that shit on Lily just after she'd buried her mom.

Worst friend of the century goes to me.

It was then I found my strength. I decided to make a change. Not to be a coward and find excuses to flush my life down the crapper. Not to hide behind the demons of the past and let me destroy my future.

So I went off the junk.

Cold turkey.

I wouldn't recommend it.

I don't really want to relive the sickness. The insects crawling on my skin. The itch that nothing but a needle could scratch. The pain of my body coming back to itself. Me descending back into the unfamiliar home of my body, which was now a stranger to me. Because that's what I'd ultimately tried to run from with the drugs at the start, so coming back to it and facing the real me, stone-cold sober, wasn't pleasant.

But I survived. People did it every day, so I would. And I did.

I hated myself, *a lot*, for being like that. For needing Lily to take care of me for the first handful of hellish days. When I'd been so sick I couldn't stand, couldn't shower. Forget keeping down any form of food. It mirrored the hell Faith went through with chemo. Though she was putting poison in her body in order to stay on this earth, to heal, I'd been doing it to leave it, further damaging my already-damaged body. I subjected Lily to that, after she'd gone through the same with her mom.

I was going to hell for sure. Withdrawal was already hell, so I guessed I had a taste of what the afterlife held for me. Totally not keen on meeting my maker any time soon.

By the time I was well enough to bathe myself and think beyond a rabid craving for junk, I was lucid enough to see what withdrawal had done to me. My pale face was almost translucent, and the circles under my eyes looked like smudged eye shadow. I looked like a cancer patient. No, I looked like a *junkie.*

It wasn't what it did to me but what it did to Lily that had me determined to stop leaning on her and take care of myself. The light that had only just come back to her pretty face was dimmed, and her dark circles rivaled mine. I didn't miss that her hunky biker hadn't been around. That could have been because I'd sworn her to secrecy, but I suspected she had further descended into martyrdom by sending him away. Sacrificing her happiness once more in order to take care of someone else.

So not good enough.

She had to work and I was planning on calling Asher and demanding he get his tight biker ass down there. I'd even lay my broken troubles at his feet if he needed convincing, which I was sure he didn't. He loved Lily; any idiot could see that. The fucker had waited for her for three years. Because he loved her, I was almost certain he'd try and get rid of me once he saw just how much I'd tainted his girl.

Rightly so.

I'd tarnished her but was too selfish to send myself away because that would mean I would be alone. Truly alone. What I had been before I'd met Lily, before I dropped out of medical school. I'd be that damaged little girl who'd had her innocence ripped from her, and the whole world would swallow me back up.

But Asher was already putting up with enough. I'd brought Dylan into Lily's life and he'd hurt her. That was on me. Now I'd introduced her to more demons.

My own.

"Lils, I'm going to be fine," I tried to reassure her. "I'm not going to run off for a fix the second you leave. You need to go to work, I know you do. I'll be okay, seriously." I was determined not to relapse, but I didn't trust myself. Not really.

And that scared the fucking shit out of me. I had an enemy, one hell-bent on my destruction. And that enemy was me.

Lily chewed her lip, furrowing her brows together. Then her face cleared. "How about you don't worry about me and try and get some sleep?" she said softly.

I frowned at her. "I'll sleep when you sleep."

I was exhausted. Was there another word beyond exhausted? Because if there was, I was that. My body was going through hell being deprived of the poison it had been surviving on. I was literally rejecting being clean. And I couldn't sleep. The moment I tried to escape the sickness and welcome oblivion, they crept back in, those taunting voices that urged me to give up.

Just one last hit.

You're never going to last.

You'll never be clean.

It took every single inch of willpower I possessed to ignore them.

Lily smiled at me, and even with bags under her eyes and wearing ratty leggings she looked like a fucking Victoria's Secret model. I was reasonably sure I looked like exactly what I was, a fucking train wreck. My hair was greasy, as I could barely stand long enough to shower, let alone wash my hair. Because I couldn't keep food down, weight was melting off me; I could see the bones in my wrists protruding. I was wearing an oversized Metallica tee and fluffy socks. It was all the weight I could take on my body. Any more was cement on my back.

"Okay, how about we both take a cat nap?" she decided. "You always feel better after a nap."

I yanked the throw up to my chin. "Or you wake up wondering what year it is," I muttered.

Lily laughed, a horrible, forced sound that fractured another piece of me.

"Sleep, Bex," she whispered, her face wiped of that terrible fake cheer. The sad, defeated look was almost as bad, but at least it was real. She squeezed my hand. "You'll get through this."

I gave her a fake smile of my own. "Sure I will," I lied. She went to pull away but I kept my grip on her hand. "Thanks, Lils," I choked out. "For everything."

She smiled again. "That's what friends are for. Now sleep."

She let me go and I resigned myself to fighting against cravings instead of welcoming oblivion. I got a delightful surprise when sleep came the second I closed my eyes.

The surprise was short-lived, however, because with sleep came nightmares.

FOUR

"When you're going through Hell, keep going."
-Winston Churchill

"**A**re you sure you don't mind staying?" a voice whispered.

"Of course I don't mind. You're actually doing me a favor. This guy seemed to find my address and he seems to think we have a date tonight. I'm happy to be anywhere but in the vicinity of my place," a different voice answered.

"Okay, just call me if anything happens and if she...." Lily's voice trailed off and she cleared her throat. "If she gets *sick*, just call me."

I tried to shake off sleep but it was too tempting to stay in the realm of half wakefulness, so the hurt in Lily's voice didn't hit me fully.

"She'll be fine. We'll be fine. I've got Pop-Tarts and *Magic Mike*. Nothing bad can happen when they're around. Now go." The woman's voice was familiar, from somewhere.

"Okay. Thanks so much for doing this, seriously."

"Yes, you're welcome. I'm amazing and we both know it. You can thank me by calling that idiot biker and restoring my faith in love and happiness."

There was a pause. "Okay, bye."

"Toodles."

I heard footfalls across our floor, then the door opened and closed.

Then there was silence and I was alone with the anonymous woman.

I creaked one eye open, then another. As soon as I welcomed reality back in, the craving hit me like a sack of potatoes covered in barbed wire. I sucked in a breath, a clean breath. It felt wrong, the air. I was too fucking lucid and there was nothing I could do about it.

Well, there *was* something I could do. One big, tempting, alluring something.

But I wasn't going to.

Once I'd fought off the craving to a manageable level, I looked up. A woman with chocolate curls wearing head-to-toe black and making me all too aware of how fucking wretched I looked banged away in the kitchen. I got up on shaky feet. She looked up, her kohl-rimmed eyes focused on me.

"Hey, you're awake," she observed. "I'm making Pop-Tarts." She held up the box. "That's my version of cooking. That and opening a bottle of wine, but from what Lily's filled me in on, mind-altering substances might not be the best right now. So sugar and preservatives is our hardest drug right now." She peered at the box. "And this particular flavor has seven vitamins and minerals in it. Score. Health." She gazed up. "Wait, you like Pop-Tarts, right? I won't be able to trust you if you say no, just FYI."

I blinked at the woman in front of me. The knockout with expertly applied makeup, wearing a turtleneck and a leather skirt that molded to her small but curvy body, chattering about fucking Pop-Tarts. And talking with obvious knowledge of my addiction. Not tiptoeing around it but stepping her kick-ass heeled ankle boots right into it.

I liked her immediately.

"Anyone who doesn't like them is most likely an employee of the Devil. Definitely not worth trusting," I said, my voice slightly croaky.

She grinned. "Awesome. We can be friends, then."

••••

"Can you do that?" Rosie pointed to the screen, where Channing Tatum was executing a pretty deliciously complicated dance move.

"In my current state? No," I answered, swallowing my fourth Pop-Tart. The first food that had actually stayed down in three days. "But when I'm not recovering from a heroin addiction? Totally."

Rosie grinned at me. "Well, the second you're better, you're totally teaching me how to do it."

When I was better. She said it offhand, like it was actually a certainty rather than a very precarious future that relied on me not fucking up.

I grinned back. "Sure."

Despite the obvious shit I was battling, I was actually having a good night with this chick. I still felt like some invisible asshole was using my psyche as a punching bag, and I wanted a fix more than I wanted backstage tickets to Smashing Pumpkins, but that small grin was about forty percent genuine. Rosie was refreshing in her authenticity. She didn't dance around the topic of my addiction, despite the fact we'd only just met. She didn't even fucking blink when I said I was a stripper, just nodded and said that pole dancing was a great workout.

She was giving me the smallest bit of hope, treating me like I was normal, not a colossal fuckup.

It was because I was starting to feel hopeful again that the pounding at the door came to remind me that I'd never be normal.

Rosie didn't jump, but her eyes flickered to me. "You expecting anyone?"

I shook my head.

She pushed up off the sofa. "You stay put, drool at Channing. I got this," she declared, dusting Pop-Tart crumbs from her skirt.

I didn't watch the screen but the door as she made her way over to it, a sick feeling in my stomach.

That feeling was justified when she opened it.

From my vantage point on the sofa, I could see Tyson clearly, taking up the entire doorframe with someone else next to him.

Rosie leaned against the frame casually, blocking their view of me. "Can I help you?" she asked sweetly, like it was two Girl Scouts in front of her, not a couple of assholes who had lost their necks to steroids.

"We're looking for Bex," Tyson grunted.

"I'm looking for a cross between Jared Leto and Charlie Hunnam." She looked them both up and down. "Nope, that's not you." She tried to close the door but a meaty arm stopped her.

"We ain't fuckin' around. She's got a job to do and we're gonna make sure the bitch earns Carlos some money. Serious money," he growled.

Great. It wasn't like I hadn't been expecting some kind of reaction from me informing Carlos I was quitting and then hanging up the phone, but I didn't expect such a swift and intrusive course of action.

I figured he'd be patient and cocky and wait for me to come crawling back. Which was not going to happen. Not if I stayed clean.

Rosie raised a brow. "Sorry, she's not here. And even if she was, I don't think she ordered steroid Barbie. How about you go and pump some iron or take selfies of each other shirtless and pretend you don't want to bone each other?" she suggested.

I had to put my fist in my mouth to muffle my laugh.

Tyson's ears reddened. "We aren't fuckin' amused, bitch. We know she's here. You don't let us in—"

"What, you'll huff and puff and blow my house down?" Rosie interrupted. "Sorry, you don't scare me, and you don't call me names unless you want me to make sure you can't procreate. Which, if you ask me, would be performing a public service. Run along now and accost someone your own size." She slammed the door in their faces only because she caught them by surprise, pushing the lock home quickly as the door rattled against its hinges.

I expected her to look panicked when she turned but her face was light. She leisurely walked to her bag as if there weren't two goons shouting threats at the door.

She rifled through her stuff, snatching her phone and putting it to her ear.

"Lucky?" she greeted, inspecting her nails. "I'm good, how are you? Oh cool, say hey to Jagger from me. Tell him if he needs a place to stay tonight, I've always got room." There was a pause and she winked at me. "Well, you don't actually have to tell my brother, you know? Grow a pair and stop being so fucking well behaved for an outlaw. Anyway, we'll fight about that later. I'm thinking I might need a little backup. I've got some wannabe goon squad assaulting Bex's door and interrupting my favorite scene in *Magic Mike*. I'd take care of it but I just got a manicure and—" She stopped talking and her eyes went wide. "Chill, dude she's fine but—" Again she stopped talking and then put the phone down, turning to stare at me.

"Okay, so you did not tell me Lucky and you have a thing."

I blinked at her, but then my attention flickered to the vibrating door. "We don't have a thing," I said. "Do you think that lock will hold?"

Asher had just installed two deadbolts because he was a man and had to take charge of such things. Our old locks would have given away the moment someone started banging. These were legit, but our door was crap. I didn't think it'd be hard to kick down.

Rosie waved her hand. "It's fine," she dismissed. "Now you and Lucky. Spill."

As if this was actually the time to have a chat about men.

"There's nothing to 'spill,'" I argued.

She raised a brow.

I sank back onto the sofa, my hand on my forehead. "I'm a stripper recovering from drug addiction. Do you think a relationship with a biker is what I need right now?"

Rosie folded her arms. "Maybe it's exactly what you need."

I gaped at her. "Lucky is, like, your family, right?" I clarified. I had learned Rosie was Cade, the president's, sister, so I was pretty sure that made her biker royalty.

She nodded. "I've known him since he was fourteen and I was seven. He rolled into town with a stupid grin, running as fast as his gangly legs could take him. I would say he's like a brother to me, but I tried it on with him when I was drunk two years ago, so that would be sick." She gave me a look. "Don't worry. He was quick to run away from me and my advances. And I mean *run*. All of those men are total pussies when it comes to me. They're all too afraid of my brother to even have wet dreams about me. Talk about twat blocking." She rolled her eyes.

I shook my head and grinned, despite the constant banging at the door jarring my shattered nerves. "Okay, so whatever he is to you, you're close," I surmised.

She nodded.

"So I'm assuming you care about him?"

She nodded again.

"Then you don't want him with someone like me."

She frowned. "Someone like you?" she repeated.

"Yep. We've already established my label as stripper and, very recently, ex-junkie." I pointed to the door. "Plus I'm the object of that sort of drama. Which involves the goons from my place of ex-employment most likely coming to rough me up in order to persuade me into solicitation. Not someone you'd want to bring home to Mom, or even your outlaw biker family. I'm too much even for your family," I said.

She narrowed her eyes. "Seriously?" she snapped. "*That's* why? That's why Lucky hasn't touched any of his normal girls and isn't joking like a twelve-year-old? Because you've got stupid shit like *that* stopping you from being with him? You think you're not good enough for him?"

I gaped at her, at her anger. Then I stood, crossing my arms. "I don't think it. I *know* it."

She rolled her eyes. "In case you hadn't noticed, we're not talking about a choirboy here. We're talking about Lucky, member of a motorcycle club. He doesn't just carry a gun as an accessory, you know? He's used it. Many times. And not to do the deeds of the common people. And even if he was a fuckin' lawyer, or cop"—her eyes flickered with something, but I didn't have time to inspect it—"it wouldn't make a difference. You're good enough," she said, her voice firm.

"You can't say that," I argued. "You don't even know me. Trust me— my life, it hasn't been good."

Rosie cocked her hip. "Newsflash, honey: life is rarely good. In fact, most of the time it fuckin' blows. But it's usually the people who have the best upbringings turning out to being the most depraved of them all. A bad life doesn't create a bad person, and usually the opposite is true. Lucky is a good fucking case study, as are most of the men in the club. Most of them came from the stuff of nightmares. They'll never be good in the conventional sense, but I'd put my life in their hands in an instant." She eyed me. "I don't know you, but I know you're not bad. I've seen that too, and you're not it."

I was going to argue with her further but there was an abrupt end to the banging, followed by sounds of a struggle.

Rosie's eyes lit up. "Boys are here." Her grin faltered. "I wish we had popcorn for this."

Okay, this chick was insane.

I crossed the living room to open the door. Lucky had his gun out, as did Asher, pointing them at Tyson and Artie. Both of them were backing away with their hands up. Artie had a bleeding nose.

Lucky turned. "Oh hey, Becky. How's life? You don't have to go to such lengths to get me over, you know. Just a phone call or a text would suffice. But it was turning into a boring Saturday night and my trigger finger was getting rusty," he said conversationally, like he wasn't pointing a gun at two retreating assholes.

He held up his free hand. "One second." He turned his head back. "You assholes come within one fucking mile of Becky again and I'll come and scalp you while you're sleeping." The change in his tone was chilling, and, because I was fucking deranged, fucking hot.

Tyson sneered. "You're not gonna be around forever. We'll get her where she belongs," he spat.

I watched the side of Lucky's jaw harden. He stepped forward, his gun level. "You're not gonna be around forever, and I'm fuckin' tempted to make your forever end now but I'm not too keen on spending date night cleaning up your brains. So how about you go back to the gutter where you belong and I'll make sure Becky remains where she belongs, with me," he growled.

There was a pregnant pause before both men edged to the stairs and retreated into the shadows.

Both Asher and Lucky waited a beat before lowering their guns. Lucky turned to me and I folded my arms. "Date night?" I repeated.

He grinned and I felt that expression to my toes. "Yeah, well, we're not exactly the conventional couple. What's a date night without guns and death threats?"

I narrowed my eyes at him. "We're not a couple. Period."

He shook his head and stepped out of the shadows, chuckling. "You keep tellin' yourself that, firefly." He patted my head.

I scowled at him. "I don't need to keep telling myself the truth," I shot back.

"Kids, can we bring the bickering inside? You're letting in the chill," Rosie called from inside. "Lucky, I've got beer for you if you don't tell my brother I'm giving Jagger somewhere to stay tonight."

Lucky grinned and tucked me into his shoulder, directing us back into the apartment. "I can't be bought with beer. I'm more loyal to my prez," he said as we stepped inside.

Rosie grinned between us and held up the box. "I've got Pop-Tarts."

"S'mores flavor?'

She nodded.

"I didn't see or hear a thing," Lucky said.

Asher shook his head, then focused on me. His gaze was shrewd as he took me in and his eyes hardened. "Where's Lily?"

I yanked out of Lucky's grip. Not because it was uncomfortable; it was too fucking comfortable. His pleasing smell of leather and tobacco made my eyes go lazy. But I'd been puking all day and my hair was unwashed. That smell would make his eyes water.

"At work," I replied, crossing my hands over my chest. I was more than aware I was only wearing an oversized tee, no bra. Granted, the tee almost reached my knees and provided more coverage than even my most conservative outfit, but I had no makeup on, my face was pale and splotchy, the circles under my eyes almost black, and my freckles made me look like a twelve-year-old with mono.

Asher obviously observed this. "You okay?" he asked, his voice thick with concern.

That hit me. Hard. Because it was genuine. I knew I wasn't Asher's favorite person, and for good reason, but there he was, coming to my rescue and being actually worried about me. It was all because of my connection to the woman who he was infatuated with, but still.

"I'm fine," I said.

Lucky seemed to shake out of his cocky delusion and saw what Asher saw. His grip was heavy on my shoulders, almost to the point of pain, as he turned me roughly so I faced him.

He took me in and his form hardened. "What the fuck?" he bit out.

"You want to let me go?" I hissed. "I like my shoulders *not* crushed by The Incredible Hulk wearing leather."

"You want to tell me what's wrong with you?" he clipped, not letting me go.

I struggled under his grip and the weight of his stare. It unnerved me, his change. Not an ounce of his previous humor lurked behind his stare.

Asher stepped forward. "Brother, you might want to let her go," he said, his hand going to Lucky's shoulder. Lucky glanced down at Asher's arm, then at his own inked hands, as if he was surprised to see them clutching my shoulders. He immediately let me go.

I rubbed my shoulder distractedly.

"Fuck," he muttered, stepping forward. Asher hovered close, as if he anticipated having to step in.

I wasn't afraid. I knew he wouldn't put a hand on a woman in anger. Men who did, they had something about them. Something people like me sensed straight away. I'd known it about Dylan the second I met him, but because I was majorly fucked-up, I took up with him anyway.

"Did I hurt you, Becky?" he asked, concerned.

I shook my head. "I'm fine," I lied. I actually welcomed the pain. It was a nice distraction from the relentless itch I was fighting, even now.

He glowered at me. "You need to stop it with the fuckin' 'fine.' You're not. Jesus, look at you. Are you sick?"

I smiled, despite myself. "Yeah, I'm sick," I agreed.

He touched my elbow, directing me to the sofa. "Well sit the fuck down before you fall down. I'll fix you some chicken soup," he said, pushing me gently onto the sofa before straightening.

"We don't have chicken soup," I informed him.

Rosie handed him a beer and a Pop-Tart, doing the same to a hard-faced Asher. "And you don't know how to make chicken soup," she added with a grin.

He frowned at her, taking a pull of his beer. "Then I'll order some." He looked back to me. "Have you been to the doctor?"

Yeah, I've been to the hospital where multiple doctors told me I'd been a hair's breadth away from death and recommended I go to some rehab facility. "I don't need a doctor. I need rest and relaxation, which means you need to leave."

His eyes narrowed. "You realize what just happened before?" he clipped. "What they wanted? What they were willin' to do to get it?"

I swallowed, not from fear, as I wasn't afraid of those idiots, but something else. "Yeah, and I know how to handle myself."

Luckily, or maybe not so, our little argument was cut short by a scream. Lily's scream.

My blood went cold and the men went into badass mode. If this were a cartoon, there would've been an Asher-shaped cloud where his body had been before he darted out of the door. Lucky was hot on his heels.

I pushed off the sofa, intent on following them. Rosie's hand on my wrist stopped me.

"Let me go," I hissed.

"You need to let the guys take care of it, as unfeminist as that sounds," she said softly.

I turned to her. "That's my best friend."

"I know. But you don't have any pants on, you're wearing grandpa socks, and you can barely stand up," she pointed out softly.

My body swayed as if to bring her point home.

Her grip became firmer, keeping me steady. "They got her," she murmured.

"This is because of me," I whispered.

Rosie's face went hard. "No, this is because of the people who are doing this. Self-blame is not good for the complexion, and I won't let you go all martyr and take everyone else's sins on your shoulders."

I kept my eyes on the door, praying for an unharmed Lily to come through it.

Like usual, my prayers weren't answered.

When I saw Lily, she was pale and gasping for breath, a familiar scene from living with her.

Lily had asthma, and when she was in a high-stress or high-exertion situation it got bad. Heck, sometimes it came out of the blue. I didn't scare easily; in fact, I didn't scare at all. But watching my best friend suck at the air and not get enough to breathe in was fucking terrifying. Especially after finding out that her attack was triggered by two men attacking her in our parking lot.

Because of me.

Fortunately I knew how to deal with this, and all my sickness and the relentless itch disappeared. For the amount of time it took to get Lily's inhaler and for her to catch her breath, at least.

Then the shake came back. The need. Because I needed this to be okay. I needed to find the contentedness that I'd found with the needle.

Because none of this was okay.

The only thing that was okay was the furious biker tenderly holding Lily in his arms like she was the most precious thing on the planet. That was okay. Because he'd protect her.

From the world.

From me.

Because even now she was trying to protect me. To pretend that she hadn't almost been attacked, or worse, because of me.

"I'm fine," she said quietly as her burly biker crowded her with his concern.

My eyes were glued to her, but the side of my body was aflame from Lucky's stare. I ignored it. I had to.

"You were just attacked in your own parking lot. No one expects you to be fine, Lily," Asher said.

"I am," she replied firmly. "I won't be if someone doesn't tell me what's going on."

Shame cloaked me, seeped into my bones.

"It was because of me," I whispered, barely able to speak through my disgrace.

"It is not because of you," Lucky growled, his face dark and eyes imprinting on me. "That's the last time you're laying the blame of this shit at your pretty little feet, got it?"

He stared at me and the way his eyes locked on me, his words so sure, seeped through the broken pieces of me. For self-preservation, I clung to them. I nodded, unable to speak. I had to look away; that stare would undo me. I was already hanging on by the last dirty, frayed thread.

"They were here because they're the scum of the earth who consider women property and don't like it when they get told otherwise," Asher cut in.

If I was in my right mind, I totally would have something to say about that. These fucking bikers might not beat their women and pimp them out, but they liked to exert some form of ownership over them. I'd experienced it firsthand.

But the difference was that ownership with them wasn't chains. At least not ones that hurt and rubbed you the wrong way. No, their chains were comfort, protection, the kind that made you never want to be free again.

Those were the most dangerous.

Lily must have mirrored my inward concerns because Asher felt the need to defend his little band of brothers and their chains.

"We never see women as property, flower. Not our club. Women aren't possessions to be owned and traded. Any fucker who thinks that is someone who needs to taste lead," he declared hotly.

Despite my best efforts, my gaze flickered to Lucky, then just as quickly flickered back to the floor. Because his gaze was still hot on me, seeing too much while at the same time not seeing enough.

If he saw enough, I'd be free from the chains I was already seeking solace in.

"And who are these specific... fuckers?" Lily asked.

I grinned inwardly at Lily's curse. She never cursed. The word sounded comical coming out of her mouth.

Lucky let out a choked sound. We all looked at him. Well, I didn't look at him, just in his general vicinity, I was careful to avoid his eyes. He waved his hand at the group.

"Sorry, shit. I'm well aware of the need to teach these fuckers a serious lesson, but I wasn't even sure you could utter the word 'fuck,' Lily," he spoke my thoughts, like he'd plucked them right out of my head.

This was getting freaky. And not in the good way.

"You know Bex's boss?" Asher asked Lily.

I was glad for the change of subject, though not at the way it was steering into reality. My ugly one. I didn't need to reveal that in front of my new friend and my... Lucky.

Not mine. No.

Lily nodded. "I've had the displeasure."

"The strip club serves as a recruiting tool for his main business, peddling flesh," Asher stated.

I swallowed bile, but knew I shouldn't be surprised. These bikers were part of the biggest motorcycle club in the state, and they had their very own strip club. They had to know what their competition was up to.

Lily nodded at this.

I hated that, that she was exposed to this shit. Women like Lily weren't born to be rubbing shoulders with women like me. With the realities that were too rough for her fragile skin. Though she wasn't weak. She was stronger than me.

"You knew?" Asher asked, surprise clear on his face.

"No, but I'm not surprised. That guy gave me the serious heebie-jeebies," she replied, her eyes zeroed in on me. The concern in them was painful. "Bex?" she probed, like she needed to know that I wasn't fucking men for money.

My blood was ice. My best friend, the only one who ever saw whatever sliver of light that was left in me, still needed reassurance that I hadn't descended further into sin.

"I said no," I stated quickly, hating everything about the moment. I swallowed thickly.

Get your shit together, Bex.

I had to play my part. Build up my shell so it wasn't transparent how broken I was. You couldn't display weakness in front of sharks or horses. Or bikers who sniffed it out and would make it their life's work to protect said weakness.

It worked for Lily and Asher.

Not for me.

Not for Lucky.

So I had to fake it.

"Or I may have used more colorful words than a one-syllable response, just to get my message across." I grinned, hoping it didn't look as forced and painful as it felt. "I thought that was the end of it. Obviously not."

"That's why those thugs were here? To bully you into prosti-tution?" she surmised.

As soon as the words left her mouth the air became heavy with two sets of alpha males emitting their own brand of fury. From the corner of my eye, I could see Lucky's entire form stiffen. Could taste the bitter fury in the air.

I had no idea how to claw my way out of this clusterfuck.

"Thing one and thing two came knocking at the door, trying to intimidate the little female into letting them in or they'd huff and puff and blow my house down. Didn't count on the fact I'd seen way worse than them. And I had bigger, badder wolves on speed dial," Rosie spoke for the first time, and I could have kissed her at that moment.

"I don't get it." Lily frowned at me. "Carlos may be an asshole, but he can't expect you to go back to work there after that. What did he have to gain from it?"

I shrugged, holding onto my mask with a death grip. "The fact I've got nothing else. That I need to eat."

She gaped at me. "You're not going back there, are you?"

No, I was not going back there. I couldn't stomach even the thought in my newly lucid state. I didn't have much self-respect left, but I had my pride. It was broken and tattered and in a sorry state, but it was still there

"Since I've been *sick*"—I emphasized the word, in order to make sure the biker searing me with his gaze wouldn't cotton onto the ugly truth—"I've obviously been missed. My ass is the only reason that place makes anything. That and my boobs."

My two greatest assets, as Carlos himself had stated. All I had. And they were melting away with the weight.

"So you're going back?" Even Lily couldn't hide the judgment in her tone.

I had been about to reassure her that even I wasn't that stupid when someone beat me to it.

"She's not fuckin' setting a toe in that shithole's direction," Lucky growled, his cold stare intent on me.

The moment he spoke for me, took away my choices and control for himself, was the second my back went up. "I am," I snapped. Of course I wasn't going back, but the very fact that he thought it was his decision to make made me want to do it just to make sure I was in control.

He tried to stare me down but that time my resolve was rock solid.

Lucky sighed and shook his head. "You wanna take your clothes off, show the world that sweet ass, you'll be doing it at our club. Where I can keep a fuckin' eye on that ass," he declared. "And where no one puts a hand on you, trying to sell that ass," he added roughly.

I scowled at him, searching for an argument where none existed. I could go back to the club where drugs were aplenty and the boss had me beaten up to try and get me into prostitution, or I could work for a club that had zero tolerance for drugs and were well known to pay the girls well and treat them with respect.

It was an opportunity to try and wrench myself out of the hole I was in. Only I wouldn't be doing the wrenching. Someone else would be doing it for me. The chains would tighten and I'd be even less likely to release myself.

So I had the opportunity for redemption. The only price was my pride.

"It's a good idea," Lily said gently. She knew what this was for me, knew my past and how I had just been tossed about by fate, unable to grasp the reins.

She had my best interests at heart, yet I still couldn't wipe the glare from my face.

All I wanted was escape. From all of this.

But that was the easy way out. I needed to learn that escape was not an option. Not anymore.

"You won't be swinging your ass around any pole until you're better. What's wrong with you? Have you been to the doctor?" He mirrored his earlier concern, that time seeming more intent on getting an answer.

I would rather die than have this moment drenched even more in the shame that came with the truth.

"I'm fine," I lied.

He scowled at me. "Bitches around here need to stop saying they're fine when they're obviously not. Every man worth his salt knows that if uttered by a woman, the word 'fine' could signify a fuckin' apocalypse," he muttered.

My blood reached the boiling point at his words, Rosie and Lily sending death glares his way as well.

He held his hands up in surrender.

"We haven't seen the last of them," Asher stated, ushering the conversation back to the more pressing matter before I could do something like scream in frustration. "Carlos knows you're my old lady. For him to authorize this, for them to do that with my bike in the parking lot…?" He paused, his face grim. "They're not fuckin' around."

"If what they said to me was anything to go by, they most certainly are not," Lily muttered.

I went stock-still at her words.

"What exactly did they say?" Asher asked slowly.

"That we haven't seen the last of them," she lied. She was a totally crappy liar. I needed to give her lessons.

"Don't get cute, flower. Now is not the time. What specifically did they say?" Asher commanded.

"Not something I'd care to repeat," she said.

I swallowed my smile. Lily was holding her own with the alpha biker. If it weren't in this particular context, I'd be high-fiving her. But this wasn't a moment to exert her newfound stubbornness, not when she was in danger.

"They said when you got tired of our… snatch, they'd take it for themselves," she finally relented under Asher's stare.

I sucked in a breath. Then another. I tried to make it invisible, the fact that the oxygen didn't seem to be entering my lungs.

"You're going to the club," Asher growled. "Both of you."

"No, we're not," Lily argued. And I knew it was for me. Because she knew that I was walking a thin fucking line. One I was already teetering on the wrong side of.

Even if I fell, even if I relapsed and never got out of the hole I'd jumped into, I wouldn't drag Lily down with me. I met her eyes. "We'll go, Lil. That's the second time you got hurt as a result of my shit," I said, trying to keep my voice even. Trying not to show how much this was getting to me. "It'll be the last," I finished, staring at Asher.

"Damn straight it'll be the last," he repeated.

I sagged at the certainty of his tone.

"I've got school here. And work. I can't exactly commute back to Amber at two in the morning. And I need that job," Lily argued.

"Well, I can solve that particular problem," Rosie chimed in from the corner before smoke could drift from Asher's ears. "Gwen and Amy have been itching to get you back, but they were waiting for the right time to ask. For things to… settle down with you." She paused, gazing around the room. "Things aren't looking to settle down anytime soon, so I'm declaring this the perfect time," she exclaimed with a smile.

This chick was awesome.

"Okay," Lily gave in under the weight of four against one, though Lucky wasn't saying anything, or smiling. He was just staring at me.

I ignored that.

Or tried to.

"But we're not going to the club," Lily added, giving me something to focus on. "I can't study, can't live... there," she said, her voice weak. I knew what hid behind her words, the memory of that day three years ago when she and Asher started this whole thing. When, the very next day, she'd found out Faith was dying. "But there's a place in Amber, somewhere no one knows about. Somewhere they, whoever they are, won't find us."

I blanched. I knew where she meant. Knew what a huge fucking sacrifice she'd be making if we went there.

I didn't think I could hate myself any more, but life was full of surprises.

"Lils," I whispered in protest.

"Where would that be?" Asher asked in a hard voice, interrupting me.

"My mom's," she said, her voice stronger and clearer than my previous broken whisper.

There was a long silence as everything sunk in around the room. As my disgrace in myself settled deeper. Took roots.

I figured I'd just have to learn to accept it.

Without any substance.

How fucking great.

FIVE

"We are all broken, that's how the light gets in."
-Hemingway

"**D**on't you have a home to go to?" I asked, irritated.

Hazel eyes locked onto mine. "No. I'm homeless and if you kick me out, you're subjecting a young, vulnerable man to a night on the streets. Someone would make me their bitch. Have you seen these thighs?" He pointed to denim-encased thighs that could crack steel. I tried to ignore the vagina flutter that those thighs caused. Lucky gazed at me with doe eyes, which looked comical on his hardened, chiseled face. "How could you sleep at night if you did such a thing?"

I cocked my brow. "I'm sure I'll find a way," I responded sarcastically. "You're not staying here," I added.

My voice was firm, but every cell in my body screamed against it. When Lucky was around I had something to distract me from the hunger. From the unbearable craving to shoot up. Because when he was around I craved something different.

Him.

I still yearned for the euphoric nothingness that the needle offered, but I also craved the complex and confusing *something* that Lucky offered. Each was at opposite ends of the spectrum, yet I could have neither.

We were moved into Faith's place, although I guessed it was Lily's place now. Since her mom was gone, she'd inherited a house full of ghosts. Asher was firmly back at his place at her side and I dug that, but I was also feeling like a fucking major third wheel. She was recovering, healing from the loss of her mom, from the shit I put her through; she didn't need my darkness hanging around, obscuring her light.

But unless I wanted to sleep on the streets, I was there, a shadow on her light for as long as it took me to save enough for my own place.

Now that I was gainfully employed by the Sons of Templar MC, or was going to be, and not shooting my paychecks into my arm, hopefully I'd be able to stand on my own two feet. And maybe even buy some kick-ass boots to stand in. And to kick ass. Because I was getting mighty sick of the bikers needing to come to the rescue. I was getting even sicker of my reaction. Of fucking wanting to be saved.

I didn't need the man who took up most of the real estate in my brain to save me.

I needed to save me.

Hence my getting very flipping annoyed at him for hanging around like a bad smell since that night, two days ago. I was annoyed at him for making it feel good. Too fucking good.

"No, you won't find a way," he argued. "You'll lie awake at night, haunted with the knowledge that I'm cold and vulnerable on the mean streets."

I rolled my eyes and the corner of my mouth turned up. "The mean streets? Of Amber?" I clarified. "Yeah, some bored housewife might hustle you into her minivan and take advantage of you, being so vulnerable and all."

He widened his eyes at me, the teasing glint alight. "Yes, and what a horrible thing to have on your conscience. I'm much safer here," he decided.

No, you're not, a voice whispered. *And neither am I, not with you here.*

Because I was already kicking one addiction, I couldn't kick the other. I focused on the TV. "I have utter and complete dominion over the remote, and you do not say anything about whatever 'game' muscle heads are playing at this point in time," I relented.

He grinned, sinking back into the sofa and putting his hands behind his neck. "I'll agree to that."

I pointed at him with the remote. "And no touching."

He held his hands up. "Hey, I can control myself. I'm not an animal. It's you I'm worried about. I've seen the way you look at this." He gestured to his body, currently clad in a tight tee and faded jeans. I almost broke a rib swallowing my laugh when I'd read his tee: *'Let's fight some ballerinas.'* It was so ridiculous and so utterly him. At odds with every other aspect of his biker persona, so much so it seemed to compliment it. Made him more attractive. He'd kicked off his boots and his cut was resting on the arm of the sofa. It was weirdly erotic to see him comfortable, to see him relaxing, and watch the way his limbs moved.

I rolled my eyes. "You're delusional."

His smile sent flutters up my spine, chasing away the itch I was battling not to scratch, even now. "Admit it, you find me attractive."

I met his gaze. "What makes you think I find you attractive?"

He raised his brows. "Um, because you're not blind."

I stared at him, and then I couldn't help it—I burst out laughing. Like proper, holding-my-side laughing. There was only the slightest edge of hysteria to it.

I finished and the way Lucky was staring at me had me shift uncomfortably. His eyes were still bright, but his gaze was deeper, more intense. "It's okay, firefly. I find you immensely attractive too," he murmured, his voice thick.

The tone, his gaze, they had me stuttering over a response for a second before I found my façade and laughed. Although that time it was forced. "Yeah, because I could totally grace the cover for *Vogue* right now," I retorted. "I'm not a huge fucking mess or anything."

I was. Sleep was a stranger to me. Especially being here, where the walls fucking seeped Faith. Her paintings, her spirit was everywhere in the colorful bohemian cottage by the sea.

It was a paradise. Tranquility. Or was supposed to be. If you weren't dragging chaos around with you. I couldn't be comforted by the ghost of her presence because I didn't want her to be a fucking ghost. A memory. She didn't deserve to have her dignity and spirit sucked away by a disgusting disease. Lily didn't deserve to lose her mom.

They were good people. And shitty things happened to them.

What hope was there for a fuckup like me?

So yeah, no sleep, which meant black smudges under my bloodshot eyes. I had managed to wash my hair, but it was still a messy mop atop my head. Food was hit or miss, which meant my cheeks were sunken in. And despite Lucky's constant presence, I didn't have the energy to hide behind my mask of makeup, to wear clothes that gave me an identity other than what I was.

Instead I was wearing leggings and a stained hoodie. I looked like a homeless person and he looked like a fucking *GQ* model.

The teasing left his eyes at my words and his jaw went hard. "You won't say that shit, not around me," he growled.

I frowned at the sudden change in his demeanor. I was getting more used to it, now that he was spending more time around me, despite my protests. Most of the time he was easygoing, almost annoying in his fucking optimism and cheer. Almost. Would have been certainly if I didn't harbor this huge schoolgirl crush on him. If I weren't addicted to everything about him.

His dumb attractive smile, the way his face darkened and his jaw hardened when the topic of Carlos came up, or when I stumbled from getting up too quickly. And when I refused to give him the details on my 'sickness.' That really pissed him off.

So much so that he'd declared he was camping out here until I 'got better' and until he was sure Carlos's goons would leave me alone. The latter wouldn't take long, I guessed. The former, well, he'd be here until the day he died waiting for me to 'get better.'

"What shit?" I asked.

He leaned forward, the motion so quick I couldn't scuttle away from his touch. My reaction times were shot to shit. He grasped my chin in his hands. "You bringing yourself down. Saying shit that pisses me the fuck off because it's not true, and because you're so fuckin' certain of it. So we'll get this straight. You're beautiful. Gorgeous, in fact. When you're strutting your stuff on stage, showin' too many fuckin' people your amazing tits and ass. When you're strutting your stuff down the goddamn street. When you smile when you don't think anyone's watching. When you laugh for me." His thumb brushed my lower lip. "When you've taken all your armor off and are just you. Even when you're spattered with bruises that make me want to kill and maim every person who had a hand in it. Even when you're battlin' some fuckin' sickness that you won't tell me about, you're stunning. So don't say anything to the contrary. Don't fuckin' *think* it. I'll know." He tapped his temple. "I can read minds. There's no end to my powers."

His eyes flared slightly with their telltale humor, but mostly there was something that wasn't common. That I tricked myself into thinking was unique to the way he looked at me.

His mouth was inches away from mine. The fix was within reach. I actually leaned forward slightly to get just one hit, but he pulled back and it stung.

"Now pick a fuckin' show," he ordered.

I blinked a couple times, letting my breathing get back to normal. Then I scowled, more to hide my emotion from the rejection. I flipped through channels till I found the perfect one, grinning wickedly.

He didn't say a thing, just leaned back, eyes on the screen.

• • • •

"Oh my fucking God. That bitch," Lucky snarled.

I was no longer watching the screen. Watching him was *so* much more entertaining. I just needed a glass of wine. But I couldn't, you know, because I couldn't replace heroin addiction with alcoholism, as much as I wanted to.

He glared at me. "Can you believe that they did that? Right behind her back. Oh, that's not cool. She better put them on the blacklist for every charity event from now to forever for that shit." He paused. "Or cut the breaks on whatsherface's new Mercedes."

Suffice to say my plan backfired. I'd thought the alpha male, tattoo-covered biker would hate watching reality television.

I was so very wrong.

"And now they're turning up to her party like they didn't potentially fuck up her marriage. That's just...." He trailed off, shaking his head.

I suppressed a giggle. "Okay, I think we need to watch something else," I declared flipping the channel.

Lucky gaped at me. "No. I need to see what happens," he snapped.

I grinned. "Some people can handle these shows. Some, like the burly biker in front of me, get too emotionally invested. I'm saving you now by cutting you off, or else you'll be here till six a.m. binge-watching and wondering why life could be so cruel to botch Michelle's nose job, trust me."

He stared at me. "Michelle gets a nose job? Why?"

I laughed and shook my head. "So can't handle it." My gaze flickered to the TV. "Much safer," I said, nodding to the explosions and car chases of some action flick.

He pouted for a while, and it was hilarious. I realized, after five minutes of being amused by his sulk, that I hadn't thought about a fix. In five whole minutes. Of course, as soon as I thought of it, that was all I could think about. I scratched my arm absently.

Lucky's bald head turned to me. "Can I ask you a question, firefly?"

"As long as it's not pertaining to Michelle and her plastic surgeries," I deadpanned.

His eyes twinkled but his face was serious. "Why?"

I tilted my head. "Why what?"

"Why the stripping? I know you're good at it—fuck, are you good at it—but you're better than that."

His words were sobering and I realized the little fantasyland I'd been in, watching TV with him, like normalcy was something I could clutch. I stiffened. "You don't know me well enough to know what I'm better than."

He regarded me. "I think I do," he protested softly. "I'm not judgin'. We do whatever we need to just to stay breathin', to make it through this fucked-up thing called life."

For a split second, I swore I saw something behind his eyes. Something dark, blacker than midnight. Something that rivaled my dark. But then it was gone, leaving me wondering if it was a trick of the light.

I retracted my claws. "I did it because it was the logical choice," I said, sighing. "I had a shitty childhood. I'm sure people had it worse, somewhere, but I didn't think so at the time. So I promised myself that I'd be better than what I'd been forced to be."

I swallowed the ash in my throat and the memories threatening the corner of my mind. I looked into his hazel eyes; they anchored me to the moment, prevented me from getting swept away in those memories. "I'm smart." I shrugged. "Nothing special, but I read a lot and it sticks, what I read. I went to shitty high schools but got good grades. And good schools like to even out their stats by sponsoring some hood rat to come and lift them from obscurity. It makes for good publicity and helps them push away the belief that fancy colleges are for the elite, white, upper-middle class." I sucked in a breath. "I had hope at first. I did well, made friends, met Lily. Almost forgot where I came from." I paused. "And then I remembered. Figured out what I was meant to be. Where I belonged. And it wasn't on a college campus, and it certainly wasn't in fucking medical school. No big, sad, tragic story. Just the truth. Just reality."

Lucky stared at me, never looking away for a second. "You're wrong," he said finally. "That is sad. Fuckin' tragic. That that's what you think. Jesus, Shakespeare could've written a play about that shit." He moved forward to cup my cheeks gently. "That the world could not only give you a shit hand, but think you, someone like you, deserves it?" He shook his head. "Fuckin' tragedy."

Then he leaned in to place a gentle kiss on my head before yanking me into the crook of his shoulder, circling his arms around me.

I was going to protest, try to escape his arms, but then I didn't. I was tired of fighting myself, so I decided to surrender to him. At least for the night. The morning would bring the light of day and hopefully I would have found enough strength in my slumber to fight him off.

SIX

"There's no drug on Earth that can make life meaningful."
-Sarah Kane

I don't need a fix. I don't need a fix.
That was my mantra, my fucking prayer. Playing on repeat while sweat trickled done the corner of my forehead and I struggled to keep my body from shaking

"Do you take Asher Breslin to be your lawful wedded husband?"

Yeah. I was thinking about shooting up while standing beside my best friend in a beautiful dress her mother bought her before she died. Craving oblivion while my sister finally got her happy ever after.

"I do."

I don't need a fix.

I would say I was going to hell, but I was already fucking there. Trapped in my own body, suffering and mentally flagellating myself for being so fucking self-deprecating on the best day of Lily's life. I had my own little Hades inside my skull.

I squeezed my hands around the bouquet of flowers, taunting me with their beauty when all I wanted was filth in my hands to shoot into my veins.

"You may kiss the bride."

For one second, beautiful clarity, the thing I'd taken for granted before, settled over me. I was freed from the clutches of the monster that had its grip on my soul to watch Asher grasp Lily and lay a hot and heavy one on her that was so not a chaste kiss. I found it in myself to grin. A real one. Happiness shined through the cracks of my damaged soul because if there was one thing I loved more than heroin, it was Lily. My kind and loving best friend.

And she was happy.

She was free.

For that split second, so was I. And then, for the second after, when Lucky's hazel eyes met mine, I was something else. Not free, but not held captive by something twisted and ugly. I was clutched by the promise in those eyes, the potential. Held hostage by a beautiful dream.

Then it was gone.

Reality burst back in at such a speed my teeth chattered together and the itch came back full force.

The cocktail of the need for my fix coupled with my disgust in myself and happiness for Lily reached a bottleneck, and traitorous tears leaked from my eyes.

Tears!

I hadn't cried since... since that night I curled up under dirty sheets, after my childish innocence had been stolen and I thought tears were something useful. That someone might hear my sobs and tear me away from the life that had become a nightmare.

No one did. That night I realized tears were useless, and I never cried again.

Until now.

And I was wearing winged eyeliner. It would fuck up my whole look. Who was I kidding? I was already a total mess; smudged makeup wouldn't do much to make me look worse. I already *was* worse.

I hastily wiped my eyes and glanced at Lily, who was getting swallowed by Lucky.

"I love you," she mouthed.

I tried my best to chase away my demons and let the warmth of this moment swallow me up. "I love you too," I mouthed back.

"No party," Asher growled, his rough voice puncturing the soft moment.

I tried to hide my grin, a real one as Lucky looked like Asher had just ran over his puppy. I also tried to ignore how the ensuing bickering over the need for a party to celebrate Asher and Lily's nuptials made me fall even deeper for Lucky. The way he was such a contradiction. The way he looked like he robbed convenience stores for fun, but then he treated my fragile best friend with a gentleness that she deserved. The way he treated me like I was something. *Somebody.*

I tried to shake myself out of it. What the fuck was I thinking? Was I falling for him?

Jesus Christ.

This wedding thing was like a drug of its own, hypnotizing me in its thrall, making me think pink sparkly thoughts that were even more dangerous than the prickly black ones I'd been swimming in. At least I could swim in those. I reckoned I'd drown in the former.

I jerked myself out of my head just in time to see Lily convince her husband—so weird that that's what the massive biker was now—that yes, they would indeed go to the party Lucky was whining about. I smiled on the inside. Lily was changing, growing. She was healing. Before, a party at a biker clubhouse would've had her running a mile, but now she was ready. She was stronger. I didn't miss that it wasn't me who made her that way, but Asher. It was a bittersweet feeling. I was beyond happy that she was slowly conquering her own demons, but I was upset that I wasn't the one helping the only person who helped me. The only thing I'd done was given her a bottle and a substance to abuse. The only way I knew how to cope was destruction.

"I'll take this one in the cage." Lucky jerked his head to me and my whole body tightened. An enclosed space with him while battling cravings that rattled my entire body? No fucking way. Especially when the threat of destruction meant the prospect of something, or *someone*, to stave off that destruction was almost as enticing as the needle itself.

"And you take your bike," Lucky continued, his attention back on Asher.

Before I could do something to get out of the situation, like fake a heart attack, Lucky's hand snatched mine and dragged me away from the blushing bride and her biker.

"You want that hand to remain attached to your body, you remove it from mine right now," I hissed as he dragged me along. The anger was for my own good more than anything else. His strong, large, and dry hand clutching my small, clammy one had me feeling some type of way. The wrong type. The pink sparkly type.

Lucky looked straight ahead, directing us out of the double doors. "I'm willin' to take the risk of dismemberment to hold your hand, Becky," he replied, a smile tickling the corner of his mouth. "Plus, I heard they're doing great things with prosthetics these days. Maybe I'll get a hook hand. I reckon I could work that shit."

A hook hand?

I struggled in vain as he led us out of the hallway and opened the door to the parking lot. I flinched back as the harsh sunlight assaulted me and caused black spots to dance in front of my vision.

Lucky stopped immediately, standing in front of me. His large body obstructed the rays of the devil ball, thankfully.

Spots still danced around my eyeballs, so I couldn't gauge the look on his face.

"Shit, it all makes sense now," he said.

I squinted at him. "What makes sense?"

He yanked me closer to his body, as if he were trying to shield me from the sun. "You're a vampire. I've never seen you in daylight, and I knew no one human could possibly look like you and do the things you do with your body. How could I not know before? A creature of the night. Of course you sold your soul to the devil. That's how you hypnotize me so," he deadpanned.

I blinked at him a couple times. He was right on one score; I did sell my soul to the devil, or I'd tried. Even he wouldn't take that mangled thing. "You're insane," I muttered.

He grinned at me. "Only two doctors have come to that conclusion. The rest just say I have an overactive imagination. Let's get my little vamp to the car." He made a big performance of lifting his leather cut in front of my face. "Don't want that beautiful skin getting scorched." He grinned at me when I scowled at him. "If you're a really good girl, I'll even let you suck my blood. I'm tasty, you know." He winked.

"You're something," I replied, almost lower than a whisper. Something was dangerous. Especially when I'd almost killed myself to escape something in pursuit of nothing.

As soon as we got in the cab he seemed to sense my unease. Though it wasn't exactly easy to hide. And I was doing a crappy job.

"You gonna tell me what's wrong, or am I going to have to torture it out of you?" he asked blandly, putting his hand over the back of my seat so he could reverse out of the lot.

I stared at the caramel, sinewy, tattooed flesh. I had an unbearable urge to lick it. That's all my body and mind was it seemed—animal urges. Lick people, get high. Whatever.

"Torture what?" I asked, my response slightly delayed as I watched the journey of his arm back to the steering wheel, hypnotized by the way his veins pulsed from his skin.

His eyes flickered to me. His voice and face may have been easy, as was his default, but the depths of those hazel irises showed something different. Something that unnerved my newly sober eyes. Everything off the junk was clearer, starker, and not in a refreshing way. The world was jarring, and it rubbed up my skin the wrong way. Seeing it without the film of a high was uncomfortable because it was reality. I thought the worst thing was looking in the mirror, but it wasn't.

It was looking at Lucky.

I'd convinced myself that my feelings for him were intermingled with my feelings for junk, and going cold turkey would wash away the daydreams of the cheerful yet deadly biker.

Oh, how wrong I could be.

The air in the cab of the truck was so stifling I felt like I might choke on it. Or throw up. I really hoped I didn't throw up.

Somehow Lucky's attention was on me even though he was in control of a motor vehicle. It should have unnerved me, but it didn't. I felt safe with him. *That's* what unnerved me. I wasn't safe with anyone, not even myself. Safety was an illusion and surrendering to the feeling was the moment you opened yourself up for destruction.

"The reason behind this," he answered my question, his jaw hard as his eyes flickered up my seated body.

I clasped my hands together at my knees. I knew I looked like shit. Even though I'd tried my best to paint my face and disguise the toll the loss of my 'medicine' had taken, it was impossible. My arms were skinny and my face was sallow. I was always pale, but now my skin had a grayish sheen to it and the bags under my eyes couldn't be covered with industrial strength concealer. So not cute.

"I ate a bad burrito a couple days ago," I lied. "What doesn't kill you makes you thinner, right?" I went for bravado but fell short. Everything was falling kind of short. It was hard to make an effort on maintaining the façade while battling the itch beneath my skin at the same time. It didn't help that a renewed itch prickled my arms with Lucky's gaze.

"You're full of shit," he ground out, not taking his eyes off me. "Tell me the truth."

I glanced at the windshield to escape his gaze. "Shouldn't you be watching the road?" I asked, changing the subject. "When I die I want to be wearing a better outfit than this. Also I'd quite like to turn up to my death a little drunk." The joke was a little too close to home. I'd almost turned up to the pearly gates, or more likely the entry to the nine levels strung out in a dirty bathroom stall.

My gaze flickered to the steering wheel as Lucky's hands tightened on it. His eyes still didn't leave mine. Seriously? The truck was still dead center in the right lane. Was he Superman under that cut?

"Let's get one thing clear here. You got a smart mouth. You make jokes, not as well as I do, but your sense of humor was bestowed on you by the devil himself and I dig that." His eyes burned into mine. "One thing you don't joke about, you don't *ever* fuckin' utter it again, is the prospect of you disappearing off the face of the earth," he growled

I was stunned silent. That didn't happen very often. I not only had a response any time someone tried to tell me what to do or say, but I had a multitude of responses, usually liberally peppered with curse words. Theoretically, a big alpha male badass telling me what to say and not to say would have exploded Volcano Bex. Not this time.

Maybe it was because I didn't have the energy to throw sass when I was too busy fighting my body's scream for junk. Maybe it was because I was feeling all weird after watching my friend tie the knot which challenged all my assumptions about true love being a crock of shit. It could have been any of those things. But it wasn't. It was the way he was looking at me coupled with the fact that sentence communicated his care for my well-being. Someone other than Lily or Faith actually giving a shit about me.

Because he was Superman, or Superman's evil biker older cousin, he sensed the intensity of the moment and my inability to handle it. A grin tickled the corner of his face.

"You especially aren't allowed to speak of you leaving this earth without giving me a taste of that sweet ass."

He winked at me and his eyes flickered back to the road, finally. We were pulling into the clubhouse. Thank Lucifer for small favors. Not thanking God because I was sure he or she had given up on me a long time ago. Or I'd given up on him.

I scowled at his profile. "You bet this ass is sweet. Sweeter than any club skank you've sunk your teeth into. But do you know where this sweet ass is going?" I timed my line perfectly as he pulled into a park. "Out of this car and away from you. Have fun watching me walk away because that's the closest you'll get."

I darted out of the car before my speech filtered into his mind. These guys were weird as fuck, taking rejection to be foreplay. Not what I had in mind. I slammed the door and sauntered towards the clubhouse. I didn't look back but I still heard his shout.

"You're killin' me, firefly."

I gritted my teeth. "Nope. Saving you, actually," I muttered.

SEVEN

"Normal is an illusion. What is normal for the spider
is chaos for the fly."
-Morticia Adams

I'd clutched my beer so hard I thought it might snap, and somehow resisted Gwen and Amy's offer for cocktails. I wanted hard liquor more than I wanted a new pair of Doc Martins, but I knew it was a slippery slope. The minute that drink trickled down my throat was most likely the minute I lost it all. So I said no. Being stone-cold sober at a biker clubhouse wedding reception was like being at a One Direction concert—not fun.

Being stone-cold sober on Planet Earth was not fun.

In addition to Lucky's stare and pretending not to watch him shrug off the girls, I had to deal with the narrowed eyes of Evie, who had been perusing me since I walked in the door. Or, more accurately, watching Lucky watch me. I'd been the object of disapproval many a time, so I recognized it on her face. Mostly, it didn't hurt; I'd learned to let such gazes bounce off the hard shell I created. But this one slithered through the cracks and stung because I knew what she was. The matriarch of this little family. Motley it may be, but this gathering of outlaws and 'whores' and the rugrats running around was a family. One Lily had been welcomed into with open arms. One that, despite my outward protests, I yearned to be a part of.

That look cemented my outsider status, despite the warmth I got from the rest of the women. Kindness was all well and good, but it wasn't real most of the time. Disdain may be uncomfortable, but at least it was real. It was too much—the happiness in the room; the hard, kohl-rimmed stare of the biker queen; and most certainly the hazel gaze that itched my skin worse than withdrawal.

I had to escape. The only reason I'd stayed that long was because I loved my best friend and didn't miss the way her gaze flickered to me every now and then. Didn't miss the way her smile dampened just a little when she took me in, concern evident on her face. Nor did it escape me that her husband, who had hold of her the entire time, glanced my way when she did, his own gaze hardening.

I tried my best for jaunty smiles when that happened. I wasn't going to fuck up Lily's wedding day with a breakdown. I'd done enough.

So it was lucky I slipped outside when both of them were heading off down the hallway to consummate their marriage, based on the look on Asher's face and the blush on Lily's.

I sucked in a breath of fresh air, flattening my back to the outer wall of the clubhouse. There was a sprinkling of men in cuts around the grassy area, most smoking and drinking beers. A couple glanced my way but didn't give me a second look. I wouldn't give me a second look either.

I tried to suck in another breath. Useless. The air was too fucking clean, too crisp. My shaking hands reached into my bag and I managed to get what I was looking for.

Sucking in the poison and smoke was a relief. One that curbed the craving—not a lot but a little. Enough that I could go on standing and not curl into a little ball in the corner.

I didn't smoke before. Abhorred it, actually. Being premed, I'd learned all about the effects of the little death sticks. Yellow nails and decaying teeth? No, thanks.

Ironic that I stayed away from cigarettes but took the needle without as much of as a second thought. They were the only things that got me through, swapping one addiction for another. Though the way I was feeling right then, an early grave was a little too enticing.

I managed about five seconds of peace with my death stick. Alone time wasn't something you got even when you lurked on the fringes of this outlaw family.

"You doing okay, sweetie?" Rosie asked softly, her brow furrowed in concern as she leaned beside me on the wall.

Like Evie's, that look punctured my shell too, but for a different reason. Because it was genuine. Because she cared. Ever since that day at our place, she'd treated me with respect and kindness, not with judgment or disdain for dragging her into my twisted world. It was unnerving, something I could get used to but something I didn't deserve. I couldn't escape it, though, as she texted almost every day and came around to Lily's, all the while acting like I was a girlfriend, not an ex-stripper junkie.

I did my best to smile at her. "Totally fine. Peachy, in fact."

She raised a perfectly plucked brow at me. Everything about the fucking women in this club seemed to be perfect. Gwen and Amy looked like they strolled straight out of *Vogue* and their outfits could fund a deposit on a house. Or keep me in drugs for the rest of my life. You know, if I did that sort of thing.

Rosie was different. From what I'd seen of her she changed personas with her outfits. Right then her chocolate curls were a mass of plaits on her head, spiraling down her back. She was wearing a vintage maxi skirt with a huge split down the thighs and a barely there crop with a multitude of tribal necklaces looking like they'd snap her skinny neck.

I looked like... exactly what I was beside her. A junkie stripper.

"Bullshit," she said, snatching the smoke from my hands and taking a puff for herself.

Now it was my turn to raise a brow at her. Normally such actions would unleash my inner bitch, but my inner bitch was in a death match with my inner demons. Even if she weren't, I didn't make a habit of being a bitch to people I actually liked. I was a bitch to a lot of people, sure. But that was because I didn't *like* many people.

She inhaled and exhaled, blowing smoke from her blood-red lips. "You look like shit," she continued. "Not as bad as you should, mind you." Her heavily made-up eyes flickered up my body. "Somehow you're working this." She waved her arm at me and my black lace 'bridesmaid' dress, which I'd paired with combat boots and winged liner, of course. "Takes a special person to look hot while recovering from what you went through." Her eyes went soft as she handed me back my smoke and squeezed my other hand. "Also takes a special kind of person to stand next to their best friend at her wedding, fake a smile and happiness while she's crumbling on the inside."

I blinked at her. Then I took a long drag of my smoke, mostly to buy some time, to find a way to chase away the fucking tears lurking at the corners of my eyes. "Lily's my best friend," I said by explanation, shrugging. "This is her day. I'm not about to fuck her life up more than I already have."

Rosie frowned at me. "Sister, you have not fucked up her life, or your own for that matter."

I gave her a look. "So having shitty taste in men, becoming addicted to drugs, and almost killing myself with a cocktail of the two is living the American dream?"

Rosie gazed at me and, to my surprise, burst out laughing. When she finished, she grinned at me. "Who wants to live the fucking American dream? I think I'd die of boredom." She reached out to squeeze my hand again. "In case you haven't noticed, it's not exactly suburbia here." She glanced around. "We've seen our fair share of ugly. Of shit. Of death." She sucked in a breath, her eyes twinkling before she shook herself and moved her gaze to me. "But we're still standing. Maybe a little bruised, maybe a little battered, but still here. And it's always the people who have been through the most who are most interesting. The best kind of people."

She let us bathe in the silence after her words, not pressuring me to respond straight away. I sucked on my smoke. "You always do therapy sessions with an ex-junkie stripper outside wedding receptions?" I asked finally.

She grinned. "Oh just every other Saturday. First one's a freebie."

I smiled back, a real one, crushing the butt under my combat boot and turning to her. "Thanks," I said, my voice barely above a whisper.

"Anytime, sister," she replied. "I mean that. Anytime. You're not alone."

It was nice, the sentiment. But despite the sincerity in her eyes and the support in her words, that's what I was. Alone. You were born alone and you died alone. And you were alone all the time in between.

"Oh and I've been thinking, about alone. I've been living alone for a while now and it's starting to get downright boring," she said. "I don't do boring. And also the chances of being targeted by a serial killer are heightened when you live alone. Trust me, I know, I watch *Criminal Minds*," she deadpanned. "And I'm guessing living with the happy couple might just trigger your gag reflex, despite it being amazing, yada yada yada." She made a mouth motion with her hands. "So how about you come and stay in my spare room and lower the chances of me being dismembered by a crazy guy with daddy issues?"

I gaped at her. Not just for some of her crazy statements said with a total straight face, but the fact she was asking someone she barely knew, someone recovering from a drug addiction, to live with her. "You're serious."

She grinned. "Oh, I'm rarely ever serious." She waved her hand. "But this is a rare snippet of seriousness. Don't tell me you can't or won't or whatever. Just say yes."

I was tempted. Sorely. To get out of the house that taunted me with Faith's presence. To let Lily live without worrying about me. "I've got a lot of baggage," I informed her.

She grinned. "Good thing I've got lots of closet space." Her gaze flickered behind me and her face paled. "Fuck," she hissed. "Got to go, babe. I just made eye contact with a guy I may or may not have bumped uglies with. I do not want to repeat that experience." She scrunched up her nose. "Two words. Back hair. Not cute. And you're totally moving in with me." She kissed my cheek, then turned on her fringed heel and darted towards the parking lot.

I watched her retreating back, shaking my head. It wasn't long after her escape that all the demons lurking under the surface emerged once more. I resisted the urge to chain smoke there for the rest of my life, namely because of the large biker with cold eyes and scar-ribboned skin who was regarding me in a way that made me uncomfortable. Not checking me out; heck, I was used to that. No, he was looking at me like he actually saw me, the twisted black edges and demons clawing from inside my skin. He'd stared at me like that when he'd come to the club, when he'd helped 'get rid' of Dylan that day Lucky shot him. But I'd been too high to notice. To properly notice.

You're imagining things. He looked a lot more like a murderer than a telepath, but I didn't like to take my chances so, with one last glance at him, I slipped back inside. I was planning on finding Lily, saying my good-byes and getting the fuck out of there, but she was nowhere to be seen. Plus, I had no way to actually get the fuck out of there. Lucky was my ride since my effing car was still at City Hall.

I was contemplating hot-wiring a car because Lord knew I couldn't afford a taxi. I couldn't afford a fucking cheeseburger. Not that hunger was something that bothered me. Not for food, at least.

I made my way through the crowd with a beeline for the ladies' room. Most big life decisions were made in women's bathrooms. My mind flickered back to that fateful night. *Or, in my case, death decisions.*

The ladies' room was blessedly empty and surprised me with its cleanliness. I splashed some water on my face in an attempt to wash away the insects underneath my skin, but they were like my mascara, waterproof and not going anywhere.

I had another handful of seconds to myself before my peace was again shattered. Though I was loath to call it peace. Alone time wasn't peace; it was the opposite. And in that handful of seconds, I realized what I was going home to. I was so desperate to escape company that I failed to understand the solitude that awaited me. Lily and Faith's house filled with happy memories and ghosts. My hands started to shake. I honestly didn't have enough faith in myself not to relapse. In fact, I had *no faith* in myself.

Get your shit together, Bex. You can do this. People do this every day. They beat it. It's possible. You're the one who got yourself into this, so get yourself out.

I braced my sweaty hands on the knees of my dress and sucked in a breath. A clean breath. My mind might have been close to cracking, my little demon aching to be broken out, but I was clean. I was sober. So help me God I was going to stay that way.

I may or may not lose my shit along the way. I just had to get through Lily's wedding night without making it all about me and my ugliness, then I'd be home free.

Or home, chained to the confines of my addiction.

Straightening, I left the stall and was about to exit the bathroom when the door burst open and precisely the last person I wanted to see in this state walked through it.

I straightened my spine in an outwards gesture of strength, or at least defiance. Inwards I was a fucking mess. "This is the ladies' room," I snapped at Lucky. "I know we're in a compound full of alpha animals who think they own the Earth, but women's bathrooms are a sacred space which no male shall breach unless he wants to suffer the consequences."

Lucky, for once, didn't grin. In fact, he hadn't grinned the entire night. His watchful gaze had been glued to me, prickling the edges of my hairline with its intensity. I'd tried to ignore it, just like I'd tried to ignore the way multiple scantily glad girls sidled up to him. I didn't judge those girls. Not for a moment. It was obvious what they were to Lucky, to the club. Some people would call them whores—the same people who would call me a white trash junkie, I guessed. I called them survivors. So I didn't judge them, as they were my sisters in a way. Women on the fringes of society who didn't live the way they were 'supposed' to. But I hated them. Not for what they were to the club, but what they were to Lucky. Jealousy wasn't an emotion I was familiar with, but it was bitter and toxic and made me want the needle even worse than before.

Lucky advanced on me and I barely had time to retreat, my back smashing against the wall beside the basin. His bulging arms rested on either side of me, caging me in.

"You need to back the fuck up," I said, my voice shaking.

Hazel eyes seared into me. "You need to tell me what's going on," he rumbled, his voice vibrating through my spine.

I sucked in a breath. "Well, currently, a biker with the manners of a Chihuahua has waltzed into a bathroom which is reserved for the opposite sex and accosted me," I snapped.

He narrowed his eyes. "You can't sass your way out of this shit, babe. I'm not fuckin' blind." His eyes flickered up my body and I felt heat with his gaze, although it wasn't sexual, more pensive. "No matter how fuckin' hot you are, you can't hide it. The weight that's fallen off you... Jesus, I'm afraid a stiff breeze will topple you. You've been hidin' it, faking it with me. But you're not getting better. Shit behind your eyes is dark. Dark enough it scares the fuckin' shit outta me. Takes a lot to scare me, Becky. So you're gonna tell me what's got the dark behind those eyes so I can kill whoever's responsible."

Despite myself, I let out a cold giggle.

"This isn't funny," he ground out.

I swallowed my laugh. "Yeah, it is. It's fucking hilarious," I hissed, leaning forward so our noses almost touched. "You want to kill the person responsible for this?" I gestured down at my body. "Get your piece out now, then. You've got your villain."

He froze. "What the fuck are you talking about?"

I used all of my laughable strength to put my hands on his chest and shove him away. I didn't move him much, just enough for me to duck under his arm and put some much needed distance between us. He frowned at me but didn't advance again, merely held his body taut.

"You've got some warped idea in that bald head of yours that you've got some claim on me. That we're *something*. That thought process needs to stop. Right now," I ordered.

He grinned at me, though it wasn't the same carefree grin that seemed to live on his face. It was something different, something I put there. Another thing to hate myself for. "We are *somethin'*, firefly. You know it. I knew it the moment I saw that sweet ass on stage. Knew it was mine then too."

I restrained an exasperated scream. "Really? While I was dancing on stage, taking my clothes off for a room full of perverts, you knew I was yours? I was *everyone's*. The fact that you felt like it was all for you meant I did my job right."

Lucky's jaw hardened. "That shit's not true and you know it."

I scowled at him. "The only thing I know is that you should be medicated because you're in the fucking clouds if you think I'm yours. If you want me for something more than a fuck. Because that's all I'm worth, and the only reason you think I'm worth more is because I haven't opened my legs for you."

He stepped forward, his hands clenched at his sides. "Maybe if you stop fighting so hard against this and give me a fuckin' chance, then you'll see I want you for a lot more than what's between your legs."

I laughed again. "Really? You're telling me you want me for what? My glowing personality? My overflowing bank account? Or how about my glitzy career where I take my clothes off for money? Yeah, I'm a fucking catch."

Lucky paused in the center of the room, taking up every molecule of oxygen with his presence. "Yeah, babe. I want to know more about the spitfire who has a fucking ocean beneath the surface, who has a dirtier mouth than me which turns me the fuck on." He paused as the sex-drenched words caused my panties to dampen. He stepped forward again. "Don't give a shit about your bank account, mainly because any man who's a man takes care of his woman, though I'll guess any man who tries to take care of you might get his face ripped off. And baby, that independence, that ferocity cloaking the vulnerability, it turns me the fuck on." Another step forward. He was quickly rendering my earlier escape little more than useless. "Your current career just happens to be my favorite profession," he continued, a teasing glint in his eyes. "Though I will admit I don't love the fact that everyone gets to see the goods." He came close enough to circle my neck with his hands. "Not the biggest fan of that. But as long as I get to be the only one who samples those goods, I'll deal. For now."

I stared at him, half hypnotized, half shocked. I knew I should've been pissed at the blatant, irritating confidence, but I couldn't muster it.

"You keep tryin' to push me away, but the only thing you're doing is pulling me closer. I'm tangled up in you and I've only tasted your lips once," he murmured. "You were right. I'm crazy, goin' 'round the bend. It's all because I'm going through withdrawals. Haven't got my Becky fix." His mouth was inches away from mine when his last sentence had me turning to stone and hurtling back to earth. He must've gauged my change because he reared back.

I lost it then, whatever control I'd been clutching to. I pushed him away once more. "That's ironic," I hissed. "Because I'm going through withdrawals too. Not in the poetic way you used the term in order to get into my pants, but the real, body shaking, throwing up, thinking the universe is going to finally kill you type of way," I shouted, and began to pace the room. "You think all the other flaws in my personality are so fucking adorable? How about heroin addiction?" I whirled to face his granite body and blank face. "Does that 'turn you the fuck on'? Does that make you want to put me on the back of your bike and have your name tattooed on my ass? Is this sexy?" I ripped up the sleeves of the flimsy cardigan hiding my arms and exposed the fading track marks in the crook of my elbow. I'd been careful when he was around, which was a lot, either hiding them with makeup or clothing. "To know that I shoot up every single day to escape my absolute train wreck of a life? That I almost ended said train wreck of a life one week ago in a dirty nightclub bathroom? You ready to claim me as yours now?"

His silence and the blank expression on his face were answer enough.

Despite expecting this exact reaction, despite saying these things with the intention of getting him away from me, it hurt. Stung through the layers of armor and steel I'd constructed through the years. Stung in such a way it punctured the wave of desperation I had for a fix.

"Yeah," I whispered, jutting my chin up defiantly, doing my best to act like the rejection didn't bother me. "I'm glad to see the ugliness of my reality has finally shown you the truth. Now that you've seen what I am, you can get on with your life and leave me the fuck alone." I stepped forward with the intention of skirting around him and running all the way to fucking Mexico.

But that plan was thwarted when his hand darted out to snatch my arm and hindered my escape. I was too surprised to struggle, to say anything, not that he gave me the chance. He whirled me around to face him and yanked me into his body, plastering every inch of his torso with mine before claiming my mouth. People said that, claiming, and I didn't understand it. Okay, I turned my nose up at those people and called them soppy assholes.

But there was no other word for what he was doing. It was him, owning, possessing, fucking branding me with one kiss. But it was more than one kiss. I'd kissed countless guys over my not-so-humble sexual career. Kissing mostly meant nothing. This was something— more than something. He was kissing me, wanting me after I just laid my filth at his feet.

He released me both too soon and not quickly enough. My brain felt like Jell-O and I was panting like an overweight Labrador.

"What was that?" I managed to choke out, blinking at him rapidly. He didn't answer, merely set my panties on fire with his gaze and hitched me over his shoulder. Yes, people did that in real life, if that's what this was.

It took me the time it took him to leave the ladies' room and walk down the hall to realize what was going on and start struggling. I wriggled and kicked, not caring that I was wearing a dress and such actions were not ladylike. I was not a lady, so who cared.

"Lucky!" I screeched.

He didn't answer me, just kept walking into the common room full with people. Fucking great.

"Put me down," I ordered, deciding to ignore the hoots and hollers as people watched his journey across the room.

He ignored me again, his arms like vises, hindering my struggle like I was a child. Despite the hoots, not many people seemed perturbed that Lucky was carting a struggling woman through the crowded room. In fact, from what I could see from my current position, everyone continued whatever they were doing without a second glance.

"Hello?" I shouted to no one in particular. "I'm being kidnapped! I thought the whole point of being an alpha biker was to help damsels in distress." I waved my hands. "Damsel, in distress."

I got a smirk from Brock, who had his arm around Amy, who winked at me. Fucking *winked*.

Rosie shook her head, grinning. I amended all my earlier thoughts about her. She wasn't nice; she was a she-devil.

We made it into the parking lot without anyone coming to my aid.

"Fucking bikers," I muttered under my breath. I'd stopped struggling, mostly because I'd discovered it was useless but even more disturbing, I'd lost the ability. My body was weak, but I hadn't realized how much. I was breathless, as well as slightly nauseous from the laughable struggle.

"Put me down, Lucky. This isn't funny," I declared as we approached the truck we'd arrived in. "Or legal," I added. Though I guessed an outlaw biker didn't exactly care about federal law.

Again, Lucky was quiet. His silence was beginning to freak me out.

My stomach whirled as he somehow managed to open the door to the truck and deposit me in the seat in one smooth move. Almost like he'd done it before.

Because I was using all of my effort not to throw up, I missed my chance of escape. Which consisted of kicking him in his crown jewels and running to God knew where. When I realized that option was available, it disappeared. It disappeared with the cold steel circling my wrist and a metallic click.

I gaped up at my hand, which was now attached to the handle on the ceiling. "Holy shit," I exclaimed. I glared at him. "You're fucking *handcuffing* me?" I shouted. "Who the heck has handcuffs in their pockets?"

Lucky regarded me, his eyes still hard as he grinned seductively. "Someone who knows how to use them in the most pleasurable ways."

The door slammed in my face and he rounded the car. I rattled the cuffs, looking for a way to pull them free. I was still attached to the roof by the time he climbed in the cab and began reversing out of the lot.

"Let me out of these. Right now," I ordered, my voice dripping with venom. It disguised the panic. Not only was I restrained in a small space while battling with withdrawals, but I was stuck with him. The one person I needed to be far, far away from. Well actually, there were two people I needed to be far away from but the second was myself, and unfortunately, you couldn't escape yourself. I'd tried. Came out with a drug addiction and, more recently, handcuffed in a truck with a hot biker.

"Can't do that, Becky," Lucky replied, eyes on the road. His body was relaxed, voice even, as if this were a totally normal thing to do.

I glared at his profile. "Um, I think you've got shit upside down. What you *can't* do is throw someone over your shoulder and handcuff them in a motor vehicle. I know you live in some alternate biker world, but I'm thinking this particular act is a universal no-no."

Lucky gave me a sideways glance before turning his attention back to the road. "The world I'm livin' in has a beautiful woman who's under my skin, drowning, struggling, and too fucking tough to ask for help. I'm not gonna let you drown, firefly. Letting your light go out? *That's* a universal no-no." He paused. "I knew you wouldn't come willingly, so I'm doing what's necessary."

I took a long deep breath. A clean one. I needed a fucking smoke. And a lock pick kit. "I'll come willingly, just let me out of these cuffs," I said, my voice even.

A grin tickled the corner of his mouth. "The moment I do that, I'll see that sexy ass running away from me. I can catch you, no doubt about that, and I'll have fun doing it, but we'll save that for later." Another pause and the grin left his face. "For when you're better."

I pursed my lips together, a thin film of shame washing over me. The silence in the cab was deafening, the truth saturating the air. I scratched my arms, the itch coming back full force.

I watched the town pass us by and houses disappear, replaced by the ocean on one side and empty fields on the other.

"This is kidnapping," I observed.

"You're not a kid, so it's technically adult-napping," Lucky replied.

I scowled at him. "You missed your calling. You should have been a fucking comedian instead of a biker."

"I moonlight. Best of both worlds, baby."

"You're impossible. And deranged," I informed him.

"I'll get that put on my tombstone."

I let out a totally ridiculous little squeal and whipped my head around to glare at the passing landscape. There was obviously no way I could try and reason with him, so I just had to buy my time and wait for my moment.

What scared me the most was that on the surface, I was desperate to escape, but the little part of me that I was trying to ignore was desperate to stay. Because every second since I'd woken up in the hospital, I'd been drowning. And now, handcuffed and going God knew where, I was treading water.

EIGHT

"She wore a thousand faces all to hide her own."
-Atticus

"Where are we going?"

"That's for me to know and you to find out."

For the millionth time, I scowled at him. "I need to pee."

"About time," he said, glancing my way. "You must have a bladder of steel. I thought women had to pee like all the time. You're always going to the ladies' room, so if it's not to use the facilities, what is it? Is there some kind Jell-O wrestling thing going on in there? You can tell me. I can keep a secret."

I decided to ignore that.

"Okay, don't tell me. I'll just use my imagination."

I ignored that too.

"Now we're coming up to a gas station. I want to establish a circle of trust. You trust me to get the good snacks while you pee, and I'll trust you not to make me chase you when I uncuff you. I've already had my cardio for the day," Lucky said, slowing down and changing lanes so he could get off the freeway and onto an exit.

I rattled my arm which was becoming numb. "Why in the name of Barbra Streisand would I trust the man who handcuffed me to a fucking truck?"

"Because of my devilish good looks and enticing charm?"

I glared at him.

His attractive face turned serious and he gave me his full attention for the first time since he started driving. "How about because I'm going to do anything and everything in my considerable power to protect you, to get you well, to chase the darkness from your eyes. Because the only thing that matters to me right now, besides a chicken burrito, is your trust."

I gaped at him for a split second, his words taking me by surprise and filling me with stupid warmth that I chased away. "Protect me? Is that what you call this?" I rattled the cuffs. "I don't need protecting. I can take care of myself."

Lucky's jaw hardened as he pulled into the gas station. "Recent events make me think otherwise."

That one stung. I didn't let on, of course. "It's obvious that you think a lot of yourself, but I'm sure even you're not delusional enough to think you can cure addiction with muscles and the sense of humor of a seven-year-old."

Lucky stopped the truck, turning his body to me. "I do have mad skills at most things, and great muscles, thanks for noticing. But no, sadly I can't cure it. But I can take you somewhere where you can cure yourself."

On that note, he got out of the truck and let me digest his words for approximately three-point-five seconds. Then my door was opened and Lucky was in my space, his scent and presence engulfing me as he reached up to unlock my cuffs. He seemed to know that my arm felt like lead because instead of it hurtling down, it was engulfed in warmth as he gently circled it with his hand and placed it on my lap. His eyes held mine the entire time.

"I got you, Becky," he murmured. "I know you're determined to face this storm alone, but give me two days. You want to leave after that, I'll drive you anywhere you want to go."

He let the offer hang in the air and didn't move, his thumb gently massaging the feeling back into my arm. I wasn't sure if the pins and needles prickling my skin were the sensation returning or my body's response to his touch. I'd like to believe it was the former, but I feared it was the latter.

He pushed a tendril of hair behind my ear. "You think about it while you visit the mythical ladies' room where the door to Narnia resides. I'll get us supplies. You want anything?"

I blinked at him. "Five Twinkies, an ice tea, and box of tampons," I said, knowing how much an alpha male would love getting feminine products.

He didn't react, only nodded. "Your wish is my command." He stepped back, letting me out of the truck. "Remember, my cardio's already done for the day and I know you wouldn't do anything as cruel and making me work out twice in one day." He winked and leaned in to shut my door before turning and sauntering into the gas station. I watched him—the way the leather on his cut moved along his muscled back, the confidence in his stride, the way two girls walking out of the store actually stopped and watched his journey through the double doors.

I didn't blame them; he was a fucking sight. Too bad he was the most annoying person I'd ever met. My gaze flickered around the gas station, noting the sign for the ladies' room. I made a beeline for it. I hadn't ruled out escape yet, but it was hard to think on a full bladder.

After I'd done my business, I stared at myself in the grimy mirror.

My hair was cascading down my back, a tumble of curls. The ends were freshly died, electric blue this time. That was about the only part of me that had semblance of order. My foundation had washed off and I was starting to worry that the purple under my eyes was permanent. The black cardigan I was wearing over my short lace dress covered my skinny, blotchy arms, but my collarbone was still visible and protruding. "Still a mess," I muttered to myself.

I splashed water on my face and reached into my handbag to rinse my mouth with mouthwash and spray some perfume. My bag was always stocked with emergencies supplies, though it was missing one thing. The thing I craved with an intensity that had my entire body shaking.

I braced myself on the cracked porcelain sink. It was insane, the itch. The need was nothing more than annoying background noise the entire time I'd been in the car with Lucky, but now I was drowning in it again as it filled my entire body with its power. I had decided to slip out the back and hitchhike back home not seconds before, but now I wasn't so sure. Whatever the fuck was going on with Lucky wasn't good, for me and, more importantly, for him. But I was selfish. Desperate not to fall down that rabbit hole that didn't lead to Wonderland. So I made my decision.

"I didn't know what to get, so I just got one of every flavor," Lucky declared, handing me a bag overflowing with feminine products.

I took it from him, expressionless. I glanced down; the bag was actually filled with every 'flavor' of tampons gas stations offered. I saw the telltale Twinkie wrapper along with about four different kinds of chocolate. My gaze went back up to Lucky, who was munching on a burrito. He held out an ice tea. I took it wordlessly.

He nodded to the bag. "I got chocolate too, 'cause I know when bitches get on the rag they need that shit. I don't know why. That, along with women's bathroom treasures, will remain a mystery to me, but I thought it would be safest to get you some too."

I didn't have a response to that, namely because it was so fucking... *domestic*. He was acting like this was something we did every month. Like he hadn't just handcuffed me to a truck after finding out about my drug addiction and subsequent overdose. It was so fucking normal and it scared the shit out of me.

His eyes flickered over me, losing the easiness to them. "You didn't run," he observed.

I swallowed. "I'm not wearing the right shoes," I lied. My combat boots would do quite well for running, and for fighting and kicking. One of the reasons I'd worn them since I'd scraped up enough cash to get them at thirteen.

But I didn't want to run. I was so fucking tired of running from everything.

Lucky nodded. "Yet another reason for me to thank the creator of those things." He nodded to my boots. "Not only are they hot as fuck but they keep you right where I want you. Perfect."

As he reversed out of the lot, I had an overwhelming urge to lick the sinewy, tattooed flesh that was inches away from my face.

Instead, I ripped open a chocolate at random, shoving it into my mouth so I didn't do anything stupider than I already had. The stupidity being staying in the truck without a fight.

"Got to say, firefly, I'm glad I don't have to use the cuffs," Lucky said as he pulled back onto the freeway. His gaze flickered sideways for a second, hunger in it. "Well, I'm not ruling out using them completely, but for that particular use, I'm glad."

I crossed my arms, namely to cover up the way my nipples hardened through the thin fabric of my dress at the pure sex in his tone. Don't ask me how the guy could be dorky, yet funny, yet dangerous and sexy as fuck all at the same time. It shouldn't be humanly possible, but there he was, living, breathing, testosterone-emitting proof.

"Where are we going, anyway? Now that I'm not being held prisoner, I should be able to know the destination. I won't be writing it in lipstick on bathroom mirrors anymore. The last message I wrote only had the license plate number on it. They're not easy to trace, right?" I asked sweetly.

Lucky chuckled, and the sound sent bolts of electricity though my body.

Get it together.

"I thought my brothers had snapped up the women with the smartest mouths in all of America, Brock especially." He glanced to me. "I was fuckin' wrong. I've hit the goddamn jackpot."

I narrowed my eyes at him. "You haven't *hit* anything. And you won't be. I'm not someone you've 'snapped up.' I'm someone you forcibly brought into your presence, using handcuffs."

Lucky shrugged. "There's only so long you can be in my presence and not fall in love with me."

I snorted. "Don't hold your breath."

My bravado hid my fear. My absolute terror that his words were a premonition.

••••

"Becky, we're here."

A soft and pleasing sensation on my jaw accompanied the rough voice puncturing my unconsciousness and I clung to it, just a little longer. Oblivion had been a stranger to me since I had become too close with unyielding darkness. Sleep wasn't something that came easy when your entire body was electrified with need, with desperation to meet that oblivion once more.

I snuggled deeper into the slumber.

That time the pressure was not soft, and it was on my shoulder. My body shook slightly. "Becky?" The voice was louder, concerned. "Wake up."

I creaked one eye open, then another. "I was busy," I moaned, cracking my neck and straightening from my slumped position in the seat. The motion also moved me far away from Lucky's proximity and his endearing scent, my sleep-addled mind having leaned into it for a split second.

He put his hand to the back on his neck, his face relaxing. "Busy?" he repeated.

I tried to subtly wipe the drool from the side of my face and tame the rat's nest that was my hair. I had a feeling I looked like a Halloween mask. One I couldn't take off. "Busy *sleeping*," I informed him, yanking my dress into place. His hungry eyes touched my bare legs, sending shivers up my thighs.

"Jesus, Becky. You sleep like the fucking dead. I was worried I'd have to get some smelling salts or some shit. I even checked your pulse. I can still do CPR, and I think you look like you need it." His grin came back, but it was crooked at the edges and didn't reach the sides.

I swatted his body away. "I'll say no to opening myself up to the plethora of STDs that reside in your saliva."

He stepped back, grinning easily in that way that didn't reach his hazel eyes.

I placed my boots on sand, then tasted the salt in the ocean air. We'd been driving the coastal road for a couple hours, so it wasn't a surprise we were by the beach. I just didn't expect to be *on* the beach. The roar of the waves filled my head and I welcomed the noise, drowning out the whispers of the little devil on both of my shoulders. There wasn't an angel in sight.

Beyond Lucky, who had his arms crossed and was regarding me, was a little bungalow thing. It was nothing fancy, which was good; I didn't do well with fancy. In fact, I despised fancy. Not that I had much experience with it.

It was small and there was a concrete footpath snaking around the front of the house, leading down to the beach. The house was mostly windows with faded black wood on the outside. A couple of beat-up old sun loungers sat on a small grassy area behind the sand.

I glanced back to Lucky. "Whose place is this?"

"Mine."

I raised my brows. "Yours?"

He nodded. "You sound surprised."

I chewed my lip and looked from Lucky to the house. I pointed to him. "Badass biker wearing a cut, covered in tattoos." I pointed to the house. "Cute beach bungalow that looks like it belongs to a person with dreads and a surfboard. Yeah, I'm surprised."

Lucky stepped forward, right in my space. The salt air was replaced by his enticing scent, which wasn't gross despite the fact we'd spent multiple hours in a car.

"I like that," he murmured. "Surprising you. Showing there's more to me than what you see. What everyone else sees. 'Cause there is, Becky. A fuck of a lot more. Just don't show it to people. But you're not *people*. Hope you get that."

I swallowed, like I was downing a handful of the sand beside my feet.

"I need coffee," I declared, stepping out of his orbit. I ran a hand through my hair. "And a shower." *And a lobotomy.* I glanced at him. "Though, I didn't have time to pack for this kidnapping, so I'm afraid my outfit choices consist of a bridesmaid's dress. That is not okay with me. In case you haven't noticed, I'm not a dress kind of girl."

Lucky quirked a brow. "Oh, I've noticed," he drawled. All residual intensity from his previous statement drained away.

I scowled at him and inwardly at myself for responding to the sex dripping in his tone. "Can you ever just speak normally?" I snapped. "Not like a fucking male phone sex operator or a caveman? There's an in-between, you know. It's called English."

Lucky's gaze darkened. "You think I sound like a phone sex operator?" he asked, his eyes dancing. "Does that mean I turn you on?"

I threw up my hands. "You're impossible!" I stomped around him and to the door.

"Becky, think quick."

I whirled just in time to catch the keys he'd launched at me.

"Good reflexes." He sounded impressed.

I ignored that and continued my stomp to the door. I had a feeling I'd have to ignore a lot for the two days I'd already begun to regret agreeing to. I'd have to ignore it or I'd be running from one destruction to another.

••••

After I'd gotten inside and caffeinated, Lucky declared he was going into 'town,' wherever that was, to 'pick up some shit.'

"Write down what you need—clothes, shoes, food." He paused. "Period-related things." He didn't even look like the standard awkward male broaching the subject.

There was a multitude of things wrong with that sentence, but the last thing caught me off guard. "Period-related things?" I repeated, scrunching up my nose in confusion.

"Well, I don't know how long all those"—he nodded to the plastic bag—"will last. I know I got a lot, but maybe you need that much? How am I to know? They could last a day, a month, a year. It's a mystery. So if you need more, or anything else that you require at this time of the month, tell me. I can get some Ryan Gosling shit if that's how you need to roll."

"Ryan Gosling type shit." I'd totally forgotten he thought I was on my period thanks to my little stunt that didn't go as planned at the gas station.

He nodded, crossing his arms and screwing up his face. "Fucked if I know why chicks are so obsessed with that shit. I personally think I could entertain you much better." His eyes flared. "But whatever, I'm not suicidal enough to argue with a woman on the rag."

"Do I look like a girl who watches Ryan Gosling movies?" I asked him, cocking a hip.

His gaze roved over me. "Well, you've got tits and a vagina. I thought that was all you needed."

I rolled my eyes. "Jesus Christ," I muttered.

"So, no Ryan Gosling." He sounded utterly pleased.

I looked back at him. "No Ryan Gosling."

He grinned mischievously. "The lady has made an excellent choice. Now write down what you need, sizes and shit." He held out his phone.

I didn't take it. "Why would I need to write that down?" I asked in an even voice.

"So I don't offend you and make you hate me forever by getting you the wrong size pants. Too big and I think you're fat. Too small and I'm trying to tell you to lose weight in order to fit into them, again making you think that I think you're fat." His gaze flickered over me again, his jaw hardening. "Which you're not. Far from it. Which is why I'm picking up every junk food known to harden the arteries of the citizens of this great nation. Put some meat on those bones."

I gritted my teeth and folded my arms. It pissed me off, the concern. Mostly because I liked it. Liked the fact that someone was worried about my skeletal frame, wanted to do something as stupid as shovel candy in my face to change that. That's what pissed me off. Then I was pissed off at him for making me feel like that in the midst this entire ordeal.

And I was embarrassed. Paralyzingly so. Because he was seeing me like this. Seeing how the junk had defeated me, broken me down and turned me into a... junkie.

So my emotions were not what most people would call stable, hence my reaction. "I'm unsure why I would need to write it down considering I'm going to be the one buying my own 'shit.' Period or otherwise. It's not your job to dress and feed me like I'm your junkie Barbie," I snapped.

His eyes blazed. "That's not what this is, Becky."

I glared at him. "Then what is this?" I gestured around the room, which I would have totally dug had I not been in that state of mind. The decorating was boho chic mixed with rock enthusiast. Alas, I was not in the mood to marvel at the décor. "You whisking me off to your little cabin by the sea the second you hear I'm 'drowning' in the sea of heroin and addiction. You think you can rescue me from it all and I'll cling to your motorcycle boot in gratitude? So you can get your masculine alpha card by saving the helpless female? That ain't gonna happen," I informed him. Well, maybe not informed. More like screamed.

He watched me for a long moment. The longest. My chest moved up and down with my rapid breaths, brought on by fury. Fury that was a little misdirected. But it was easier to shout at someone than look at myself.

"I offered to get your shit because you're dead on your feet. You dropped off like a fuckin' stone the moment you relaxed enough to let sleep claim you. Never seen anything like it," he said quietly. "Guessing that entire delicious package, that sharp mind included, is on its last legs. Been holding yourself together for so fuckin' long it's inevitable. You need to sleep, Becky. Pure and simple. That's the reason why I was gonna go in alone. That and I guessed you needed some time here, alone. To fight sleep like a gladiator and to snoop around this place. Then have a moment to let the shit you've been running from catch up to you. Process it without anyone else around." He glanced around. "There's nothing here." He paused, his eyes cutting to me. "Nothing to tempt you. And I know you well enough to know you're stubborn as fuck. Once you make a decision, it'd take a lot to make you stray. So I'll guess you won't go runnin' for a fix if I leave you alone for a couple hours. That's what that was. But you want to fight off oblivion and the rest for a couple hours to walk around a shitty department store to get no-doubt shitty clothes, be my guest."

He then opened the door, gesturing me to go through it.

I blinked at him half a dozen times, looking for the words.

Sorry. That's the word you're looking for.

I pursed my lips together and made my combat boot move. It felt like it was laden with cement, that's how tired I was. Now that he'd mentioned it, it was hard to ignore. As was the constant itch, but it was better with him 'cause I was either pissed off, amused, or turned on when I had him around. Not craving. But I didn't say that, nor that five-letter word. I just walked through the door to buy shitty clothes I couldn't afford.

But Lucky didn't hold a grudge. He whistled in the truck on the way to the town—smaller than Amber, little more than a strip mall and a handful of shops—tapping his tattooed fingers on the steering wheel as if he didn't have a care in the world. As if he hadn't inexplicably taken on a recovering junkie and her boatload of baggage. Like such an endeavor was a hobby, like stamp collecting.

Me, I silently seethed beside him. See, I could hold a grudge. I was an expert at it. I still hadn't forgiven the girl who stole my sticker collection in my third foster home. Hannah, that total bitch. I was directing my anger at him and his irritating cheerfulness when, even at the height of my fury, I knew it was at myself. For being such a colossal bitch and him being nothing but nice. Weird, off-the-charts cuckoo and also fucking hot as balls, but nice. And alpha. It was a very strange mix, one I didn't think I'd ever seen in my life. And I'd seen men. A lot.

It was in the Target snatching up some clothes—all black, of course—that I finally released my anger.

I had deliberately wandered away from Lucky when he had his back turned, inspecting the various sugary snacks while muttering something about how it was better to be prepared in the event of PMS. That should have been offensive for not only me, but for womankind in general. But the way he said it wasn't derogatory and dripping in patriarchy. It was like childhood naivety wrapped up in a male deliciousness with a low, raspy voice.

Hence the reason I escaped, so I didn't pounce on him in the candy aisle in front of a family with a child on a leash.

That child was already going to have enough problems by the look of the way it was struggling against that leash. I didn't need to add to them.

I was mentally calculating how much was in my bank account—I was pretty sure it was nowhere near triple digits—and how many pairs of underwear I could get away with getting. And ignoring the fact I was getting the most expensive shitty lace black ones instead of sensible cotton that came in ten packs. Like I was playing with fire, expecting to get someone to see that.

I'd already played with fire and gotten burned; what was another scar? At least this one would be enjoyable to get.

I absently scratched my arm. Lucky was no longer in smelling distance, which meant my craving was amped up about a thousand percent.

I glanced around, half expecting him to be standing somewhere, watching me with his arms crossed, grinning. I didn't think it was possible to sneak away from alpha bikers. Didn't they have like twelve senses or something? By the way Lily talked about Asher I would have thought so.

"We have a lost child in the store," a voice sounded from the speaker phone. "Would a Rebecca Flannery please come to checkout five. Your"—there was a clearing of a throat—"*father* is here waiting for you." There was no mistaking the slight dreaminess to the woman's tone. She was most likely wagging her tongue at the sexy, grinning, idiotic biker standing in front of her.

There was a muffled sound on the speaker. "Firefly, come back to me. I have snacks," Lucky's husky voice sounded through the entire store, no doubt causing womb flutters everywhere. Even the middle-aged woman wearing a muumuu and inspecting the cotton underwear ten-pack snapped her head up the moment he started speaking.

"Also, cleanup on aisle three." There was a pause. "I've always wanted to say that."

Despite myself, and the insects crawling up my arms, I smiled.

I made it to the counter where Lucky was leaned over, his amazing denim-clad ass and the grim reaper on his cut all I could see as he talked to the near-drooling checkout chick.

As if he had Bex radar, he straightened and turned, eyes finding me in a second. His face lit up and his grin intensified. "I found you."

I made it to him, holding back my smile. "I wasn't exactly lost."

His eyes twinkled. "Yes, you were, firefly." His face was bright, but the multitude of meanings weighed me down.

The checkout chick, who indulged in too much bleach and was wearing a uniform two sizes too small, gaped at me, then Lucky. "That's your daughter?" she asked in disbelief.

I started to speak but Lucky slung his arm around my neck.

"Yep, isn't she adorable? She looks old for her age, and I look great for mine, obviously. I had her young. Even at twelve, my swimmers were world-class." He winked at the checkout chick, who was still gaping.

I snorted. I couldn't help it. The look on her face was fucking priceless.

"Okay, it's getting past this one's bedtime, so let's get our shit and go," Lucky said, snatching everything out of my hands to dump it on the counter.

Both the checkout girl and I were dazed by the man in front of us, albeit for different reasons.

Surprisingly, she recovered quicker than me. Which meant by the time I came to, Lucky was handing over a wad of cash.

"Hey!" I protested, stepping forward. "You're not paying for me."

He glanced at me. "Funny, 'cause I just did."

I scowled at him. "I can take care of myself. I don't need you buying my shit."

Arguably, I couldn't take care of myself—my mess of a life and bank account was a testament to that—but still. My life was my own to fuck up. And my bank account was mine to empty.

He ruffled my hair. "We need to get you home and wash your mouth out with salt, young lady. You know better than to fucking curse." He took the bags and walked us towards the double doors.

I glared at him. "You're not doing that," I snapped.

"What's that, beautiful?"

"That alpha, 'I take care of everything because I have balls' thing. I can pay my own way. I'll never be a 'kept' woman. Or a prostitute," I added.

That made Lucky stop and turn to give me his full attention. "I paid for that shit because it's my fault that you need it. I 'kidnapped' you, which means I should foot the bill. I don't pay for sex, and you sure as shit don't ever need to fuckin' charge for it. I'll never let that shit happen." His voice turned serious at the end. "And even if I did ever pay for the pleasure of your company, you'd be worth a fuck of a lot more than cheap lace underwear, which I totally fuckin' approve of by the way. No matter how cheap, your ass will make that shit look ace." He winked at me. "We good? Or you gonna nurse another snit in the car. I'm good with either option because you're cute as fuck when you're angry."

I fought with the combination of a smile and tears threatening my fragile emotional state. Instead I managed an eye roll and stomped towards the car.

"I'm taking that as us bein' good since you didn't swear at me or call me a misogynistic prick," he shouted after me.

And with my back safely to him, I smiled.

NINE

"Damaged people are dangerous. They know how to make hell feel like home."
-Unknown

"Wow, someone got out of the wrong side of bed this morning," a gravelly voice observed. That was after he had shaken me from my blissful slumber and I'd used every curse word in my extensive vocabulary when he hadn't let me roll back over.

I hadn't had any success in killing someone with the power of a glare before, but I tried my darnedest right then. "It's six a.m.," I gritted out after my glare only intensified his grin. "There's only one side of the bed to get out of at this time." I glanced up and down at him. He was wearing cutoff sweatpants and a white wifebeater that was drenched with sweat and clung to every inch of his muscles. Even my barely awake body responded to that. I reasoned someone in a coma would appreciate that.

"You're a morning person," I observed in disgust, swallowing the half-comatose Bex reaction to launch her sleep-addled body at those washboard abs. I resisted.

"You say that like it's akin to being a suicide bomber," he replied.

I glared at him. "There are a lot of people I don't trust in this world." I held up one finger, starting my list. "People who finish their shampoo and conditioner at the same time." I held up two fingers. "Couples with joint social media accounts." I held three fingers up. "Anyone who puts clothing on dogs." I tried to ignore his amused smirk and how hot he was while doing it. I managed, mostly because I remembered what time it was and that smiling hot fucker was the reason why I was awake. "Morning people round out the list of people never, under any circumstances, to be trusted. It's unnatural," I informed him seriously.

I didn't expect it, but his grin disappeared and he stepped forward, clasping my forearms lightly. His eyes searched mine. "You can trust me, Becky," he murmured. "Even if everything else doesn't make sense, shit turns upside down. That's one thing that's gonna stay constant," he promised.

Okay, it was way too early morning for that shit. The 'hearts and flowers, eternal promise' type shit that caught me unexpected and almost broke a rib with the force in which it made my crumpled heart beat.

Then I finally registered where I was, in a bed, and a very comfortable one. Lucky was standing over me and I was sitting up. The room around me was bathed in gentle morning light that was blazing through the open blinds. I frowned at the offending brightness, though it was hard to frown at the unobstructed view of the ocean. The room was a lot more hippy and a lot less rock than the other rooms. There was a multitude of antique mirrors artfully splayed on one wall like a fucking Pinterest project and a Moroccan-looking rug on the wooden floor. I didn't have time to fully take catalogue of the room because I moved slightly and realized what I was wearing—or not wearing. I was no longer wearing the dress I had on the day before. I pulled out the fabric at my chest to get a better look at it. It was not one of the crappy garments I'd purchased either, and it had a telltale smell.

I glared up at Lucky. "What am I wearing, and how did I get here?"

"Well, you got here because I carried you in here. Lay off the candy, why don't you? You're fucking heavy," he deadpanned. "You crashed on the way back and weren't waking up. I knew you were alive 'cause I took your pulse. And did the mirror thing with the breathing. But I wasn't too hot on bringing you out of that shit 'cause it was obvious you needed it. Didn't think you'd want to sleep in the dress that you hated, so I put you in my tee. Promise I didn't look. Much." He didn't even have the decency to look sheepish, grinning from ear to ear.

I threw the covers back so I could stand toe to toe with him. I had planned on giving him a piece of my mind, but I hit a hiccup when my vision went black and everything went kind of sideways.

A strong hand gripped my arm, stopping my descent.

"Fuck, Becky. You okay?" Lucky's voice lost all hint of humor as he yanked me closer to his body so he could grasp my chin.

I blinked away the stars and tried to shrug out of his grip, which was kind of impossible considering his hands were like vises and I was still struggling to chase off vertigo. "I'm fine," I lied.

His frowning face came into focus. "When was the last time you ate? You were in stasis last night so you missed my delicious dinner, and I didn't see you indulge in a bite of any road snacks yesterday, apart from the chocolate you shoved in your face to stop yourself from licking my muscles."

It took me a second to recover from his last sentence, but I managed. "I had coffee when I got here."

He frowned. "Coffee doesn't count as a food group."

"In my world it does."

"Jesus, firefly, you need to take care of yourself." His voice was hard. "You're not fuckin' invincible, you know."

I found enough balance to yank out of his grasp. "Trust me, I know."

We stared at each other for a long moment and I was sure he was going to address the elephant in the room, but then his face changed. "Let's go. You'll be treated to what most people usually have to pledge their firstborn children for." He paused dramatically. "My chocolate chip pancakes."

"Chocolate chip pancakes?" I repeated. My gaze traveled his muscled and tattooed body once more. "Is this a *Freaky Friday* situation? Are you actually a forty-year-old housewife who crotchets and somewhere in suburbia a woman is wearing an apron and cursing and throwing knives at her husband?"

Lucky chuckled deeply, sending little shivers down my spine. "Nope, I'm just a very complex man. There's more to me than meets the eye." He winked, then turned his back, walking from the room. "Pancakes in twenty, so get that hot ass showered and dressed. You can keep the tee," he yelled over his shoulder.

"I don't want your smelly shirt," I called after him.

I inhaled once more. I was totally keeping the tee.

••••

"Now you're just fucking with me. That's not a word," I said.

Lucky glanced up, grinning. "It is a word."

I quirked my brow. "Use it in a sentence."

He didn't even blink. "I, the king of Scrabble, used the word 'muzjiks' to kick Becky, the poor little Scrabble peasant, out of the running for supreme ruler."

We were playing Scrabble. Fucking *Scrabble*. And I was enjoying it. Despite the fact that Lucky was an absolute menace at the game and so far had used three words that I didn't even know existed in the human language. He showed me via an online dictionary that they did indeed.

I gave him a look.

"Okay, muzjiks were called Russian peasants under the tzar," he said with a straight face.

I gaped at him. "You hustled me. At Scrabble. You hustled me."

He shrugged. "I'm in it to win it, baby. No place for morals in board games."

I froze just a little at the term of endearment and the casual use of it. No doubt it was offhand, and he most likely called every girl he banged by that name. I'd had my fair share of guys use it, most likely when they forgot my name. But this was different, especially doing something so domestic, so intimate. Especially after the day we'd had.

It was a good day.

I hadn't expected it.

Good days were few and far between in my life, even more scarce since I'd decided to self-medicate. Totally absent since I'd decided to stop self-medicating. But defying the odds, junk didn't ruin the day for me. Sure, the craving lurked under my skin like a constant itch that only one thing could scratch, but I managed it. And without wanting to throw up or scream or murder someone.

Lucky wasn't screwing around. His pancakes were the shit. So much so, I had two servings. My first bite reminded me how hungry I was, how ravenous. It'd been a long time since I'd had any kind of appetite for anything but heroin, but there it was. For chocolate chip pancakes made for me by a friggin' biker.

"Who taught you how to cook like this?" I asked through a full

ANNE MALCOM

mouth. A lady I was not.

He had been watching me, leaning against the counter with a small grin on his face. The grin dampened slightly. "My mom," he said flatly.

I barely noticed it. "Thank her for me."

Then I went back to my breakfast, not thinking twice on his reaction.

After breakfast he declared he was going surfing.

"I've got an extra board. Want to join me?" he asked after I'd recovered from seeing him shirtless.

No, I didn't recover exactly, just found a way to act like I did. Hours later, I was still recovering from his fricking eight-pack, his caramel skin mingled with tattoos and art.

I'd managed to snap my head up and not lick the V cut out of marble and hugely visible in his low-slung board shirts. "Are you joking?"

He grinned. "Always."

I shook my head, mostly to get images of me pressed against that naked torso out of my mind.

"There are sun loungers, and a shit ton of books in the living room. Saw you had an overflowing bookshelf at your old apartment. You read?"

I nodded. Before I started screwing up my brain and ability to concentrate, I'd loved to read. Reading was a healthier form of escapism than drugs. If only I'd stuck to that.

"Awesome. Well, read or fantasize over my godlike body. I won't be long." He leaned in and kissed the top of my head. "Don't worry, I'll be fantasizing over yours too." On that note he left the kitchen and walked outside, leaving me blinking like an idiot in his wake.

I'd done as he said, fantasizing about his body and reading. Spent the entire day doing both, in fact. I didn't have a swimsuit to lie out in, but considering I was pale and got scorched in the sun, that was probably a good thing. I slathered on the SPF and hid from the rays under the umbrella while I immersed myself in a book from the decent collection Lucky had. I didn't imagine he read Virginia Wolfe, which had me curious about who lived here. It was obvious a female had, as the woman's touches were hard to miss. The fairy lights strung above the vintage patchwork sofa. The scented candles on the coffee table, which was also littered with motorcycle magazines. Because I was too wrapped up in myself, I hadn't asked about this place.

I didn't get the chance to ask Lucky, since he left me alone with my book the entire day, which surprised me. I was sure he'd be like a Jack Russell puppy, constantly biting at my ankles, demanding attention. He wasn't. He only approached me to deposit snacks—which he did on a regular basis, muttering about how I needed fattening up—and lunch. He seemed to sense I needed the ocean and escape, and a little slice of peace, even if it was tinged with the chaos inside my head.

He'd yanked the book from me when the sun started to kiss the horizon.

"All right, I don't want your eyes going square," he'd declared.

I squinted at him. "That's from the TV."

He shrugged. "Same thing. Dinner time."

"I just had lunch."

"Four hours ago," he corrected. "Now up or I will force feed you. I can't promise you'll enjoy it, but I will."

So I did as I was told, without sarcasm or protesting or anything. I surprised even myself. The conversation was light and easy the entire dinner, the elephant in the room still sitting there. Then it was Scrabble time. Which led me to now.

"Are we ever going to talk about it?" I asked in exasperation, looking up from the board.

"The fact that you would starve if you ever had to make a living playing word games and I am the king of such games?" Lucky teased, his eyes bright.

I eyed him levelly. "No, the fact that I'm recovering from a heroin addiction, almost killed myself with an overdose, and then you spirited me away here the moment you found out, despite the fact we're...." I trailed off, looking for the words to describe what we were. I swallowed; I knew what we weren't, at least. "Nothing. Despite the fact we're nothing."

All teasing glint left his face and his jaw went hard. "We're far from nothing, Becky. You know that."

I didn't lower my gaze, even though his stare was getting

downright scary. I forgot, what with his easy attitude and stupid jokes, that underneath was the face of something much more sinister.

"No, I don't know that. You stalk me at the club, speak in monosyllabic grunts when I get in trouble, act like there's some kind of brand on me I haven't noticed."

He gritted his teeth, looking like he was going to spout into those monosyllabic grunts, which I didn't have time for.

I held up my hand. "That's not what we're talking about now, but trust me, we will talk about it." I took a breath. "We're talking about the elephant in the room. The fact you've been treating this like it's some kind of vacation. That I'm not... an addict," I finished.

"I know that," he gritted out after a long silence, his voice tight. "Despite the fact I wish it weren't the fuckin' truth, I know that shit, Becky."

"So why did you bring me here when you found that out?" I asked. "You have a life, one I presume is much more exciting than this." I held my hand out to the board. "Playing Scrabble with a drug addict."

"Stop," he growled, his body stiff.

I tilted my head. "Stop what?"

He leveled me with his gaze. "Calling yourself that."

I didn't back down. "That's what I *am*, Lucky. If you can't handle hearing it out loud, then drive me back to Amber and let me take care of my own shit." My voice rose to a near shout while I ignored the little blossom of fear at him doing just that. I didn't understand that fear. Of being alone. Of being without him. So I ignored it.

"Take care of your own shit?" he repeated, his quiet voice juxtaposing my shout, but somehow holding more volume to it.

I nodded.

"Taking care of your own shit almost got you fuckin' *dead*!" he roared, pushing out of his chair so hard it rattled to the ground.

I didn't flinch at that. The rage. I was used to it. Welcomed it, in fact.

He stalked around to me, yanking my own chair around and bending to get in my face. "There's no fuckin' way I'm leavin' you alone with this shit. Riskin' a repeat of your overdose and this time you actually pump enough shit in there to actually leave this earth," he growled. "So, to answer your earlier question, no, I don't have anything fuckin' better to do than make sure my firefly's light doesn't go out."

I blinked at him. Again. And again.

"Yours?" I repeated on a whisper.

He nodded, his face still inches from mine. "Yeah. Mine. Since the moment you bared your tits on stage and threw your sass off it." He paused, and for one terrifying and glorious moment I thought he might cross the distance between us and kiss me. Instead, he spoke. "And I can't hear you call yourself that shit, not again. Not because I don't know it's true. I'm more than fuckin' aware of that truth." His gaze flickered down to my bare arms. "I can't hear it again because I know that, despite your best efforts to appear otherwise, you're fragile as fuck. So fuckin' desperate to appear hard when you're the most breakable. So I can't hear it 'cause I've got a tenuous fuckin' hold on my rage, and if I hear it too much, I'll let go and break you without meanin' to." He reached up to brush my hair out of my face with a tenderness that didn't match the fury on his face.

"Your rage?" I repeated. "You're angry? At me?"

He nodded. "Fuckin' furious."

"Why?" I whispered. My heart sank with his admission, which was very un-Bex of me. Usually I didn't give two shits if people were angry at me. In fact, I preferred that so idiots I didn't want to waste time on didn't talk to me. But Lucky wasn't in that category. Despite everything, he was the only guy I wanted to waste time on.

"Because you're blind. Blind to what you are. What you really are. If you could see what I see, no fuckin' way would you go so deep into the darkness that you have to inject yourself with poison to see again." He paused, and I was pretty sure it was because he could hear the way my heart was beating out of my fucking chest. I didn't know it did that in real life. Didn't know guys could actually make that happen. But there we were. It didn't feel nice either. It felt uncomfortable, painful, like I might have a heart attack.

Lucky was unaware of my potential coronary. "I'm angry at myself for not finding you earlier, not being there to steer you away from that shit. Now I can only just watch and do everything I can to help you find your way out. 'Cause no matter how much I wish it was different, it's not up to me. It's up to you and you only. So you're here to make that decision, and I'm here with you to watch you hopefully make the right one."

The air turned cold as he pushed away from me, turned on his heel, and left, along with the elephant left the room. And yet it still felt so full I couldn't breathe.

•••

I stayed longer than two days.

Almost two weeks, in fact. It wasn't just Lucky's huge admission that had me reluctant to leave, though it was a huge fucking factor. It was the peace.

I'd never had it before.

Peace. Quiet.

Since birth, my entire life had been chaos, had been loud. It had been constant motion. Stopping meant destruction. Quiet usually meant that something, somewhere, was gearing up to strike.

But not there. Not in that little cabin with the biker I'd promised myself I wouldn't let in.

I let him in.

Not literally, though I craved that on about the same level as the junk. Actually more because there in the peace, the craving slithered away. Not completely, of course; it would always be there, present, taunting, tempting. But enough so I could take a breath without pain.

I guess you could say I wasn't really recovering, just replacing one addiction with another, but whatever.

Not that Lucky was making any moves. The opposite, in fact. He still cooked me breakfast, told stupid jokes, and treated me to my daily ab show when he went surfing, but no funny business. I didn't normally wait for something; if I wanted it, I went out and got it. Even with guys. *Especially* with guys. I didn't believe in gentlemen making the first move, mostly because I had no experience with gentlemen, but still.

But it was different with him. Every fucking thing was different with him.

I talked to him. Actually *talked* to him.

I didn't talk to anyone except Lily. And, more recently, Rosie.

But even with them I didn't share like I did with him. Sometimes it was easy, just stupid surface stuff. Mostly bickering and me insulting him for liking Nickelback. But other times it wasn't surface.

"What made you do it?" he asked suddenly, making me look up from my book.

It was after dinner, another great one he'd cooked and I actually ate.

"Do what?"

He gave me a serious look, one that said exactly what he was asking.

I sighed and put my book down. I should have told him to fuck off. Mind his own business. Or even walked out of the room. That's what the old Bex would have done to anyone else. Heck, that's what this new, clean Bex would still do to anyone else. But he wasn't anyone else.

"Why does anyone do anything that threatens destruction and yet promises escape?" I looked anywhere but him. "Because I was willing to risk it all just for a moment of escape. And then I couldn't stop." I shrugged.

I felt his presence more than saw it. But I couldn't avoid his gaze anymore when his hand came to my jaw, bringing it down to meet his eyes. He was close, bent down in front of me. Inescapable.

"What's so bad that you needed to escape, Becky?"

I laughed nervously. "Um, in case you hadn't noticed, I wasn't exactly living the dream. I was—no, wait, *am*—a medical school dropout who took her clothes off for money. Though, now I'm a medical school dropout, unemployed stripper, and ex-junkie. I was wrong. I'm totally living the dream."

Lucky searched my face. "Why did you drop out? Of medical school? Really tell me, none of the 'I just didn't belong' crap."

I shrugged. "I realized it was never going to work out. That I was never going to work out. It had been a dream, trying to be something better than I was born to be. Seriously, me? A doctor? Could you actually see me doing that? Saving lives? I can barely save my own. Actually, I wasn't even the one who did that," I said quietly, remembering waking up in that hospital bed.

Lucky grasped my neck. "I can see you doing that," he argued. "I can see you doing anything that you fuckin' want to do. The only thing that doesn't suit you, no matter how fuckin' good you look doin' it, is taking your clothes off in some shithole for a bunch of perverts. Only thing you're not born to be is someone who lives in the shadows."

I swallowed the tears that he seemed to fish out with his words. "You don't know that. Can't say that. I was born for the shadows. You don't know where I come from," I whispered.

"Don't need to know that. I want to, one day, when you feel like tellin' me. But for now, I don't need to know where you come from to know you deserve more than the scraps of life you give yourself. I know that where you are, *what* you are, means you deserve more."

We were at that moment again, that moment when his face lingered inches away from mine and his lips were as intoxicating as any substance, chemical or natural.

That time I didn't give him the chance to pull away. I dived in, unable to fight the craving any longer.

His lips crashed into mine in a beautiful collision, and the high was instant and magnificent. It wasn't tender or gentle like his words. It was fierce and crazy, a furious struggle between the two of us for control.

Then it was nothing.

The hands at my neck tightened and he pulled away, using gentle force to pry our lips apart.

"Hey," I protested.

He rested his forehead against mine. "I won't do this, not now," he rasped, his voice thick. "Not until you've fought this shit off and I don't feel like I'm taking advantage of you."

I fought against his hold. "You're not taking advantage of me," I argued.

He held firm but the veins in his neck pulsed. "Yeah, I would be. Plus, I'm a selfish bastard. I want *all* of you. I want you to give me everything. I'm not takin' it when you're still strugglin'." His eyes burned into mine. "That doesn't mean I don't want to. I fuckin' want to. I should get a fuckin' medal for my restraint right now. But I'm willin' to be patient 'cause I know you're worth it." He stood. "Now I'm going for a drive 'cause I can't be in the same room as you right now." His eyes burned into mine. "If I stay much longer, all my self-restraint will disappear and I'll fuck you into oblivion right there on that sofa."

Then he left.

Fucking *left* after saying that.

The asshole.

I was angry. Pissed. I'd paced, sworn, and sent mental daggers to wherever he was. I'd planned on staying up and unleashing my anger. But he didn't come back, not until I was long asleep on the sofa. I only awoke to his arms encircling me and laying me down on my bed. Because I was sleep-zombie Bex, I wasn't myself. Which was how I explained away clinging to him when he tried to let me go.

"Don't leave me," pleaded the stranger Bex.

And he didn't. The sound of boots hitting the floor followed and I was bundled up in strong arms. I nuzzled deeper.

"This is nice," I mumbled.

A hand stroked my head. "Sleep, firefly."

"I do," I whispered, already half in the dream world. "Knowing I'm with you, near you. I sleep for the first time since it happened. I'm safe."

Then I drifted off and didn't feel the way his body stiffened at my words.

And in the morning, he was gone.

TEN

"Do not fall in love with me, for I'll break your heart, long before you realize you are going to break mine."
-Atticus

I got it. Peace. Just a taste. Nearly two weeks of it. The only slice I'd ever have. Because everything comes to an end, right?

The good news is nothing lasts forever. That's what I'd tell myself when I was at a shitty foster home where we got dressed in dirty clothes and slept in scratchy sheets. That's what I told myself... after, when I thought I'd go crazy with the demons pounding at my skull that night. They were still pounding, even now. But it wasn't forever yet; there was still time for them to leave the building.

That's what I told myself now, that forever wouldn't be fighting the urge for a craving, counting every second as a small victory in an exhausting fight.

Then there was the bad news: nothing lasts forever.

My peace was shattered two weeks into our little stay. Or, more aptly, I shattered it. Two weeks was a long time to be cooped up in an isolated cabin with someone, but I wasn't getting cabin fever. I was starting to like it. Too much.

I was starting to like Lucky.

A fucking lot.

He'd just come in from his surf, wearing low-slung board shorts and nothing else. You'd think I would've found a way not to be struck silly by his washboard abs covered in tattoos. And I mean *covered*. There was only a small space above his heart that was naked, unblemished skin.

It was getting harder not to pounce on him. Especially when I needed something. Needed escape.

But he didn't promise escape.

I think he promised damnation.

So something had to give.

"Why?" I snapped at him as soon as he closed the sliding door.

He threw a towel onto the counter and shrugged. "I don't know, I was just born this beautiful. Sure, I work out, but this bone structure?" He gestured to his face. "God-given."

Now that I was sober, my emotions were volatile, like constant PMS. Which was why I may have let out a shrill, frustrated, embarrassingly girly scream.

"Be serious for once in your fucking life!" I shouted, stomping into his face. "Why? Why did you bring me here? Hit the pause button on your life for two fucking weeks for someone you barely know? And don't hit me with the romance novel 'you are mine' bullshit. We're not in a fantasy world. This is the real world and that's not how it works. This"—I gestured between us—"doesn't make sense. I'm not someone anyone 'falls' for. So give me the fucking reality, Lucky. The sense. The why."

His eyes were blank, unflinching in the face of my—potentially unreasonable—fury. "I can't," he answered, his voice flat.

"You can't what?"

He ran his hand over his smooth head in frustration, turning to regard the sea. "Give you a reason. Sense. I fucking got none. All I know is that this"—he turned so he could gesture between us like I did— "isn't fantasy. It's reality. Because it's not nice and easy and good. If it was good, I wouldn't be a man who knew what life looked like leaving a man's body, to be the one taking that. And you wouldn't have darkness behind your eyes, track marks on your arms, and a job that took a little of your fuckin' soul every time you took your clothes off." He stepped forward so he could clutch my neck in his hand. "It's not good. But it's reality, and it's inescapable. I don't fuckin' want to escape it, no matter how difficult this shit is. I don't want to escape. I want to save you."

His words punctured me. Struck me dumb, and I didn't know which of my raw emotions would win its race to the top.

Anger won.

ANNE MALCOM

Which was good.

Safer.

"You brought me here to save me?" I asked shrilly, yanking from his grasp.

"I took you here for you to save yourself. I'll do anything I can to help with that."

I let that bounce off me. "Well, you're twenty-three years too late, buddy," I said, my voice like ice. "You think it's just a little drug addiction that damages the image of whoever the fuck you see out of those baby browns?" I laughed. "Yeah, tip of the iceberg. See, I was born damaged. I'll die that way, and everything in between is gonna make sure I stay that way. I don't pity myself. There are kids in Africa who have to drink poisoned water and who most likely won't make it to their twenties. Being abandoned at birth and bounced around from shitty to shittier foster homes isn't exactly the worst thing that could have happened." I swallowed. "It could have been worse." I chased away the memory of the creaking of the door in the darkness and the horrors that happened after the door creaked shut again and the darkness settled deeper into my soul. "I was the one who picked up that needle, I know that. That's on me. I was the one stupid enough to overdose, and I'll take all that." I leveled my gaze at him. "What I won't take is some perpetually happy biker spiriting me away for God knows why trying to make me better when he has no fucking clue what he's talking about."

Lucky's jaw was granite and not an ounce of humor lurked behind his eyes. It was unnerving, and I found myself almost regretting my monologue. I opened my mouth to do something I didn't have much experience in doing—apologize.

He beat me to it.

"You know why I'm called Lucky?" he asked.

"'Cause you always win at bingo?" I retorted sarcastically.

"Because the first time I ever shot a gun, it plowed through the skull of some guy in a rival crew. Luckiest shot my homies had ever seen," he explained in a flat voice. "I was twelve."

I gaped at him. At the transformation of his attractive face. The strength was still there, but everything else was stripped away and I saw what he'd been hiding, what I hadn't even made an attempt to see. His demons. His damage.

"Didn't exactly grow up in suburbia, Becky," he continued. "I spent the first thirteen years of my life in an area of East LA where you either get a crew or roll the dice with your life." He paused, eyes far away. "I got a crew. Thought I was hot shit, fuckin' invincible. The big man with the weight of a gun in my trousers when I hadn't even shaved." He shook his head. "Was a stupid fucking kid. My momma hated it, but she couldn't do much. She was working two jobs to put food on the table, trying to raise my two little sisters and control my wild older one. She loved me, which meant she hated what she knew I was going to turn into. I loved her too. My little sisters. Alexis, despite the fact she got into trouble every time she left the house. Which was exactly why I picked up the piece in the first place. I loved them and knew I needed to protect them. I was the man of the house since my dad was facing life in prison after he fucked up a burglary, shot a cop." He paused again. "Dad wasn't a bad guy either, at least not what I remember of him. Just made some fucked-up choices and panicked at the wrong time. He told me before he died that he saw the face of that cop every time he closed his eyes. I didn't understand it at the time. Not until I earned my nickname and took my first life." He stared at me, unblinking. "Not until I closed my eyes that night and saw that kid's face for that night and every fuckin' night since. Though, he's not the only face I see." He swallowed visibly, his fists clenching at his sides.

I knew it then. Something was coming. Something terrible, something fucking horrific. It was like the air churned with the expectation of it, tasted bitter. I knew it because horrors in different people have a way of recognizing one another.

"Lucky," I whispered.

He jerked, like he didn't realize I was still there. "It's Gabriel, actually," he said. "That's the name my momma called me, despite everyone else going with the nickname I earned with blood. That was what *they* called me. Sofia, Camila, and Alexis." He choked their names out like they were daggers on his tongue. "Alexis was the oldest. Fifteen going on twenty-five. A handful, and not one either me or my mom could contain." He smiled, not at me but at a memory. "She had spirit. Fire." His eyes settled on me. "You remind me of her. Chaos and spirit barely contained in one human being. Beautiful. Disastrous."

I flinched. Not because I was insulted but because I was touched. He'd found it. My soft spot. By comparing me to the sister he obviously loved. Adored.

"They were twins, Sofia and Camila," he continued. "Six years old. I was meant to take care of them that day. It's what I thought I was doing. Out in the streets protectin' our turf, making the neighborhood safe for them." He sucked in a breath. "Our house was shit. No matter how much Mom tried to make it different, it was shit. It was small, falling apart, and gray. Only color came from the girls. We didn't have much except a front yard where the girls liked to play in the sunshine. Every day they played out there, pretendin' they were somewhere else, somewhere they deserved." His voice was hard, cold. But I wasn't fooled. I could feel the sorrow drenching the room. I don't know how the heck I hadn't seen it before. I thought I was good at hiding my demons, but this guy was the fucking king.

And it broke my shriveled heart.

"'Cause I wasn't where I was supposed to be that day, taking care of my girls, they did get to go somewhere else. Somewhere I hope to every fucking thing that is holy is somewhere better. That's the only thought that keeps me upright. That and the knowledge that they didn't feel a thing. Didn't know what was happening until they left this world." His hazel eyes weren't liquid; they were solid and they punctured through me. "See, the guys searchin' for retribution for their fallen homie were good shots too. Not lucky, like me. Practiced. Ruthless. Didn't fuckin' blink at putting bullets in two little girls' heads." His face was a mask. "Though they did regret it. I made sure of that."

I shivered at the ice in his tone, the violence. It was a stranger to me. The person those demons transformed Lucky—no, Gabriel—into.

"Tore me apart, Becky. Till there was nothin' left. Broke my momma. She never spoke to me again, still won't." He swallowed roughly and found a way to meet my eyes. I got sucked into them. Entangled in his nightmare. "Alexis overdosed a few months later. Not on purpose. She loved life too much, even with the babies gone." His eyes glistened. "She was tryin' to live. Burned too bright too quick and she exploded, like a supernova," he whispered. "I went dark after that. I went fuckin' black. Fell deep into a world that still gives me fuckin' nightmares. That makes this one look like Candyland. Chanced upon Asher after a few years in that world. He was running from his own shit. Not my story to tell. But somehow, both of us recognized that we couldn't stay where we were without turning into the monsters who'd taken my sisters from me. So we got out. And the rest, shall we say, is history." He didn't move his gaze from mine. "So it wasn't fantasy that drew me to you. It was reality. My ugly, dark reality. And that's why I dragged you here. To fuckin' save you, even if that pisses you off. 'Cause I'm not lettin' another supernova explode in a ball of brilliance and leave my world just that bit darker."

The silence that descended after he finished speaking was so heavy it seemed to darken the room, despite the sun shining through the windows. I was shocked silent, shocked still.

God, I'd been such a bitch to him. So self-important about my own suffering, so sure I was the only person between us battling demons so I had the authority to act how I wanted. How could someone who seemed to derive so much joy from the stupid aspects of life be someone who'd tasted the worst suffering this stupid ball of water had to offer? How the fuck could he spend the day laughing when the universe gave him every reason to turn into a monster?

"I'm not sayin' this for pity, Becky. Or to belittle your own shit. I'm only saying it so you understand you're not alone. You're not the only one the devil took some shots at while the big guy was lookin' the other way."

"You believe?" I asked in shock. "In God, in something bigger than this, after what you've been through?"

"You got another option for slogging through the shit that's unfortunately a part of life? 'Cause death's a part of life. Shouldn't have been a part of Sofia and Camila's, not for a long fucking while. Or Alexis's. But since it was, and I can't change that, I've got to believe that someone, somewhere, is takin' care of them. Only thing that'll keep me sane. That and the knowledge of the fact I got my revenge.

Guess it's kind of a paradox in believing in heaven when my revenge got me a one-way ticket to hell. But I'm okay with that, if they're in that place and the people who put them there are roasting with the Devil himself."

It broke then. My shield, my armor, whatever it was that stood between me and him. Fell into a thousand pieces, and I didn't give a shit. I didn't have words. I wasn't a warm and tender woman who could heal hurts with soft whispers. So I did the only thing I knew to do, the only thing that came to mind, that felt natural.

I stepped forward, kept walking until my body pressed to his. I soaked it up, every ugly and thorny emotion rolling from him. I moved my hands up the sides of his neck and gripped it tightly, pulling it slightly so I could reach his mouth, so we were inches away from each other.

"Becky," he warned.

"No talking," I murmured.

Then I pressed my lips to his. It was a first for me, kissing someone like that. Kissing someone I actually gave a shit about. Kissing them and wishing that my lips would do something, cure something. A sensation rolled from that kiss, spreading to every part of me.

I didn't have time to inspect it. The pivotal change that came with that kiss. The earthquake it triggered between us, changing the landscape of our relationship. I didn't have the time nor the brainpower because seconds into the most gentle and profound kiss of my life, it changed. Gabriel's hands moved to my hips, biting into the flesh as his mouth took control of the tender kiss. Though it was no longer tender. It was carnal, animalistic. It was the earthquake that didn't just change the landscape, but shattered it.

He growled into my mouth and moved back. "Fuck, Becky. You got to stop this now if you ain't ready. If you want me to be the gentleman. 'Cause I'm fuckin' seconds away from losing every ounce of gentlemanly thoughts and taking you hard and fast against that wall." His voice, his words, the bulging cords in neck, the sex in his eyes all set me alight and drenched my panties.

"Take me," I rasped. The meaning was clear—I wanted him to take me, and not just against the wall.

His mouth claimed mine once more, his hands going to my ass and lifting me. I didn't hesitate to wrap my legs around his waist. My tee rode up and my entire body shuddered when the thin film of my panties rubbed against his hardness with a ferocity that bordered on insanity, needing the friction, the release, more than my next breath.

My back slammed against the wall, hard. The tingle of pain that came with the impact only made me burn hotter.

Gabriel's hand moved to my arms, yanking them up my body and holding both my wrists together in his iron grasp. He moved his mouth from mine and I glared at him for the loss.

His smile was that of a predator, his eyes midnight.

"Don't stop," I commanded, rubbing my body against him.

I didn't think it was possible, but his eyes turned darker and his hand circled my neck so my legs and the wall were the only things keeping me attached to him. He exerted a small amount of pressure, a whisper of what he was capable of, but enough. "You're not in charge here, firefly," he growled. "That spirit makes my dick harder than marble. But here?" He pressed his torso into me so he rubbed against me in the most delicious way. I let out a strangled moan. "This? I'm in charge of this. You get it when and how I say. And you're going to fucking love every minute of it."

I already was. Every fucking second of it. Of him taking control. Of him taking over everything and me being at his mercy. Despite everything I was outside of that moment, it was something I craved, something I didn't even know I wanted.

Domination.

He flexed his fingers once more. Then his hand at my neck moved and I could breathe easy. He grasped the bottom of my shirt, his other hand still at my wrists, and rolled it up. I stayed where I was thanks to the fact I was used to gripping poles. The shirt went over my head and up my arms. I expected him to let go of my wrists in order to discard it, but instead he did some sorcery and turned my tee into a binding, fastening my arms together above my head. Both hands moved back to my ass, sinking into it and plastering my body even closer, rubbing every inch of my naked torso against him.

"You're going to keep those arms precisely where I put them," he ordered. "They ain't gonna move until I say so. You aren't allowed to come until I decide that pussy is going to get its release." His hands tightened, bordering on pain, and he captured my nipple between his teeth.

I cried out at the pleasure of the pain they inflicted, the perfect cocktail, bringing me to the edge of oblivion without even paying any attention to my soaked core. I itched to bring my hands down, to rake my nails down his back, to clutch him closer to me.

I didn't because Gabriel was in charge, not me. That knowledge was not only hot as shit but a relief that made it possible to embrace every inch of the pleasure.

"Fuck, Becky, you're fuckin' soaked. My girl likes this," he growled in my ear as his expert fingers delved into my panties.

"I love it," I hissed, my voice little more than a rasp.

He found the magic spot in an instant and I slammed my head back against the wall, my arms coming down of their own accord.

His hand was at my wrist in an instant.

"I didn't say you could move these," he rumbled. He kept my hands in his viselike grip while he worked me with his other hand, capturing my mouth roughly. "You gonna be a good girl now?" he asked against my lips.

I couldn't speak, could barely breathe with the fire he was building. I could only nod.

He moved his hands from my wrists to circle my neck once more. "Open your eyes, Becky."

I snapped them open at his command, unaware I'd even closed them. His were liquid and intense on mine. "You're not going to come, are you, Becky?" he murmured, rubbing his thumb against my collarbone.

I let out a groan as he quickened the pace between my legs.

"Because I didn't say you could do that either." He nuzzled my neck, his stubble scratching the skin on my cheek. "Not until I'm inside that sweet pussy and I can feel it tighten around me. Then you can. Then you'll do it again. Later I'll taste your fuckin' climax on my tongue. Now, you will not. You get me?"

All I could do was nod.

"Good," he growled.

Then his hand was gone, as if he could sense I was teetering on the edge. I was half insane with need, widening my eyes at him in a silent plead. He grinned hungrily, like a predator. "You'll get my dick soon, firefly."

One hand went back up to my sagging wrists while the other went to his shorts. The few seconds he took to free himself yawned into forever. The overwhelming craving for him, for release, took every cell in my body hostage.

Then I got it. What my empty body screamed for. Filled to the hilt.

It was a magnificent mingling of pleasure and pain as I got used to his considerable size.

He mistook my cry for pain, and his entire form froze, the cords in his neck pulsing. "Becky, you okay? Did I hurt you?" His mask slipped, the hunger and domination mingling with concern.

I nodded rapidly. "I'm good. Only if you move."

I barely got the last word out before he heeded my command. Boy, did he heed it.

All concern was gone as he slammed into me, brutal, unyielding, fucking beautiful.

"You're gonna come now," he rumbled in my ear.

I wanted to whisper that I was going to come when I was good and ready, but I was too far gone for that shit. My body was at his mercy, and it obeyed his order.

Everything exploded into a thousand different colors, better than any high I'd ever ridden. Cleaner, purer.

Right.

He didn't stop as I came down. If anything, he quickened his pace, building me up before I even had the chance to come back to earth.

He captured my mouth to taste the last of my cries. Through stars dancing in my vison, his midnight gaze penetrated. "I'm far from fuckin' done with you, firefly," he growled, slamming into me.

Oh, he was far from done with me. He fucked me into oblivion, taking me to the stars and away from any coherent thought for hours to come.

"Thank you," I whispered against his chest, trailing my fingers along the ink of his pec.

He turned me so our eyes met. "You don't have to thank me for every orgasm I give you. I plan on giving you many, many more. It'll get exhausting to thank me every time. A blow job would suffice."

I smacked his pec and he grinned.

"It's impossible to have a conversation with you."

He bundled me in his arms. "Sorry, firefly. What are you thanking me for?"

"For bringing me here. For putting your entire life on hold. For Scrabble, chocolate chip pancakes. For the peace. For giving me something I couldn't give myself. A space to get clean. A second to breathe."

He was quiet for a long time, his body rigid. The only thing telling me he hadn't drifted off to sleep was the back and forth of his fingers on my spine.

"Why are you thanking me now?" he asked finally, his voice thick. "You plannin' on runnin' off in the middle of the night now that you've had your wicked way with me?" His words were teasing but his tone held something else.

Fear.

I moved to meet his eyes, and not a hint of humor twinkled in them. "No, I'm not planning on that. Sneaking around in the dark isn't really my style. It's just... I thought I'd tell you now when I'm mellow and not irritated at you. Which I'm sure I will be approximately twelve hundred times between now and when we leave. And I don't want the fact I'm stubborn and a bitch when irritated to stop me from letting you know how much this means to me. So I'm thanking you now to cover my bases."

He blinked at me a couple times.

The silence started to make me uncomfortable. "You know, it's customary when a person thanks another person to say you're welcome."

Gabriel squeezed me. "You're welcome," he whispered, pulling me up his body so my delicate flesh rubbed against his concrete abs. I let out a hiss as my sensitive nipples stood to attention. His face darkened with desire.

"Though I've got to admit, my actions weren't exactly pure in bringin' you here, babe. In fact, they were downright selfish. You see, I want you." His hand moved to cup my bare ass. "I want this," he said against my mouth. His other hand moved to stroke my head. "But I also want this," he murmured. "And I kind of wanted both in one piece. So I brought you here to find the pieces. Get you put back together so I could have you for myself."

I paused my stroking, not eager to give up the moment for reality. But I had to. "You can't," I whispered.

His eyes hardened. "Can't what?"

"Have me for yourself." I silenced his protest with a hand on his lips. "Because I don't even have myself. Don't own myself. So I can't jump into something like this. Not until I've gotten to know the stranger whose body I've been living in for twenty-three years."

He frowned at me, moving my hands off his lips. "I'm not givin' you up," he said, voice firm.

If now's the time to be candid, I guess I better do it right. "Me neither. I can't," I admitted. "I just can't give you everything."

He yanked me to his front, cupping my face. "I'm happy with what I got, for now," he murmured.

I swallowed against the promise—and warning—in his tone. Before he could capture my mouth and take me away from reality once more, I pulled back slightly. "I'm sorry," I whispered.

He grinned. "I'm not exactly getting the raw end of the deal, babe. At least my cock isn't. He's not feelin' sad at all."

I didn't grin. "No. For Sofia and Camila. Alexis. And for Gabriel. I'm sorry you lost them." My voice was a soft whisper I didn't recognize.

He stiffened at the mention of their names. "I didn't lose them. They're still here." He glanced around the room. "I hope not now," he joked with light eyes. "I hate that they're gone, but that anger, that fuckin' rage that ate me up, killed the boy I'd been. I had to let it go. To survive, you see?" His finger trailed my temple. "I don't think Gabriel is lost either. I think he was just waitin' for someone."

And then, luckily so I didn't have to respond to that, he kissed me. And more.

From that day on, he was Gabriel to me.

••••

"I don't like this," Gabriel declared, frowning at the house in front of us like there was a bomb inside.

I unbuckled my seatbelt. "Well, thanks for offering that little gem. But it does nothing at all to change reality. It often goes on whether you like it or not."

He moved his gaze back to me and it rooted me to the spot. I actually froze in place. Ever since I'd let him in, really let him in, body and soul, I gave him power over me. It scared the shit out of me. I didn't even have power over myself.

Which is why I needed distance. A lot of it. Despite the fact my skin itched at the thought of it, my heart hurt at the prospect.

My fucking heart.

What was he turning me into?

He leaned forward to capture my neck in his hands. My stomach dipped at the contact.

Yes, I so needed to get away from him.

"I want you to come home with me," he mumbled. "I want you in my bed."

I scowled at him. "Yeah, like I said, the world doesn't spin the way you want it. Nor do I do what you want."

He regarded me. "You want it too."

"No, I don't," I lied.

He yanked me closer so our mouths almost touched. "You're a liar. You want it. You're just too fuckin' scared to admit how much."

I pulled back, which was a herculean task considering how addicting those lips were. What came out of them? Not so much.

"I'm not scared," I argued. "I'm not afraid of anything."

Lie.

That was a great big lie. I didn't used to be afraid of anything. When you've been in a foster home where a kid held a knife to your throat for taking their seat in front of the TV, you learned that fear helped no one. Especially not the little girl who met monsters in the dark, the real kind. I wasn't afraid of monsters, or anything for that matter.

Until Gabriel.

I was terrified of him. Of what he made me feel.

So I needed to run. I needed him to be as far away from me and my fucking truth as possible. Away from my monsters.

Gabriel's jaw hardened. "Everyone's afraid of something. It's not a bad thing. It means you've got something to lose."

I gathered my bag. "Not me. I've got nothing to lose," I lied again.

He eyed me. "You're clean now. If you're not gonna admit what's between us, then admit that. That's something to lose."

I bristled. "That's it?" I hissed. "Why you don't want me out of your sight? You think I'm just going to run back to being a junkie?"

His eyes blazed. "That's not what I fuckin' meant and you know it."

"Whatever," I said, using irritation to hide my hurt.

I tried to get out of the truck but a hand at my wrist stopped me. "This isn't the end, Becky. You don't get to push me away now that we're back to reality."

I raised a brow. "So *now* you're acknowledging reality? Welcome to the real world, where I can do whatever the fuck I want. And short of handcuffing me to the steering wheel, which you've already tried to do, you can't make me do anything." I ripped my hand from his grasp and leapt out the door before I could let anything on his face tempt me to apologize and take him up on his offer.

It took every ounce of strength I had to walk down that path and not look back.

But I did it.

Both for me and for him.

ELEVEN

*"She was the prettiest Hell I'd ever been in.
I didn't mind burning at all."*
-Matt Baker

"**W**hat are you doing here?"

I jumped, not only at the low growl but the familiarity of it. I managed to regain my composure by the time I turned around.

He looked good.

Fuck, did he look good. He was wearing all black, a sinner and a saint all mixed in one. Soulful eyes and covered in tattoos. I didn't know whether I wanted to try and redeem myself to get the saint part or sell more of myself to the devil to meet the sinner.

Despite, of course, his stupid fucking shirt, which made me want to smile and set my panties on fire. It read 'I taught Christian Grey all that shit.'

Boy, did I know what he taught. The discipline he demanded in the bedroom. What I had fucking craved.

I swallowed. "What are *you* doing here?" I paused, looking around. "No wait, that's kind of a stupid question. It's a strip club, plus you're here to visit Julia. Or perhaps Cadence?" My voice was sickly sweet. "Or it could be Charlotte." I folded my arms, mostly to help cover my lack of attire. Not that he hadn't seen it all. And tasted it. "You see, I found out that I'm part of a club. Not like yours. We don't ride big bikes to compensate for some other shortcomings. But this one is a special, and quite large, sisterhood. All the girls you've fucked. Most of who were convinced they had something special and unique. Until they found out about the other three girls, or four, in some cases, you were also dating, who all felt equally unique." I sucked in a breath. "Who am I *lucky*"—I spat the word—"enough to be sharing a rotation with?"

I had been informed of Gabriel's dating habits on my first day when I met all the girls at Diamond Lounge.

Outwardly, I'd rolled my eyes and laughed it off. Inwardly, I'd crumbled. I fucking hated that it was that easy to smash the house I was trying to rebuild, but it was. I was barely holding on to my sobriety. Which Gabriel had given me.

I thought, despite my bravado, my denial, that he had given me more.

That we were more.

I had actually hoped for it.

It was my own fault, really. Hope had been snuffed out of my world the moment the door creaked open that night. I'd been a fucking idiot to try and relight that particular flame.

So I'd ignored the various calls and texts from him and hid, actually fucking hid, when he turned up at Rosie's. Luckily she covered for me with minimal inquisition.

"It's complicated," I told her after I'd straightened from my position from behind the sofa.

She nodded, sad understanding flickering in her eyes. "Isn't it always?"

I had been uncharacteristically going to ask what she meant by that, what hid behind her multiple personas, but she spoke.

"Should we watch zombies rip apart what's left of the human race and drool at Daryl in all of his unshowered glory to make us feel better?" she asked, flopping down on the sofa.

I grinned. "Yeah."

So I hadn't gotten to the deep and meaningful behind Rosie and her serial dating, but I thought it might have something to do with a certain law enforcement officer who'd turned up at our place and she was the one hiding behind the sofa.

"Wow," I muttered when I opened the door to captain handsome.

"You're Bex," he greeted, his voice smooth and deep.

Very pleasing to the ears.

He was very pleasing to the eyes too, all tall and muscly and bone structure. A little too clean-cut for me.

I raised a brow, surprised he knew who I was. I'd kept a pretty low profile since I'd moved in with Rosie, but it was a small town. "You're a cop, seriously? Or are you looking for a bachelorette party? Because you've got the wrong house. Have a nice night, though. Ginuwine's 'Pony' is always a good opening." I winked at him and tried to close the door.

His police issue boot stopped the motion. His eyes twinkled and the corner of his mouth twitched.

Again, I was surprised. I didn't expect Captain America to have a sense of humor.

"I'll keep that in mind for the future, in case this line of work doesn't go to plan. For now, I'll stick to my current profession, enforcing the law."

The way he said that rubbed me the wrong way and had all warm fuzzy feelings for Officer Hottie dissipating. I frowned up at him. "Well, enforce away. I think you have to seek crime in order to do that," I replied.

He regarded me. "I'm looking for Rosie."

I leaned against the doorframe to communicate how unwelcome he was inside it. "As far as I know, she hasn't committed a crime. But she starts cooking meth in the kitchen you'll be the first person I call."

He frowned at me. "It's not exactly preferable to joke about the cooking of drugs in front of the police."

I put my hand on my chest. "Why, I'm ever so sorry, Officer," I declared, with only a hint of sarcasm. "Drugs are bad and wrong. I know that. I did D.A.R.E in high school."

He stared at me.

I stared back.

"Shouldn't you be, you know, fighting crime, sending out bat signals?" I probed.

He folded his arms. "I'm lookin' for Rosie."

I nodded. "You mentioned."

He sighed, obviously losing patience. I was surprised it took that long. If I were him, I would've gotten my gun out and winged me right here right now. "She here?"

"You got a warrant?"

His eyes widened. "Jesus," he muttered. "You're serious."

I nodded. "As plaid on a golf course."

Cue another stare off.

I totally won.

He yanked his very attractive cop aviators down onto his face. "You'll let her know I came by?"

"It'll be the first thing I do," I told him with a smile.

He shook his head, then turned on his heel.

He might not be my flavor, but it didn't mean I couldn't enjoy watching him walk away.

So we were both hiding from men.

It just sucked mine had actually found me.

It sucked even more that I was glad he'd done so.

Gabriel's brows knitted together. He stepped forward, intoxicating me with his presence. "It wasn't any of them I spent the last two weeks with. Shared my fuckin' deepest darkest secrets with. Who I've had to damn near stalk just to see her beautiful face," he murmured, his face close to mine. "Who I haven't been able to get out of my fuckin' mind." His eyes turned hard. "Now I see you here, not exactly the best place for you, given all the shit you've just come out the other side of. So I'll repeat my earlier question. Why are you here?"

"Deep breaths," I muttered, looking from his intense stare to my boots.

His brows furrowed. "What?"

I snapped my gaze up. "I'm not talking to you," I barked. "I'm talking myself out of making a scene or committing murder." I glanced around and noticed Gage leaning against the bar, chugging a beer but watching our exchange with his calculating gaze. "Though, given the ownership of such an establishment, I doubt I'd be the first to spill blood here." I pulled myself away from him. "But I'm starting fresh. Trying my best not to do things like murder. Or drugs," I added harshly. "And to address you're earlier statement, I'm here to *work*. And I'm sure you'll have some kind of caveman opinion on the woman you've deluded yourself into thinking you own taking her clothes off for money." I paused, raising my brow. "But I'm going to tell you now, that opinion isn't going to change a damn thing. So how about we skip all the chest pounding and arguing and go straight to you storming out of here once you've realized you can't change who I am, or what I do for a living?"

He stared at me. And stared. It started to get unnerving, but hell if I was going to be the one to speak first.

He finally stepped forward and grasped my hips tightly before I could scuttle away. I may have been gaining weight and muscle thanks to movie nights with Rosie and my last few practices with the pole, but I was no match for him.

"You think I want to change you?" he murmured. He brought his hand up to brush my newly dip-died purple ends. "You can't change a wild thing. You try, you get yourself damned for trying to alter something so chaotically beautiful it hurts to look at. So you may drive me to fuckin' drink, baby, but I'm not looking for eternal damnation. I've done plenty of things that might damn my soul, but this won't be one of them."

I lost my breath, my argument, my fricking sense at his words. He took advantage and closed the distance between us to savagely claim my mouth.

I was afraid he had already claimed everything else.

He pulled back when I was seriously about to climb him like a tree, right there in the middle of the club.

His eyes were liquid gold. "I don't accept this." His gaze flickered around the actually well-decorated and classy strip club. "This is not where you belong." His eyes moved down my body, taking in my barely clad body. "And no one's eyes but fuckin' mine belong on that body. It makes my blood boil thinking of that." He yanked me to him. "But as long as I'm the only one fuckin' you till you can't see or remember your own name, I'll deal."

Fury mingled with melancholy at his words. And temptation. Something I craved but couldn't have. He needed to know that. So I didn't struggle, glancing up to meet his eyes. "I can't reconcile what I am with what you want me to be. I want to be her, the woman you think I am, but I'm not. The sooner you realize that, the sooner we can both exit this delusion and get on with our lives."

I let myself have one more moment in his arms before stepping back.

He glared at me. "I don't want you to be anyone but who you are."

"Really?" I scoffed. "Look around." I held my hands out to the stage, the pole. "Look at me." I gestured down to my bra and panties set. "Is this what you want from your 'old lady'?" I asked honestly.

His gaze set me on fire. "Yes. It's exactly what I fuckin' want."

Then he pressed his mouth to mine once more before letting me go, turning on his heel and leaving me standing there, all hot and bothered and wondering what the fuck just happened.

TWO MONTHS LATER

What had happened on that Monday afternoon two months back was Gabriel claiming me. Or trying to.

What happened over the next two months was me fighting tooth and nail against that claiming.

I was barely my own, still finding out who sober Bex was, what she wanted from life.

I think that's why he didn't go full alpha. Why he only *looked* like he would kill every man in the audience every time I worked. And he was there almost every time. I tried my best to ignore him, to act like I wasn't dancing for him, but he was like a magnet.

Nothing could change that.

Since I couldn't change the laws of attraction, I controlled what I could. I made sure we didn't do any couple shit like eat meals other than breakfast and midnight snacks together. Not that breakfast was a meal we normally had together, despite how good his pancakes were and how much Rosie loved them.

No, I set the parameters, which he begrudgingly accepted. Another surprise, which I called him on one night while mellow and sated.

I was tracing the rider on his back as he lay on his stomach. It was a tattoo all the men in the club had, spanning from shoulder to hip. The club insignia, a grim reaper riding a bike on a road of skulls. But his was different, the insignia was shrouded in angel wings that came from the top of his neck, almost protecting the rider. On closer inspection, I saw three names etched into the wings.

Sofia. Camila. Alexis.

"I'm surprised," I said, trailing my nails down the inked feathers, swallowing my tears at the names on his back.

"That I'm mortal, despite what I can do in the bedroom?" he answered, his voice muffled by the pillow.

I grinned because he couldn't see my face. "That you're not fighting for control."

He rolled around so he pressed me to the mattress in one swift move. My breathing quickened, despite the fact he'd only just finished rocking my world. "In case you didn't notice, I've got control," he rasped, focusing on the headboard he'd only just uncuffed me from.

Yes, *uncuffed me.* I'd gone willingly into captivity. Anyone would if they experienced the nirvana of Gabriel's body ravaging theirs.

"In here," I agreed, my voice less than a whisper. "But not out there." I nodded to the door.

His eyes didn't leave my face. "No one has control out there. I control the things I can, and the things I can't, I protect."

I swallowed at his words and managed to find my own. "So you don't itch to give me a property patch, and it doesn't piss you off that you can't make me your little old lady?"

His face hardened, just a smidgeon. "We don't have property patches, firefly. If we did, you reckon anything would get Gwen to wear one? That bitch takes what she puts on her back seriously. I don't even think my prez could get a patch on her. Not that he would," he said, a teasing glint to his eyes. "I also take what I put on my back fuckin' seriously. Before I put on this leather, my life was fucked. Spiraling, full of demons. So I know the value of the club, what it means to me. What it gave me." His hand circled my neck. "Since I know the value of where I belong, I know how fuckin' hard it is to belong to someone. Something. You're just figuring out how to belong to yourself. I'm willin' to wait however long it takes for you to figure out you belong to me too. I'm willin' to accept whatever you can give me, and this." His hand snaked down my torso, stopping for delightful torture on my nipple and then moving lower. Way lower.

My eyes rolled back, my sensitive flesh exploding from his touch.

"This is a fuck of a lot more. It's enough." He kissed me, then hovered above me. "For now," he warned.

I didn't get the chance to argue the 'me belonging to him' statement because he made sure my mouth stayed busy.

••••

I was soaring. Fucking flying.

High.

Not in the way I was used not. No syringe was needed for this high.

Only him, my new addiction.

"You're not gonna come yet," he growled, the veins in his neck pulsing as he pounded into me.

My body was screaming for release, but at the same time it wanted to topple over the edge, it itched to prolong the feeling of hovering just before something magnificent. To grasp onto that ledge and last facet of control before it was all lost and the abyss swallowed me.

So I teetered.

My hands were bound by my own fucking bra. Yes, he'd torn it off and used it to restrain my wrists. They were burning from being held above my head for a prolonged amount of time, but the pain was exquisite. It made everything, the pleasure and the way my body reacted to that pain, so much more intense.

Beautiful and ugly at the same time.

He pressed our foreheads together, bringing me in for a brutal kiss, his lips smashing against mine as he swallowed my screams.

"As much as I hate it," he growled against my mouth, not stopping his thrusts, "you exposing your beauty to all those fucks." His eyes met mine. "And I fuckin' *hate* it... but I love it." He surged into me harder and deeper than I thought possible, and I saw stars as he bit into my neck. "I love that those fuckers are goin' home with only the image of your sweet ass in their minds, burned into their fuckin' retinas, and I'm the one who gets to hold it." He squeezed my ass roughly to make his point. "I'm the only one who gets in here." He paused his motion, filling me up and stopping me from finally tumbling down.

My breathing came in pants as he refused me the release he'd built up since my eyes met his half an hour before. Since I'd strutted on stage and danced for him. Taken everything off for him.

There was something darkly erotic about stripping for the man you were screwing while a roomful of people watched. I'd been damp with desire by the end of my set.

Fucked-up, I knew, but I didn't care.

Because Gabriel was equally fucked-up. The moment I left the stage he was there, dragging me to a barely concealed corner of the dressing room, behind a flimsy door. And with the chattering of the girls and the thump of the bass in our ears, he began ripping my clothes off, what little clothes there were, and surged into me.

He had been frantic, furious, animalistic. Brutal.

And I fucking *loved it.*

Without warning he pulled out of me. The emptiness and loss of him and my own release was painful.

I didn't have time to protest as he roughly turned me, pressing my cheek into the wall, spreading my legs and plunging into me once more.

I panicked.

I couldn't be taken like that.

Pressed facedown, being assaulted by some unknown attacker.

It hurtled me back to that night. That horrific night when my innocence was stolen while I was pressed facedown on the bed.

I'd learned to reclaim my sexuality since then, mostly by fucking a plethora of different guys I chose, taken back through sheer promiscuity.

Some therapist would love to unpack that can of worms, I was sure. But it was how I coped. Survived.

And by making sure no one took me like Gabriel was taking me now. Having me fully immobile, helpless.

I panicked because, despite the way dirt sank into my naked body with the memories that hurtled into my mind's eye, so did arousal. It mingled in a way that had me feeling more turned on than ever before, and filthier too.

"Come," he growled into my neck, his breath hot on my ear.

And I did. It was glorious and horrible and mind-shattering all at once.

He grunted his own release into my neck and I barely noticed it.

I barely noticed anything until I came down. Then all I saw was disgust in myself.

And I needed him out. I needed it to be gone. The grime that covered every inch of my fucking body. My insides.

"Fuck, baby," he muttered into my neck, breathing heavily.

"Untie me," I croaked, pleaded.

He registered the panic in my voice immediately, stiffening before he did exactly as I requested.

He massaged my wrists, turning me around. He came out of me as he did so and the evidence of my depravity leaked out of me.

"Becky?" he asked, his voice dripping with concern, face painted with regret. "Fuck, did I hurt you?"

I regarded him coldly. "Get your hands off me," I snapped.

I had to hide behind her. The bitch. She was the one protecting the little girl inside, who was sobbing in the soiled sheets.

He did so immediately and I pushed past him, gathering the remains of my clothes. Precious little, but enough to cover me up.

I heard the rustling of his belt but set to my task.

"Becky, talk to me. You're freakin' me the fuck out." His voice was thick.

I luckily had the coat I'd started my routine with; otherwise, I would've been fucked. *Thank God for trench coats.* I tightened the tie and made for the door.

He stopped me. "Becky, don't fuckin' run."

I started to shake, my hold on sanity tenuous. I needed out. "Let me go," I pleaded, my voice shaking.

Again he sensed it, the desperation that came with that plea.

I didn't look his way again. I found the door, my escape, and I ran. Ran to try and get clean.

•••

"Dude, I'm totally with you on not talking to the rat bastard, even though I have no idea what he did," Rosie said, her eyes on me. "I don't

ANNE MALCOM

need to know. I saw what state you were in when you got home." She shivered, as did I.

State was a good word for it. I was almost fucking catatonic. It was the surprise that got me. I hadn't expected it to hit me so hard. I thought I'd made peace with that particular demon years before, found a way to fight it. Not defeat it, that'd never happen, but keep it in its corner. Turned out I hadn't. It had been biding its time, waiting, lurking, until the opportune moment came to tear at the shreds of innocence I had left.

It was safe to say there was nothing now.

Rosie had blanched, actually fucking paled, the moment she saw me. I was pretty sure I would have too. Naked except for a fucking trench coat, muttering about how I needed to be clean and shaking so hard I'd bitten my tongue and actually drawn blood.

"Shit," she'd exclaimed. "Bex, what did you take?" Her voice was calm, purposeful.

I let out a frenzied and hysterical giggle at that. I supposed I must've looked like I was on the edge of overdose. And in a way, I was. I'd overdosed on him. On us. On the depravity he didn't even know he'd unearthed, the depravity we'd shared.

"Bex," she repeated. "Do I need to call an ambulance?" She had her phone in her hand though she was biting her lip, knowing my hatred for hospitals.

I shook my head quickly. "I haven't taken anything. I promise."

Something in my voice must have been convincing. "What do you need?"

"Clean," I choked out. "I need clean."

To her credit, she didn't look at me like I was crazy, which most likely would have sent me over the edge. "Okay, we'll get you in the shower."

She led me into the bathroom, turning on the water for me. "You need me to stay?" she asked, her voice even.

I shook my head. "I'm good."

She didn't look convinced.

Yeah, I so wasn't good.

"I'm not going for the razorblades, I promise. I just need to be clean," I said, my voice stronger. I was coming out of that terrible abyss with the calm Rosie was emitting, and the steam filling the room.

"Okay," she said. "I'll be right outside. Making tea and Pop-Tarts."

She gave my hand a final squeeze and left the room.

Left me to get clean.

When I emerged, as clean as a shower would ever get me, she handed me a steaming mug. I took it.

"Drink," she ordered.

"Is there tequila in this?" I asked hopefully.

She gave me a look. "I did think about it, but I didn't know how tequila would taste with Earl Grey. And I also don't know the rules for giving a recovering drug addict hard liquor, so I went with no, sorry."

I smiled at her. "Probably a good call."

I sipped the tea, sitting on the sofa.

"Want to talk about it?" she asked, sipping her own mug which wasn't steaming like mine. I had a sneaking suspicion she didn't have Earl Grey in hers.

I didn't. Like would rather get a bikini wax with duct tape kind of didn't. But I found it all pouring out anyway.

When I'd recited the whole gory and thankfully short story, she sat in front of me, a tear streaking through her makeup. "Fuck, Bex," she whispered. "I don't know what to say. I'm so sorry that happened to you."

I shrugged, feigning nonchalance. It was my coping mechanism. "It's life. I dealt." I paused. "Or thought I did. Then that happened with Lucky and I kind of... freaked out."

Rosie nodded. "Understandably."

I gaped at her. "You don't think I'm a total fucking head case?"

She gaped back at me. "Babe. You're standing. Breathing. Living. You know how to do winged eyeliner better than anyone I know and have a kick-ass sense of humor, all despite that fucking nightmare. You're a miracle." She leaned forward to squeeze my hand. "Freak-outs, they're normal. I have one every second day when my hair doesn't cooperate. People lose their shit. Fucking necessary. It's only when you try and swallow all that down, keep it bottled up, that it turns to crazy."

I blinked at her. "I've never thought of it that way before."

She smiled. "Probably because you've never thought too hard on it before. We never do about our ugliest shit. We run from it. Try not to look too closely. But it catches up, forces our gaze."

"Yeah, I guess so," I agreed.

"You know he's not going to leave you alone," she said gently.

She'd barely managed to keep him from storming in not an hour before. I'd heard his shouts.

But she did.

"No, I don't think he will."

The thought terrified me. Of seeing him. Trying to explain what it was that had me running like I'd been afraid.

Me? Afraid.

Because I loved him.

Fuck.

There are two things completely free from logic in this world. Fear and love. Two things I promised myself I wouldn't surrender to because lack of logic in my world meant lack of life.

So I didn't love. And because I didn't love, I had nothing to fear. I'd already discovered nightmares were real before I'd reached high school, experienced the horrors that happened in the dark. Yet there I was, bursting with love. And fear. I'd given into both and couldn't do anything about it. More importantly, I didn't *want* to do anything about it.

And that had me wanting to escape. Myself, him, everything.

But life had other ideas.

More precisely, death.

TWELVE

"She had been innocent once, a little girl playing with feathers on the floor of the Devil's lair."
-Laini Taylor

He caught up with me the next day. At the grocery store, of all places. I was being a total coward and ignoring every single call—all twenty-seven of them—after letting Rosie deal with the bellowing alpha the night before.

But I was still recovering.

It was like aftereffects of a migraine. The actual episode was over but the fragility of my head still remained. My sanity. The pain was a shadow that was hard to forget. So I was hiding from him until I found a way to build up my walls again, to forget that pain.

Without drugs.

How fun that would be.

That choice was taken away when I was deciding between skim and two percent.

Both milk bottles were ripped from my hands and set back down roughly. Then Gabriel had me by the wrist and was dragging me bodily from the store.

I struggled against him. "Let me go," I hissed.

He didn't look my way. "Not happenin'."

I struggled again and people looked, but no one came to my aid. Probably because this was a small town and everyone knew Gabriel and the leather on his back.

I just didn't know that the cut of leather gave him carte blanche to manhandle women in the fucking grocery store.

Obviously it did.

"Don't worry. Only a woman getting dragged out of a grocery store by a fucking biker. Nothing to make you actually do something about," I shouted at no one in particular.

One woman wearing a low-cut pink dress that looked like it belonged on a Vegas stage, not in a grocery store, actually grinned at me.

Grinned.

Not even the security guard did a thing, just nodded pleasantly at Gabriel as if we were strolling past hand in hand and I wasn't getting dragged while struggling like a banshee.

"This fucking town has some serious fucking issues," I said as we reached the parking lot. "Serious fucking issues," I shouted back to the store.

We made it to Gabriel's Harley before he turned.

"Get on," he ordered.

"Not fucking likely," I snapped back.

He stepped forward, toe to toe with me, his face granite. "Becky, get on." Everything about that action was meant to intimidate—his voice, his height, his face devoid of the light humor that was his default. That, as I'd learned in the cabin, was his mask to hide his true face. The damaged, dangerous, broken man before me.

I didn't back down. "I'm not scared of you," I hissed. "And you may be able to drag me bodily out of places on account of the fact you have too few manners and too many muscles, but you can't command me to do anything. So unless you want to hog-tie me to that bike, I'm not going anywhere." I crossed my arms.

He held my stare like he was considering it, actually *considering* tying me to a motorcycle and driving off.

"Fine," he relented, and I tried to hide my triumphant smile.

"Okay, now that we've established you're a fuckin' nutcase and this town has zero issues with kidnapping as long as the kidnapper is wearing a Sons of Templar cut, I'm going to go. Preferably over state lines." I made to leave but he caught my wrist.

"I said fine to not putting your sweet ass in danger by forcin' you on a bike, but I ain't lettin' you leave," he growled. "Not until you've talked to me. And if it has to be in a fuckin' parking lot, so be it."

I struggled against his hold but he didn't let go. It wasn't painful, but it was firm. "You're seriously doing this?"

Not a spec of his trademark humor danced behind his eyes.

"You're seriously doing this," I muttered.

"I've got no fuckin' choice," he growled. "You won't answer my calls, you got Rosie as a fuckin' sentry, and that bitch is scarier than Gage when she wants to be. This was a last resort. Not one I'm particularly comfortable with, but it's necessary 'cause I've been goin' fuckin' insane with worry, and anger, over what happened last night. What I did." As if the reminder was enough, he let me go, stepping back. He ran his hand over his bald head and I noticed the way his eyes were slightly bloodshot, indicating lack of sleep.

"Talk to me, Becky. What the fuck happened?" he asked, his voice softer. "How bad did I hurt you?"

I was taken aback. "You think you hurt me?"

His face was blank. "Babe, you recoiled from my touch seconds after my cock slid outta you. I was takin' you rough, but fuck, I thought you could take it. I never would've fuckin' done it if I knew you couldn't." His voice was laced with regret, and shame. Despite myself, I stepped forward, itching to comfort him.

"It wasn't you," I murmured. "Or what we were doing," I added. "I can take it. With you, it's better than I've ever had. The best, in the worst way," I admitted quietly, aware of how exposed we were in the fucking parking lot. But I knew it was now or never. If I had time, a bike ride to think about what I was about to tell him, I'd pussy out.

His head tilted and he stepped forward too, his body brushing against mine. "Then what, Becky? The way you looked at me scared the fuckin' shit outta me," he admitted.

I sucked in a breath. "I wasn't looking at you," I said quietly. "I wasn't even *seeing* you." I gazed up to his hazel eyes, needing them to anchor me to the moment. "I was seeing *him*."

His entire body froze as if he sensed what was coming. "Who?" he gritted out.

I wanted to look away from him, escape the intimacy of his gaze. But if I looked away the darkness of the memory would swallow me up, and without the cushion of narcotics, I'd get lost in the abyss. So I kept his gaze. "The man who raped me when I was twelve years old."

ANNE MALCOM

The words flew out with the breeze, which carried them on the air and polluted every molecule they came into contact with. It was visible, tangible, the effect they had on Gabriel. Every inch of his body turned to stone and his eyes deepened with emotion, with intensity.

Then I wasn't seeing his eyes. Or even him. I wasn't even me. I was a stranger. A little girl still clutching the last soft edges of her childhood that hadn't been filed off.

I couldn't sleep because I was hungry. It wasn't unusual, going to bed with no dinner. Mostly because there wasn't enough food to go around in these stupid prisons they called foster homes. The fat 'parents' stuffed their faces and gave the kids the scraps.

It should've been illegal, or something. But I guessed the fancy people making the laws didn't care about orphan hood rats getting all Oliver Twist up in there. I was going to make sure they did, when I was older and out of this craptastic place. When I wasn't bundled under itchy sheets and trying to ignore the rumble in my stomach. I was totally going to get one of those fancy suits and fancy hairdos and go on the TV and tell kids like me they weren't forgotten. I'd help them.

Not just the one little girl clutching a dirty rabbit, like the one I'd given my dinner to earlier that night.

All of them. I'd help them all. I was smart, read a lot. I could totally do it.

I was contemplating trying out my lock-picking kit and going for the padlock on the refrigerator since the whole house was asleep. Then I could hoard some stuff for me and bunny girl. You didn't learn names here. Names meant attachments, friendships. You couldn't do that. Nothing here was for the long time. Everyone was only visitors in each other's lives. Nothing was for good.

But I liked bunny girl, despite my rules.

So I guessed it was her who was creeping into my Harry Potter-esque cupboard of a room. I rolled over, about to let her into my bed as I had for the last four nights she'd been there.

She couldn't sleep alone. Think it might've had something to do with the fact she'd been alone in her apartment after her mom offed herself.

Brutal.

But the kid was cute and small; someone would adopt her. But for now, she had me. And I'd take care of her.

But it wasn't her small form that stood over my bed. This one was much bigger, the shadow taking up the whole room.

I scuttled back, already scrambling for the knife I kept hidden in my boot.

Another kid gave it to me when I was ten. Leather jacket was his name. He was older, cooler. He smoked a lot. I didn't like that, but I liked him. He'd given me the knife the day he left.

"You hide this," he ordered.

I gaped at the glittering steel he held out to me. I took it, trying not to do something stupid like cut myself. That would be embarrassing.

His smoke-tainted hand went to my chin, tilting it up to meet his eyes. "Kid, you listening?"

I nodded rapidly.

"You hide that." He nodded to the knife. "When the time comes, you use it. The time will come. You're a cute kid, a life in the system ahead of you. There's all kinds of men—monsters, not men. They like cute, green-eyed little kids who don't have anyone in the world." He gave me a hard stare that kind of scared me. "You use that on them. And don't you dare be scared of them. Ain't no use for fear in our life." He let go of my chin, stepped back, and was gone.

I hadn't realized what he'd meant, but I kept the knife.

Now I knew. But it was useless in my boot because a sharp pain erupted in my head and I was slammed down roughly on my cardboard bed.

"Not so fast, Rebecca," Walter whispered.

His breath stank of the food he'd gulped down, rotting in his big fat stomach.

I struggled, but he was big and strong and his body was on top of mine, swallowing it.

"You don't say a thing," he rasped in my ear, his hands moving down my body, touching me in wrong places. Bad places. Places that were dirtied by his hands.

I wanted to cry. To scream.

"You be quiet, be a good girl, and I'll give you extra dinner. You just have to give me something."

He turned me over so my face squashed into the pillow. I couldn't breathe, and his weight at my back meant I couldn't move. Panic settled over me like spines from a cactus.

Then he didn't wait for me to give him anything. He took it all. Everything I didn't even know could be taken, stolen.

I'd wanted to scream. But I didn't. I stayed silent and horrifically awake through it all. It seared into my brain, my soul.

I rubbed my arms. The air was warm, but the past surrounded me with the chill of the memory. Of the nightmare. "It only happened once," I whispered. "Once was all he got before I ran." I blinked away the memories of living on the street for two days. Two days of homelessness was better than two seconds in that house. I would have spent two decades there if possible. I sucked in a breath. "They caught me, the people trying to help." I laughed bitterly. "Yeah, to help. But luckily they didn't take me back there. I got into another home where I stayed until I was old enough to escape. Or try to." I stared at him. "Once was enough. More than enough to make sure the chains of that night would ensure escape was impossible."

I waited for the poison to set in, for him to rear back and create distance between himself and those ugly words.

It didn't come, the distance. Instead he yanked me to him, circling me in his embrace so tight it was as if he were trying to meld me into his body. His scent engulfed me, clean laundry mixed with tobacco and leather. It chased away the bitterness of *his* breath that came with the memory. His arms, instead of making me feel caged in, set me free from *his* grip.

He pressed his lips to my head. "Shit, Becky," he murmured.

Too soon, he let me go. Not fully, but enough so he could meet my eyes. "Really hate that we're havin' this conversation in the fuckin' parking lot of a grocery store, but I guess that's kind of my fault," he said, his voice even. I didn't miss the way he held his body, the fire burning behind his eyes.

Despite all that, I let out a small choke of laughter at his words. It was cleansing, a release of some sort. "Yeah, but is there an ideal place for you to hear that?"

His grip tightened. "No. Except in a place where time travel exists so I could go back and rip that fucker's dick off," he clipped.

I shivered at the iciness of his rage, despite the fact his arms were warm around me.

He met my stare. "He got a name? You remember it?"

I laughed again. "I remember his fucking Social Security number." I rattled it off, my voice robotic. I'd done it for as long as I could remember. When the darkness got be too great, I concentrated on the memory, promising myself I would never forget because one day I'd use the information to get revenge.

Then he did something I didn't expect at my words. He grinned. But not like I was used to seeing, with light and humor, making me squirm at the *GQ*-ness of it all. No, this one was dark, velvet evil that promised murder. And still, because I was fucked-up, it made me squirm. "Excellent," he hissed.

Without letting me go, he reached in his pocket and grabbed his phone, pressing a couple of buttons before putting it to his ear.

"Who are you calling?" I frowned.

He put his finger to his lips.

My eyes widened. "Did you just shush me?" I asked dangerously.

He ignored me. "Wire. Hey, bro. I need a location on a Walter Asper," he greeted, rattling off the Social Security number I'd memorized.

There was a pause as he waited, and it hit me.

"Gabriel," I whispered.

He kissed my head. "A second, baby," he murmured, his eyes far away.

He stiffened as I heard the muffled voice of someone else. "Good. Text the location through to me." There was a pause. "No, I don't need backup."

Then he hung up the phone.

I stared at him. "Is there a reason why you just got the location of the man who fucked up my childhood?"

Gabriel kissed me lightly on the mouth. "Oh yes, there's a fucking reason."

Releasing me from his arms, he leaned over, opened a bag on his bike, and retrieved a leather vest. He held it out to me.

I stared at it. "That doesn't go with my outfit," I said finally.

He looked me up and down.

I was finally able to wear tank tops and was making the most of it. Though it was little more than a scrap of fabric, I compensated for the fact it showed a lot of belly and considerable cleavage with high-waisted jeans and my signature boots.

"Yeah, as much as I don't want to cover that up, we're goin' on a road trip and you need protection."

I didn't miss the double meaning behind his last word, but I didn't focus on my feminism being fucked with.

"Road trip," I repeated.

He nodded.

"Where are we going?" I asked, even though I knew the answer.

His eyes were dark. Midnight. "Can't time travel, but we can do what should've been done eleven years ago," he said, his voice velvet.

I stared at the leather. I knew what was going to happen if I took it. Where the final destination would be. It would be another mark on my soul, and I would be blackening his.

I took the jacket without hesitation.

THIRTEEN

"Life is rough so you gotta be tough."
-Johnny Cash

"Please," the coward choked out, tears and snot streaming down his face.

I didn't blink at his plea, merely leaned forward, placing the bloodstained knife at his flabby neck. "Funny, I remember uttering that same word eleven years ago. When you had me pinned to the bed. When you stole something that wasn't yours to take, you sick fuck," I hissed.

I ran the blade along his collarbone, feeling immense satisfaction at his shriek of pain. "How many girls?" I asked when he stopped screaming.

His bloodshot eyes darted from me to Gabriel, who was leaning against the wall, casually swinging his gun between his thumb and forefinger. I knew he was waiting. Waiting for me to finish exacting my revenge so he could finish the job. Do the dirtiest of the dirty work.

He'd been clear about that before we came.

"You deserve to make this guy hurt," he'd said after he'd tied him up in some abandoned warehouse in Reno. Reno. The guy had been living one state over. "That's your right. But you're letting me end him."

I stared at him. "How is that your right?" I asked, weirdly calm over the fact we'd just kidnapped a man and were now discussing his torture and murder.

Maybe it was because of the little girl I'd seen playing in the front garden of the same house that held my lost innocence. Though she wasn't playing. She was sitting on a swing set, staring into space, her eyes empty, devoid of anything. A look far too tortured and adult for a

ANNE MALCOM

little girl. A look I recognized.

She couldn't have been more than twelve.

I guessed that's why I was calm. And angry over Gabriel declaring he be the one to get to send this monster to the underworld.

"Why? Because you're the big strong man you get to do the killing? A woman can't? We get equal pay and the right to vote. We should be allowed to pull the triggers too."

His eyes were hard and the corner of his mouth twitched. There was no smile, though. There hadn't been since the moment I told him. His face had been eerily blank.

I had no fucking clue how he organized an SUV to transport the guy and a place to store and presumably kill him. The perks of belonging to a national outlaw motorcycle gang, I thought.

"This isn't about fuckin' women's rights," he replied. "I got nothin' against a woman killing someone who deserves it. I got somethin' against *you* doin' it, but not for the reasons you think," he said, holding his hand up to stop the protests he knew would come with that statement. "It's 'cause I want a shot at this guy for what he did to you. More than anything, it'll bring me immense fuckin' joy to send him to the reaper. It's somethin' I've done. Many times. Saw the life filter outta someone's eyes, been the one to take that life." He regarded me, cupping my face. "I already got those marks on my soul and I'll pay for them, whenever my time comes. But you, you've already got enough shit scarring yours, shit you had no control over. I'm not gonna let you have that on you, not gonna let him put another mark on your beautiful, scarred soul. He can't have that."

His words struck me dumb, which I think he took as agreement. He kissed me soundly and handed me a blade. "Don't cut yourself," he warned, grinning wickedly. "Go nuts." He stepped back, revealing the overweight, naked, and balding man tied to the chair in front of us.

I did. Go nuts, that was. I hadn't even known I'd have the stomach for it. Revenge. I'd dreamed about it, plenty of times, making him pay for what he did to me, what he took from me. I'd fantasized, but I never had the courage to do it.

But I'd found it. Gabriel gave it to me.

And I found that I could do it. Get my revenge in every way I'd imagined.

"How many?" I repeated, my voice rough.

"I-I don't know what you're t-talking about," he stuttered.

I eyed him, the monster in the dark all these years. He wasn't scary now that I'd stripped away everything and exposed him for the coward he was. The overweight, beady-eyed waste of space who cried the second he lost the upper hand. The second someone fought back.

"How many little girls have you fucking raped while you got paid to take care of them?" I seethed. "How many lives have you ruined?"

He started shaking as he sobbed. "I'm so-sorry," he cried. "I'm sorry. I can't control myself. Please don't kill me. I'll stop. I promise I'll stop—"

His pleas were cut off when a garbled wet sound erupted from his throat. I stepped back, not wanting blood on my tank top.

"No, you won't," I said to his twitching, dying body.

Gabriel clutched my hips, bringing my body back to his front. He gently pried the knife from my hands, tucking it into his belt.

"Jesus, Becky," he murmured into my neck. "I thought we'd fuckin' established I'd be the one to do that."

I stared at the body, my mind numb. "No, you saying something does not establish it as law," I informed him. "Despite your thoughts to the contrary, my soul is already damned. And even if it weren't, giving this guy the death he deserved should be counted as a good deed, not a sin."

I thought back to the little girl on the swing set. Then the little girl I was eleven years ago. I didn't save them, but at least I avenged them.

The numbness started to recede and the reality of what just happened set in.

I'd killed someone.

The blood in my veins sped through my body hotter than before, my heart thumping and pushing it through at record speed.

Gabriel whirled me around so his hand circled my neck. "You're not damned," he growled, his eyes wild.

"I am," I argued, my voice hoarse. "Or at least I will be, after I do this."

"What?"

I didn't tell him what. I showed him. I yanked his head closer to mine and crashed our mouths together. I knew Frenching your kind-of boyfriend after killing a man wasn't exactly a sane move, but I had to. The blood and adrenaline flowing through me needed an outlet.

I expected him to pull back, but my body burned when he yanked me closer, his fingers diving into my hair and tugging at the strands.

"Fuck," he growled, pulling my head back so my eyes met his wild ones. "If this is fuckin' damnation then I hope to never find redemption." And then his mouth was back on mine, slamming me back into an icy concrete wall. The impact scratched my arms but I barely noticed. Cold wasn't something I even registered.

Because I was hot. Burning.

Gabriel's touch was setting me aflame.

His hands moved roughly to yank my tank top off. I held my arms above my head obediently, knowing where this was going. Loving where this was going.

But he surprised me. The tank top fluttered to the floor and he clutched my neck.

"No, baby," he rasped. "Not tying you up, leavin' you helpless to me. You're not that. You're never fuckin' that. I need to feel those warrior hands on me. Those fighting nails on my fuckin' back as I fuck you so hard you forget everything but us. But me."

My breathing quickened. I'd been fucked up in my sexual preferences for as long as I could remember so that's why I'd responded to how Gabriel did it. Did me. More than responded. I'd just never thought he'd turn me on beyond anything by demanding this.

Normality.

Apart from the dead body in the corner.

But this was as close as we'd get.

And I loved it.

He claimed my mouth again before kissing down my neck, paying attention to my nipples. Then he moved down with deliberate slowness. Gentleness.

His hands that knew fury, brutality, and murder gently undid my jeans, like such an act was a blessing, an honor. Then his mouth fastened between my legs, working me to the edge of the earth.

To the edge of life.

Then he brought me back.

In more ways than one.

••••

Something changed after that. Something integral, pivotal, between us. You couldn't kill someone together and go back to hearts and flowers.

Not that we ever were that.

You'd expect doing such a thing would create distance, a yawning chasm of guilt and sin. It was the opposite.

We hadn't spoken after, apart from Gabriel informing me someone would 'take care' of the body as I dressed myself. I stood on shaky legs. Not from the act that had blood staining the concrete floor, but from the act that Gabriel had performed on me against that same floor.

I trusted him to have it taken care of and take care of me, so I didn't end up facing the rest of my life behind bars.

He'd never let that happen.

I was sure of that.

We rode back in the dark, the air biting against my skin, prickling it with its chill. I embraced the cold. And the warmth of Gabriel's back, and the hand that covered mine for most of the ride.

We went back to his place. It wasn't a question.

Then we made love.

I fucking hated myself for that description, but that's what it was. There were no handcuffs, no commands, no fury. Just us. Slow. Devastatingly so.

And afterwards we'd talked. Like *really* talked. About everything. And nothing.

I gave him everything I could, more than anyone had ever gotten. More than I thought I had to give.

It happened after chocolate chip pancakes with Gabriel not wearing a stitch of clothing and me wearing nothing but his tee.

"Your mom," I said quietly, staring at the pancakes. The ones she taught him how to make. I glanced up to regard him over his kitchen counter. His eyes shuttered immediately. "Is she still...?"

"Alive?" he finished for me, his voice brisk.

I nodded.

His face was blank as he leaned forward and rested his elbows against the countertop. "Yeah. She's alive. Still in the same house. Doing the same job. Holdin' on to those same demons." He shrugged. "I don't like it. In fact, I hate that she still ignores the man I am because of the boy I was." He didn't betray an ounce of emotion, which was weird—heartbreaking, in fact. Because he couldn't contain it when he witnessed my shit. When he met my demons. But his face was emotionless in the face of his. Even when he'd told me about his sisters, he hadn't feared the memory, flinched at it. In the face of it all, he was dauntless.

"I don't like it, but I understand it," he continued. "My mom had two men in her life who let her down. My dad and me. Stole her daughters from her."

I pushed off my stool, shoving the pancakes away from me. "You weren't a man," I hissed. "You were a fucking kid. A kid trying to survive and trying way too fucking hard to be a man in a world that doesn't seem to recognize age as a reason to give someone a break." I paced the room, anger pulsing through me. Fury. "It wasn't your fault that your sisters died," I said fiercely. "None of that is on your shoulders. It's on the people who pulled the trigger on Camila and Sofia, and as much as I hate to say it, on Alexis." I ignored the stiffening of his jaw. "She was a baby, a kid. But she was old enough to know better. We're always old enough to know better when life touches us with bitter reality. There's usually a limited amount of choices to take. The one your mom did, finding a person to blame, the wrong person. Your sister, looking for escape and finding destruction. Or you, looking for destruction and finding redemption." I paused. "Because that's what you are. You may have done some bad things, but that doesn't cancel out the good. Good means something different when you're brought up in a different world than conventional America. Good is relative. And you're good. And bad. But you're still redeemed." I unintentionally quoted Johnny Cash, but it was apt so I rolled with it, tears threatening the corners of my eyes. "Your mom can't see that, but I can. So fuck her."

Because my emotions were exposed to the nerve and I had about as much control over them as a plastic bag in a snowstorm, a wayward tear leaked down my face. I wiped it away angrily.

"You're crying," Gabriel observed, rounding the counter.

"I'm not," I snapped, scrubbing at my face, not giving a shit about my eyeliner.

He stepped forward and clasped my hips lightly. "It's okay to cry. It's human. Hell, I bawled like a baby when One Direction broke up."

I scowled at him. "Don't make fun of me."

"I would never. It was a tragedy. What was Zane thinking, going out on his own? Solo careers never work. Just look at the Spice Girls."

"You're talking about the Spice Girls right now?" I asked in disbelief.

His gaze turned serious and he frowned. "I guess I am. See, I'm still that fuckin' kid at heart, so I say stupid shit like that. It's my only character flaw," he admitted. "When did you get so old and wise, firefly?"

I gave him a long look, tossing up between giving him some smart-assed answer or giving him more.

He got more.

But not before I stepped from his grasp.

I sighed. "I feel like I was born old. Like the universe decided to rob me of my innocence the moment my parents abandoned me. My chance of being young was taken away before I could even be young. At the same time, I feel like I've never really grown up because I had to make every decision since I can remember about how to keep myself alive." I picked up a photo frame on the mantle, more for distraction than anything else. I didn't get distraction. Two little girls with dark hair and hazel eyes were hugging a bigger girl wearing too much makeup, her beauty still shining through even though she was scowling at the camera.

I swallowed coal and put it down with a shaking hand, not looking his way even though his stare was burning into the nape of my neck. I kept wandering around the edge of the room. Taking in his cluttered living room, motorcycle parts, beer bottles, and magazines swallowing the coffee table in front of his leather sofa. "It's a terrible paradox," I continued. "I'm old without the peace and wisdom that comes with age. I'm just jaded." I regarded the mirror I'd wandered to. I didn't have the lines of age, and my pale skin was in surprisingly good condition considering the fact I more often than not slept in my makeup, barely got any sleep, and shot poison into my veins. My jet-black hair was similarly healthy, shiny, and tumbling down to the faded ends I dip-dyed when I needed a splash of color in my gray world. It was my eyes. That's what sold it. "Old, jaded, and hard," I said to my reflection. "And I'm so terribly fucking young because I make decisions based on what's directly in front of me. Don't consider consequences. Or other people, for that matter." My mind went to Lily, the way I'd started to drag her down into my downwards spiral before Asher yanked her out.

Gabriel had been silent for my whole monologue. So silent that, if it weren't for the heat at my back from his stare, I would've thought I was talking to myself.

Which I kind of was.

I sighed. "You know, I used to think drugs gave me clarity. That I could see the world for what it truly was when I was high." I laughed. "Yeah, I was that deluded. Now I'm clean." I fiddled with the fireplace pokers. "Or at least trying to be. And I can see everything so much clearer than I ever have. I don't exactly like it, but it's me. So I've got to deal."

Suddenly he whirled me around and clutched my neck roughly, his eyes alight.

"Know your secret babe."

My heart dipped and acid crept up my throat. "My secret?" I repeated in a small voice, all traces of bravado gone like a plastic bag in the wind.

His hands circled my hips, pulling my body flush to his. He regarded me in a way that made me want to freeze the moment. I'd never had anyone look at me like that in my entire life. Like I was someone worth something. Worth the devotion that glittered in the backs of those eyes. "Yeah, firefly. The secret you keep to your chest." His finger trailed my breastbone lightly. "Beneath all the hardness you put so much effort into building up. Beneath that hard beauty. There is the most beautiful and caring soul I've ever encountered." Somehow the look in his eyes became more intense and I felt myself unable to tear my gaze away, as much as self-preservation screamed at me to.

"The hard, babe, it's for the world out there. A world that was hell-bent on destroying you. I get that. In fact, I stand here utterly fucking shocked that I'm not holding the broken pieces of that beautiful woman I've been dreaming of since I laid my eyes on your sweet ass." His eyes twinkled. "Somehow, by some miracle, you're not broken. You're whole. Beautiful. And soft. Most beautiful kind of soft 'cause the rest of the world gets hard. I get this." He circled the area above my heart, sending a wave of heat to my toes. To the place I thought would be icy cold forever.

"I may hate that you've had to build that shield, babe, that life has made it necessary. Another part of me is glad as fuck it's there 'cause without it I wouldn't be holding you in my arms, wouldn't be able to taste how sweet it is beneath that." He paused his monologue to press a chaste kiss on my mouth. I yearned for more, for it to deepen, the fire in my belly burning brighter than ever.

He pulled back slightly, his nose still brushing mine, and I watched him as if his impossible words had hypnotized me. "Don't worry, firefly. I'll keep your secret. I just want you to know that you don't need all that hard. To use up all that energy trying to shut out the world. That's my job now. To protect that soft, all the while making sure no one knows about it 'cause then I won't be able to do a damn thing all day but knock motherfuckers out who try and get my girl." He gave me a look. "No motherfucker's gonna get my girl. Therefore, I need to hide the evidence that, in addition to being a fuckin' knockout with tits, ass, and legs, and a beautiful vocab to boot, you're also soft and beautiful on the inside. That's for me. Only me." His hand moved to my neck to grip it firmly. "Also, I have other things I want to do with my days apart from knocking motherfuckers out. Though, it is good for the soul to punch a douche every now and again." He jutted his chin up in false thought. "I can think of one thing I'd much rather spend my days doing. Making love to my girl."

I was about to open my mouth and ruin that beautiful moment by declaring I was most certainly not his girl.

My words were swallowed in a kiss.

As was my protest.

Because the way he fucked me all night long had me believing I might just be his girl.

Until I woke up, at least. And the grim light of day exposed his beauty... and my reality. So I snuck out before I was tempted to say 'fuck reality' and lose myself in that beauty.

If I had the luxury of seeing the future I wouldn't have snuck out. Wouldn't have left that beauty. I would've clutched it in a death grip if I'd known it was the last slice I'd ever get. Before ugliness swallowed me whole.

••••

I closed the trunk of my car and tilted my head towards the sky, smiling. Yes, smiling. And doing something as simple as appreciating the warmth of the sun.

Of course, such a gesture would most likely singe my pale skin and open me up to potential melanoma, but for once I was seeing the silver lining.

I was basking in the light.

I was doing well.

One could almost cautiously say I was doing great.

I still craved it. Every single day. But I was learning how to handle it. Learning how to fill my life up with other things. Healthy things. No, I wasn't drinking green juices or foregoing Pop-Tarts—that would never happen—but I was being more outgoing. Hanging with Rosie, and with Lily when she wasn't studying or wrapped up in her husband. I was making friends with some of the girls at the club, despite the fact they'd fucked the guy I couldn't admit was a huge factor in how well my life was going.

Of course, since it was going well, when the sun was beginning to rise, that's exactly when the eclipse hit.

No, that's when the whole entire sun exploded in spectacular, painful disaster and I was wrenched into permanent darkness.

I'd just finished a grocery shop. One I could actually pay for and have some left over. I was toying with the idea of treating myself to some new boots when a figure blocked out the sun in front of me.

When I saw who it was, my good mood dissipated. "No. Not happening," I said, trying to skirt around Dylan's steroid-abused body.

A hand at my arm stopped me. Pain erupted from the tightness of his grip.

"Let me go," I hissed. My eyes darted around the empty parking lot.

Just my fucking luck. Right when I might welcome a hero, there were none to be seen.

"Not so fast, bitch. Carlos would like a conversation," Dylan growled, yanking me into his face.

"Well, considering I'm no longer employed by that dickweed, I don't have to come running when he calls. And because I'm no longer too high to care about things like self-respect, I'm not screwing you anymore. So let me go," I commanded.

His eyes turned to slits. "It wasn't a fucking request."

Then there was nothing. The sunshine seeped away.

I'd never feel its warm glow again.

FOURTEEN

"Hell is empty and all the devils are here."
-Shakespeare

LUCKY

He woke up without even realizing he'd been asleep. It was a strange feeling. Like surging up from underwater and still having liquid seeping into your lungs. He thought it was from some bender he'd been on, a particularly bad hangover. He reached for her.

Then he realized some things. He didn't 'do' benders. Not anymore. Not since her.

Since he'd found his beautiful, wild, and fucking damaged girl. One who had so many demons behind those green eyes he'd be fighting them the rest of his life.

She'd tried to fight one set of demons with a whole other monster. One who'd almost taken her off the face of the earth.

So he didn't tie one on anymore. Didn't abuse any substances apart from the fucking intoxicating pussy she had him addicted to.

It was out of respect for her and because he didn't fuckin' *want* to. He mostly partied and fucked different women to escape his own shit, the darkness he spent every second of every day hiding.

He didn't have to hide with her, and he didn't want to escape with her. It was because of his own darkness that she was herself with him.

That's where he recognized the second thing. She wasn't there. Not because he couldn't touch her but because he couldn't smell her. And from his experience of sleeping with her, despite her insistence of giving them 'boundaries,' she'd clung to him in unconsciousness when her waking hours were spent pushing him away.

So he almost always woke up with his little spitfire attached to him and her scent imprinted on him.

The only thing he smelled was a harsh chemical. Something he recognized. He also recognized he couldn't move his hand, and there was a fuck of a lot of cotton in his mouth.

He fought against the heaviness of his limbs and managed to open his eyelids. The first thing he saw was a tube attached to his arm, and that's when the memories came back.

Fucking Carlos in the club. He and his goons had Lily. Shot him. He'd remembered that. It hurt. A lot. He was sure he was a goner. You didn't survive a bullet wound to the chest.

And when he'd lain there, the life seeping out of him, he'd been scared. Terrified. Not at meeting the reaper; that was something he'd expected ever since he'd patched into the Sons.

Everyone was living on borrowed time. Putting a patch on and a gun every morning just made it stolen time.

Someone was stealing it back.

That also didn't scare him.

It was the fuck's words that echoed in his brain before the pain had exploded into his chest. It was the gloating smugness that had been behind those words that haunted him before Carlos tried to turn him into a ghost.

He'd been ordered to go to the strip club to get accounts or some shit. A prospect job, surely, but he'd go. Because he knew, and Cade knew, he'd take any fuckin' excuse to go there. Or to find some reason to burn the place to the fuckin' ground in order to stop Becky from taking her clothes off for money.

Yeah, she was good at it. Had a fuckin' talent for it, like she was born to it.

But she wasn't. She was born for more. So much fucking more. To conquer the goddamn world with her fire and beauty, and to bring him along for the ride.

She was born to be his. He knew that. He'd known it since he'd fuckin' met her. He just had to wait for her to realize it.

He'd been brainstorming ways to speed up that particular process— whipped cream featured heavily—when he ran into Lily. Then he ran into trouble. Big fucking trouble. Trouble being Carlos and his fuckin' goons ambushing them in the deserted strip club in the middle of the fuckin' day.

Biggest of trouble being the last words Carlos had said before someone plugged him with a bullet.

"I'm afraid Rebecca won't be coming to the phone right now."

Then there was nothing but white-hot pain.

The memory was like an electric shock to his limbs. He tried to move but it was beyond a struggle, like someone had attached cement blocks to his arms and legs.

"Easy, brother," a voice warned.

Lucky glared at his best friend and struggled against his hold, but he was weak. Apparently getting shot took it out of you. It was laughably easy for Asher to push him back to horizontal.

"Lily?" Lucky asked with concern, memories of the club coming back in a flash. Not just Becky in danger, but Lily.

Asher's jaw hardened and Lucky's form tightened. If anything happened to his best friend's wife, it would haunt them both for the rest of their fucking lives. Lucky would blame himself for the rest of his fucking life.

"She's good," Asher reassured him.

He allowed himself to sink back into the lumpy bed.

"You get to her in time?" Lucky asked.

Something worked behind his brother's eyes. "Not exactly," he said, his voice thick.

Lucky sensed the heaviness in the air. It made him more than a little uneasy. "What happened? Obviously the big guy upstairs, or downstairs, has bigger and better things planned for me, hence me being awake and still stronger than you," he teased. "What did I do? Drag my bloodied body to Carlos and snap his neck?" he asked hopefully.

Asher shook his head but didn't smile.

Lucky was unnerved even more.

"Brother?" he probed.

Asher sighed and rubbed the back of his neck. "After they shot you, they tied Lily up, set the place on fire," he explained, his voice flat.

"Fuckers," Lucky hissed.

Asher nodded. "Lily managed to get free. Dragged your lazy ass out of there before you could get barbequed."

"Lazy?" Lucky repeated. "I'd been shot. I deserved a cat nap. Tell me Lily's okay."

Asher's eyes darkened. "She's good. She got a burn on her hand. It'll scar."

Lucky could feel his brother's fury; it mingled with his own. "Please tell me they're dead. And that you left one for me to play with. And that Becky made sure whoever was stupid enough to try and catch her is sterile."

There it was again, that look. It was something more than his woman's life being threatened, though there was plenty of fury on that score. Something else hid behind Asher's cold eyes.

Something that turned Lucky's own blood.

"Not exactly," Asher said.

Lucky sat up, grunting at the effort. "Tell me," he gritted out.

Asher eyed him. "How about we wait until the bullet wound isn't quite so fresh?"

"Fuckin' spit it out," Lucky ordered.

"I tell you, you gotta trust that the club's got it covered."

Lucky nodded.

"Need your word."

"Fuck, you've got my word. You know I'd trust the club with my life. Spit it out. I need my beauty sleep." He could feel darkness edging closer to the center of his vision.

"We didn't get her back. By the time we got to the club all traces of Carlos were gone. He's in the wind." Asher said quietly.

Lucky froze. "What?"

"Bex," Asher muttered, his eyes dark. "The whole club's already out. We'll find her—"

Lucky ripped out his cords and shit to push out of the bed. Asher had to stop talking in order to restrain him.

All sorts of machines starting ringing with a shrill beep.

Lucky ignored it and fought against Asher's grip. "Fuckin' let me go!" he roared.

Asher didn't stop. "You said you'd trust the fuckin' club."

Lucky might've had a bullet in his chest, but that meant nothing,

nothing, when he knew they had her. It'd take a bullet to his skull to stop him from fighting to get to her.

"I trust the club with my life. Not with hers. I trust no one with hers. Let me go, brother, or I'll fuckin' kill you!" he yelled.

Doors opened and doctors rushed in. Lucky ignored their shouts. He had one destination in mind.

Becky.

Hers was the last face he saw when they injected him with tranquilizer.

And it wasn't the beautiful face he was used to. This one had been overcome by demons she was just beginning to chase away.

THREE WEEKS LATER

"I need it to be said that I highly advise against this," the doctor said, frowning.

Lucky shrugged on his cut, not wincing at the pain that came with the movement. He embraced it. The pain was his fucking fuel. He felt a renewed sense of power with that leather on his back.

"So noted, Doc," he replied.

The doctor stood in front of him, blocking his way. It took a fuck of a lot of restraint not to push him bodily. It didn't matter that the guy was pushing fuckin' sixty and was a goddamned civilian, one who'd saved his life at that. His rage didn't discriminate. This man was an obstacle standing between him and Becky. Obstacles were to be eliminated.

He clenched his fists at his sides.

Two more seconds. What it would take to shake this guy off. That was two more seconds Becky was wherever she was.

There it was again. The pain. Not from the wound inches from his heart. It originated a couple inches to the left.

She's strong. She'll last.

It didn't matter that even the strongest souls could be defeated.

"You run the risk of infection, blood poisoning, even cardiac arrest," the doctor listed on his fingers.

Lucky shrugged again. "I'm feeling fit as a fiddle. If I feel like I'm goin' into cardiac arrest, I'll give you a bell." He tried to step past him.

The doc grabbed his arm.

We don't kill civilians.

"You go into cardiac arrest, you won't get to 'give me a bell.' You'll die," he informed him gravely.

"Then I'll tell the big man hey from you," Lucky said. He pulled out of the man's grasp and didn't look back.

"What did the doctor say?" Brock asked as soon as Lucky left the room. He didn't slow his pace as Brock and Gage stepped on either side of him.

Lucky looked forward. "I'll be running marathons and kicking your ass better than ever," he grunted.

He felt his friend's gaze. "Bullshit," he said. "You were shot in the chest. Less than three weeks ago."

Lucky kept walking. "I'm aware."

Brock grabbed his arm, bringing him to a stop. There was a fuck of a lot more pressure there than the doctor. Lucky glowered at him, his temper barely under control. Brock was lucky he didn't have his piece.

"You ain't no use to her dead, brother," he said quietly.

Lucky met his gaze. "I'm goin' for my woman. You try and stop me, then I'm not responsible for my actions."

He wasn't responsible for his actions if he found her and it was too late. He was damned for fuckin' life if they found the broken pieces of her.

Then he'd be as good as dead.

I'm coming, Becky. Hold on.

TWO HOURS LATER

After Bull kicked in the door and Lucky rushed in, he froze. It was only for a split second, less than that. But for the rest of his life he would torture himself over that split second. That slight hesitation. Because that moment, however fleeting it was, was another moment his firefly had to go through *that*. Another moment he could never get back, one that would be seared into his memory. Torture his soul for the rest of his life.

He hesitated, and then he moved. He didn't make any conscious effort to do it, every part of his being pushing him towards that rickety bed where *that* was happening. His vision, which had been red around the edges, was completely tainted with vivid scarlet. He barely felt the pressure at his knuckles, or the blood splatter his face as he kept going. It was red. Everything was red.

He felt strong hands at his shoulders, pulling him back, robbing him of his revenge.

He made a guttural sound at the bottom of his throat and fought off the thief of his vengeance, kneeling once more to batter the thing that had been doing that.

"Brother." A voice was urgent in his ear as hands clutched his shoulders, yanking him to his feet.

He breathed heavily, eyes not moving, vision still scarlet. Mind still only on one thing.

"Brother," the voice repeated, a large hand twisting his neck to move his face away from the crumpled red form on the floor.

He took in Bull's face like a lion might glare at a competitor for his prey. At that moment, Bull wasn't his brother, one of his best friends. He was the man stopping Lucky from punishing the thing who had been hurting her.

"Lock it down," Bull commanded.

"Fuck off," he snarled, struggling to wrench himself from the iron grip.

Bull's hands didn't move, and neither did his blank gaze. "You need to lock this shit down, or we'll lock it down for you. You don't want that," he said, demons dancing behind his flat gaze. "She needs you." He nodded to the side.

Lucky slowly followed his gaze. The red subsided just enough so he could register the small form in Gage's arms. The horrifyingly empty look in those eyes. The way her inky head was bowed and a shaky hand traced his brother's arms. She did not take in anything else around them.

He looked at the legs draped over Gage's elbows. Little more but skin and bones. Filthy. Naked. Covered in bruises. *Handprints.*

A slice of agony so intense rippled through his entire body he was surprised he stayed standing. He did. And he swallowed that pain. Embraced it. A white-hot calm settled over him and the red left his gaze.

He met Bull's eyes once more, nodding once. "I'm good."

Bull regarded him for a long second, searching for the truth in that statement. He must have found it because he nodded and the hands on his shoulders left, Bull stepping back.

Lucky very calmly reached into his cut, took out his gun, and emptied the clip into the body on the floor. The echoing silence that followed the rapid shots seemed to yawn on forever. He could feel the pulse of energy rippling off his brothers.

Then the silence was gone. "We've got to go," Cade declared, his face hard.

The prez's voice seemed to jolt everyone out of the terrible clutches the actions in that room had over them.

"We need to get the fuck out of here," Cade continued. His hard gaze turned to Gage, the bundle in his arms. Lucky watched as a glimpse of what he was feeling inside flickered on his prez's face before he moved his attention to Gage. "You got all your shit in place?" he asked.

Lucky knew what he meant—the various explosives he had scattered around the warehouse before they had stormed the place.

Gage nodded. For once he didn't grin at the prospect of blowing something sky-high, eliminating people who had hurt the club. Looking at his brothers now, they had *crippled* the club. Opened up old wounds that barely healed, no matter the fact that years had passed.

"Yeah, we get Wire to make the call... *boom,*" he said softly, the last word echoing through the room.

Cade nodded briskly. "Good."

Lucky finally jerked out of the state that had frozen him in place, a spectator to his nightmare come alive, rushing forward. "Give her to me," he ordered Gage tightly.

Gage didn't do as asked. Instead he looked at him, at the blood that Lucky barely registered which covered him almost to his elbows. He was regarding Lucky like a mother to a child requesting to hold a newborn baby, like he was measuring whether he would drop or harm the precious bundle.

"Give me my fuckin' woman," he gritted out, wanting to snatch her. The only thing stopping him was the fact that he worried such a movement might harm her more, if that were even possible.

She didn't seem to register their presence, the fact that they were talking about her. She merely continued tracing patterns on Gage's scarred arms with a look of vivid concentration.

"Let's get out of here, get her to a hospital," Gage answered, still not giving him his woman.

Lucky clenched his fists and swallowed a bellow of frustration.

The moment he was considering forcibly removing her from his brother was the moment her matted head snapped up and he visibly flinched at her face.

"No hospitals," she hissed, her eyes focused on Lucky. What haunted him was the fact she was looking right into his eyes but wasn't *seeing* him. Her pupils seemed to take up every inch of those beautiful irises. She wasn't seeing any of them, but something else. She was face-to-face with demons.

"No hospitals," she repeated, her voice rising. "No hospitals." Hysteria mounted on her croaky, almost foreign voice.

With massive amounts of effort, Lucky managed to clear his face of the fury, the utter devastation eating at him. He turned it soft, looking into those dangerously empty eyes. "Okay, firefly, no hospitals," he soothed.

She gazed at him for a long moment, long enough to shred his insides. She nodded briskly and bent her head once more to trace Gage's arm. She didn't seem to have any desire to leave those scarred arms. Those empty eyes showed not one glimpse of recognition. So, with even more effort, with pain that almost floored him, he stepped back.

"Let's get out of here," he said, not making eye contact with anyone in the room. Those empty eyes were the only thing he thought of. Utter fear at the prospect of being able to fill them up again. After *that*.

If he couldn't fill them, there was one thing he could do.

Kill every single motherfucker responsible for this.

Slowly.

LILY

Asher hadn't stopped his bike when I flew off, my feet barely touching the ground as I sprinted past the various bikes parked outside the clubhouse. My heart was in danger of beating out of my chest. I didn't stop until I made it into the common room. One that was always filled with laughter, with easy atmosphere that engulfed you in its warm glow the moment you stepped in. The utter silence had my heart silencing. Stopping.

"Where is she?" I demanded in a hoarse voice.

The men I had at first feared and then come to consider as family were scattered around the room. They were all in various positions, nearly every single one of them clutching a bottle of alcohol of some sort. Every single one of their strong gazes was tainted, etched in defeat.

I struggled to stay upright as fear blanketed my entire body. For these men to be beaten down to this, it had to be bad. Bad was what I'd been prepared for. Bex had been missing for weeks, so I had known it wouldn't be good when we found her. But I hadn't been prepared for how bad. My mind hadn't been able to entertain that. Until now. Until I was confronted with it and couldn't escape it. Something bad had happened to my best friend, my sister, and I wasn't sure if I'd survive it.

I felt hands at my waist, yanking me into a hard body. "Flower," a voice murmured. A voice that usually soothed me no matter what. Arms that took the weight off my chest the moment they made contact with my skin. They didn't that time. Not with the ice running through my veins. Not with the weight of a thousand tons that settled on my chest the moment I registered the energy in the room. When I realized what that energy meant for Bex.

My entire body started to shake involuntarily as my gaze landed on Lucky. Or, more accurately, the top of Lucky's head. It was bowed down, cradled in his large hands that rested on his knees. He hadn't even moved when I spoke. Something about that position, a position of defeat, teetered me closer to the cliff I was in danger of tumbling off.

"Where is she?" I repeated, my voice raw, almost a screech.

Something in my tone, maybe the despair, registered and Lucky's head snapped up. I physically recoiled at his face. At the emptiness there. There was no grin. No twinkle in his eye. Nothing. It was as if something had come along and sucked every inch, every possibility, of happiness out of his body and replaced it with something horrible, something ugly. Fury simmered underneath it, vengeance.

"Flower," Asher said, his voice soft. Concerned. Knowing.

"Don't 'flower' me," I snapped. "I want to know where my best friend is. Right now."

Cade stepped forward, his eyes first over my shoulder, meeting Asher's gaze, then focusing on me. Their edges were crinkled slightly, soft. But the emptiness, maybe not the same gaping chasm as in Lucky's but a fraction of it, was still there.

"She didn't want a hospital," he explained slowly.

Some part of me, some distant part, relaxed a smidgeon at the fact she was okay enough to communicate what she didn't want. Another more aware part of me sank at the knowledge that she'd needed a hospital. At the flatness of Cade's voice, mirroring an echo of the defeat on Lucky's face.

"We've got someone we trust in there, treating her." He lifted his chin to the door, where they held their 'church.'

I nodded and stepped out of Asher's arms, one destination in mind.

A gentle but firm grip on my shoulder stopped me. I glanced down at Cade's hand and then glared at the owner.

I didn't glare at anyone, apart from Asher because I was confident enough to come out of my shell with him. No matter how far I'd come from who I used to be, I was far from actively glaring at men who radiated badass-ness, despite their kind eyes. But this man, no matter how scary, hot, or intimidating he may be, was barring me from going to her. I'd engage in a physical altercation with him if need be. Not one I was likely to win, but I'd fight tooth and nail.

"You don't want to see her right now, Lily," he almost whispered. "It's... not good."

His words had a physical effect on me, stabbing me with daggers of meaning. I straightened my shoulders. "It's not about what I want. Or what you think I want. It's what she needs," I hissed, then shrugged off his hand and strode purposefully towards the door, praying to be as fearless as I knew Bex would have been in my situation.

ASHER

Asher moved to follow Lily as she darted towards the door. The one he knew held more pain and suffering for his girl. Pain and suffering he intended to protect her from as best he could. He couldn't protect her from this and it almost killed him. She didn't need any more blows. He knew she was strong enough to handle them, but she shouldn't fuckin' have to.

And despite Bex's downfalls, she was a good person. Asher knew she had waded through some epic shit in her life. Not the details, but he saw it in her eyes. People didn't become heroin addicts because they'd enjoyed a cloud-free existence. He'd been furious at her for putting Lily in danger at the start, but then he saw how much Lily meant to her, how much she meant to Lily, and he managed to swallow that anger. He'd even begun to respect her for the way she was turning her life around, trying to beat the demons at her back.

Now they were back, in full force. And all he could do was witness her and his wife battle them. A hand on his shoulder, much firmer than it had been on Lily's, restrained him.

Asher stopped, his eyes on the blonde head disappearing behind the door. He raised his eyebrow at Cade in warning. He really didn't want to have to break his president's nose, but he would if he stopped him from going to his wife. If he made it so she had to face this alone.

"No, brother," Cade said quietly.

The two words gave him pause. The way he said them, reminiscent of the tone he'd heard from him years before. When he'd come back from the hospital to let them know that Laurie had faded away, unable to survive the brutality inflicted on her.

His gaze snapped to Cade. "No." It was more of a prayer than a question.

Cade nodded slowly.

Asher closed his eyes for a split second and felt physical pain, not only at the fact he knew what this meant for Bex, for his wife, but for his best friend. Lucky sat like a statue, like a man who had lost everything rooting him to the floor and the world was in danger of tearing him away from himself.

"We've got Sarah in there with her. She understands the need for... discretion," Cade told him.

"Is it bad?" Asher managed to choke out.

Cade gave him a long look. "It's bad, brother."

"Fuck," Asher hissed under his breath.

Cade stepped forward, close to him so he could speak quieter. "They kept her high. Strung out so she didn't even know her own fuckin' name." He paused, taking a huge breath. "When we stormed the place, she was chained to the bed. Naked." He sucked in a harsh breath, fire in his eyes, defeat sagging his shoulders. "Some fucker raping her," Cade explained in a flat voice. Asher didn't miss the fury that barely stayed contained. That turned the air thick enough to swallow.

His entire body turned wired. He knew. The moment he had walked into the room, he knew. But hearing it, hearing the words, hearing the strongest motherfucker he knew so shaken, it got to him.

His gaze flickered to the door his wife had disappeared behind. Every inch of him was screaming to go to her. To be there.

"Fuck," he repeated.

Another thing that would try to bruise his flower. To destroy her.

He swallowed it, that animal need to go to his woman. Barely. The thing that stopped him was the gaze that settled on his best friend; on all of his brothers. They were all feeling this. Bleeding from this.

He gave Cade another long glance and clapped him on the shoulder. Cade nodded to him and stepped aside.

The men gave him somber chin lifts as he waded through the room, through their fury. Brock was clutching a whisky glass so hard his knuckles turned white. Ranger was murmuring quietly into his phone, his eyes hard. Asher guessed he was talking to his woman, Lizzie. Each of the men might be hard motherfuckers, but their world was the club and their women. Seeing the shit that Asher guessed they'd seen, he knew they'd need to make sure their old ladies were going to chase away their demons.

He stopped in front of Lucky, who was staring between his knees. He hadn't even flinched as Asher made it to him.

"Brother," he said quietly, no fuckin' clue what else to say. He didn't do girly comforting words. They didn't have fuckin' heart-to-hearts. But his brother was bleeding. His best friend. Fuck if he would just stand there and watch it happen.

Lucky's head slowly moved up a good few seconds after Asher spoke, as if it took longer for words to get through his head.

Asher flinched, actually fuckin' flinched, at the look on his face. It was like what Bull had been wearing since the moment Laurie was dumped outside the club, since she died. The one that had only just faded away when he met his wife. It was always there, though. A shadow over him. A scar. You didn't escape that shit; it was tattooed on your soul forever. It had been hard seeing that on Bull, but it almost fuckin' killed him to see it on Lucky. They'd patched in together, grown up together. Fuck, they'd screwed their first girls on the same night when they were tangled up in a world they'd escaped together. Like Asher, Lucky had a fuckin' rough childhood. He'd had to do some serious shit before he'd even gotten his dick wet. He turned into a ruthless motherfucker when needed, but most of the time he was smiling. Laughing. Not letting the shit of his past turn him into something else.

That's why it got to Asher. Seeing everything torn away from his face. Everything.

"Fuck," he muttered, locking eyes with the wild animal that used to be his best friend. "Let's—"

He didn't get to finish his sentence because Lucky moved. Surged up and pushed past him without a word. Asher turned to watch him storm out of the clubhouse and then heard the roar of his bike as he left the lot.

"Fuck," he muttered again.

Then he welcomed the rage, let it fill him up. "We're getting blood for this," he said to Cade, who'd approached after Lucky left.

Cade's gray eyes met his. "Oh there will be blood," he bit out. "A fuckin' ocean of it."

There was only one problem with that statement.

They were already swimming in that ocean of blood.

Drowning in it.

FIFTEEN

"Some women fear the fire. Some women simply become it."
-R.H Sin

BECKY

ONE MONTH LATER

"**R**ebecca, you've been attending group for three weeks now and still haven't shared. Have you got something to add today? To get off your chest?" The rehab counselor asked me in her throaty voice.

Get off my chest? Yeah, how about the weight of the world, lady.

"Bex," I said instead.

Her overgrown brows furrowed. "Excuse me?"

"Well, I've been here for three weeks and for that time you've called me Rebecca while I've repeatedly told you it's Bex." I thrummed my fingers against my jean-clad thighs in irritation.

I needed a smoke.

I actually needed a fix. A fucking huge one.

They didn't offer that at this particular facility, hence me nearly smoking a pack a day.

Not the healthiest coping mechanism, but what was a little more tar on my already blackened insides?

She regarded me with those kind eyes that made me want to strangle her with one of her many tiny scarves. "Does something about your given name upset you?"

I didn't lower my gaze, though I felt everyone else's heavy on me. I didn't like it, the attention. Precisely why I hadn't spoken a word in this little circle jerk that I was subjected to daily. The group session of depression, of people's addiction sob stories, would make even the most cheerful person want to eat a bullet just to escape it all.

"Besides the fact that the stupid name was the one and only thing my asshole parents gave me before dumping me on the state? It's not really my style," I said, leaning back in my chair. I inspected my nails instead of looking at the people who were staring at me.

The black polish had chipped off, the nails bitten down almost to the skin. They were a testament to how fucking ruined my insides were. Black and peeling, chewed and torn.

"You don't know your parents, then?" the counselor probed.

I glanced up. "You think I'd be here if John and Judy Cleaver raised me and Mom baked cookies every day?" I was being a bitch. It was my default. Plus what little cheer I possessed had been well and truly beaten out of me. Only sarcasm and venom were left.

The counselor jostled in her chair. "It sometimes doesn't matter what background we come from. Addiction happens to everyone. It doesn't discriminate. But I'm intrigued to understand how you think your own addiction is connected to your childhood. Was it hard?"

I laughed, the first time since…. It wasn't a pretty laugh; it sounded ugly, like nails on a chalkboard, like the soundtrack of my soul. "My childhood? No, it was a fucking breeze."

She furrowed her brows. "It's a safe space here, Bex. You can tell us."

"Safe space?" I repeated. "There's no such thing. You think 'cause we're here spillin' our guts, making the world a much grayer place with our addiction horror stories, that we're safe? The very fact we're here is a testament to the fact we're *not* safe. Never will be. No matter where we are. That's the whole fucking point, isn't it? The monkey will always be on our back, always a shadow no matter how bright our life may seem. We're never safe from that."

A pregnant pause descended after I spoke. The counselor leaned forward onto her elbows. "Despite the experiences that have led to this belief, which I'm sure were traumatic, it's not as dreary as that. Your future can indeed be bright and you *can* overcome your addiction. I can promise you that."

I laughed again. "Can you promise that?" I asked, my voice flat. "Can you promise sunshine and rainbows for everyone in this room?" I held my arms out. "To the guy who almost killed his daughter? Can you say that's not gonna haunt him every fucking day for the rest of his life? Or how about the girl who tried to slit her wrists? You think those scars are gonna fade away to nothing overnight?" I paused. "Or what about the girl who grew up in the system, had her virginity stolen by a sweaty drunk when she was twelve years old, and had to fight *every day since* just to survive. And that fight got her a drug addiction." I sucked in a breath. "That fucking fight got her chained to a stained mattress, strung out but not enough to forget the men who raped her in that cold fucking room to the point she can still feel their hands on her skin *right fucking now*?" My voice was a shrill shout, scratching against the silent air. I pushed up, my chair rattling to the floor with the force. "I don't think any amount of kumba-fucking-ya is going to make that shit go away. So if you'll excuse me, I'm off to live my cloud-filled life. Good luck with your sunshine and rainbows," I said to the silent room. "Say hey to the Easter Bunny for me."

On that note, I stormed out of the room as fast as my combat boots would take me, praying that the ocean of tears brimming at the corners of my eyes wouldn't escape. 'Cause if they did, if I gave in to that sorrow, I knew for a fact I'd drown. And no one, not even the hazel-eyed biker I'd done everything to forget, could save me.

I knew I was expected to stay longer to be 'cured.' The concept was laughable. I would never be cured.

Clean.

It did its job. I was 'clean' in the sense I no longer had drugs coursing through my veins. The need for them would always course through. It was about managing that need.

I guessed my relapse hadn't been precisely that, considering I had been forced to take the drugs I had previously kicked. My body didn't know that, though. The only thing it knew was that it had been robbed of the thing it needed.

So my body needed to be stuck somewhere it couldn't get the better of my mind and suck me into a hole of addiction.

Because I knew if I touched any drug again, it was the end. Those three weeks broke me, and I knew drugs would shatter me.

I was in pieces, but I wanted to carry them around a little while longer.

Which was why I was there.

And why I was leaving.

I could barely stand being stuck in my own crazy, barely managed to fight my own demons. I didn't need to be surrounded by other people's. I didn't need to know that some guy had been so high that he left his two-year-old daughter in a hot car for two hours. Didn't need to think about how a woman had nearly killed a whole busload of people while driving drunk.

Luckily it wasn't some sort of prison where they locked the doors and stopped you from leaving.

I knew I wanted to leave but didn't know where I could go. I wanted to go nowhere. Be nowhere. Feel nothing. Problem was nowhere wasn't a place. As much as I wanted to disappear into the sunset and make everyone's life better for it, I couldn't.

So I went back.

Rosie, insane as she was, not only let me move back in to where I had been living *before* but had insisted on it.

Like I said, I didn't like it, spreading my dirt around good people, but I didn't have much of a choice.

I had money saved, thanks to not spending every cent of it on drugs, and earning a crap-ton more than I had stripping at the Sons' club than I did with Carlos.

It wasn't enough, though.

So my plan was to somehow work up the nerve to work again, get enough money, and then disappear.

When I was strong enough to walk out the fucking door, that was.

••••

"Want to talk about it?" Rosie asked, speaking for the first time since she'd yanked me into her arms an hour before. She glanced up at the rehab building, shuddering. "Let's break you out before Nurse Ratched comes out and drags us both in."

I kept staring at the rain trailing down my window. Mother Nature matched my mood. How adorable. "Really, *really* don't," I replied. My words were clipped, and I probably should've cared about not being a bitch to the person who had dropped everything to pick me up from rehab when I'd called on the edge of breakdown two hours back. Actually, I should've been groveling at her feet considering she hadn't asked whether I really should be leaving or requested some certificate of sobriety before bundling me into her car. I just didn't have the energy. I was using everything I had to inhale and exhale, and to brace for the pain that came with that motion.

I saw Rosie's curls bob in my peripheral vision. "Fair enough," she replied, her voice light. "How about a cheeseburger?"

I glanced at her. I didn't smile, but I tried. "I'd kill for a cheeseburger."

Rosie grinned back. "Well, let's get you one before you get into a state penitentiary just hours after I sprung you from rehab."

If the prospect of holy matrimony didn't turn my blood, I would seriously consider marrying that woman.

Comfortable silence descended. Rosie could talk better than any politician I'd ever met, but she also knew when to shut up. I'd learned that living with her in the months... before. I'd also learned she had a different date every weekend, and a different persona to take with her on each one. Her easy sense of humor and filthy mouth had her quickly becoming one of my closest friends. Plus the rest of the women who came along with the family Lily had adopted. Despite all my reservations and hatred for groups of girlfriends who had perfect lives and eyebrows like the ones in said family, I'd liked them all. I'd tried to keep my distance but it didn't exactly work, especially with Rosie.

I chewed over all of this on the drive. I hadn't seen any of them considering I'd been delirious the first few days of my freedom, and then when I was lucid enough to understand how I'd be suffocated by kindness, I'd convinced Lily I needed the confines of rehab. I was pretty sure I'd broken her heart by demanding to be taken to a facility full of shrinks and addicts instead of letting her 'take care' of me. She'd insisted she could do it, but I couldn't let her. She was married, went school, had a life. Lily was finally coming back to life. I wasn't sucking that vibrancy from her.

I could see it happening, even through the film of my despair. The way her eyes sparkled with agony every time she was around me. It was fucking horrific. Not just for her—I wasn't that much of a martyr—but for me too. I'd probably be heading for a long stay in the loony bin if I had to see the effect of my shit on my best friend. See the reality of it.

It was hard enough when she came to visit as soon as she was allowed, which was thankfully only once a week.

Another reason I'd escaped pretty much as soon as I'd stopped shaking from withdrawals was *him*. I knew he wouldn't stay away.

That was ingrained in these men. To save the flailing. To fix the broken.

So he'd come. To fix me.

I didn't trust myself not to seek him out in my damaged, shattered state. He'd put me together once before, and I craved to be whole so bad I knew my resolve would shatter. But I knew I'd never be whole. Sometimes people were broken in such a way that there was no repair to be had. Just finding a way to live a life as jagged edges of a person who once used to be whole.

Rosie was driving closer and closer to all that I'd tried to escape. I hadn't truly realized that until now, too busy trying to get away from the place that I thought would be some kind of retreat. It may have hid me from the people who would make me think too hard about reality, but it unveiled what I was trying so hard to hide from—myself.

Catch-22, really. The only reason I'd called Rosie and not a cab to the airport was because I had no other choice. I'd used up pretty much all of my meager savings to fund my stay at the Silver Farm. Lily had, of course, tried to insist she pay for it. Or, more aptly, her husband pay. Which he'd been happy to do. That residual hardness that he used to have around his eyes when looking at me was gone. He'd treated me like some little broken dove ever since I'd woken up and realized that consciousness wasn't an escape from my nightmare. No way I was letting them pay for what I'd gotten myself into.

So I'd used the money I'd been saving to finally get myself out of the gutter. Maybe I was destined to live there forever.

I turned to Rosie on that thought. "Look, I completely understand if you don't want me living at your place anymore. I'll pack up my shit as soon as we get back—"

I was cut off by the jolt of the car slamming to an abrupt stop. I braced my hand on the dash to stop my head from rebounding on it. Rosie pulled over to the shoulder of the deserted highway.

I glanced at her. "Give a girl some warning! I almost Frenched the dashboard. I'm not wanting dentures just yet."

She didn't smile, glaring at me instead. "If you *ever* think of moving out because you have some fucked-up reason about why I wouldn't want you living with me, I'll find you the second your shit leaves my place. Seriously, I can be like Liam fucking Neeson when I want to be. I'll find you, and I'll drag you back to my place and make you watch *Sex and the City* with me for twelve hours as punishment," she threatened, her tone serious.

I blinked at her, unsure of what was going on here.

Her face softened slightly and she reached out to give my arm a quick squeeze. "This is the one and only time I'll bring this up without you saying something first. You went through hell, Bex. Hell," she repeated, shuddering. "Breaks my heart every time I think about it. And somehow, you're sitting here, whole and not a basket case. Somehow you survived it with your sanity intact. I'm in total awe of your strength, seriously, sister." She paused. "But no matter how strong you are, you can't get through this alone. I know you're a strong independent woman who don't need no man, but you need your girlfriends. And even if you don't think that's true, they need you. *I* need to have you around, under my roof, for my peace of mind. So I know you're okay, you're here. Lily needs you five minutes' drive away so she doesn't go back to those three weeks where she thought she lost her best friend. Okay?"

I nodded slowly, her words prodding at those numb pieces of me that were lying inside my shattered psyche.

She nodded too, pulling the car back onto the highway. "Since that's sorted, it's cheeseburger time."

And just like that, I was taken back to a family I hadn't asked for, but one I craved just the same.

And taken back to the man I hadn't asked for, but breathed for, just

ANNE MALCOM

the same.

ONE WEEK LATER

I stared at my reflection with effort. I had made a point of avoiding reflective surfaces for the past month. Avoided looking directly at them. At me. Or whatever was left.

They say—whoever the proverbial assholes *they* are—that the addict looks in the mirror one day and does not recognize the face of the drug-stricken loser before them. I had a lot of free time in the junkie house, so I set about reading every addict autobiography and memoir out there.

Depressing shit.

That's where I got that particular theory. Maybe that's not exactly what *they* say, but I took some artistic liberties. I recognized myself every day I was high. *Every time*. Sometimes I was blurry around the edges. Sometimes I couldn't tell where the reflection ended and I began. Another time, when I was seriously fucked-up, I thought I was trapped in the mirror.

All of these times, I couldn't mistake myself. Not on the outside, at least. The inside may have been twisted, gnarly, and positively ugly, but I couldn't see that from my glorious spot on my rainbow high. I could only see what the mirror showed me. Nothing underneath. Drugs gave me a wonderful little blind spot to my true self.

Now, stone-cold, horribly sober, I couldn't place this... thing. Even worse, I could see the gnarly, thorny edges of my insides. My blind spot was gone.

I blinked at the sallow face staring back at me. Makeup-less, I hardly recognized myself. I was always wearing my war paint, whether it was waking up with residue of the night before or a fresh coat. It was my armor. Another thing to add to the persona I had created. Black hair, usually with sharp streaks of color which changed routinely. Black combat boots were a staple. I had four pairs in various states of disarray. My eyeliner was always thick and black. I was always on. Always a construction. Never just me. I needed all that stuff, to cover the dirt.

I didn't have any of it right now. My hair hung limp around my shoulders, dipping almost to my bra strap. It was stringy because I couldn't remember the last time I washed it. The ends were such a faded pink they just looked orange now. My face was pale, almost transparent under the bathroom lights. My frame looked skeletal and my face had angles I didn't recognize. Quite simply, I looked like shit. But the outside was nothing like the charred and broken inside. I felt like my body was this empty shell and the ashes of me lay in a pile, rotting with every passing day.

"Get yourself together," I whispered to the sad and pathetic-looking girl in front of me.

I couldn't stay like this forever. The problem was I didn't know what else I could do. How I could change. It was as if I was locked in place, my mind a stark wasteland, my identity stripped away from me ever since I'd finally left the drug addled ocean five weeks ago.

But how did I change? How did I get clean when the dirt set like concrete on my soul? How did I shake the craving, the utter desperation for that escape, that nothingness the needle offered?

I eyed my hair, directing all my anger at those greasy strands. My hands moved of their own accord, opening the bathroom cabinet behind the mirror, momentarily taking away the image of the girl I didn't know. She quickly came back when I found what I needed and slammed the little door shut.

I didn't think. Just started cutting.

SIXTEEN

"I desire things which will destroy me in the end."
-Sylvia Plath

"Wow, diggin' the pixie cut, babe," Rosie declared when I walked into the room. She was sitting cross legged on the floor flipping through a glossy magazine.

I gave her a look. Unlike many movies, when the heroine has some sort of moment of fierceness and decides to assert that independence by giving herself some fabulous new 'do, mine did not look fabulous. I was not a hairdresser. I had never cut hair in my life. I was a mess, so right now, my hair served as some sort of communicator for the utter disaster of my insides.

Rosie put down her pen and pushed herself off the floor, eyeing my hair as she approached me. "Okay, so we're not going to be letting you enter any hairstyling competitions, but I like the spirit of the idea," she said, circling me like some sort of predator.

After some deliberation, she walked to the breakfast bar to drag a bar stool into the middle of the room.

"Sit," she commanded.

I raised my brow at her.

"Are you thinking I can make this any worse?" she asked with a small grin.

"Good point," I answered with no returning grin. I didn't grin, smile, or smirk anymore. I wondered if it was physically impossible. That I had finally gone through enough horrors to make my body chemically unable to produce anything resembling happiness.

"Okay, you stay there while I get the scissors and we'll make this fabulous," Rosie declared, squeezing my shoulder.

That was the only form of recognition for the reason behind my rash hair decision. There was no sad look, no probing questions. Not with Rosie. I was beyond thankful for that. She acted like such actions were completely normal. Though, she was slightly insane, so maybe things like this *were* normal in her world.

I doubted having an ex-junkie, ex-stripper, ex-human as a roommate was normal. One who barely spoke these days, one who had turned into some kind of zombie who sat on the sofa watching documentaries on serial killers. But she didn't make it feel any worse. I didn't think it would be possible to feel worse anyway.

"Okay, I'm thinking early 2000s Halle Berry meets 2015 JLaw at the Oscars," Rosie declared, reentering the room with scissors and styling implements. "What do we think?"

I shrugged. "Whatever."

She didn't seem perturbed at my lack of answer considering she'd had enough experience with it. Her eyes lit up. "Free rein, excellent."

I let myself relax as much as was possible as she ran her hands and then scissors through my newly short locks. I gritted my teeth against the occasional touch of her fingers against my scalp. The touch. I didn't do well with that. The sounds of the chopping seemed to work as some sort of meditative instrument, my mind wandering out of the room and over the events of the past month.

Well, not too far. I didn't like to think of those first few days back to *reality*, if that's what this was. The days before I spirited myself off to rehab as fast as my boots would take me.

I couldn't remember parts, which I was thankful for. It took days for me to fully come off whatever cocktail of drugs I had been given. That I had taken. The withdrawals of those had been bad.

Bad.

Worse than the first time I went off, and that had been horrible enough. I had thought my body would shut down without the poison it had grown accustomed to, come to rely on.

At that point, one month ago, I was certain of death. If not my physical body, then my mind. It felt like someone was forcibly ripping it apart from the inside. Images would tear through the shields that I had built up since birth. Images of that room. Of that bed. Of what they did to me in that bed. I had scratched my arms raw at one point, desperate to open my veins, to see if the filth of those memories would pour out with my blood.

Then they had tied me down. That was worse. Being immobile. My mind was already surrendering to helplessness, crippled, and my body was now too.

I had come down enough to realize the reason for it. To gain some sort of coherent thought.

ONE MONTH EARLIER

Lily's hand was tight on mine, resting just above the makeshift bindings they had tied with scarves. Those scarves struck me as ridiculously funny.

I was unable to contain the hysterical bubble of laugher that came out when I saw the vibrant designs.

Lily's head had snapped up at the sound, her eyes instantly alert as she took me in. Sleep didn't seem to hide behind them.

"Bex?" she asked cautiously, hand not letting go of mine.

The way she looked at me, the hesitation behind it, punctured me. It didn't make me stop laughing, though.

"It's the scarves," I choked out finally, not recognizing my scratchy voice.

"The scarves?" she repeated, sitting up a little straighter.

I nodded. "Doesn't it strike you as just... silly? I'm tied to a bed with vintage scarves. With ones that should be on the neck of some fashionista or tied around some stupidly expensive handbag, not used to restrain... me."

A small, sad grin crept at the side of Lily's mouth. I suspected it might be for my benefit more than anything else. This suspicion was due to the utter despair which was poorly hidden behind her ice-blue eyes.

"I guess it is quite... *silly*. I didn't exactly have anything else lying around the house, and it was necessary." Her eyes touched on my upper arms.

I glanced down at my forearms, which had been wrapped in

bandages. I vaguely recalled some dull pain at some point in the murky past. Scratching. I'd been scratching my arms, the intention of ripping off my filthy skin and letting them out. The insects crawling under my skin.

To the outsider I guessed that looked pretty fucked-up.

Hence the scarves.

"Yeah, well, I didn't really expect you to have bondage gear on hand, kid." I winked at her. "Unless you've got some real dark side you've hidden from your best friend."

My teasing tone fell flat, even to me. Maybe because the moment I said the words I wanted to swallow them right back up. Lily, my innocent and all-around good best friend, wasn't the one with a hidden dark side. No, that was me. Only it wasn't a side, a slice of me corrupted by the black. It was the entirety of me. It *was* me.

She squeezed my hand and tears welled in her eyes. "Bex, I don't know what to say. I'm so sorry," she choked out, the raw pain in her voice making me flinch.

I couldn't watch that, couldn't look at the pain in my best friend's eyes. I didn't get respite from the consequences of my dark side corrupting the only person stupid enough to care about me. My eyes rested on the glove on Lily's hand. The medical one.

Cloudy memories assaulted me at that moment.

I had been fighting. Fighting hard. With every inch of me. Then all of a sudden my limbs didn't work anymore and every part of me was still. Apart from my mind, pounding at the outer reaches of my skull, desperate to get out.

Dylan's face dipped close to mine, his eyes alert with something I recognized—arousal, and narcotics.

"We got you now, bitch," he hissed, grinning. He moved to touch my body, I saw him do it, but I couldn't feel it. "We've got you. We're going to break you," he informed me, his eyes darting around as if he couldn't keep them still from excitement. "It's going to be brilliant," he declared.

"Ghuoh phuck yoourseelf," I managed to blurt out through numb lips.

He didn't stop grinning. "I knew you'd fight. Just knew it. Pity your little mouse didn't put up much of a fight. Your biker dog neither. They both burned with little effort," he told me with satisfaction.

ANNE MALCOM

Every inch of my mind stilled. I stopped pounding on the corners of my skull. Dread. Pure dread had me paralyzed in my mind.

Dylan grinned. "That hit a nerve, didn't it? You'll get to live with that. Know they burned because you're a stupid whore who didn't do what she was told," he sneered.

Then he did things. Did things I couldn't feel physically, that I couldn't stop.

"Your hand," I croaked, trying to push up.

Lily glanced at it. "It's nothing," she tried to soothe me.

"It's not," I gritted out, wincing at the pain that was utterly foreign to me. The physical pain at least. My mental pain was a constant companion. "They did that to you," I stated flatly.

"I'm fine," Lily said firmly.

I pursed my lips. My body stilled. "Who else? Who else got hurt because of me? Did someone...? Did *he...?*" My voice trailed off into despair.

"He's fine," Lily said quickly, chasing away my thoughts. At least some of them. "Lucky's fine." She swallowed, eyes weary. "It was touch and go. He got shot, in the chest, but he's too stubborn to let that slow him down."

My heart stuttered. The air left my lungs.

Shot.

In the chest.

"But he's okay?" I croaked.

Lily nodded. "He's okay." She made to stand up. "In fact, he's asleep on the sofa right now. It's quite difficult to make him do such things like sleep, eat, leave your side. It's a rare moment right now. I'll get him."

My hand tightened around hers like a vise. "No," I hissed frantically. I used every ounce of my meager strength to keep her in place. Like my life depended on it. Not *like* it did—my life *did* depend on it.

She frowned at me but sat back down.

"I don't want to see him. I don't want him around, not anywhere near me," I declared.

Lily gazed at me. "Bex—"

"No," I interrupted. "Promise me. Promise me you'll make him go away. Lily, I can't—" I sucked in a breath. "I can't have him anywhere near me. Around this. I don't want you to have to be around this either, though I know you'll stay, despite everything I've put you through. I love you more than words for that. I'm so sorry I have to put this on you, tarnish your life even more."

Lily's face turned hard. "No," she ground out. "No. You do not say anything like that, not now, not ever," she commanded. "You do not lay any blame at your own feet. This is not your fault. They took you. They—" Her voice broke and I knew she knew about what *they* did. "This is not your fault," she said finally.

"But—" I argued.

"No buts. You don't want to break my heart by trying to find some way to blame yourself for this. There is no one to blame but the *animals* that don't deserve to exist in this world. The only thing you need to do is focus on getting better," she instructed, as if that were possible. "On letting other people, people who love you, help you get better."

I relented. I had to. Arguing with the woman who was the only family I had was pointless. She may be convinced she was weak, but I knew she was strong. Stronger than me by bounds. So I no longer verbalized my absolute certainty that all of this was because of me.

That she had almost died because of me.

That she was scarred for life because of me.

That *he* almost died because of me. That he was shot because of me.

That I had been further ingrained with dirt as a result of my own choices.

I didn't verbalize it, but that didn't mean it wasn't always on my mind.

But I stayed there. For Lily's sake. I wouldn't harm her any more than I already had. Harming myself, that was fine. Inevitable, inescapable. Her? That was unacceptable.

She did try to fight me on something else I wouldn't budge on. Not even for her.

"He loves you," she said quietly after silence had descended, cloaked us for a long while.

I sucked in a painful breath.

"You can't shut him out," she continued. "I've never seen anyone like that. The way he was. I've never seen someone that destroyed. Never. Especially not someone as strong as that. Someone like Lucky," she whispered. "He's been here, every moment, as much as me, Bex. He won't go anywhere. I don't think a nuclear missile would move him from your side."

Her words punctured me like a million little needles on my soul. It took great pains to hide that from Lily. "He doesn't love me," I stated in an empty voice. "He feels responsible. That's what these bikers do, it seems. Take on every hit that poor defenseless women are suffering, take it as some personal affront. We were nothing," I lied. "It was just fun for us both. Had this not happened, it would have fizzled out at some point. Now I've been... used. Sullied. That's a hit on these alpha-male types. He thought since we were fucking that meant I was blanketed in an invisible testosterone blanket. They breached that."

Lily looked at me for a long time. Long enough to know she didn't buy my blasé attitude. "That's not true. You forget you're my sister. What you feel, I feel." Her voice broke. "You went through hell, and I feel that, Bex. It hurts me. I also know what you feel for him. You can't hide that, not from me. I know you care," she said firmly.

I closed my eyes a moment, contemplating further protests. I opened them, making my decision. "I can't," I choked out. "I can't have him near me, Lils. I can't see myself through his eyes. I can't. It'll kill me," I confessed. "It'll destroy whatever's left."

Lily's frame jolted and her face softened immediately. Her small bandaged hand came up to stroke a hair from my face. "Okay," she whispered in a tortured voice. "Okay."

She'd done it. Somehow, she'd made it so I didn't have to lay eyes on him. I heard it, though. The moment she'd spoken to him. I'd heard the shouts, the curses, the smashing of some unknown furniture.

I heard it all and felt it all. Just more wounds to add to my bleeding soul.

I was selfish, I knew that. And possibly cruel for not seeing him.

But I was being cruel to be kind.

As much as the decision not to see his face was for me, it was also for him. He needed to be as far away from me as possible. I seemed to be like some contagious disease. Get close to me and you're tainted with my affliction. I fucked up every life I came into contact with.

I didn't miss the fact there was always a Harley outside Lily's house. Lily and Asher's house. That's where they'd taken me after I had been treated in the clubhouse, not that I remembered.

I knew I had not been taken to a hospital. I was thankful for that. Being somewhere so sterile, so full of bright lights, where my filth would be magnified, might've made me go insane.

PRESENT

"There," Rosie proclaimed, standing back to inspect her work. "Beautiful."

I highly doubted that, but I let myself be directed to the mirror above the dining table.

"Wow," I said when I saw my reflection.

Despite the sallow, almost gray skin, sunken cheeks, and lifeless eyes, my hair looked good. It was slightly longer on top and she'd put some sort of goop in it to spike it up. It looked funky and edgy, reminding me of Pink.

"I know, you're a knockout. Not many people can rock short hair," she informed me with a grin.

"Let's not go crazy. You've managed to make my hair look a lot less scary, and I thank you for that, but knockout I am not," I replied, turning.

Rosie frowned at me, her hazel eyes hardening. "We can agree to disagree there," she said sharply.

I rolled my eyes, unable to muster the energy to fight with her. It was impossible. I was saved from any further conversation on this particular topic with a knock on the door.

"I'll get it," Rosie declared.

As if there was a question. Since I got back I didn't do things like answer the door.

Or leave the house.

I wanted to. I didn't want to become a hermit and stew in my own

ANNE MALCOM

misery. That was just fucking depressing.

But the one time I'd tried to leave the house, my foot had hovered over the threshold, my lungs seizing up as the sunlight hit my face. Every single molecule of air in my chest had been stolen and I'd been sure that was how I was going to go. Suffocating on the doorstep.

There were worse ways to die. I'd survived them.

Unfortunately.

Lily had been there and had been able to convince me I wasn't, in fact, dying, just suffering from a panic attack.

She had enough experience with them to talk to me in soft tones and let me know that I wasn't alone and this wasn't permanent.

It helped, a lot. I also had a renewed respect for my best friend. She struggled with that every day and still managed to function, to live? I'd known I couldn't escape the events of those three weeks unscathed, nightmares and constant itching beneath my skin evidence of that. But I hadn't realized the depth of the terror that would clutch me in its blackened grip.

How it would sequester me indoors for a fucking week, watching grim documentaries which failed to scare me.

I didn't think anything would scare me now.

I didn't answer the door either, because he'd taken to knocking on it.

Every day.

Rosie got rid of him. Or Lily did.

Every day.

So I was staying far, far away from that door and the multitude of terrors it held at bay.

Because that's what I was most afraid of. Seeing him. What he'd turned into because of me. Seeing myself reflected in his eyes. My true self. It would be more confronting than any reflective surface. I so wasn't ready for that.

I was planning on avoiding him until I was ready. So, until the end of time.

"Wow, Bex, your hair. It looks... amazing," Lily said, her eyes widening as she walked into the room.

Rosie followed her. "Yes, it's my genius. I'm the Leonardo Da Vinci of hair."

Lily grinned at Rosie. It didn't reach her eyes. Didn't convince me. That killed me. The haunted gaze poorly hidden behind a crooked smile.

She reached forward and squeezed my hand. "You look good, better," she lied. She quickly released my hand, knowing how I felt about human contact these days.

Avoided it all cost.

I rubbed my hands on my leggings. They felt even dirtier after Lily touched them. "I am," I lied back. "Feeling great."

She gave me a sad smile and started unpacking snacks from her bag. "What are we watching today?"

Rosie snatched a Twinkie and sank on the sofa. "Okay, we've either got the world's deadliest women or real life inspiration for the most famous horror movies," she said, squinting at the screen. "I'm voting for the world's deadliest women. Might give me some tools to escape the latest clinger." She winked at me. Rosie had only just resumed her dating routine since I got back, and it took serious urging from me before she did so.

"Sounds good to me," Lily agreed, taking her place on Rosie's floral armchair and placing a hefty textbook on her lap.

I regarded them both. "Don't you guys have something better to do than babysit me and watch this crap?" I nodded to the TV. "Lily, you've got school and a husband to ravish you." I looked to Rosie. "You've got a job and a population of men to conquer. You don't need to be here waiting for me to break down. Just keep the loony bin on speed dial, leave me the number, and I'm set."

Rosie frowned at me, then Lily. "I happen to like finding out how various serial killers evaded capture and their murder techniques. It's valuable information. I don't have work today, and my conquering will wait. Lily?"

Lily looked at Rosie. "I like it too. And it serves as a valuable study tool for my current subject." She held up the textbook on psychology. "Plus, my husband is busy so he can't ravish me. I'm exactly where I need to be."

I looked between them, sighing. There was no convincing them

ANNE MALCOM

when they were ganging up on me.

I rolled my eyes and sank beside Rosie. "Okay, serial killers it is."

My tone may have been nonchalant but I was selfishly thankful for each woman's presence, despite the fact I was disrupting their lives. I didn't quite trust myself with solitude just yet.

••••

"This is unacceptable," I said, sitting up from my reclined position on the sofa.

Rosie kept her gaze on the TV. "If you're talking about that dress with those shoes, I totally agree."

We'd moved on from serial killers to real housewives. Not much of a change, though there were less severed limbs in this one.

"No, not that." I glanced to the TV. "Okay, not *just* that. This." I gestured down to my body. The oversized and stained tee I was wearing, the blanket I was clutching like a five-year-old held onto a safety blanket. I let it go and it fell to the floor. "Me hiding inside like a... coward," I declared.

Lily sat up, her face hard. "You're not a coward, Bex. You're the strongest person I know," she argued.

I gazed at her. "Because sitting here binge-watching TV shows and not changing my shirt for two days is brave?"

"Breathing is brave after what you went through, babe," Rosie put in, her attention no longer on the TV.

"Yeah, well, life's more than just breathing," I said to both of them. "Let's do something."

Lily looked concerned. "What?"

I rolled my eyes. "Calm down, Lils. I'm not suggesting we go and score some hard drugs."

She didn't look amused at my joke, although Rosie grinned because she was insane.

I thought for a second. "I want to get a tattoo."

"I'm in," Rosie said immediately. She stood. "I'll text my guy and put on my tattoo-getting outfit." Then she left the room, presumably to put on her 'tattoo-getting outfit.'

Insanity loved company.

Lily looked less keen. She chewed her lip. "Do you think this is the best idea?" she asked softly. "Making such a permanent decision when you're so...."

"Such a fucking mess?" I finished for her.

She leaned forward to squeeze my hand. "That's not what I was going to say. When you're still recovering."

I looked at her. "I'm always gonna be recovering, babe. That's my life now. I can wallow in it, or I can live in it." I paused. "I need something permanent when everything else feels so temporary. When I feel so temporary."

Her eyes flickered with understanding. "Okay, we'll do it."

I raised a brow. "We?"

She grinned. "You're my best friend, my sister. You think I'd let you do anything alone?"

••••

"Okay, when your husband kills me, can you tell him to keep away from the face? I want an open casket," I spoke over the buzzing of the tattoo gun.

Lily scowled at me. "He's not going to kill you." Apart from the scowl, she looked relatively relaxed. Who would have thought little Lily wouldn't even blink as a man injected ink into her skin.

I gazed down at the design. "Um, yes, I think he will. You're his 'delicate little flower.' I'm leading you astray and marking your pretty virgin skin. He's totally going to kill me."

Lily regarded me. "If Asher's going to kill you, then Lucky's going to kill me."

I stiffened. Actually froze.

"He's not going to anything," I replied, trying to stop my voice from shaking. "Because he's not going to see this." I glanced down at the fresh tattoo that was bright pink around the edges.

It was on the inside of my arm, covering my favorite vein. '*Perfer et obdura, dolor hic tibi proderit olim.*' Be patient and tough; someday this pain will be useful to you. Underneath the sloping script was an intricate and beautifully lifelike skull. It had taken hours and four cans of Coke. For me, that is, not Lex, the artist. Winding, growing from the skull were dark roses. Not red but black, torn and frayed and almost dead.

Almost.

I looked up from the ink. "He's not going to see it because he's not going to see me."

She frowned at me. "You can't hide from him forever."

"I can try."

SEVENTEEN

"The scariest monsters are the ones that lurk within our souls."
-Edgar Allan Poe

Time is poison. Toxic. It doesn't stop for anyone, unyielding, unchanging. Time was my enemy. It didn't change the desperate need for a fix, didn't lessen my cravings; if anything, it made them worse. It didn't chase away the demons that no one could see, the ones that promised to be conquered with one little needle. It didn't wash off the dirt on every part of me. Amongst all of this, time didn't make me forget *him* either. My traitorous mind would not even give me that. Wouldn't let me kid myself into thinking I wanted to see him, that I needed to see him.

It was crumbling willpower that stopped me. The determination not to go anywhere near the man who held what was left of my ashy heart. The man who led the dirty life but was squeaky clean. I couldn't see him. Look at his easy smile, get hypnotized by his eyes, let his strong arms touch me. It would make the dirt visible, unbearable.

I was sitting cross-legged on the sofa, sucking on a Diet Coke with my eyes glued to the TV. I was doing my best to ignore the constant itch and focus on the dull burning in my arm from the tattoo. It was comforting, having constant pain to focus on.

Lily had managed to text me after we'd dropped her off at home.

> **Lily:** Asher is not going to kill you. In fact, he says he's eternally grateful to you for being so impulsive and rash.

I'd grinned at the phone. So the biker didn't mind his little flower getting marked. Though it wasn't surprising since she'd inked their wedding date on her wrist in roman numerals.

ANNE MALCOM

Rosie had gotten a peace sign, made from birch and flowers, with a gun pointed at it, also threaded with roses. That's something a therapist would have loved to dissect. Me, I gave her a thumbs-up and let her be. If she wanted to tell me, she would.

Because my attention was so transfixed on meerkat mating rituals, I didn't even notice the door opening and closing, or the footsteps in the hall. Well, I noticed but I didn't decipher that the footfalls were not gentle clicks from Rosie's heels, but hard thumps from motorcycle boots.

Given my track record, it was probably a bad thing being that unaware, but whatever.

"Get up," a deep voice ordered.

I jumped, or more likely crawled, out of my skin and spilled Diet Coke everywhere at the unexpected presence.

My heartbeat returned to normal when I realized it was not a murderer standing in front of me.

I glared at him. "What's your fucking trauma? Ever heard of knocking?" I hissed. "Or announcing yourself when you enter a room?" I added, standing and trying to wipe the sticky soda off my hoodie.

Gage stood at the edge of the room, arms crossed. "I thought the slamming of the door might have given you notice that someone was entering the house."

I glared at him. "I assumed it was Rosie—you know, the woman who actually *lives* here? Most other, normal humans who don't reside in a dwelling *knock* to alert their presence." I stomped into the kitchen to get a cloth to wipe up my mess.

Gage's eyes followed me. "Would you have answered if I knocked?" he asked in a flat voice.

Good point.

Since I had gotten back from my little holiday at Thousand Acres or New Beginnings or whatever the fuck it was called, I had sequestered myself in Rosie's house. Luckily she was totally down with that, and dutifully watched David Attenborough documentaries—I'd moved on from serial killers—with me whenever she was home, which was a lot. When she wasn't here, it was Lily.

Now and then, it was Gwen and Amy, or Lizzie, with her two weird kids, who I kind of liked. Despite the fact I hated kids.

Other than that, I did not see anyone else. I knew there was a Harley constantly parked outside Rosie's house, though I didn't peek often, just in case I caught a glimpse of *him*.

"That's the whole point of knocking," I informed him. "You give the person inside the choice to answer or not."

"You don't need that choice. You're coming with me. We're going to a meeting," he declared.

My eyebrow rose, the only outward reaction to his words. Inside, my stomach dropped and my mouth went dry. "A meeting?" I repeated.

He nodded. "Yep. Get shoes on."

I didn't move. "I'm not going anywhere. I don't want to go to a meeting," I informed him sharply.

He didn't move. "I didn't ask whether you wanted to or not. I said we're going."

I felt my hackles rise at yet another alpha throwing his weight around. It was better than the shame of every single one of these people knowing about me. Knowing what I was. An addict.

"You can't make me," I declared, crossing my arms and regarding him with defiance. With confidence I was faking.

He could. He mostly certainly could make me do whatever he wanted me to do. The thought soured in my stomach and made my skin crawl. He was big. Every biker in the goddamn club was big. Not all were tall like this motherfucker but almost all were built like brick shithouses. Some of the older members had let themselves go and a beer belly covered what would've been a healthy six-pack in their heyday, But even with the extra pounds they held muscle. I could only think of two men who didn't conform to the 'must be muscled and menacing to enter badass club' rule. Wire, the skinny guy who constantly had an energy drink in his hands and spent most of his times with computers, and Skid, the gangly prospect I'd met what felt like years before.

Gage was like neither of them. He was much taller than me, but that wasn't saying much.

He was attractive, another rule of the club. Though it was in a darker way than most of the other men. They were badass motherfuckers, don't get me wrong, but there was a hardness to Gage that I recognized. His muscled arms were decorated with various ribbons of scars, a hint at the reason for the dark that lay beyond those eyes.

"I could," he answered, reading my mind. "But I won't," he added and, despite myself, I deflated slightly. "You need to go."

I scowled at him. "You have no fucking idea what I need," I hissed, anger starting to bubble past everything else in my mind, which was good.

"Got some idea," he replied mildly.

I stepped forward. "What? Those eyes have some kind of magical mind-reading power?"

"Nope." He moved his hand to his pocket and threw me the small item.

I caught it on reflex. I stared at him a beat, then moved my attention to the small plastic object in my hand.

"Four years sober," he said quietly.

My head snapped up at his words.

"No one's demons are the same. Helps to know that people other than you are fighting their own, though."

I continued to stare at him in disbelief. Then I moved my gaze back down to the chip in my hands, contemplating it. I couldn't fathom it. Since Lily had hooked up with Asher—and, by extension, the Sons of Templar MC—I had met almost all of the men in the club. Got to know them. One rather intimately. They were all strong, solid. Dauntless. And most could be romance cover models. That was neither here nor there. I never considered any one of them having the weakness that I was ashamed to possess.

And if I could have picked one, Gage would have been my last. Granted, his icy eyes were unsettling, and sometimes almost devoid of anything human, but he seemed stoic, unflappable.

"Shoes," he repeated.

I wanted to argue, throw sass. Stamp my feet. Anything but actually agree to go. But something in his gaze, in his admission, had me throwing the chip back to him and soundlessly padding to my room to put on shoes.

••••

"Does anyone else know? About you?" I asked after we'd been driving in silence for a good ten minutes.

Gage had silently waited for me to put on my wedged sneakers—not for everyone, but I thought they were kick-ass—and quickly change my top.

I wanted to swamp myself in another huge baggy hoodie like the one I had been wearing before Gage made me spill soda all over it. I wanted to cover every inch of my body in something shapeless that I could hide behind.

I didn't.

I wouldn't.

I wouldn't give those men power over me. What they did to me irrevocably scarred my soul, my insides. There was no changing that. But I would not let them stop me from at least outwardly being who I used to be. Even if the tight black jeans and cropped racer-back tee were an illusion of strength, a way of denying the depth of those scars, so be it.

I hadn't been able to look in the mirror. I couldn't be confronted with myself again. I felt dirty looking at my scantily clad body. The shower was the worst, naked and exposed to it all. I fixed that by putting the water to scalding and scrubbing myself until I was raw. I had three showers a day. It was an improvement on a week before when I damn near lived in the thing. Rosie and Lily hadn't said a word about it.

"No," Gage replied roughly, his voice jerking me back to the present.

I glanced at his profile in the cab of his truck. "It's a secret?"

Gage kept his eyes on the road. "No secret. My shit's my shit. I keep it tight," he replied.

"Are you going to tell me that if I tell anyone, you'll have to kill me?" I asked, only half joking. I had an inkling that Gage wouldn't hesitate in killing someone. Maybe not people he cared about, but something about him was chilling. At the same moment, I felt weirdly at ease around him. Maybe because I, like him, was fucked-up. In a way there was no going back from.

Gage looked at me sideways. "Tell people. Don't tell people. I don't give a fuck. Though, I doubt you're around anyone to be runnin' your mouth. You've shut yourself off from everyone. Not that there's anything wrong with that. I get it." He paused. "It's just harder being alone with your problems. Took me a fuck of a long time to realize that."

I chewed over his words. "Why are you taking me? Why are you here?" I asked finally, deciding not to talk about the being alone part. That I'd be going it alone as soon as I could muster the courage to get back on stage again. Earn again.

He met my eyes. "Been through a lot of shit, babe. Shit that would give most normal people nightmares rest of their life." He moved his gaze to the windshield, seeing something other than the road in front of us. "That day. A month ago. It was some shit. The worst kind. I admire the hell outta you. You've managed to somehow get back on your feet after that. But I've been worried 'bout how long you're gonna stay upright without someone steppin' in," he paused again. "Not talkin' 'bout your girls, know they've got your back. I'm talkin' 'bout someone who knows what it's like to crave the needle. The fix. Crave it more than your next breath. Don't know what the other hell you're going through is like." He visibly flinched. "Can't imagine it in my own nightmares. I can't see how dealing with those demons, plus the hunger for the fix, is taking you anyplace good. So I'm here," he explained.

I stared at him for a long moment, a prickly sensation under my skin at the fact he'd taken it upon himself to help me. To be there for me. It was foreign. Unwelcome. And at the same time, it filled me with warmth.

"Thank you," I whispered finally, looking out the window. "I'm not closing my eyes or chanting, and if anyone tries to hug me I'll throat-punch them," I added defiantly as we pulled into the parking lot of a church.

Gage surprised me by chuckling. "Wouldn't expect anything less."

There was a small silence as he parked beside a beat-up Camaro. He turned to me. "I don't expect anything from you in there." He nodded towards the building. "No one does. You choose how this works for you. You sit, you watch, you listen. You feel like it, you talk. You don't want to, fine. But you will come with me every week, we clear?"

I swallowed the angry retort that was almost instinct at anyone ordering me around, especially an alpha male. This wasn't someone ordering me around because of some freak gene. "Okay," I said quietly.

Gage seemed surprised at my placid response, but then he nodded. "And don't worry. No one's getting close enough to breathe on you," he declared fiercely, surprising me with the intensity in his voice. He opened his door. "Let's go."

LUCKY

"We finally found the connection between Carlos, the Tuckers, and how they've suddenly got enough resources to start a war and then turn to fuckin' ghosts," Cade declared, leaning forward and clasping his knuckles together. His hard gaze flickered around the table and settled on Lucky.

Lucky didn't have a reaction, not visibly at least. He might have clenched his fists, gritted his teeth hard enough to shatter, but nothing else. Inside, the fire of his fury blazed as hot as it had for the past month.

"Devlin," Cade continued simply, and the entire room turned wired.

Brock's face turned into a mask of fury. Obviously this was the first the VP had heard of this. Only Steg, sitting on the other side of Cade, looked like he wasn't shocked at this knowledge.

"That's not possible," Brock ground out. "I slit the fucker's throat myself."

Something danced behind Brock's eyes. A shadow of what Lucky was doing the tango with. The fear and rage that came with knowing someone fucked with your woman.

Cade regarded him evenly, but it was Steg who spoke. "Fucker had a son. One who's obviously been building up the remains of the empire we shattered. One who's chosen now to strike." He paused, sighing. "And he seems to have done his research. Figured out who the players are, who's stupid enough to strike out against us. What our weaknesses are."

Lucky felt the old man's gaze on him, but for once he stayed silent. He didn't speak much these days. He sure as fuck didn't laugh. Joke. Now he spent his time trying not to unleash the dragon that had awakened inside of him two months back. One that needed revenge. Vengeance. Thirsted for it.

"So we fuck them all up," Gage put in simply.

"We don't have the numbers, not this charter," Cade explained, gritting his teeth.

"We may not have the numbers, but one of us is worth ten of those fuckfaces," Gage replied.

Cade leaned back. "We've got to be smart about this. They're targeting *women*." His gaze landed on Lucky once more before he continued. "No fuckin' way am I doing anything that even has a one percent chance of blowing back on my woman. My family," he declared.

"Agreed," Asher said from beside him, his jaw hard.

"We call in other charters," Cade told the table. "Then we go to war. And burn them all."

For the first time in months, Lucky smiled.

••••

"Brother." Lucky felt pressure on his shoulder as the rest of the men filtered out of the room.

He turned to Bull. "Got shit to do," he bit out.

Bull's hand stayed firm. "A minute," he requested, though it seemed less of a request with his hand at Lucky's shoulder.

Lucky couldn't take him, he thought. Bull was a big fucker. Strong. Lucky was no small-fry either, he could take care of himself. Before, Bull might have been able to take him. But now that he had that dragon inside him, Lucky wasn't sure if his brother would win.

He didn't fight him, though. He had a tenuous hold on the rage inside him, enough to make sure he didn't come to blows with his brothers. Just enough.

Lucky sighed and nodded, surrendering.

"Make it quick," he bit out.

Bull raised a brow. "What? So you can rush off to the bar and continue your efforts to put Jack Daniels out of business? Or so you can cruise around beating up every tweaker and small-time player in the game, looking for info and askin' to get fuckin' arrested?"

Lucky gritted his teeth. "My dad died in prison ten years ago. Don't have a mom, not anymore. And I don't remember havin' a third parent lookin' anythin' like you."

"I'm not your parent. I'm your brother. And I know what you're goin' through."

Lucky clenched his fists. "Do you?" he hissed. "Because from where I'm standin' you got yourself some peace. In your new fuckin' family. Knowin' Laurie isn't livin' with demons of that day. She got peace. My woman? She's gonna live with chaos for the rest of her fuckin' life," he yelled. "And I can't do a thing about that but kill everyone who put that chaos there. And I can't even fuckin' do that."

Bull's eyes went black. Alien. He stepped forward. "Because I know you're hurtin', I'm not going to break your nose for insinuating that Laurie is somehow better off six feet under," he said quietly, his voice deadly. "I'm just gonna tell you that Bex is not. She's living, breathing, and bleeding. So instead of goin' around searching for more blood to spill, how about you try and fuckin' staunch the flow of hers." He gave Lucky a long stare before leaving him there, in the clubroom where life and death were dealt.

Where he would make the decision between the two.

EIGHTEEN

"She never seemed shattered; to me, she was a breathtaking mosaic of battles she'd won."
-Matt Baker

BECKY

It was my fault. I was trying new things, forcing myself to start becoming a functioning member of society. Society I'd never belong to, but I had to exist in. I was planning on going back to work in a couple days, so I kind of had to do things like answer the door.

I don't know who flinched first, me or him. I guessed I looked different since he last saw me, what felt like a lifetime ago. I'd lost weight, gotten a new hairstyle, and my face was devoid of anything I could describe as life, as vibrancy.

But him.

Fuck.

I barely recognized the man in front of me. He was the same, physically, I guessed. Tall—not huge, but taller than me. He was dressed in all black—jeans, motorcycle boots, tee, and leather cut. That in itself was cause for pause. Usually he was wearing blue jeans so faded they looked like they were made for him. And most of the time, apart from when he decided he needed to ramp up the badass, he was wearing some stupid tee under his cut.

It wasn't just the lack of stupid tee that had me physically recoil. It was the lack of *anything*. He looked like he had somehow gained more muscle in the two months I hadn't seen him, but he had lost everything else. His jaw was covered with substantial stubble, hiding half of his attractive face. His cheekbones seemed more angular.

But his eyes. They were haunted. Destroyed. The humor that

constantly twinkled beyond them was gone.

"Fuck," he rasped, looking over me much the same I had him.

I didn't have time to think about shutting the door in his face, turning on my heel, and running or bursting into tears. I didn't have time for anything because suddenly, he wasn't on the doorstep. He was everywhere. I was in his arms.

I sank into them immediately, like the only place I had belonged. Home.

"Fuck, baby. Fuck," he muttered before I felt him kiss my head. We didn't say anything else. Didn't move for what felt like an eternity. It was as if by stepping into his arms I had stepped into some sort of void in the universe where nothing existed. Not even my own thoughts.

He pulled back slightly, enough so his hands could run through my hair and his tortured eyes could meet mine.

"Different," he whispered. "I like it."

It was as if his words jolted me out of whatever madness had me sinking into his arms in the first place. I suddenly realized what he was doing, and I felt it. Filthy. Corrupted. Insects crawled under my skin.

I yanked myself out of his arms, and although his jaw hardened underneath his stubble, he let me.

We stared at each other once more.

"You shouldn't be here," I whispered. "You *can't* be here."

He shook his head. "Here is where I should've been the entire time," he replied softly. "Staunching the bleeding."

His last words confused me for a second before I stepped back so I hit the wall. "You need to leave," I ordered in a shaky voice.

I hate that my voice shook. That I retreated. That I was weak the moment I was faced with him.

He shook his head again, stepping forward. "No. I need to stay. For selfish reasons, like sanity. Firefly, I'll go fuckin' insane if I leave right now, with the image of you like this. Beautiful. Still hauntingly fuckin' beautiful, but broken." He paused, evaluating the distance between us as if he wanted to close it. Thankfully he didn't move. "I'll go insane if I don't stay and help repair you. Fix you," he muttered.

I blinked away tears. "I can't be fixed," I declared, my voice firm, resolute.

His fists tightened at his sides, the veins in his arms in danger of jumping from his tattooed skin with the effort I guessed it was taking not to move them. Not to touch me. I knew he wanted to. Ridiculous as it sounded, I could taste it in the air, the charge, the electricity. I knew he wanted to because I wanted him to, more than anything.

But to survive, to be able to handle this moment sober, he couldn't touch me. I still had the memory of how dirty I felt under his touch seconds before. Even under his gaze, in his presence, I was itching to escape my own body so I didn't have to swim in the filth anymore.

His jaw was granite as his caramel hazel eyes hardened. "You can be fixed," he gritted out. "You will be. You fuckin' *are*. You're standing right in front of me. Different, in a way that almost kills me, but still beautiful, still breathing, still surviving. You, right here, right now, is proof that you can be fixed. That you will be. I'll make sure of it."

I stood stock-still as his words hit me physically. As his eyes branded my soul. "This is not something you can badass your way into. That an alpha male attitude, some muscles, and a cut can fix. What they did...." I didn't miss his flinch. Didn't miss the way the air turned bitter with his fury. I managed to find a way through it, to meet his eyes. "What they did, it didn't wound me or break me. It *disfigured* me. Permanently changed my core, my identity, every part of who I am. I'm not ever going to heal, be whole, be someone who is ever going to be worthy to stand beside you. I'm always going to be this... *thing* they turned me into. That I turned myself into. Nothing's going to change that."

"Okay," he said, the amount of emotion in that word turning his voice foreign and almost unrecognizable. His head was bent down to regard his feet.

"What?" I whispered.

He looked up, and I flinched at his eyes. There was no film, no filter between him and me. His demons were right there on the surface for me to see. "Okay," he repeated. "Breaks every part of me that's still left whole. But if that's what you are, if you are so fuckin' sure you can't be fixed, that what's in front of me is all I can have, I'll take it." He stepped forward. "What's in front of me is beautiful in every fuckin' sense of the word, just in case you'd forgotten that. It's also mine. No act on this earth is gonna change that, and I'll take you however I can have it."

I blinked through my tears at his words. I couldn't surrender to them. I wouldn't.

I sucked in a breath. It was choked and strangled as the very air around me seemed to scrape the sides of my throat as it traveled down my lungs. Existing was hard, impossible, when the mere act of breathing clean air was excruciating. I blinked up at him, the man in front of me who'd haunted my nightmares. Who I promised myself would only exist in my nightmares.

"I don't sleep," I whispered.

He jolted and his face was a contortion of agony.

"And when I do, when my body loses its fight with exhaustion after a couple days, they come," I continued. "The nightmares." I looked up, to escape his eyes and in an attempt to force the tears threatening the corners of my eyes back where they came from. It was a long moment of silence before I found the strength to lower my gaze once more. "Though nightmares isn't the best description. Nightmares aren't real. You wake up from them and thank whatever you pray to that they exist only in the land of darkness and night." I sucked in another mouthful of glass. "These are real. And they don't leave me when I wake up. They're always there. *Always*."

As if he were unable to hear this anymore, he stepped forward. Like I'd coordinated it, I stepped back just as quickly. It was hard enough to get oxygen into me with him in the same room. I wouldn't be able to do it if I could smell him. Taste him. He didn't try to move forward again, but every inch of him was etched in stone.

"You're in my nightmares," I choked out. "Always. You're always there, surrounded by the filth, elbow-deep in it. Saving me. You already did that. It's done. I'm saved. You can sleep easy. At least one of us can. So you need to stop trying to save me, 'cause this is as close as it's going to get. Leave." The last word was a prayer.

Gabriel looked at me. Branded me with his gaze. It wasn't comfortable, or enticing, or full of desire. It rubbed me the wrong way, like sandpaper on the psyche, with the depth of fucking sorrow in it.

"Sleep easy," he repeated, his voice gravel. "I haven't had a moment of fucking peace or easy since I woke up in that hospital room and learned that you were gone." His fists clenched at his sides. "My nightmare, firefly, was being strapped to a fucking table while unable to go to you. Chained up while you were.... That's what I'll live with. What'll keep me up at night. Every night for the rest of my life. So the only fucking way I'll ever sleep easy if you're next to me, and when I get shaken awake by my own nightmares, I'll have you in my arms to chase them away."

There it was. Him, basically begging at my feet. Offering me something I'd dreamed about since the moment I was lucid enough to realize my nightmare was never going away. Safety. He was offering me himself. Even though he knew what had gone on those three weeks. What they did to me. And he still wanted me. Or thought he did.

He wouldn't. Not once he saw how deep the dirt went. How fucking shattered I was.

I didn't even want me.

"I can't chase away your nightmares," I choked out. "I'm too busy with my own. Now, I need you to leave."

He stared at me, and for one horrible moment I thought he wouldn't leave. That he'd stay and I'd lose the battle I was waging with myself, take him up on his offer. That I'd cling to his fucking leg and never let go.

He rubbed at his head like I knew he did when he was frustrated. "Baby, I know you've been through—"

"You have no fucking idea what I've been through!" I shrieked, interrupting him. I tried so hard to sound strong, but my words seemed to break as I said them. *I* seemed to break.

Gabriel stepped forward and I scuttled back against the wall. He frowned at the distance between us, obviously wanting to close it, but he must've seen something in me because he stayed rooted, his hands balled into fists at the sides.

"You're right, firefly. I have no idea what you've been through," he began quietly. "I only know what *I've* been through. The deepest depths of hell I've been living in, suffering in, for the past two months. The pain that seems to kill me, but somehow I keep breathing. The anger that I can't swallow no matter what. That's all I know, Becky." He paused, his eyes never leaving mine. "I know all that shit, what I'm feeling, is nothing on what you're battling. That what I feel is a drop in the fuckin' bucket compared to your pain. I can't understand how something can be worse than what I'm going through. The living hell. It makes me sick, physically sick to my stomach to know that's what you're feeling, what you're living." He couldn't seem to stop himself anymore, closing the distance between us so he framed my face with his hands. I couldn't say anything, couldn't move. If my words had broken me before, his touch shattered me. Destroyed what was left.

"There's nothing I can do to stop it. To fix it. That'll haunt me to my dying breath. There's nothing I can do but love you. And kill every last person on this planet who had a hand in hurting you. I'll do it, babe. Every single person is going to die by my hand, I promise you that. But you gotta make me a promise. They'll die by my hand, but I gotta live by yours. I've got no right to ask anything of you, but I'm doin' it. Humans are hardwired to do whatever it takes to survive." His gaze burned into me. "So here I stand, doing the only thing I can to survive. Touching the only fuckin' thing in the world that'll keep me breathing, other than the thirst for blood. I can't exist on that thirst alone, or I'll fall back into that hole I clawed my way out of fifteen years ago. I know this time, if I go anywhere near that thing, I ain't comin' out. So I'm here. Survivin'."

His words were bullets, shattering me into smaller pieces. I couldn't do this, be reminded of his demons, try to conquer them while struggling with my own. It was one or the other. And for someone who spent her whole life with the singular goal to take care of herself, to survive, I was finding myself wanting to do the opposite. To save him. To give him what he wanted, even if it destroyed me.

"I'm going," he said, searching my eyes.

My body sagged. Staving off destruction for another day.

"But for today. Not forever. I'll be back here every fuckin' day for the rest of forever if that's what it takes. To remind you that everything may have changed, turned ugly, broken. Everything but what I feel for you."

His newly foreign eyes burned into me for a second more, and then he was gone.

I stayed standing until the door closed behind him.

ANNE MALCOM

Then I crumbled to the floor.

ONE WEEK LATER

"See you next week," Gage said as I unbuckled my seatbelt.

"Yeah, can't wait," I muttered.

We had just gone to another meeting, and despite my flippant attitude, it helped. Not with the dirt, the feeling of filth—nothing would help that. But with the cravings I was ashamed of. The cravings I sometimes questioned whether I was strong enough to fight. Whether it was worth fighting.

I glanced up at him. "They don't... suck," I said, my voice contradicting the sarcasm of earlier.

Gage only nodded.

I swallowed, my eyes going to the ribbons of scars on his arms. "Is that from junk?" I asked, nodding to them.

He glanced down, his face turning hard. "Everything's because of junk, isn't it? When it all boils down to it. The good, the bad, the ugly. Everything after that first taste is a result of that choice."

I was taken aback by his answer. Or lack of it. Maybe he hadn't explained his scars, but he had explained something exponentially more profound.

"Yeah, it is," I whispered. "A biker and a philosopher," I mused.

Gage stared at me. "What happened to you, that wasn't your fault," he said, his voice impossibly soft.

I gave him a long look. I didn't do this. I didn't talk about those three weeks. Not with anyone. Not Rosie. Not Lily. Not the fucking therapist Lily kept insisting I should see. Not Sarah who treated me, no matter how understanding she may seem.

People may seem understanding, like they want to help. Talk. But once I unveiled the truth, the ugly, vile truth, there wouldn't be any understanding. There wouldn't be anyone there to help.

"Whatever you say, big guy," I muttered, hiding behind sarcasm.

I went to get out of the truck, but a hand on my shoulder stopped me.

"I don't want to put this on you. Understand you've got your reasons why you're doing this, but he's my brother," he started, and my body stiffened. "He's fucked-up, babe. It's tearing him apart, not being able to see you. Help you."

I laughed, a bitter, ugly sound. "That's where he's wrong. He can't help me. The best thing he can do for both of us is forget me. The best thing I can do for him is to make him forget me," I told him coldly. I jerked my shoulder out of his grasp, jumping out the door before he could tear any more of my wounds wide open.

Because I had so hastily gotten out and slammed the door, I didn't hear what he muttered while he watched me storm into Lily's house.

"Problem is he'll never forget you."

••••

"Bex," Lily yelled from the kitchen. "Do you want another piece of pie?"

"Do you even know me at all?" I yelled back, cradling my hot chocolate and staring at the waves.

Yes, hot chocolate. I was sipping it with a million marshmallows like I was a five-year-old. I would have loved a nice eight-dollar bottle of Pinot, but I didn't think that was a good idea.

I heard someone enter the room, assuming it was Lily, I didn't move my gaze from the perusal of the waves. "God, I hope one day I'll have enough of a hold on this addiction beast that I'll be able to indulge in cheap crappy wine," I exclaimed. "If not, just shoot me now."

"I think my wife and best friend may object to that course of action," a deep voice answered.

I moved my sheepish glance to Asher, who was leaning on the doorframe of the conservatory of his and Lily's home. The place I'd come to consider my home. The only one I'd ever had. Where Faith lived in the walls, her paintings, her energy still holding her life force, despite the fact she was gone.

Asher had been careful around me since everything, keeping his distance as if he sensed my reluctance to have strong and dangerous males in my presence. Even now, he stayed leaning against the door.

I tried my best for a jaunty grin. "Jeez, ever heard of sarcasm? It'd be valuable to learn the distinction. I'd hate to think of the amount of people you've shot unnecessarily."

He shook his head, not smiling. Then his face turned even more serious. "I'm proud of you, Bex."

I gaped at him. "Proud of me?"

He nodded, walking forward to the windows to regard the wild ocean like I had been before. "For still findin' the ability to say shit like that. For figurin' out a way not to run back to the easy way out, even though no one would blame you if you did." He turned to face me. "For getting through."

I blinked at him. "Your pride is a little premature. I'm not exactly 'through' yet. I'm barely past the starting line."

"You'll get there," he said with certainty.

Before this could get any deeper and we stared braiding each other's hair, Lily came through with plates. She eyed us both. "I've got pie," she declared.

"Then I'll totally marry you if you ever decide to leave your biker and jump the fence," I deadpanned.

She grinned at me. "Sorry, I kind of like him."

Asher moved to his wife, taking the plates and setting them down so he could yank her into his arms and kiss her hair.

It was like a fucking shampoo commercial, the two of them so attractive and shit.

"Yeah, I kind of like him too," I muttered.

Asher let her go and gave me a small smile. "I'll go and watch the game, let you girls talk about... girl shit," he said.

Lily rolled her eyes. "Girl shit?" she asked dangerously.

He motioned to the living room. "I'm leaving before any blood is spilled."

He left and I laughed. Some of it was even genuine.

I took the pie Lily handed me. "He's totally scared of you. The big biker who most likely chews bullets for fun is totally scared of his little wife."

She grinned at me, chewing the pie. "It's how any marriage should be," she declared sagely.

I wanted to grin back, but I'd used up all my faux happiness for the night.

"I want it," I confessed.

Lily focused on me, her face soft. "What, honey?"

"Everything," I whispered. "I want to have some dumb nickname that only one man calls me and it mean everything. I also want my own name and not be belittled by a stupid term of endearment. I want to give my everything to him at the same time as owning every part of myself. I want him to take care of me and I never want to entrust my own survival to anyone else." I blinked away the tears. "I want to sleep without nightmares. Heck, I just want to *sleep*. An entire night. I'm so fucking tired. I want to embrace oblivion without the fear of my own mind, and I want to do it the only place I feel safe, next to him. But I also want to be able to sleep that entire night alone with my demons and find a way to conquer them myself." A single tear trailed down the side of my face. "But most of all, I want him. Pure and simple. And I'd give anything I have or will have to feel worthy of him. To be able to have him without feeling dirty and tarnished when I have him."

Lily blinked at me and moved forward like she wanted to hug me, but caught herself when she realized my body stiffened at the potential contact. "You're not dirty. Or tarnished," she declared fiercely. "You're strong. You're my best friend. And you're not allowed to say things like that. Ever. Not when you're wrong. I'm so effing proud of you, Bex. I know for a fact Mom would be too," she choked out, her eyes glistening.

I swallowed. "You and your hubby have one mind or something?" I asked, trying to break the tension. I couldn't deal with all the pride and inspirational talk.

She tilted her head, looking confused, but then her eyes focused on the doorway, going wide.

"If that's the president coming to tell me how proud he is, can you tell him to come back tomorrow?" I asked, taking a bite of my pie.

There was silence and I turned.

Gabriel was leaning in the doorway, much like Asher had. But his posture wasn't easy, relaxed. He was the stranger who had showed at my door a week ago. The one I dreamed of. The one I craved.

"What are you doing here?" I managed to choke out.

"You weren't at home. Rosie said you were here. So I'm here," he explained, his voice rough.

"That's not an answer," I snapped. "Did Gage tell you I was here?"

He stiffened. "No," he said slowly. "How the fuck does Gage know you're here?"

I sensed the danger in his voice. "He doesn't," I lied. "Why are you here?" I repeated.

"You're here. I'm here. That's the only answer I got," he said. He glanced at Lily. "Can you give us a minute, squirt?"

She glanced to me in unease.

I resisted the urge to use her as a human shield. "I'm fine, babe," I lied.

She furrowed her brows before getting up. "I'll just be inside," she said. "Watching the game or fighting with Asher over the remote."

Then she was gone and it was just me and him. The second time... since. And it wasn't any easier than the first. He was still hard to look at. Almost impossible.

But I managed. And because I made myself look, I finally realized what all this had done.

"I've stolen it from you," I whispered.

His brow furrowed. "What?"

"Your happiness, your life. What you had before," I croaked out. "Before me you were happy. Your life wasn't... *tainted* by me—"

I stopped abruptly because he was no longer leaning against the door. He was there, right there, in my space, taking away whatever buffer distance had offered.

"Don't need to hear any more of that, babe," he growled, his eyes dark. "I was happy before," he agreed, almost reluctantly, "but it was a hollow sort of happiness, like I was only living my life on the surface." He swallowed. "That's the only thing I could do. Going any deeper meant meeting my demons, and I was happy for them to be strangers till I died. Then I met you, found out what it was like to be filled up, how to go deeper. Since meeting you, I'll admit, I've gone deep, so deep I didn't think it'd be possible to get out. But you were always there, my firefly. My light." His finger trailed along my jaw. I was frozen to move, yet the feeling of ice followed with his touch, exposing the dirt below. "I'd take our most miserable, darkest day together over a thousand of those happy ones I had alone," he said. "Real happiness, the kind that penetrates right down to the core, that's all coiled up in pain. In knowledge of how fuckin' ruthless and unyielding the world can be. How it can be so full of pain you're sure that's all you'll ever feel. Real happiness is comin' out the other side of that and holding something beautiful in your arms. That's you, babe. I wish to fuckin' Christ that you didn't have to go through what you did." His eyes were haunted by the demons of my past. "I'd have taken it all from you in a second. But the only good thing that's come of this nightmare is I get to feel real happiness. I get to hold on tight. And now that I know what happens if I don't hold tight, I'm never fuckin' letting go."

His words, the closeness, all of it was too much. Way too fucking much. I pushed off the sofa and as far away from him as I could get.

"You've got to let go," I told him. "Because I'm not chaining you down, dragging you into this. You don't deserve that."

"Fuck!" he yelled, and I jumped like I fucking scared squirrel. I hated that. Everything that took me by surprise, the fucking wind pushing trees against the window, made me jump. Fear, an almost unknown acquaintance *before*, was now a constant companion.

He saw it, sensed the way my body vibrated with the stupid emotion, and immediately his face gentled. He stepped forward but didn't make to touch me. He'd learned about that.

"This isn't your fault, Becky," he murmured. "Jesus. The fact you're dealin' with this shit and laying all the blame on your fragile shoulders eats me up inside. You're the victim—"

"Stop!" I screamed, my voice shrill. It was his time to react bodily to my words. Though it might not have been a full-on jump, there was a flinch. "I'm not that," I hissed, leaning forward. "I'm not a fucking *victim*," I spat the word. "I know that's what you want me to be. Help this train wreck of a situation catalogue in your mind because if I'm a victim then you can be the hero. You have a purpose. To save me from the big bad wolf. To use that"—I nodded to his cut where I knew he had a gun underneath—"to exact revenge and save the victim. I'm not that. And you can't fix me. I can't give you purpose or let you sling me on the back of your Harley and ride off into the sunset. By calling me a victim you're making me helpless. You're taking away my power and giving yourself control over me, whether that's your intention or not. I can't be helpless. Not now, not ever again. Because that, that'll kill me." I'd petered down to a low whisper. "Do you know how much of an effort it is just to stand up? To physically hold my body upright? Not to sink to the floor and beg it to swallow me up? It takes everything I've got left. I'm not going to give in. I'm not giving them that power to hammer the final nail in my coffin. Because I'm not a fucking victim. I'm a survivor." And on that note, I turned on my heel and walked out of the room.

LUCKY

He watched her leave. And it took every ounce of his considerable strength to stay rooted to that ground she said she wished would swallow her up.

Lucky's heart threatened to smash through its cage. He swallowed roughly. He couldn't go after her. Not now. Not if he wanted to keep her.

And fuck, did he want to keep her.

"I'm a survivor."

He smiled. Someone who knew him well wouldn't recognize such a smile on his face. One didn't exist there until before her. Before her, his smiles were happy, naïve, empty. A concentrated observer would see this wasn't empty. It was full. Of melancholy, anger, hurt. And love. Not the puppies and bunnies Hollywood love. The dark, gritty, heart-wrenching, blood-drenched kind. The one that either gave him a reason to fight for his next breath on the same earth she existed on, or welcome the embrace of death which had already taken her.

It wouldn't. Not for a long fucking time if he had anything to say about it.

So he didn't follow her. Didn't make chase.

He wrenched his phone from his cut.

"Skid. You're on Becky. Every fuckin' minute, every fuckin' second.

If you so much as glance up to marvel at the starry night's sky and make a wish on a shooting star, you'll be burning up in flames just like one," he growled.

He hung up, not waiting for a response.

Because he had another destination in mind. Another person to direct his anger at.

••••

"What the fuck, bro?" Gage protested as Lucky grabbed the sweetbutt on Gage's lap and deposited her on the floor. She scowled at him but knew better than to say anything in protest. All the girls gave him a wide berth since they'd found Becky.

He knew he scared them. He didn't give a shit. Plus, he had no fuckin' plans of getting anywhere near them for whatever remained of his life.

He clutched Gage by the collar. "Why the fuck have you been hangin' around Becky?" he clipped, barely restraining his urge to punch the fucker. He'd shelve that urge. It'd come in handy.

Gage regarded him with that icy, empty stare that was the motherfucker's default. "She tell you?" he asked mildly.

He clutched his cut tighter. "I'm asking you," he clipped. He had been beyond furious when Becky had refused to tell him why. Not at her; fuck, not even at Gage. He trusted his brother. Even now, his anger wasn't really being directed at the right place. He was furious at himself for being unable to swallow this fuckin' dragon, this white-hot rage that simmered every minute of every day.

"You're askin' the wrong person," Gage replied.

Lucky got in his face. "That's my woman," he said quietly, dangerously.

Gage nodded. "Yeah, and she's a good one too. Which is why I'm not betrayin' her fuckin' trust." He shook Lucky off with ease. "Frankly, I'm insulted you think I'd try shit on with her. Not because she's your woman, but because of the shit she's been through. She ain't ready for that shit. Not from me. Not from you. Even I got fuckin' boundaries."

On that, he turned his back on Lucky and tagged the girl who'd been hovering on the edge of their conversation, disappearing down the hallway.

Lucky stared after them.

Fuck.

He was more fucked-up than fuckin' Gage. *Gage.*

That thought chilled him to the bone. But that didn't stop him from plannin' on seeing Becky. Nothing would, short of a bullet to the brain.

NINETEEN

"She wears her strength and darkness equally well. The girl has always been half goddess, half hell."
-Nikita Gill

I stared at the building, my nails biting into my palms so hard I was pretty sure I'd draw blood if they weren't bitten to nothing.

"You're sure you want to go in there?" Gage asked.

I didn't look at him, just nodded.

"Interesting choice," he said, staring at the script above the double doors.

My gaze snapped to him. "What's that supposed to mean?"

He met my eyes, his cold and calculating stare giving nothing away. "It's meant to mean interesting choice," he said evenly. "Not many women would go back to this after what you went through."

"Yeah, well, I'm not 'many women,'" I said, gathering my bag and my confidence.

"I'm aware of that," he muttered.

Gage and I had established a rather unconventional friendship. Though it was a stretch to call it a friendship. Could people really be friends with sharks? That's what he was—a predator. Something vital was missing from him. I'm guessing what the junk took away.

That's why I felt so at ease in his company. Something vital was missing from me too.

And he hadn't even fluttered an eyelash when I'd requested he drop me here on the way back from our meeting.

"I'll be here when you're done," he told me as I opened the door.

I turned my head. "You don't have to stay. I can walk." The prospect of walking out in the open, clean air had my chest feeling tight, that didn't matter. I had to do this shit at some time. I couldn't be afraid of

ANNE MALCOM

the big wide world forever.

"I'll be here when you're done," he repeated.

I rolled my eyes. "Bloody bikers," I muttered as I climbed out and shut the door.

Yeah, bloody bikers. In the week since our confrontation, Gabriel made good on his promise. He was there, at Rosie's, every single day. Not for long, and he didn't even come in, though I knew he wanted to. Come in and try to save me from it all.

But he didn't.

It was as if he sensed that trying to save me would be the very thing to destroy me, that being in his presence for more than a handful of minutes was a mixture of torture and ecstasy I was only just mentally competent enough to handle.

So that's all he gave me.

Those minutes were too much and not enough all at the same time. Mostly he asked how I was doing; told me to eat more; gave me the long, soulful, demon-filled stare; and left. Showing me what had changed about him.

Everything.

And what had changed about how I felt for him.

Nothing.

The previous morning, it changed.

"I made a mistake," he said, jaw hard. The outburst came out of the blue, but the impact of the words hit me hard. So hard I was happy I stayed upright.

"A mistake?" I repeated. "Yeah, that tee with those jeans? Not cute." I shook my head at him, trying to hide behind the bravado that served me so well in the past.

His gaze tattooed my soul. "I tried to make you mine. Tried to play by a book that was already written. Written for somebody else." He stepped forward, clasping my hands in his and I let him. Despite the ice that settled under his grasp, the dirt that sank in, I let him. His touch was pain, but I feared the absence of it may be agony. "That's where I fucked up. Rules for trying to win you, trying to make you mine, aren't in any book ever written. 'Cause you ain't one in a million, firefly—you're one in a lifetime. I thought I could make you mine, make you belong to me. I didn't see that you don't belong to anyone but yourself. That's why I could never grasp you in two hands... before." His eyes flickered with demons before he chased them away. "Now I intend to keep you in my arms for good. And not as something that I own, that I possess, but that you give me. As a gorgeous, chaotic soul, with warrior's eyes and a fuckin' saint's heart. I can't possess your chaos, but I can let it possess me." He lifted my hand up to his lips. "And it does. Every inch."

Then he stepped back and walked away.

Fucking walked away.

I'd stood there like an idiot, shivering at the loss of his touch and the icy grasp of the flashbacks that came with it.

So that's when I made the decision that brought me here. Gabriel, and his words, and his fucking soulful stare drenched in sorrow.

I kept my back straight and my steps purposeful as I crossed the parking lot. Tried to tell myself I wasn't going to freak out.

Fake it till you make it.

Which was what I did when I walked through the doors and passed my old place of employment. I purposefully averted my gaze from the stage in the middle of the room.

I wasn't ready for that just yet.

It was empty, eerily so.

"Bex," a low voice rumbled.

I almost crawled up the wall until I saw the owner of that voice.

Cade's expression was how I imagined a ranger might approach a wild horse—cautious, ready for it to bolt. "Sorry, didn't mean to scare you."

I straightened my spine. "You didn't scare me," I lied.

He gave me a contemplating look before nodding, then gestured to a seat at the bar.

I sat down. He sat beside me. "How you doin'?" he asked, his voice softer than I ever imagined he'd be capable of. I didn't exactly know the biker 'prez' except in passing when I'd worked here. He'd technically been my boss, since the club owned this place and he was in charge of the club.

But since I'd become employed, Gabriel seemed to magically take over the running of this place, namely making sure the patrons didn't get within breathing distance of me. Killed my tips, but they paid well so I hadn't complained.

Obviously he didn't run the place anymore, which was a huge fucking relief. When I'd told Rosie my plans, she had looked at me sideways for just a second before putting me in touch with Cade.

"I'm fine," I lied, glancing anywhere but his kind yet hard eyes.

He nodded again.

"I want my job back," I blurted, wanting to do away with any talk of my current state of mind.

The only change in his expression was a slight raise of his brows. "Thought that might be the case."

I drummed my fingers on the bar, mostly to distract me from my unease, from the constant itch.

"You sure you're up to it?"

I narrowed my eyes. "I'm here, aren't I?"

He regarded me. "Yeah. It won't go down well. With him."

I stopped drumming. "Yeah, well, it's a good thing this has nothing to do with him."

"Babe, it has everything to do with him."

I gave him my best level stare. "Nope. I know you guys take this ownership thing pretty fucking seriously, despite the women's protests, but this woman"—I pointed to myself—"isn't owned by anyone, not even Gabriel. Especially not Gabriel. Men have been in control of what they do with my body, and I didn't like it. Not one bit."

I ignored Cade's flinch.

"So I'm here, controlling what I'm doing with my own body. Me. No one else. And if you won't give me my job back, I'll go somewhere else."

I made to stand up, though my threat was empty. I didn't have anywhere else to go. I had no money, and there wasn't exactly a plethora of strip clubs within spitting distance. I sure as shit wasn't going back to Carlos's. I couldn't, even if I were deranged enough to go back to the employer who had me kidnapped and raped—and trust me, I wasn't. I heard he dropped off the face of the earth and the club had burned down to ashes not a day after this one had.

Faulty wiring was the official story.

Cade's hand on mine stopped me. I flinched as his skin came into contact with mine and he clocked my reaction immediately, taking his tattooed hand away.

I let out a breath.

"You can have your job back," he said quietly. "If that's what you want."

"It's what I want."

He stood and I did my best not to fucking freak out at his size and the way he towered over me.

I managed. Just.

"We're opening again on Friday. You up for that?"

I didn't miss the way his gaze flickered down my body. He was taking in my tight jeans and equally tight cropped Henley. Not in a male way—I was pretty sure all women were invisible to him except his hot wife—but in a way like he was mentally calculating if this physical form could hold itself up on stage.

I'd put on weight. Not a lot but enough to hide my protruding bones. And my most important assets for this job, my tits and ass, were full and healthy, so he had nothing to worry about.

Friday was two days away. I was so not up for that. "Yep." I hitched my bag on my shoulder. "All good if I come tomorrow to practice?"

He nodded. "Cadence will be here."

Cadence was the manager of the dancers and a bitch.

We got on famously, despite her having screwed Gabriel.

She'd even visited Rosie's a week before. She brought tequila and flowers, and a Glock.

Like Rosie, she was insane.

I nodded. "Awesome. Well, I'll see you. Say hey to the wife from me." I went to leave his presence and this fucking place. It was making my skin itch like nothing else.

"We'll get them." His voice was a low boom.

I froze but didn't turn.

"They're gonna pay for what they did, I'll promise you that," he continued.

I sucked in a breath and then kept walking.

Yeah, they'd pay. I just hoped I got to make them do so.

••••

I'd been practicing my routine for two days straight, and every inch of my body screamed in protest at the abuse I was putting it through.

Stripping, despite what people thought, wasn't just gyrating on stage and shedding your self-respect along with your clothes.

It was hard, really fucking hard on your body. There was a reason housewives and idiots who drank green juice started doing it for workout purposes.

And my body had been abused and battered in the most brutal of ways for three weeks. Not as bad as my mind, but still not good. Add to that one month of doing not much at rehab and even less at Rosie's apart from serial killer marathons. It was safe to say I was rusty.

I wasn't bad, but I wasn't good.

Plus, my body hadn't exactly recovered and it pissed me right off that I landed on my ass when I tried moves that used to be a piece of cake...before.

Just another thing those assholes had ruined.

I was sitting on the stage, my feet hanging off it, trailing the new wood. It was all new, thanks to the fire that had been started the day mine went out. But I could feel the skeletons underneath it. It was where Lily almost died, where Gabriel almost died.

My throat started to close up.

"Here," a voice interrupted my thoughts, thankfully, and a bottle of water was shaken in front of my face.

I glanced up at Cadence and took it. "Thanks."

She hoisted herself up to sit beside me. "You sure you're up to this?" She nodded to the pole.

I narrowed my eyes at her. "Don't I look up to it?"

"No," she said bluntly. "Don't get me wrong, I dig the hair and you're still better than half the girls here, but you're runnin' on half a tank, babe. Understandable, considering what you went through. It's heavy shit. You think this is the right place for you after...?"

"After I was kidnapped by my ex-employer and fed drugs while they did unseemly things to me for three weeks?" I finished for her, my voice sharp.

She didn't flinch as I expected her to. Most people didn't do well with being confronted by ugly reality, but Cadence looked like she'd seen enough ugly reality to be jaded by my world, which scared me slightly.

"Yeah," she agreed.

I shrugged. "This is where I want to be. The only place I feel like I can be. As crappy as my old job used to be, when I was on stage, I had a sort of power, you know? Before I fucked myself up on drugs. I didn't exactly love the reality of it, but being on stage is...." I searched for the word.

"Freeing?" she finished for me.

I nodded. "Exactly."

She didn't press, didn't try to dig deeper and have a big heart-to-heart, which I fricking loved. "Okay then. That's all I need to hear. You do what you gotta do." She jumped back down onto the floor. "It's good to have you back."

I smiled at her. "It's good to be back."

It wasn't.

It wasn't *good* to be anywhere right now. But I figured if I faked it for long enough it would be.

"You," a very masculine and very angry male voice echoed through the empty club.

Both Cadence and I whipped our heads to the red-faced, bald-headed, tattooed biker stomping boots in our direction.

"Angry male approaching is my cue to leave," Cadence declared, leaving just as Gabriel made it to us.

"What the fuck are you doing here?" he clipped.

I scowled at him. "Hello to you too."

He snatched my arm and hoisted me to the floor, then began to drag me towards the door.

His hand on my bare arm immediately drenched my body in ice. The dirt came to the surface and I struggled to get free. "What are you doing?" I shouted. "Let me go."

He kept dragging me. "I'm gettin' you the fuck out of here and

ANNE MALCOM

somewhere where I can shake some fuckin' sense into you," he growled, bursting through the double doors and into the parking lot.

I started to panic as the dirt became unbearable and his touch had my mind flickering between the parking lot and that room.

The room where I was covered in dirt. Nothing but dirt and ice.

"The man who is dragging me bodily is talking about sense?" I shrieked. I kept struggling against his grip. "Let me go," I ordered.

Gabriel ignored me, just kept dragging me through the parking lot.

I didn't notice anything except the way his hand on mine made the grime unbearable. It was creeping up my arm like a flesh-eating virus and it had to stop. I wrenched my hand from his grasp but it didn't work, so I stopped, forcing him to stop too. It was either that or drag me. The look on his face might've been foreign, but I didn't think he was about to drag my limp body on the ground through a parking lot.

"Let me go!" I screamed, unable to hold the panic and terror in anymore. Because the longer his touch remained on me, the longer I was in that place, in that room.

He did so immediately. My voice had been unrecognizable even to myself.

"You can't touch me," I said, my voice lower, hoarser. "I can't have that." I rubbed my arms in an effort to get it off. "I can't have people touching me," I muttered, trying desperately to escape that little room.

"Fuck," he whispered, all rage gone from his voice. Only sorrow and regret was left. I felt him more than saw him step back.

I blinked and was back in the parking lot, looking at Gabriel put his hands to the back of his neck, his face tortured.

There was silence in that moment, enough of it for me to get my breath back, to convince myself that there was nothing under my skin.

His eyes burned into mine and he moved his foot an inch, then froze, as if he realized I needed the distance. "You're safe, Becky," he whispered, his hands clenched at his sides. "No one's touching you. No one's hurting you."

I clung to his words like a life raft.

"I—" He took a breath. "Fuck, I didn't mean to come in there like that. Do this to you." His gaze flickered up my body. "I'm sorry, Becky. So fuckin' sorry. I didn't realize—"

"It's fine." I was finding my strength now that the images were gone. Now that his touch was gone. "I'm fine," I lied.

He wasn't convinced.

"Apart from being moderately pissed off that you came into my place of work shouting and acting like a maniac," I added icily.

He clutched the back of his neck once more, his jaw hard. "I didn't mean to lose it, Becky. I fuckin' promise. Jesus, I know I need to handle you with care. I only just got you back. I didn't recognize that." He nodded to the building. "But when Gage told me you were going back to work, I saw red." His eyes went hard. "What the fuck are you thinking, Becky?" His voice was soft, but the edges were rough with fury.

I folded my arms. "I was thinking that this is my life and I'm in control of how I live it." I paused. "And I'm totally not inviting Gage to my next sleepover. That mute can't keep a secret."

The cords in his neck pulsed, I was guessing at the effort it took to stay calm. "Yeah, babe. It's your life. I want you to live it. You don't, I don't fuckin' live mine," he declared. "So I don't want you self-destructin', doing something you think you need to do to prove to people, to yourself. Jesus." He ran his hands over his head. "After what you went through? Puttin' yourself on stage?" He shook his head. "I can't let you do that, Becky."

I glared at him. "I wasn't asking permission." I sucked in a breath. "I didn't ask for any of this." I waved my hands down my body, between us. "For you to come into my life. To get so wrapped up in you I don't know where you begin and I end. I certainly didn't ask for that.... I may have set events in motion to make it so, but I didn't ask for them to take me. To do what they did to me. To turn into this person, this thing I am now. No, it all just happened. I had no control. I don't have control over any of that shit. Over the fact I can't even stand my best friend fuckin' hugging me because any human touch sends me right back into that room. That all hurtles out of my control. That"—I pointed to the building—"is something I can control, screwed up as it sounds. It's the only thing I can control right now. So I'm doing it, whether you like it or not. And I'm sorry if it hurts you or damages your ego or whatever, but I don't care. I can't take on your shit as well as mine. I've got to be selfish right now or I'll lose it."

I was breathing heavily by the time I finished on a whisper. I didn't exactly mean to blurt all of that out, but it had come to a bottleneck.

Gabriel wasn't breathing heavily. He didn't look like he was breathing at all. He was a statue, a beautiful, damaged statue, coated in rage and regret. The moment yawned into silence that filled the open air with my words. I was tempted to do something to break it, but I'd said enough. Far too much.

I was also tempted to wave my hand in front of his stone eyes to make sure he hadn't left the building.

"Okay," he said finally, his voice low and rough. "I get it, not havin' control. 'Cause that's all I want, to be able to control every single thing you can't. To make it better, or at least kill the people who made it that way." He clenched his fists to his sides. "And because I've got no one to kill, no way to control what they've done, I want to control you. Yeah, it's fucked-up no matter what way you look at it, that need to control everything you do to make sure you're never hurt again, but that's me. That's the real me. Fucked-up in ways I didn't even know I could be. And I don't want to be normal 'cause that means I won't be tangled up in you either. So I can't control you. I won't like it." His hard gaze traveled from me to the building. "In fact, I'm tempted to finish what that fucker started and burn that place to the ground so you won't have anywhere to go but to me. But that's 'cause I'm selfish too. But I'll find a way to get right with it, only 'cause I can't breathe without knowin' you're safe. This month, not being able to see you, has been hell. Having everyone see you?" He shook his head. "'Spect that'll be similar. But I'll deal."

I drank in his words, sweet and bitter at the same time. Everything I wanted to hear but nothing I could handle.

"I can't stay away from you, Becky," he whispered, his voice hoarse.

I stared at him. "I don't want you to," I admitted, sick of lying to myself. "But I don't know how to be around you now. I barely know how to be around myself. It hurts to see you. What you are. What I turned you into. But it hurts so much more not to see you."

He stepped forward, careful not to touch me. "You didn't turn me into anything," he growled. "They did. And they'll die a thousand fuckin' deaths once I get my hands on them, you can trust that. You're sayin' *you're* selfish? I gotta be too. I can't not be around you, babe. Just can't. I'll wait for however long it takes for you to get to know yourself. I'll wait a fuckin' year just to get you to hold my fuckin' hand. But I'll be waiting here." He pointed to the ground between us. "Not close enough to touch, but close enough to fuckin' feel. Feel the way the bitterness on my tongue goes away knowin' you're here, breathin', existin' survivin'. And I won't go 'cause I know, underneath it all, you don't want me to either."

My shaking hands went to my hair and he followed their journey. "Okay," I whispered.

He jolted.

"But I don't know how long I'll take. You could be old and fat and gray by the time I'm ready."

A shadow of his old grin tickled his face as he rubbed his flat stomach. "Can't fatten a thoroughbred." He winked. "You look wiped. Can I walk the lady to her car?"

I nodded, slightly thrown by the change in persona. It was something I was coming to expect, but the effect was that much more jarring when I could see through the transparency of his actions.

We started walking together in silence until we got to my beat-up car.

He faced me. "Any chance you've changed your mind about getting up on stage?"

I raised a brow. "In the thirty seconds it took us to reach my car?"

He nodded seriously.

"No. I'm stubborn. You know that. And it's what I'm going to do, like it or not."

His eyes flickered. "I'm gonna go with not. But I'll deal."

"'Deal' does not mean you shoot anyone in the audience."

He scowled at me. "When was that agreed upon?"

"I think that's just something universally known. You don't shoot people for patroning a strip club," I said, rifling through my bag for my keys. I was driving now, all by myself, with only one panic attack that had me parked on the side of the road for half an hour. But I dealt. I found them and glanced back up at Gabriel. "One you seem to own, so I think shootings might hurt your bottom line."

He clenched his jaw. "I don't give a fuck about my bottom line. I give a fuck about you."

I sucked in a breath, trying to find a way to navigate this situation. Gabriel beat me to it when his eyes zeroed in on my arm.

"Becky," he said quietly, almost a whisper. "You get a tattoo?"

I couldn't quite understand his tone, so I turned my arm up for him to inspect, careful to keep from touching distance. It was healing now, flaking at the edges, but still looking pretty kick-ass.

Tattoos were definitely something I could get addicted to.

Though that wasn't saying much. I could get addicted to anything— Pop-Tarts, serial killer documentaries, people. More accurately, the man in front of me tracing my new ink with his hazel eyes.

"*The Walking Dead*, I dig it," he said finally.

I frowned at him. "I'm kind of used to following your train of thought, but even I'm lost now."

His eyes met mine. Something twinkled from underneath their new hard shell. "The quote. It's from *The Walking Dead*. Great show. Glenn is, like, my spirit animal. You're definitely Maggie."

I blinked at him. "Okay, I have no clue what you're talking about, but this quote isn't from a zombie show. It's from a book. Ever heard of them?"

He pretended to ponder. "They're just like really long magazines, right? Without the pictures?"

I wanted to smile. I almost did. That stupid little line gave me hope that Gabriel was still there. That this stranger was temporary and I hadn't damned him for eternity.

My hope was quashed when he stepped forward. When the stranger stepped forward and Gabriel disappeared. He made sure not to touch me.

"Why, babe?" He nodded down to the ink.

I swallowed. "I'm covered in scars that I didn't get a choice in." I glanced down at the one on my arm from where the handcuffs had scraped my wrist almost to the bone. "Most of them you can't see. Which is good 'cause if you could, that's all you'd ever see. The ribbons of scarred skin, the ruins of me. I wanted to put something permanent there that I designed, that I controlled. I've got a mostly blank canvas on the outside, so maybe if I cover it with beauty I can disguise the ugly, even from myself."

He stood there for a long time after I said those words, digesting them. "I hate this," he rasped, his voice rough with emotion. "That you can't see that you are beautiful, with or without the ink. Though, I can admit, the prospect of you covered is fuckin' brilliant." He gazed at me. "I hate that this darkness has settled over you, swallowed you so you're blind to your magnificence."

I stared at him. "I hate it too. But it's life. And I'm here. And that's it," I whispered.

"I'm gonna get you out, baby. If that's the last thing I do, I'll tear you out of the shadow of this fucking thing."

I stared at him. "That's the thing. I don't need the light, and I don't need saving. I'm learning to love this darkness because I've realized it's always going to be me. There's no changing what they did, only learning to accept what they made me. What I've turned into to survive. And I think the only place I can survive is the hell I'm in. I'll make it homey, chuck in some throw pillows. I think I can survive here. Maybe even live, actually *live.* Not as the same person I was before, but as someone who kind of resembles her." I glanced down at my arm. "Or maybe someone completely different, a whole new stranger I'll get to know. Either way, I've got to find a way to embrace it all. The ugly, shitty, and uglier."

He nodded. "Okay."

"Okay?"

"If I can't bring my Becky back into the light, then I'll just have to make the dark comfortable as fuck. Make it better than before. If you're settling into hell, then I'll make it our own version of heaven. Let the darkness come."

This was a lot.

Too much.

"Why do we always have these conversations in fucking parking lots?" I huffed.

He shrugged. "'Cause mostly our shit's too big to be contained in one room. We need the open air to swallow it up, give us a chance to breathe. And we will. Breathe, that is." He leaned in to take the keys from me. His tattooed hand just brushed mine, but it was enough to set my skin afire with ice. I stepped back, hitting the side of my car.

He pretended to ignore that and unlocked it for me, putting the keys in the ignition. "Go home, babe. Breathe," he ordered softly. "'Cause I know this, us, even without the monsters in your head, is hard for you to fathom. So go have some time. Some. Not a lot. Then we'll take it slow. Take the darkness. Make it ours."

He moved forward, like he wanted to kiss me. I stiffened and he caught himself. Instead he gave me a stiff nod and walked away.

I watched the leather of his cut as he did so. Watched the darkness trail behind him like invisible smoke only I could see.

I sucked in a breath. Then another one.

Then I got in the car. And it wasn't empty. It was full with my monsters. The ones I was yet to tame.

LUCKY

He leaned forward on the table, clenching his fists. "She can't deal with anyone touching her," he bit out. He kept his head down but felt the atmosphere in the room change. "Even Lily. Her fuckin' best friend. Says she can't even stand her touch. Makes her feel *dirty*," he spat, his body shaking. He snapped his head up, meeting his president's troubled gaze. "Why the fuck don't I have anyone to punish for that, Cade? Someone whose skin I can rip off their fuckin' face? It's been *weeks*. And I don't get that. It's easy. Track down scumbags. Kill scumbags. Rinse, repeat."

Weeks of false leads. Of sitting on his fucking hands, going insane. That's what it felt like. His sanity came back and forward.

He'd lost it the second he found out from Gage that she was going to be stripping. Jesus, he'd put his hands on her, in anger. He'd made her feel *dirty*. He'd put that look on her face, the one that would go along with the other images of her in that room, chipping away at his sanity.

He was surprised he'd lasted that long without going around the bend. Giving in completely and utterly to the darkness that had beckoned him since he'd kicked that door in.

She'd stopped him from welcoming it, knowing she'd need him. He fuckin' needed her, more than anything. Those snatched minutes he'd had on her doorstep weren't enough—fuck, he didn't even know if havin' her chained to his side would be enough—but they were something. They took the edge off. When he saw her strength, saw glimpses of his old Becky glistening through the cracks of the new, beautiful, broken one, he had hope. Found some strength of his own. He needed her more than breath. Even more than revenge. But he still wanted that. He needed it if he was going to avoid a padded room.

Cade leaned forward. "You know why," he said, his voice even. "We've got no fuckin' intel on Carlos since this shit went down. He's a fuckin' ghost. Same with the Tuckers. They've gone underground, got lackeys runnin' their businesses who don't know shit. Now that they've got the money and firepower behind them, they've got the upper hand."

Lucky crashed his fist down on the table. "Well, we need to get it back," he roared. "I don't care what it takes, who I have to end to get that fuckin' intel. I'm doin' that. I'll go rogue if that's what it takes. In a fuckin' second. So we're gonna spill some blood. Or I'm gonna spill *a lot*. Either way, I'm sending some fuckers to the reaper."

He stood and stormed out of the room, leaving it behind with one destination in mind.

The bottom of a fucking bottle.

TWENTY

"I think Hell is something that you carry around with you.
Not somewhere you go."
-Neil Gaiman

"Are you flipping serious?" Lily exclaimed when I emerged from my room.

I glanced to Rosie, who was doing her lipstick in her compact. "I guess she told you."

I glanced back to my best friend's furious face. She had her arms folded. "Yeah, she told me. I was hoping that she was joking or suffering from a mental break." She glanced to Rosie. "No offense."

Rosie shrugged. "None taken. It could totally happen. Sanity's not something I've got an ironclad hold on. I'm at peace with it. "

I put my hand on my hip. "I thought you said you supported my decision," I snapped at her.

"I do. But mostly when I support decisions, there should be a red light flashing somewhere. Right about there." She pointed to the wall above my head.

I rolled my eyes and moved to pick up my other boot which I'd been searching for. It was the last thing I needed to leave the house. The last little piece of armor.

Lily snatched it from my grasp before I could get it.

I straightened, scowling at her. "Give me my boot, Lil."

She scowled back. "No. I will not give it back until you tell me you're not going."

"Well then, I'll have to find some new footwear. Because I'm going," I said firmly.

"No, you're not," she argued.

"Yes, I am."

"Fuck!" she shouted and I flinched at not only the volume of her voice, but the word itself. Lily didn't curse. Hardly ever. And there she was, cursing, injecting a shitload of feelings in that one ugly word.

She stepped forward, her eyes glistening. "You can't go back there," she croaked. "To that, after what you went through. I can't let you."

"I have to," I whispered. "That's the only place I can go back. Where I can make sense. Scramble up a bit of fucking normalcy. I can't hide away in here for the rest of my life, going insane. Only rich people get to wallow in insanity. Everyone else has to figure a way through it, make bank. This is my way through, Lils."

It was the reopening of the Diamond Lounge. It had almost burned the day... my mind stuttered. When they'd taken me they'd lured Lily there, tried to kill her and Gabriel. I swallowed ash at the prospect of going there, literally dancing on the spot my best friend and my... he almost died.

It wasn't like dancing on their graves since they were both alive, but it was like dancing on mine because that was the place I'd been before. The person I was before.

"You're only just getting back on your feet. You're getting through. Considering what happened to you...." Lily's eyes were pleading.

"Considering what happened to me, reclaiming my body for myself is the best thing for me to do," I said firmly. I reached forward to squeeze her hand, ignoring my own discomfort at doing so. She needed the contact, so I breathed through it. "Lil, they've still got it. Got me in that terrible fucking room. I've got to do something to steal it back from them. To show them and show myself I've got some fucking agency over my own body. Taking my clothes off for a room full of horny men doesn't seem to you like that's what I'm doing, but that's what it is for me. Normal."

She blinked at me a couple times and then nodded, handing me my boot.

"Thanks, babe."

"I'm coming," she declared.

"No, you're not," I said firmly. No way was I subjecting her to flashbacks of that shit.

She folded her arms. "You can't stop me. You're gonna take back your body? Well, I'm gonna take back mine too."

I straightened from putting my boot on. "Well, shit. I love that biker most of the time for helping you realize how kick-ass you are, but I kind of hate him now. You're giving me a run for my money."

Her face went sad. "No, you'll always hold the title for most kick-ass," she said quietly.

I shook the moment off. "Well yes, because of my choice of footwear. Much better ass-kicking attire than those." I nodded to her pink open-toed stilettos. They looked expensive, no doubt a gift from Asher. He did that often. Gave her shit, shit that she never could have afforded. He spoiled her.

I loved him for that too.

••••

"Does Lucky know about this?" Lily asked in the car on the way to the club.

"Yeah, he knows," I muttered.

"Oh I sense juice," Rosie said, tapping the staring wheel.

"How did he take it? Not the best, I'm guessing," Lily asked.

"You could say that," I muttered, my body going cold at his violent reaction. "He's dealing."

Lily gaped at me. "Lucky's dealing?" she repeated.

Rosie met my eyes. "Does *dealing* mean he's going to brandish his gun at the door and make sure no one with a dick enters the premises?"

I folded my arms, frowning. "No, we spoke about that. He promised not to shoot anyone."

Rosie grinned. "Yeah, he promised not to *shoot* anyone. That still doesn't rule out threatening to shoot."

"Fuck," I muttered as we pulled into the parking lot. I grabbed my phone.

Me: You are also forbidden from brandishing any kind of deadly weapon to intimidate people tonight.

I gathered my stuff and got ready to exit the car. Lily's small voice stopped me. "Are you sure you want to do this, babe?" she asked, her face pinched with concern.

"Why does everyone keep asking me that?" I whined.

Rosie raised her brow at me. "Maybe because it's only been a month and a half since you've gotten back from Dante's Inferno and you're ready to strip in front of half the male population?" she deadpanned.

I scowled at her. "I'm not sure what everyone expects me to do. Hide away in my bedroom, too scared to face the world in case it presents me with horrors? Not really my style." I didn't add that, alone at night, in my bedroom, was where the worst horrors were presented.

"And that's why I want to be you when I grow up," Rosie said, smiling sadly.

"Oh trust me, you do not want to be like this."

She frowned. "Agree to disagree, babe."

I rolled my eyes and looked back to Lily. "You understand why I've got to do this?" I asked quietly.

She chewed her lip. "Yeah," she whispered. "But I fucking hate that I understand it. I hate that you have to."

Her tears hit me hard.

She managed to pull it together. "But I'm also proud. And I know Mom would be too."

Okay, right in the heart. Or the lump of coal that was lying in my ribcage. My phone dinged.

> **Gabriel:** No fair :(That means I can't come at all because my entire body is a deadly weapon. Take it back.

I would have thought such an expression was impossible after Lily's words, but I grinned down at the text.

> **Me:** You're officially an idiot. I'll clarify to say no physical weapons of any sort to be used.

ANNE MALCOM

"What's so funny?" Lily asked as we walked to the doors.

I glanced up. "Just Lucky."

She smiled. "Remind me to kiss that man when I see him."

Get in line, sister.

••••

I was fine with the multitude of stares from the girls and bikers in the club when I arrived. Even with the old lady posse who swarmed me as soon as I walked in. Though, thankfully, they must have been clued in on my 'no touch' rule because they kept their distance. I was fine putting makeup on in the crowded dressing room, fielding the stares of the fellow dancers, pretending not to hear their whispers. They weren't malicious, but I didn't think they expected me there.

I was fine slipping into my costume for the night.

Well, fine wasn't exactly it. I was desperate for a fucking fix. I sat in my dressing chair, tapping my feet and fingers just so I didn't scratch my arms raw. Doing this sober, while trying not to think of what I was doing and how much it affected Gabriel, was not a breeze.

But I managed.

Just.

> **Gabriel:** Break a leg.
>
> **Gabriel:** Please don't actually break anything.
>
> **Gabriel:** Now I'm worried about the safety precautions of this place. It doesn't have a good track record. I heard someone got shot here.
>
> **Gabriel:** Take good care of those legs please.

His rapid-fire texts not only gave me something to concentrate on, but something to smile about. Not actually smile, but almost smile.

"You're up, babe," Cadence said.

My blood ran cold but I stood, reluctantly placing my phone and my connection to Gabriel down.

She looked me up and down. "You look hot."

I did. Slathered in heavy makeup and red lipstick, my newly cropped hair spiking out in all directions. My outfit wasn't much, all black with suspenders, ripped fishnets, and combat boots, but it was me. And me was good.

She glanced to the curtain. "There are a lot of people out there. A lot of guys from the club, though I hear they're all under strict orders to look at their feet the moment you strut your ass out there." She grinned. "It may or may not have to do with a certain biker sitting front and center who just asked me what our history was with people tripping on loose floorboards."

I rolled my eyes.

She went serious. "You don't want to do this, no one's gonna judge you."

I straightened my back. "I can do this," I declared. "People are gonna judge me either way."

And as if on cue, my music sounded.

I was fine the entire walk done the T-shaped stage. The music was pulsing in my ears, the lights obscuring most of the audience. Then I got to the end. To the pole. And the lights were bright. There was no hiding under makeup or costumes—they showed it all. The dirt, the filth, the spots where fire had eaten away the wood I was standing on. The blood. His blood. His life nearly draining away on that exact spot.

The spot where I was going to shake my fuckin' ass and strip.

I tasted bile.

People were watching. I couldn't see them, but I could feel their stares and I knew they saw.

The music faded away. The lights. The cavernous room.

Everything was colder, darker, smaller. More painful.

I was there, with them, and I couldn't escape.

●●●●

I blinked awake in a second. Everything was there in a rush, jarring and slightly unnerving.

Gabriel stood immediately once he saw me push myself up from the bed.

He rushed forward, moving like he was going to cup my face, but he stopped at the last minute.

"You're awake." The two words were drenched in relief.

I frowned at my surroundings, understanding where I was due to the motorcycle paraphernalia and the musky scent of the sheets.

I was at his place.

In his bed.

The knowledge was both comforting and disconcerting.

"I wasn't aware I went to sleep," I said, my voice thick with confusion, my head foggy.

His face turned blank and the cords in his neck pulsed. "You didn't exactly... go to sleep. Babe, you just kind of left the building. Terrified the absolute shit outta me."

I remembered. The club. The stage. The lights. It all melting away and the room replacing it. "Shit," I whispered.

He nodded tightly. "Yeah."

I put my hand to my head. "I'm such an idiot," I groaned.

He went still. "What?"

"I pretty much went cationic in front of a room full of people. That's it, my job is toast."

And my paycheck. And any chance I had for earning enough money to give me a chance to stand on my own two feet. Or, as it seemed, collapse on my own two feet.

"Who gives a fuck about the job? About the people? I'm worried about you," he growled, stepping even closer to the bed. "Becky, I saw it. You were there, beautiful, magnificent, hot-as-fuck Becky. Then it all drained away, like someone pulled your plug and you were just... gone." He shuddered, actually fucking shuddered. "I thought it was bad seeing the pain, the brokenness in your eyes, but I'll take it over not seeing anything."

"I don't even know what happened," I whispered.

"Flashback," he clipped. "Never seen one happen like that, but that's what it was. Something triggered it when you were up there, sucked you outta that room and back... there."

The silence that bathed us was uncomfortable and prickly, both of us knowing where 'there' was.

"So I guess I was wrong," I said finally. "I don't even have control over my body, what I do with it. My body has control over me." The thought was exhausting and rather depressing.

Gabriel gritted his teeth. "It's killin' me not to touch you right now, babe."

I stiffened at the prospect. I wanted him to. Wanted some illusion of safety that his tattooed arms offered. But my skin felt like it was made of tissue paper. If his callused hands touched me, it might just tear.

"I won't," he reassured me, noting my reaction. "But you've got control over that. Over me. Hold onto that, if nothing else. You may not be able to control how your body deals what you went through, but you control me. I breathe because you breathe, babe. You ask me to walk through the streets wearin' nothing but one of those Borat suits, I'll do it. I won't like it, but I'll do it. Plus, we both know I'd wear the shit outta that thing."

I let out a choked laugh, despite the situation.

His eyes twinkled. "There she is," he murmured. "You're not lost, or gone, Becky. You're still there, in your cocoon, waiting for the time that you've evolved enough to come out. Patience, my dear grasshopper. Patience is all you need."

I quirked an eyebrow at him. "Patience is a virtue, and we both know I don't have any of those."

He narrowed his eyes. "You've got many, many other more valuable traits than boring old virtues." He paused. "I know I don't have the right to ask, and if you want me to take you home, I will in a fuckin' second, but do you want to stay here? I'll take the couch," he said quickly. "Gentleman that I am."

I gazed at him for a long moment. "No," I whispered.

His eyes hardened at the edges. "No problem. I get that you want to be with your girls.

"No," I said again. "You won't have the couch."

His face changed. "Becky," he rasped.

I looked from side to side. "This is a big bed. Big enough for the both of us. I want to stay. I don't think I could be anywhere else but right here with you. If I go anywhere else I'll be...there." I paused. "So I need you."

Those four words were terrible to say, to admit, but I did it. For my sanity.

And maybe for his too.

He nodded and made his way over to the other side of the bed. I listened to the thud of his boots, the bed jostling as his weight hit it.

I turned on my side to watch him get in. Once he was on, he did the same, his face so close to mine I could feel his breath. He didn't touch me, though. It was as if there was a small glass barrier between our two bodies.

His eyes searched mine. "This okay?"

No. It wasn't okay because all I wanted was to smash that glass.

But that thought sent trails of ghost hands up my legs. They weren't gone yet, and I wasn't letting him touch me while the memory of their grip remained.

"Yes," I whispered. I could have left it there, but I didn't. "It's the most okay I've been since Reno."

His eyes flared with heat and something else. "Good," he rumbled. "Me too."

LUCKY

THE NEXT DAY

Cade put the phone down, his face blank.

Lucky jerked his knee in frustration, knowing he couldn't shoot his president, one of his best friends, out of impatience, but he was fuckin' tempted.

"Tuckers want a meet." He'd addressed the table, but his gaze flickered to Lucky.

He laughed. "They got a fuckin' ounce of sense? They want a meet, they'll get one. They'll be meetin' the fuckin' reaper."

Gage slammed his fist down on the table. "A-fucking-men."

Cade's eyes focused on him. "They say they had no hand in what went on in that warehouse."

"They're fuckin' liars," Lucky exploded.

Cade nodded. "I expect they are. But they're also not stupid. They know we've got our brothers in from different charters." He nodded to Jagger, who was there from New Mexico, the rest of his crew set to arrive in the next few days. The scarred brother grinned back. "So we're not outnumbered. They're rats jumpin' from a sinkin' ship. Devlin's sinking ship."

Brock cracked his knuckles, his fury palpable. Devlin's father had kidnapped his old lady, nearly killed her. Now that his son was in charge, the brother was intent on ending the entire family line.

"We'll take the meet," Cade decided.

I can't shoot my president.

"Are you fuckin' insane?" Gage clipped.

Cade smiled. "No, but you are."

••••

The balding man in a suit, a fucking pinstripe suit, leaned back in his chair. "We regret this entire chain of events, Cade. Made bad decisions in our choices of business partners. That's all. Our family had nothing to do with your... misfortunes."

Lucky stood behind his prez and had to restrain himself from reaching for his gun. The itch was so bad his body was shaking.

"Misfortune?" he spat, stepping forward. He ignored how the fuck's goons stood with his movements. "You call kidnapping and almost killin' my woman misfortune? I call it suicide." He didn't even notice the guns pointed at his head until Cade's hand lifted in a lowering motion.

"Easy, brother," he muttered. Lucky's gaze flickered to the old man, who hadn't even stood. The fuck was arrogant enough to think he was untouchable. He would soon learn. "Mr. Tucker," Cade addressed him. "You'll kindly ask your sons to lower their guns." His voice was even but there was a threat in his tone, as if he were the one holding the firepower. Which he technically was, but they weren't to know that—yet.

Tucker jerked his head at the men, who immediately complied. "I understand tensions are running high, but you will believe me when I say our family was innocent in that crime. And as a show of regret of how we connected with the wrong people, we're willing to give you all the information we have on Mr. Devlin. As a gesture of peace." He nodded to the man at his left, who laid a paper on the table.

"And Carlos?" Cade asked.

"We have nothing on him, I regret to inform you. But shall he crawl out of whatever hole he's been hiding in, I'll let you know."

Cade nodded, holding his hand out for the folder.

Tucker held it at arm's length. "And we have your word that you'll forget that we made questionable business decisions, and understand that we had nothing to do with this horrible event?"

Cade nodded once. "My word is my bond."

Tucker looked relieved and handed him the folder. The minute Cade had it in his grasp, Bull and Brock stepped forward, planting two bullets in his son's brains while Lucky did the same with the white-haired piece of shit.

Gage and the rest of the brothers were exterminating the rest of the Tucker family off the face off the earth, making sure to leave Dylan for Lucky.

Cade stepped over to the jerking body in front of him. "My word's not my bond. Fuckin' bullets are." He lifted his piece and the man stopped jerking.

Brock rubbed his hands together. "One lot down, three to go."

Carlos and Devlin were likely to be harder to pin down, but they'd get them.

Bull stepped forward, lowering his phone from his ear. "Got news." His gaze was fixed on Lucky.

"What the fuck happened now?" he gritted out, his mind immediately going to Becky.

"They got all the Tuckers. Except one."

He knew who it was before Bull confirmed it.

"Dylan."

"Fuck!" he roared in frustration.

He found a sense of calm. They'd get him. He'd get him. Because he had to.

It was that simple.

TWENTY-ONE

"Love her, but leave her wild."
-Atticus

ONE MONTH LATER

"I want you to move in with me."

I shifted my eyes from the skin that was turning into something beautiful, covering the ugly—on the outside, at least—to Gabriel's honeyed gaze. "What?"

He frowned at me. "You heard me."

I frowned back. "Yes, I heard, but I was giving you a chance to rectify your Tourette's."

He grinned at me, reaching out to play with my fingers.

That was okay, that touch. We'd worked our way up to it, and his patience was reminiscent of a monk. Night spent watching stupid movies at opposite ends of the sofa, that invisible glass between us. There were moments, a lot of them actually, when he caught himself about to stroke my face, bring me to his body, kiss me. He stopped himself before contact was made.

Every time, every single time, I was both relieved and disappointed.

And each time, there was a little more disappointment and a little more relief.

I was healing.

It was a slow process.

Snail's pace.

A frustrating one at that. Even now, a month later, I still had the constant itch, constant need for nothingness when I woke up and went to sleep overflowing with the weight of it all. Of everything. And no matter how much sleep I got—which ranged from not enough to too much—I couldn't beat the exhaustion. Because from dawn till dusk, I was fighting. And the battle was rough, and gritty, and ugly.

But I was winning.

I think.

Obviously I didn't go back to stripping after the whole fiasco that everyone kindly pretended didn't happen.

Cade had walked up to me in Gabriel's kitchen the next morning, his eyes soft. "You good at math?"

I frowned at him through my coffee mug. "Math?" I repeated. I'd only had two coffees, but even at full Bex I reasoned I'd still be confused by the greeting. These macho bikers had their own language that I needed to become fluent in if I planned on living in their world.

I was finding I kind of was.

Maybe.

"Accounts, expenses, that type of shit."

I nodded slowly. I had been premed, and I had a logical brain. All that chemical and number crap had come easy to me. It had rules, limitations. I liked that in the limitless world I was living in. It was comforting.

He gave me a small smile. "Good. We need someone since our current bookkeeper is useless." His gray stare flickered to Gabriel, who was leaning against the stove, sipping from his own cup and wearing low-slung sweats. And nothing else.

I should have gotten an award or something for maintaining eye contact with Cade the entire conversation.

Okay, not the *entire* conversation. Maybe like eighty percent of it.

"Words hurt, you know," Gabriel shot back in a faux wounded voice.

I rolled my eyes and focused on my coffee.

"So?" Cade asked, looking back to me.

My eyes, which had crept back to Gabriel's abs, snapped to Cade. "So?"

He did the mouth twitch. "You want the job?"

He had my full attention then. A job where I didn't have to sell my body? I didn't want to seem too eager, like jump up and down or anything, so I took another sip. "What's the pay like?" I asked, playing it cool

"More than what you got on the stage."

"I got pretty good tips."

"Including tips. It's still generous."

I nodded. "And the benefits?"

"Full."

I took another sip, and then something occurred to me. "Just so we're clear, this isn't charity, right? Because I don't need that."

The mouth twitch disappeared. "No, it's not," he said firmly. "We need someone who won't run our business to the ground, and Gwen mentioned you'd been premed so I figured you'd be smarter than someone who didn't graduate high school." He gave Gabriel a look, though not at his abs like I had been. He moved his attention back to me. "We need you. It's not charity. I'll expect you to work."

I gaped at him. "Wow, I think that's the longest and most complete sentence I've ever heard you say."

The mouth twitch came back. "So that's a yes?"

"That's a yes."

He was right; it wasn't charity. It was hard work. The books were a fucking mess and it took me a week to get them in order again. But I loved it. Got lost in the numbers and the logic of it all. I could find it there, some form of escape from my world free of logic.

So that was a part of it.

Not the biggest.

He was the biggest. And now he was sitting there, asking that. Something that would shake up my only just-settled world. Or as settled as chaos could be.

He kissed my fingertips and I shivered with the contact. "I'm not askin' in the way you're thinkin'. I've got the spare bedroom cleared of shit and ready for you, if you want it."

I glanced at him and then down to Lex, who was concentrating on my ink. I was getting kind of addicted to it. Since that first prick of pain with Lily and Rosie, all I'd wanted was more. More of the pain to distract me from everything else, more of the ink to cover the scars that wouldn't heal. More control over my body, even if it was just what was happening on the outside.

So I was getting a full sleeve done. I had known immediately what I wanted—a fairy tale, right there on my arm. Because I couldn't have one, but I could make one. Though this was a little different. I had the trademark castle on my shoulder, which had been done last week. It was beautiful, intricate, a peaceful array of pastels and rainbows. Half of it was, at least. The other half was black shadows, a stormy sky, gargoyles coming to life from the turrets.

A confluence of what I wished for and what I got.

A reminder that I could have both and neither. That I was pulling myself off that dark place in pursuit of the sunshine and rainbows. But I wouldn't exactly get that. I'd have somewhere in between.

And as soon as Gabriel had heard that's what I was doing, he'd insisted to come 'to hold my hand.'

"I don't need anyone to hold my hand," I'd informed him, frowning.

He'd grinned. "But I need someone to hold my hand."

So he came, and right then, he was holding my hand.

And I'd never admit it out loud, but I needed it.

"You're really going to have this conversation in front of Lex?" I nodded to the heavyset, tattooed man bent over my arm. "You'll make him uncomfortable.

He didn't look up. "I'm not uncomfortable."

I scowled at his tattooed head. "Dude, I thought we were friends."

"We are friends," he replied over the buzzing of his gun.

"Not anymore," I muttered.

He chuckled and continued his work silently.

Gabriel grinned at me. I was getting used to that too. The way his grin had changed, warped from the easy one I'd been used to, to something different. Something darker.

It's where we lived now, the darkness. It wasn't exactly comfortable, but I was getting used to the shadows.

"So, Lex approves. What more do you need?"

"It's not what I need," I argued. "It's what *you* need, which is a reality check. We are not even properly together and you want to move in together? Like that's not a recipe for disaster."

Gabriel's eyes darkened. "We're fuckin' together," he growled. He exerted gentle pressure on my hand. "I want you at my place, where I can see you all the time. Know you're safe," he declared.

I didn't lower my eyes, even though his stare was making me uncomfortable, confronting me with reality. Yeah, we were together, and that thought filled me with equal parts joy and dread. I swallowed both with effort. "Well, I want a lifetime supply of Chunky Monkey and a Golden Globe. Life doesn't always give us what we want," I stated matter-of-factly.

When in doubt, use sarcasm.

Gabriel clenched his jaw and glanced to my arm, not saying anything.

Score, I'd won. Why didn't victory taste sweet?

Because you wanted him to fight harder. Even though you know how fucked-up it is, how much you'd tarnish him even more by moving in, you know it's a fantasy, but you want it.

"Done," Lex grunted, moving my attention outwards.

He wiped the ink and blood off my arm to reveal my latest piece. I stared at it, as did Gabriel.

"Wow," I muttered.

It looked awesome. On the inside of my arm, above my very first tattoo, was an intricate and beautiful picture of a girl, a princess. Everything innocent and beautiful about her face, right down to the crown—on one half, at least. On the other side of her head, the crown wasn't shiny and glistening; it was tarnished and cracked, dark and sharp. Her face was no longer innocent but half a skeleton, decaying but still somehow beautiful.

Right above my favorite vein was me. I wasn't the skeleton, and I sure as shit wasn't the princess. I was both. A reminder of what I'd turned into from the moment I injected it.

"Fuck," Gabriel exclaimed, rubbing his mouth roughly. He glanced to Lex, who was rustling and putting his shit away. "You're a genius, bro. Didn't think you could make that skin any more beautiful, but you did."

Lex nodded. "It's my job."

Gabriel grinned. "Well, as soon as I find a blank space on this beautiful canvas"—he gestured down to his body—"I want that." He nodded to my arm.

I sucked in a breath. "You want this?" I held up my red and aching arm.

He nodded. "Fuck yeah, I do."

I glared at this. "But this is *my* tattoo. This is me. Why the fuck do you think I'm going to let you get it?" I hissed, anger bubbling from my words.

"I'm just gonna wait outside," Lex declared.

Gabriel's eyes didn't move from mine. "Yeah, good call, bro. Assume brace positions."

I scowled at him even deeper, pushing up and wrenching from his grip. "I can't believe you want to take my tattoo from me," I seethed, pacing the room.

He stood, striding over to me. His hands settled at my hips, stilling me. "I'm not takin' it away from you, Becky," he murmured.

I bit my lip. "That's what it feels like."

He reached up to stroke my face. "Yeah, well, it's not that. It's me havin' a piece of you where I can see it. Remind myself that you're here. That you're fighting. That you made it through. I've got all that tattooed on the inside, but it's gnarly and ugly." His hand skimmed past the tattoo to hold my wrist. "I need somethin' different on the outside. Just like you do."

My anger fizzled away quickly as his words touched me. And his hands touched me. And it didn't feel dirty or wrong.

It was right.

Maybe slightly fucked-up, but it was right.

••••

The next day, Gabriel got the tattoo.

The fucking next day. And he got it on the only blank space he had—above his heart, where the scar of the bullet wound marred his smooth skin. He'd insisted I be there, to hold his hand.

But really, I needed him there to hold mine as I watched Lex cover the evidence of the past. Of both of our little deaths.

We'd gone back to my place, me on the back of his bike. I could do that now, ride on the back. Have my whole body pressed against his without drowning in the filth of the contact. It was still there, but I could paddle in it.

His fingers twined in mine as we opened the door to Rosie's place. Once he knew I could handle that contact, he made sure to keep us connected almost every second we were together.

Which was a lot these days. He came over every night and watched movies, or watched me watch movies. His gaze was electric and weary, like he was waiting for something. For me to break, maybe. Or for someone to try and break me again. I didn't miss the way his eyes scouted all public spaces we went to together, how he insist he do a 'walk-through' of Rosie's before I went in. Which was what he released my hands to do now.

I knew they were on the revenge train. It was kind of hard to miss the previous week's news that the entire Tucker family had died in a 'tragic fire' at their family compound.

I hadn't mentioned it to Gabriel. Not yet. Because they were very intent on getting revenge for me. I was even more intent on getting it for myself. I just didn't know how to do that. Luckily, Rosie 'knew people' and had 'put out feelers.'

I had a feeling that chick had a lot more to her than ever-changing outfits and a revolving dating door.

A lot.

So I was playing the part. The one of the woman who needed the men in cuts to fight her battles for her. One in particular. I knew he needed it to somehow find comfort in the darkness, just like me. Because he was healing too, and I wanted to give him that. But I wanted to take it for myself.

"No monsters hiding in my closet?" I asked, folding my arms as he walked back to the front door.

He grinned wickedly. "Oh, there's plenty. But they're friendly."

I wish.

"So," he started, stepping forward, "do you want help packing, or will it break some kind of chick rule for me to handle your unmentionables?" His gaze went hooded. "Though if it doesn't, I'm requesting that exact job."

I scowled at him. "I'm not moving in with you," I told him firmly.

"Yes, you are," he argued.

I restrained my urge to fight, to swear my way out of this situation. Namely because I didn't want to fight with Gabriel. We were both fighting enough battles; we didn't need to fight each other. So I took a breath, glancing down at our boots, inches away from each other. "I have to figure myself out before I can give you anything. I have to find out who I am without the drugs, without the stripping, without the filth. That new person is just being made, coming to life after I died those months ago." I found my strength and glanced into his glittering eyes. "Because that's what happened. I died. A part of me. A big fucking part. The part I held most precious because it was the part I thought had survived everything. Would survive everything." I paused, sucking in a breath. "I need to find a way to come back to life before I can make anything with you. I need time," I whispered.

His eyes still glittered, twinkled with emotion that I couldn't place, and his usually expressive face was blank, the small twitch in his jaw the only thing distinguishing him from a statue. That and the way my blood sang for him, yearned for him.

He stepped forward, so close his body brushed mine and I was engulfed in his musky scent. He didn't touch me, though, at least not physically. Though he held me just the same, every inch of me, whoever 'me' was.

"You didn't die," he rasped, his voice like sandpaper. He lifted his hand and trailed it lightly down my cheek, his eyes watching its progress. "You, my little firefly, turned into a chrysalis, a cocoon that protected that soft, beautiful part of you that somehow survived what would destroy most people." His hand moved down to my collarbone. "It took a while for the outer parts of you to heal, but now you're comin' out of that cocoon, becoming what you've always been. Evolving into something more beautiful than before." He took a breath. "You need time to get to know this new beautiful thing you've turned into, you got it. You want to learn to love the woman you see in the mirror every day, fine with me." His hand circled my neck and pulled me gently so our foreheads were touching and his eyes burned into mine. "You can have all of that, but I'm not going anywhere. You see, I've always known that beautiful thing you've turned into, always seen it. And I don't need to learn to love the woman you see in the mirror." His nose rubbed against mine and I struggled to breathe. "'Cause I already do. Have since the moment you talked about nuts covered in piss."

Before I had the chance to respond, he pulled back and stared at me. I expected him to say something else, or to pressure me to say something. Instead, he gave me a small, dark grin.

"See you tomorrow, firefly."

Then he was gone.

That guy so knew how to make an exit.

TWENTY-TWO

*"Sometimes the most courageous act a human can do
is to let somebody love them."*
-Michael Xavier

"Great. More fucking visitors," I muttered to myself. I walked through the hallway to the door it felt like I'd just closed on Lizzie. I'd contemplated ignoring it, but then I thought it might be some big bad biker man who would take my not answering to mean I'd been kidnapped or was hanging from a shower rod. Then he'd take it upon his muscled shoulders to kick the door down and stomp in and save the day. I heard they did that sort of thing rather frequently. So to save Rosie's door, I answered.

I couldn't have been more surprised at who the knocker was when I burst it open. Instead of some biker man, it was a biker chick. *The* biker chick. Or queen, to be exact. Evie was someone I'd only met in passing and she'd made it more than clear what she thought of me, which was not much. Not that I blamed her. She was hard. There was something behind those only slightly wrinkled eyes that saw through the bullshit.

Which had been dangerous before.

Now it was downright terrifying.

She quirked a brow. "You gonna invite me in or just stare at me like that?" she asked, her voice husky and raw.

I was taken aback by the greeting. Everyone had taken to treating me with care since I'd been back, like I was breakable. Fragile. Rosie was a slight exception, but even her concern cracked through. They meant well, I knew, but the best way to make someone feel weak was to treat them like they were about to fall apart.

It seemed Evie wasn't going to do that. I opened the door and she strutted through it, her large fringed leather handbag swinging in the crook of her arm. I dutifully followed her back into Rosie's living room. It looked like a hippy, a biker and a fashionista had vomited all over it. The whole room was an identity crisis, but like Rosie herself, it worked.

Evie sat herself down on the white sofa, pushing a furry throw pillow out of the way.

I stared at her.

She stared back at me.

"Can I get you something? The blood of an infant, bottled unicorn tears?" I asked uneasily.

She quirked a brow, obviously not finding me funny. Then she looked me up and down. "I get it," she declared. "Why he picked you."

I immediately knew who she was talking about and I stiffened.

She either didn't notice or ignored it. "The fact you're still up and about, wearing crop tops, shows you've got guts. You're not hard on the eyes, either. Too skinny, though."

I frowned at her. "I'm not sure where this conversation is going, but then again I was lost before we started."

She eyed me. "I'm here to check on a girl who went through the hellest of hells and came out the other side. Not unscathed, I'm guessing, considering the boy I consider a son is full of fucking scars that will never heal."

I flinched at the no-nonsense tone of her husky voice.

She didn't miss that. "Yeah, I see you've caught them too. They're hard to miss. Though I guess impossible to miss when you see them in the mirror."

I didn't think she required an answer, so I moved to sit down in the sofa. Only so long I could stay standing under the weight of her words.

"You clean?" she asked.

I gaped at her. "You really don't do bullshit, do you?"

She shook her head. "This life, there is no bullshit. A lot of blood, bullets, and chaos, but no bullshit."

"I dig that." I eyed her. "I'm clean," I said. "Though I'm more depraved now than I was when I was using." I had no idea why I added that little personal gem. Maybe because I was tired of the bullshit

ANNE MALCOM

myself.

"That's called love. The most addictive and destructive substance out there. If used right, it can create." She looked at me shrewdly. "In your case, recreate." There was a pregnant pause. "If used wrong, it can flatten everything in your life and turn what remains into a gray wasteland."

I raised my brow. "I don't exactly understand what you're trying to convince me of here. That I should run back to the needle?"

She lit her smoke. "There a promise of anything going right with that needle? Way I see it, the only thing it promises is a barren wasteland, right or wrong." Her kohl-rimmed eyes narrowed on me. "What you've got with the kid, what he's offering you? Sure, if it goes bad it might resemble the wasteland that addiction is. But you give it a chance, you give him a chance, you might just find an oasis."

I chewed over her words as she puffed on her smoke, not bothered that I was silent. She arched her brow at me. "Though you decide that shit, you do it soon. Stop fuckin' him around. He'll follow you around like a lovesick puppy and feast on every scrap of hope you give him. Those men"—she nodded to the curb where Skid's bike was visible— "they don't love like normal men. Not in this life. They've chosen a life outside the lines of the coloring book called society. They live rough and hard. They love hard too. And mostly, it's for life. Even if you two explode into a blaze of disaster, he'll still hold the burning embers till the day the reaper takes him. I can see that in his eyes."

Cue girly stomach flip. Not a time to mull over that while I was getting life lessons from the biker matriarch.

"I've known him since he was a prospect runnin' from a street gang and used his good looks and smart mouth to guide him through the shit life threw at him. He's a good man. And if you hurt him, I'll run you over with my car and make it look like an accident," she declared, like she was mentioning she might have me out for dinner one night. It wasn't an empty threat; I'd heard plenty of those in my life. This was a promise. And despite the fact she was promising my murder, I liked it. I liked that for Lucky, that he had someone looking out for him. That he had a family. I liked that for Lily too. She lost the only family she had left when her mom died and was saddled with the junkie stripper fuckup for a best friend. Now she had a family that would kill for one another.

Not exactly Thanksgiving with Grandma, but it was good.

And on a little shelf in the dusty corners of my mind, I liked it for me too. That I might find a way to fit. Because this was Evie's roundabout way of welcoming me into the fold—with a death threat, but with a promise of family too.

I nodded slowly as it all sank in and I nurtured the little hope I had. "I won't hurt him. Not on purpose, at least." I had to cover my bases.

She put out her smoke and stood, hitching her bag on her shoulder. "I don't expect you will." She walked over to me and cupped my face in her manicured hand. I didn't flinch away like I had with most human touch recently. It didn't make my skin crawl or the dirt that more unbearable. It was kind of nice.

"What I see behind Lucky's eyes, I see it behind yours too. You're hiding behind your demons, baby. I know they're bigger and scarier than most, and I'll personally castrate the person who put them there given half the chance, but they're not indestructible. You're in charge of whether you let them win or not. Whether you give yourself a chance at something more than the shitty plate that life decided to hand you." She leaned in and I smelled vanilla and coconut as she kissed my head and straightened. "We got family dinner at my place next Sunday. You make the right choice, you'll be there."

On that note, she turned on her caged heel and left the room.

I put my head back on the sofa. "Well, fuck," I muttered to the ceiling.

••••

The next day, Gabriel turned up at my office, sauntering in and dripping his hotness all over the place. He leaned against the desk, staring at me.

"I can't concentrate with you just leaning there, being all hot," I snapped at him, not looking up.

His grin was palpable. "Well, I'm sorry, but hot is the only thing I know how to be. It's a blessing and a curse. Mostly a blessing 'cause I get to distract the beautiful Rebecca Flannery," he said, placing something on top of my budget sheet.

I glanced up at him, my stomach fluttering at the look on his face. And the stomach flutter was good. Or mostly so.

"What's this?" I asked, fingering the envelope in my hands.

His eyes twinkled. "Open it and find out."

I did as he instructed, and after a couple seconds scanning what was on the page I moved my head up to meet his eyes. "Is this for real?" I asked in disbelief.

He grinned. "Well, I don't know if it's technically going to be a *lifetime* supply considering ice cream could become obsolete when we turn into oil-consuming cyborgs. But for now, you'll never want for Chunky Monkey."

I gaped at him. The piece of paper was a delivery schedule from Ben & Jerry's, which stated a new delivery every week.

"Oh, and I would like to present you, Rebecca Flannery, with this." He pulled out a statue-like trophy from behind his back.

I took it automatically, surprised at the weight. My eyes near popped out of my head. "This looks surprisingly real," I said slowly, looking at the fake Golden Globe in my hands.

He merely shrugged.

"This is a fake, right?" I asked while reading the inscription.

He shrugged again. "Let's just say I know people. Who would you like to thank? The academy? Your agent? Or your positively amazing old man and soon-to-be roommate?"

I stopped my perusal of the statue and gave him my full attention.

"My body is my fortress, my dominion. When we lost Faith, I lost faith. Whatever shred I'd been clutching. Lost all control. Of everything apart from my body." I hugged my arms around my ribs. "I became the dictator of it. The dictator bent on destruction. Not because I was suicidal but because even through destruction came control. I was the agent of my own destiny, or in this case my own demise. In a world that gave me a life I had no control over, my body became my kingdom in which I ruled. There was a kind of brutal comfort in that. Then *they* came. They did those things. My control was lost. I held no dominion over myself. The one thing I had left to possess, even through the darkest depths of my addiction, was lost. They stole it. I became a stranger, a prisoner to myself. Now with you, this, the same thing is happening. I don't have control over this, over us. It could mean a destruction that isn't in my hands. It's in yours."

"I'd never fuckin' destroy you, baby. I'll treasure you."

"I know. At least I hope. But I can't trust that. Not now. Not when I've only just gotten the dominion of my own body back. I don't think I can pass over the keys to the kingdom just yet."

The cocktail of emotions in his eyes was enough for me to battle against the prickle of tears at the backs of mine. I wanted to throw myself into his arms, tell him I was his, now and forever. To give in to the fairy tale. To believe him. I almost did; my arm actually twitched. But I held stock-still because this wasn't a fairy tale. This was life. This was *my* life. The one I'd only just got back. The only one I had. And I couldn't lose myself in another addiction just as I'd kicked the last one.

"I get it," he said finally. "Fuckin' kills me, but I get it. You've got the keys to the kingdom, baby, and I'll wait for them 'cause it's prime real estate. Mine. And you can have your kingdom as long as you reside in my house."

I frowned at him. "I don't think you get me."

"Oh, I get you. But I'm havin' you under my roof. You'll get your own room. No funny business, I promise. I can keep my hands to myself, you know. I'm not an animal. Though I can't say the same for you, having my manly deliciousness within licking distance." He waggled his eyebrows and I couldn't help but surrender to the grin that tickled the corner of my mouth.

He was tempting me. With his stupid grin, with the fact he didn't blink at giving me what I wanted, even if it was ice cream. He wanted me. Me. After everything.

And I wanted him. After everything. I wanted nothing more than to move in with him. To be normal. Free from my nightmares.

But I was scared.

Terrified.

Not for me, for the grinning biker in front of me who apparently was willing to steal Golden Globes for me. To sell his soul for me.

"I'm never going to be free," I whispered. I didn't let the hardness of his jaw penetrate, and I straightened my back so I didn't look like I was hunched over feeling sorry for myself. I wasn't. Self-pity was an ugly emotion that I had no room for. "I'm okay with that. I'm at peace with that. I was born captured by a shitty childhood, and from then onwards I would live in captivity. I chose to chain myself to the needle. That's for life. I'll always be an addict, never be free of that label. It was a choice. It was on me, and I accept it." I sucked in a breath. "What they... did, I'll never be free of that either. It's something I've survived but I'll never be free from. I've accepted that too." I found the courage to meet his hazel eyes. "But you can be. You can be free from all of that. I have to live in captivity because I've got no choice. It's my life and I'll live with it, but I won't chain you down too. I won't. I care far too much about you to do that." I didn't say how much because admitting it to myself was another set of chains I couldn't accept. Because those didn't scratch at my psyche and jar me with discomfort. They felt nice. Right.

I swallowed. "I care too much about you to let you be captured by all of that shit. You deserve freedom."

My words floated into the air and hung there as his eyes never left mine, his gaze heavy on my face. That gaze said more than the mouthful I'd just uttered. It captured me in a way that I'd give away my freedom in a second to stay in it forever. Then he was in front of me, yanking me out of my chair so every inch of his body imprinted onto mine and his mouth covered mine, working against it with a ferocity I had no choice but to surrender to.

Just before my knees buckled, he let my mouth go, and I restrained a groan of protest. His forehead rested against mine.

"I care far too fuckin' much about you to let you live in captivity alone. I'd gladly take a cage with you than an open world without you. Freedom's just another word for nothing left to lose, and baby, I've got a fuck of a lot to lose."

I blinked rapidly at his words, my heart thundering in my chest. Then my brows knitted and I squinted up at him. "Did you just quote Janis Joplin?"

A shadow of a grin tickled the edge of the intensity on his face. "The woman's a wordsmith. I may have borrowed a line to get my point across," he murmured, cupping my chin. "You want to chain me up to you, baby? It's already been done. I'm yours. Only chains I'll ever want are the ones connecting me to you. So just fuckin' agree to move in with me."

••••

I moved in.

I was weak. It was either move in or run.

I wanted to run. I really did. For both our sakes. Because I was certain that this spelled disaster.

But I couldn't.

So I moved in. Not into the spare room that he'd offered. I moved in.

"If I'm going to do this, I'm going to do this," I'd told him the day before.

He rubbed his hand over his mouth. "Fuck, babe, you sure?"

I raised a brow at him. "You're objecting?"

He stepped forward, lightly clasping my hips. "Fuck no. I'd be jumpin' for joy if I weren't so fuckin' conflicted." He rubbed his hand on my bare hip. It was nice. Not completely, the residual dirt still lingering, but it was nice enough. "We haven't gotten to that yet. I don't want to push you into any shit you're not ready for."

"I'm not ready," I admitted. "Not for that." The mind-blowing, soul-destroying kiss we'd shared in my office was the first and only one we'd had. We were like two teenagers, the lust and desire hanging between us, but something heavier obstructing it. But he'd stayed over. A lot. He kept to his side and let me make the moves, which I hadn't done much of. I curled up to him in my sleep and that was it. My unconscious mind craved his touch while my waking mind couldn't handle it. But he'd respected the fact that just having him there, present in the dark with me, was all I could handle. "But I want to try and do this. I don't do shit half-assed. If you don't want me in your room if I'm not—"

He clutched my neck roughly, the first time he'd made such a sudden movement since... then. "I fuckin' want you," he growled. "Don't say that. Don't even think that. I want you any way I can have you. Always will," he promised.

I'd nodded. "Okay" was all I'd been able to choke out.

Rosie was equal parts happy and sad about this turn of events. We'd spent the previous night having a ceremonial good-bye to being roommates. It was bittersweet. In fact, I'd had a tiny freak-out while watching a documentary about inmates on death row.

"I can't do this," I said suddenly.

"What? Watch this? This is like crème de la crème of our documentaries," she replied, her eyes on the screen.

I turned to face her. "No, I can't do this. Go and play house with a fucking biker who wants to save me. Who I want but can't have because I can't find a moment of fucking quiet in my head, and if I can't find that he can't give it to me. No one can. I'm just bringing him into my freak show. I can't do that. I have to leave. To run. Do you 'have a guy' who does passports?" I asked seriously, beginning to panic.

"Of course I do," she said. "But I'm not calling him. You don't need to run. I won't let you, and Lucky sure as shit won't."

"But I can't. I can't take what he's offering."

"It's not him who's offering anything," she said. "Quiet is a gift. So is peace. And love. And salvation." She eyed me, the glitter-rimmed lashes not hiding the wisdom behind those baby blues. "They're all gifts you've gotta give yourself before anyone else can."

"How can I find quiet when my demons scream at night? How can I find peace when chaos is all I know? How can I love myself when I can barely stand the feeling of my own skin?" I paused, sucking in a strangled breath. "How can I find salvation when I'm already damned?" I wiped away a tear angrily. Angry that I let it escape, at the vulnerability in my voice, the fact I'd just let myself be so weak. "Jesus," I muttered. "I sound like a fucking Britney Spears song."

She reached across the sofa to squeeze my hand. "Sweetheart, salvation only comes to the damned." She grinned. "Hey, sometimes the best wisdom is hidden in catchy pop songs."

So she convinced me to not flee the country.

Barely.

And I tried to give myself peace.

I got it when I moved into Gabriel's small but warm house by the sea. It mirrored the little cabin that felt like it existed in a dream but it lacked the boho vibe of the other one. This was all rock and roll and all Gabriel.

All my fears melted away the second we got inside.

"Welcome home, baby," he murmured quietly from behind me.

"Yeah," I replied, looking at the ocean through his living room window. "Home."

Then I moved my gaze to him, or more precisely, his denim-encased ass. And I got it. A flutter. A twinge that made me want to do something about it. Then came the dirt, chasing away whatever good feeling had been there.

He bent down behind the breakfast bar so he was out of sight but started talking. "I thought we'd start this off right," he called.

Then he lifted two heavy coolers onto the bar, grinning from ear to ear.

"Please don't tell me there's body parts in there." I nodded to the white containers.

His grin widened. "Of course not," he said. "Red is for body parts, white is for food." He tapped the side.

I shook my head and wandered to the breakfast bar to get a better look.

"I present to you our dinner, breakfast, and lunch for the next seventeen months," he said, eyes on me.

The he took the lid off both bins. Inside, amongst the ice, were cartons of Chunky Monkey. A crap ton.

I gaped at them. Then at him.

"You were serious?" I asked.

He nodded. "I'm always serious about two things, frozen goods and my firefly." He paused. "And *Golden Girls*," he added.

I smiled at him. Actually smiled at the warmth he was spreading just by being him.

"There she is," he murmured, his eyes dancing with demons.

Before the moment could get too much, he shut the lids.

"Right," he declared. "I'll take these out to the big freezer, move some body parts around, and be back." He gave me a look. "I'll give you some quiet just to, you know, settle." His arms pulsed lifting the coolers and I tried not to drool as he walked into the door leading to his attached garage.

Rosie was right. Quiet was only something you got if you let it in.

And I let it in.

It was nice.

For about five minutes.

Then the noise came back.

It was when I was unpacking my things in Gabriel's walk-in closet. Yes, he had a walk-in closet. I'd called him on it, not five minutes before.

"It came with the house," he protested.

I'd grinned and shook my head and he went to get us beers. Or him a beer and me a soda. I was still swearing off any mind-altering substance. Well, not any, considering I'd just moved in with the most dangerous substance of them all.

Whatever.

While depositing my underwear in a drawer, the glint of metal sparkled in the light and caught my eye. Once I focused on the object I froze. Not just my body, but every molecule of my being.

I was no longer in the cluttered yet comforting, warm room. I was caged in by concrete walls, cold, the bitter air sucking every inch of life from my naked body. The steel rubbed against my wrists and I could barely stand it, the pain. No, the pain I could stand; it was the filth I couldn't. I couldn't escape it. Those cuffs held me in place, kept me from trying to escape the dirt. Try to get clean.

I started to shake. I couldn't stop and it racked my entire body. I was paralyzed but inwardly I writhed, trying to get free of that prison inside my mind. I was trapped, and the thought had me wanting to sink to my feet. To run. To find it. Nothingness.

"Becky?"

The voice made me jump but I didn't turn. Didn't speak. I was too busy fighting.

He came closer, his heat at my back. "Babe?" he asked, voice thick with concern.

It was his hand on my hips that did it. The gentle pressure of him pulling me back into his hard body. His clean body.

I ripped out of his grip, finding my motor skills then.

"Don't touch me," I half shrieked. My feet moved, my body working on pure survival instinct. I ran towards the bathroom, one destination in mind.

One goal in mind.

To get clean.

I didn't even realize he'd followed me, too busy on my mission. I reached to turn the shower on and started to strip down.

"Baby. What's going on? Fuckin' talk to me," he ordered, his voice hoarse.

I could feel his presence but he didn't touch me. Thankfully.

"I can't talk. I've got to...." I trailed off, yanking my shirt off my head. "I've got to get clean," I muttered, more to myself than him. On autopilot, I divested myself of all my clothes, everything in the room going soft around the edges. It blurred so I was half in the dirty room, chained to the bed, and half in the bathroom filling up with steam.

Then I was in the shower.

I wasn't sure how I got there, considering I didn't exactly remember turning on the shower or stepping in.

I met hazel eyes.

Gabriel. He was in the shower with me, fully clothed and holding me up. "You're clean, baby," he murmured.

It was then I realized that something soft and rough was moving over my body. Not his hands but a pink loofah, trailing suds everywhere.

I watched his hands move it up and down.

"You have a pink loofah," I observed.

His eyes stayed on mine. "I do," he agreed.

"Don't they sell matte black ones? I feel like that'd be more suitable for you." I paused. "For me."

His eyes were hard. "No. This is perfect. For you. For me."

He let the words and the weight of them hang between us as he cleaned me. The best he could.

••••

We were lying in bed afterwards, me wrapped in his arms. That was a feat in itself. To be curled against his chest, him stroking my back, without wanting to crawl out of my own skin?

A miracle.

Catching a glimpse of the cuffs in his closet had been horrific. An instant ticket back to that room.

It had also been something else.

Him seeing it. Me. I was an 'it' now. Stripped down raw to the nerve. He saw it and yet there I was, in his arms.

We hadn't spoken as he climbed out of the shower, cradled me in a fluffy towel like a child, and put a clean-smelling shirt over my head. He'd changed from his soaking clothes and there we were.

"The fuckers who did that to you, they're monsters." He broke the silence, his voice sandpaper.

My head lifted from his chest and I met his eyes, shaking my head. "No, there's no such thing as monsters. *People* did that, which I think is worse. Monsters were conjured up as a way to excuse the treachery that man is capable of. Because there are some acts that we want to put on an inhuman creature rather than admit that our fellow man is able to do such a thing." I stared at him. "Monsters, real ones, the ones made of nightmares, they don't exist here." I held my arm out into the open air. "They exist here." I moved the same arm to point to my temple, swallowing hard. "Sometimes there's so many of them I don't know if I can fight them anymore. Then I look in your eyes and I see the same monsters. They haven't killed you. You're still here."

He tightened his arms. "Yeah, I'm still here," he rasped. "And I'd die for you, firefly."

I held his eyes, even though it caused me physical pain to see the devotion, the truth in them. "Don't say that," I whispered. "Anyone can promise death. To die for someone is a split-second decision, an instant. I don't want you to die." The thought of a world without him turned my tongue to dust. How close to reality that had been. Because of me. "I don't want you to die for me. I want you to live. Make a conscious decision every day. That's so much harder. Means so much more, to brave the shit of this world and keep going. That's it."

He kissed my head. "Okay, I'll live. Only if you make that same promise."

I stared at him. "Okay, I promise."

Or I'd try my best.

TWENTY-THREE

"The demons are back and stronger than ever. They are looking for a fight. Looking to win. And this time, I might just let them."
-K.C.W

ONE WEEK LATER

It was Sunday night, and we were at Evie and Steg's.
And I was drowning.

The entire night, I was wrapped in the warm glow of the unlikely family. And there was a lot. In addition to Gwen, Amy, Mia, and Lily and their hubbies, there was Rosie, her friends, Lucy and Ashley, and about the whole freaking club. And me and Gabriel.

Evie and Steg had a huge fucking compound out on a plot of land. They needed it, to fit everyone.

And everyone fit. Literally and figuratively.

Except me.

Because I was embraced in the warmth at the same time as the ice settled over my insides. The dirt.

Gabriel's arms around me were almost too much to bear. I'd come so far, but I felt like a rubber band that had snapped back into its original form.

I lasted through the whole night, somehow.

Then, like the universe was giving me a sign, Gabriel pulled me away from Gwen and Amy, who I'd been chatting with, playing my part to.

"You okay, Becky?" he asked, frowning at me.

"Peachy," I lied, doing my best not to flinch away from the simple touch.

He didn't seem convinced but nodded anyway. "We've got some

club shit to do. You okay if Rosie takes you home?"

Home.

That wasn't real.

Just another place I didn't fit.

I couldn't speak so I nodded.

"I shouldn't be too late," he promised.

I nodded again.

He frowned once more, kissed my head, and left.

And when Rosie dropped me 'home,' I got straight in my car and looked for something.

Nothing.

••••

I was staring at it. Or it was staring at me. I wasn't sure which. All I knew was that its presence, its fucking allure, filled up the entire room and I couldn't actually move.

I was terrified of moving.

Because if I did, I knew exactly what I'd do.

Without hesitation.

I'd fall headfirst into the fire that I'd only just escaped.

The door opened and closed and the sound of motorcycle boots wafted into my muffled ears.

I felt him enter the room but didn't look up.

"Hey, babe, what you starin' at so intently? Trying to move something with the power of your mind? Waste of time. Telekinesis is something that manifests when you're a kid. Trust me, I already looked it up on—" I'm guessing he stopped because he saw the syringe full of heroin sitting on the coffee table.

Inches away from me.

My hand twitched. Even with him a few feet away. Him. The man who promised salvation.

Salvation and damnation within my reach, and I couldn't move because I was scared of what I would choose.

Or what would choose me.

I expected him to lose it. To transform into that man I knew lurked underneath the façade that droned on about telekinesis.

He didn't say a word but his rage filled the room, mingling with the presence of the heroin and tasting bitter as I sucked air in.

His boots echoed as he rounded the coffee table and came to sit next to me. He didn't touch me, just sat there, right there, resting his elbows on his knees and staring in the same direction as me.

I was jealous. His stare was a choice. Mine was not. It was like being up on stage before the true nightmare began and having that magnetic force pulling my attention to him. This wasn't natural chemistry, nature trying to yank me closer to something that promised light. No, this was something wholly unnatural that I'd chosen and would have that seducing pull to venture back down that dark path.

The allure of nothing.

My hand twitched again.

Nothing. No pain. No memories. No nightmare. No filth. I wouldn't feel trapped under my own tarnished skin.

There'd be nothing.

A tanned, tattooed hand settled over mine, encompassing my small pale one in its strong grip.

He didn't say anything, but he didn't need to.

If I got nothing, then that meant no Gabriel. No stupid jokes about penguin's knees. No soulful glances. No falling asleep in his arms and feeling safer than ever. No chance of anything... more.

I stood, my decision made.

Gabriel stiffened and I bet he itched to stand too, to stop me. He stayed. I picked up the junk I'd gotten off one of my old dealers. Then I dropped it to the ground and crushed it under my combat boot.

Out of the corner of my eye, Gabriel's entire body sagged with relief. Mine did not.

He stood, slowly coming to stand in front of me, his face etched in stone. "Why?" he asked. There was no judgment in his voice, not an ounce.

"Tonight," I replied, my voice thick. "Everyone was just so... right. They fit."

Gabriel's eyes flared. "You fit too." It was almost a growl.

I shook my head, stepping back as my emotions whirled in my

stomach.

"I'm never going to be this old lady version of Mary Sue all your brothers seem to have," I said, pacing the room before stopping in front of him. "Birds don't help me dress in the morning, and I don't wake up looking like a supermodel. I wake up looking like a 'before' picture on *Extreme Makeover*, or a swamp creature, depending on the hair situation. I don't have a fancy designer wardrobe or some strange superpower to wear white while rearing sticky-handed toddlers. I don't like toddlers. Or kids." I started pacing again. "I don't smile at people for no reason. I don't like *people*. I'm pissed off at the world most of the time, and I just can't find it in me to make the effort with people I don't think are worth my time. A lot of people think I'm a bitch." I gave his amused face a meaningful look. "*A lot*. When I get PMS, I'll either cry at an insurance commercial or seriously consider murder over someone if I don't like the way they breathe. There's no in-between." Lucky grinned at that and I ignored it. I had to. "I'm not funny or quirky or...." I searched for the word and somehow, something in me broke. "*Clean*," I said finally. "It's ironic really, that that's the name for being sober. Clean." It even tasted bitter on my tongue. I laughed a humorless laugh. "It's a sick joke. I'm not clean. I'm so covered in filth, in dirt, that the word shouldn't be used in a sentence next to my name. I'm broken. Used. Tarnished," I listed in a detached tone. "I'm so fucked-up even your most ruthless brother looks well-adjusted next to me." I laughed again. "I'm too dirty for even the outlaws."

My laughter stopped and I gazed up at Lucky's tight form. The amused look was wiped from his face and it was taut. His fists were balled at his sides. I took it in, then continued.

"You deserve Mary Sue," I whispered, my voice finally cracking. "You deserve someone who wasn't broken the moment she was brought into the world. Someone who wasn't born dirty. Someone who had their innocence stolen before she knew to protect it. Someone who didn't get corrupted, defiled before she even knew what was happening." I sucked in a breath. "Someone who didn't take her clothes off for filthy men. Who didn't shoot filth into her veins as if the dirt covering her soul wasn't thick enough before that. Someone who wasn't...." My mind ventured somewhere even I wasn't strong enough to go. I took a deep breath. "Someone who wasn't *raped*. Repeatedly. Raped and was too high to even care," I spat out the words, like maybe if I said them, they'd stop torturing my soul, bouncing in my head, taunting me. Lucky's body flinched each time I said that ugly word, as if it were a bullet piercing his skin. "Do you know what I was thinking about while they were doing *that*?" I asked, trying to ignore the way rage had seeped into the air and seemed to thicken it, turning it into something to swallow and not breathe. Something bitter. I'd had experience with bitter—it was my life—so I sucked in a breath. "*Nothing*. Nothing except my next hit. Except the next time I could chase away the filth and fill it with the void."

"Stop," he growled. His head jerked up and I flinched when I saw wetness in his eyes. "You need to stop fucking talking," he commanded. I never thought pain could manifest in one word. Encompass it. Until that moment. I never thought I'd feel fear either, not until that moment. Terror choked me as I belatedly realized what I'd done. Laid my broken, used, ugly soul right at his beautiful feet. I'd done it. Presented him with the true me. Now he would rear away in disgust. I felt physically sick at the thought of losing him. I welcomed the loss of my left arm before that.

He came forward, yanking me to his body. "None of that is true," he growled. "None of it. That shit that happened to you, it's the stuff of fuckin' nightmares. I can't take it away, but I can show you, tell you every single day how beautiful, how clean you are. Always have been." He paused. "And you were, even when I first saw you, strugglin' with demons I couldn't see, you were breathtaking. You were like autumn. I was so caught up in your beauty, the fuckin' colors." He touched my cropped hair. "I was so fixated on that shit that I didn't see that you were withering away. Thank fuck you made it through to summer, baby."

I flinched at his words. "Is this summer?" I asked in a flat voice. "Despite everything I was before, despite how broken and totally fucked-up I was, I was always *alive*. I always had some sort of spark, even at the depth of my addiction. Even lying in that hospital bed after I'd almost killed myself, I had fight left. Not a lot but enough.

Something. Now I don't feel it, the fight, the zest. I just feel tired. So fucking tired of fighting. Of everything. I'm not going to swallow a bottle of painkillers or anything, but I just can't fight anymore. Even if I could, there's nothing to fight. Just darkness. You can't punch a shadow. So I don't know what I am, because I'm not living. And in the absence of life, there's death. Not the six-feet-under kind, but something different, something worse."

He clutched my face, pulling our foreheads together. "No, babe, in the absence of life, there's fuckin' *love*," he rasped. "The love I got for you, it's gonna burn well after I'm in the ground, till the world turns to dust," he promised. "You feel like you've lost your fight for now? I say for now 'cause I know this shit is temporary. That you're gonna come back to me, light up my world again. Find your zest. But for now, you don't want to fight? I've got enough fight for the both of us. I'll fight for you, firefly. I'll never be too tired, too old, or too fuckin' anything for that. I'll fight for you till my last breath. Or until you're ready to fight for yourself again."

I should have said no to that. To someone fighting my battles when he had his own to focus on. But I was weak in that moment, having fought the hardest one, crushing the syringe under my feet.

"Okay," I whispered.

His body sagged and his arms tightened around me.

"I need you to come somewhere tomorrow," I said to his chest.

"Anywhere."

He was right on that. And since he'd already ridden to hell with me, group sessions should be a breeze.

•••

I stood at the front of the room, the weight of the attention on me almost too much to bear. It wasn't that I wasn't used to people looking at me. I fricking danced on a stage naked for a living. I was used to it. But I'd never been naked, really naked, in front of anyone but Gabriel. Even then I had a film over my true self so he didn't see the raw fucking mess I was when I was stripped to the core.

I didn't even let myself inspect that.

ANNE MALCOM

But there I was, in a room full of strangers, except Gage and Gabriel, stripped, to the core.

Nothing had ever been so fucking terrifying in my life.

I swallowed, finding the strength from the man who I'd refused to let give it to me, until now. My gaze touched on Gage. His face was impassive but he gave me a small nod. I nodded back.

"Nat introduced me to it all," I said, not knowing where to start, but the beginning seemed best. Not the real, ugly beginning—I wasn't ready for that—but one of the beginnings. "The drug scene," I continued, scanning the room but not really seeing anyone. Instead I saw the back room of the club and Nat grinning while handing me a little white pill. "She did it in a way that made it seem like nothing, no big deal, no worries. Like the opinion I'd had on drugs my entire adult life had been misplaced and they weren't as serious as I'd built them up in my head. Like I was only now just getting in on the secret that everyone but me knew. Drugs were okay." That night, that first night, I got it. This was how people got through life. I'd been stupidly naive in thinking anyone could get through it sober.

I moved my attention back to the room. "She was like my spirit guide, giving me pills to fly me high, giving me more to bring me back down. And finally giving me the syringe that changed it all." That was another night burned into my existence. Some crappy party. No, not even a party, just a handful of sketchy people in an even sketchier apartment. I'd been anxious to leave but Nat had convinced me to stay. She'd held out the syringe to me and I'd paused. Who would have thought what a ripple effect that pause would have? How much hung in the balance? If only I'd just gone with my gut instead of taking the vial that held my doom.

"I'm not blaming her. I guess that's what a lot of addicts do, search desperately for someone, anyone, to point the finger at, lay the blame on. God forbid we actually take responsibility for flushing our own lives down the crapper.

"I'm under no such illusions. She may have offered, but I accepted. I swallowed those pills. I injected myself. I was the master of my own destiny." I paused, the slideshow of horrors from that little room playing on repeat in the front of my mind. I struggled to escape it, to find my way back to the room. My throat was raw as I spoke my last sentence. "In this case, I was the master of my own demise." My gaze touched on Gabriel's for the first time since I'd gotten up here. "Or so I'd thought. Someone very important to me pointed out that all of that shit was winter. Drugs stripped everything off me, like leaves from the branches on a tree, and it looked like demise. I didn't believe him. Then." I stared at him, seeing myself in those eyes across the room, and for once, I didn't hate what I saw. "But now I think, if you'll excuse the *Game of Thrones* undertone here, summer is coming."

••••

I walked into the clubhouse and froze the moment my eyes hit the common area—more specifically the sofa and TV. Even more specifically who was on the sofa and what was on the TV.

For once, the common room was empty of prospects, club girls, any old ladies, and any patched members I begrudgingly accepted as family.

Right then there were only two people—three, including me. Gabriel was on the sofa, leaning back with one of his long, sinewy, and tattooed arms draped along the top of the sofa. The other lay softly on top of a dark head which was situated on his thigh. The head of a beautiful little girl who was lying on her side, using Gabriel's impressive, denim-clad thigh as a cushion. Her little face was scrunched up, a thumb in her mouth, and her eyes were closed in sleep.

I'm not one for womb clenches at any moment, especially at the sight of children. I didn't like children. I had no desire to have them. No way, no how.

Right then, I seemed to have forgotten that fact. Because looking at Gabriel, thoughtlessly giving such a young girl easy affection, the image of him, in his cut with tattoos and the innocent, beautiful little human, my womb clenched.

Then my gaze moved back to the television.

"What are you doing?" I asked, finally realizing I was turning into some sort of Peeping Tom, though I was sure Gabriel knew I was

ANNE MALCOM

there. He had badass skills.

The way he jumped told me his badass skills were on vacation. Amazingly, the little girl on his thigh stayed in her current position, still firmly gripped by the sandman. I felt a pang of envy at how little people welcomed oblivion so easily.

You could welcome it that easily, the devil on my shoulder said. *All it takes is one shot.*

I shook the thought away with great effort, my hands shaking slightly.

"Shh," he hissed.

I raised a brow. Belle didn't wake up with him almost crawling up the back of the sofa, so my simple question probably wouldn't wake her. But then, he wasn't looking at Belle. His gaze was glued to the TV.

My mouth had a mind of its own and a small grin tugged at the corners. "Did you just shush me in order to keep watching *My Little Pony*?" I teased, my eyes on the ridiculous pastel cartoon.

"I'm not watching *My Little Pony*," he scoffed, though his gaze didn't move. "I'm watching Belle, who happens to like Rainbow Magic. I'm just being an awesome uncle and letting her have her way."

My grin turned into a full-blown smile. "Babe, Belle's asleep," I pointed out.

Gabriel suddenly tore his gaze from the TV. It didn't go to Belle, as I expected, but came straight to me. I felt his eyes at my smile and I couldn't even take it off if I tried. Something moved beyond them before he quickly glanced down at the sleeping toddler on his lap. Registering that she was, in fact, asleep, he quickly fumbled for the remote and turned off the TV.

"You're a Brony," I said, on the edge of laughter.

Gabriel's gaze shot to me. "No, I'm not," he argued. There was a pause. "What's a Brody?"

That's what did it. I burst out laughing. Real, bent-over, gut-wrenching, tear-bringing laughter. I finally got hold of myself, still too far gone to see the way he was looking at me. "A '*Brony*,'" I said between giggles, "is a full-grown man who derives pleasure from watching Rainbow Magic," I explained. "Never in my life would I think a biker, a big bad Sons of Templar biker, would also be a Brony," I teased.

Gwen entered the room before he could defend himself, her hair slightly mussed. "Thanks for watching Belle, Lucky," she said. "Hey, babe, what's up?" she asked me.

I grinned. "Well...."

Gabriel surged off the sofa, thrusting the sleeping kid into Gwen's arms.

"We were just talking about how incredibly manly and strong I was and how Becky couldn't control herself around me. I had to remind her that we were in the presence of a child, but that didn't stop her." He shrugged at Gwen. "What can I say, I'm irresistible." He was at my side in a flash, his hand over my mine. "We've got to go now, bye." He ushered me out the door before I could utter a word.

"How much do I have to pay you to keep that under your belt, Becky," he murmured in my ear, yanking me to his side.

I grinned and glanced up at him. "About a million dollars. But I'll take it in installments."

"Let's get my baby on the bike."

"Or we could ride unicorns?" I teased.

"They're fuckin' ponies," he snapped, and I full-on laughed.

I didn't think I'd ever be able to, but there was Gabriel, proving me wrong.

TWENTY-FOUR

"She has been through hell. So believe me when I say, fear her when she looks into the fire and smiles."
-E. Corona

"I don't want to go to a party," I whined, climbing off Gabriel's bike. He grinned and took off my helmet, then ran his fingers through my spiky hair. I closed my eyes. I was getting better at it, letting him touch me. Letting the warm feeling wash over me and not feel *their* hands disperse ice through my limbs. Since that night, three days before, when I'd fallen apart almost completely, it was like I could finally start putting myself together again. I didn't miss the way Gabriel watched me, his eyes guarded and intense. I knew I scared him with the syringe. I'd terrified myself. I'd looked right into the hell I'd clawed my way out of and seriously considered going back there. But I hadn't. And that was something pivotal.

I'd been getting better. I wasn't ready for everything, but I was getting there. I freaking hoped so, because living with someone who looked like Gabriel, sleeping next to him and his abs, had me feeling all pent-up but unable to do anything about it.

Just another kind of hell.

He cupped my chin in his hands, bringing our foreheads together.

"A wise woman once said something about reality," he murmured. "Something like, 'Nothing at all to change reality. It often goes on whether you like it or not.'" He quoted me. To me.

I sucked in a breath. Not at his words—I barely noticed them—but the proximity of his mouth. It almost brushed against mine as he spoke, and it was like I was a stupid fucking schoolgirl who had never been kissed. I wanted him, with a need that was physical. Yearned for him. At the same time, I wasn't ready, wasn't rid of that feeling of uncleanness.

He didn't kiss me. I was equal parts relieved and disappointed.

He stepped back, twining my hands with his as he directed us towards the entrance.

I grinned at Rosie and Lucy, who strutted past us as if they were on a catwalk. They certainly looked the part. Rosie was going for grunge, wearing tight ripped jeans, a Grateful Dead tee, and boots she'd borrowed off me. The girl was a chameleon. Lucy stayed true to her *Breakfast at Tiffany's* elegance in drainpipe tailored pants and a tight-fitting black top which slid off her shoulder.

"Um, I know you would have indulged in a few cocktails already, since you're alcoholics, but the party's that way," I informed them, pointing in the opposite direction.

Rosie slowed. "Sorry, we got a better offer from somewhere where my brother won't kill my game." She winked at me, and then her eyes went to Gabriel and my intertwined hands. Her grin widened. "Have fun, lovebirds. Don't do anything I'd do." She blew us a kiss and Lucy did a finger wave before they left in the direction of Rosie's convertible.

Gabriel squeezed my hand. "You sure you don't want to go and troll the town with Trouble One and Trouble Two?" he teased.

I gazed up at him. At the eyes that had become darker and deeper since I'd met him. Since we'd bathed in each other's darkness. "No. I don't need to go looking for trouble when I'm staring right at it," I whispered.

His eyes went deeper and he grinned. "Ditto," he murmured.

As loath as I was to leave the moment—I wanted to live in it—something flickered in my mind. "Shoot," I muttered, glancing over to where the girls had almost reached Rosie's car. "Rosie has my lipstick. I've got to get it before they leave." I tried to run in their direction but the grip on my hand tightened.

"You sure that's not just an excuse for you to run and escape from me?" he asked, not teasing any longer.

I gave him a long look and held my breath. Before I could think about it too much, I went up on my tiptoes and pressed my mouth to his. It was quick and closed-mouth, but it did something. Something good, something that had my heart beating just a little quicker. And something bad. Something that had my skin prickling with goose bumps, and not the nice kind. The mixture of the two was an exquisite cocktail that I didn't drink too deep of, not yet.

I stepped away and left him standing there with a hungry, dumfounded look on his face before turning to run in Rosie's direction.

"Hey, bitch, don't run with my lipstick," I called.

She and Lucy had been chatting and staring at the man who just got out of an SUV, who was seriously yummy and frowning at Lucy. Both snapped their attention to me.

"Okay, I'll give it back, but only if I can keep the boots," she yelled back.

I shook my head and slowed my pace. It didn't look like they were getting in Rosie's car anytime soon. By the way the hulking Maori man was eating Lucy up with his eyes, she wasn't going to find anything better anywhere.

If I didn't have my own caramel, hulking man I'd totally fight her for him. But as impressed as I was with his muscles, his height, and the tribal design snaking down his sinewy forearms, I only appreciated it in a detached kind of way. Not just because men had been ruined for me from those three weeks in that cell. Or maybe they had.

All men except one.

"Who's the hunk?" I asked when I reached the women.

Lucy chewed her lip and Rosie grinned wickedly at her. "Lucy's boyfriend," she said, her eyes on the man who was leaning against the SUV, looking like he was happy to lean there for the rest of time.

Her head snapped to Rosie. "He is fucking not." Her violet eyes focused on me. "He's my stalker."

I grinned, holding my hand out for my lipstick, which Rosie gave me. "Yeah, well, if I were you, I wouldn't be so cut up about having such a hunky stalker. At least when he ties you up in the basement you've got something pretty to look at." I winked at her and my phone vibrated in my pocket. "So I'm guessing you'll be sticking around for the party after all?" I surmised, grabbing my phone and glancing down at the unknown caller ID.

"No," Lucy snapped.

"Yes," Rosie declared at the same time.

They scowled at each other.

"Well, you two have fun working that out. I'll see you inside."

I turned my back to their bickering, grinning at Gabriel, who was leaning against his bike, arms folded, waiting for me.

Such a normal moment, having him staring at me like that, having the itch down to a manageable level. Going to a party where I actually started to feel like I belonged had me feeling something I knew I shouldn't.

Something that was dangerous.

Deadly.

Hope.

And then when I answered the phone, that hope was shattered into a thousand pieces.

"Yello," I greeted, my voice light.

"Hey, baby," a familiar sickening voice drawled.

I stopped in my tracks. My smile froze on my face and my throat closed up.

"No greeting? Not even your trademark smart mouth?" he continued. "I'm surprised. Delightfully so. My boys managed to fuck it out of you." There was a loaded pause and his heavy breathing filled my ears. "That's until those biker fucks came in and killed them all. Blew up our fuckin' house. Now that was just rude," he hissed. "Turnabout's fair play. Your boyfriend blows up my friends, kills my family, I blow up yours. Though I am disappointed to let such two hot pieces go to waste." He sighed.

I found control over my body at his words, at the chilling realization of what he meant.

Lucy and Rosie had just finished their fight and looked like they were about to get into their car.

I dropped my phone, not needing the poison of his words anymore. I had bigger things to worry about.

"Rosie!" I screamed, my voice shrill. "Get away from the car."

I didn't wait for my words to penetrate, just started sprinting towards them. The man at the SUV did the same and Rosie and Lucy reacted immediately, running from the vehicle.

I got to them.

Not soon enough.

Or maybe just in time, depending on who you asked.

Because just as the man snatched Lucy out of her run and dove on top of her, the world exploded into face-melting heat and the air became a dump truck, pushing me through the air.

I was flying on the scorching air.

Then I wasn't.

The ground came at me at a surprising speed.

Then it didn't.

Because then there was nothing.

••••

It was the ringing that woke me. The ringing that was so loud and so shrill it rattled through my forehead.

I blinked, trying to shake the sound out. Gabriel's face was the first thing I saw, terror cloaking it. His mouth was moving, but all I could hear was the ringing.

I blinked again and tried to move.

Gabriel's hands were around me and he said something else, his other hand going to my face and pulling it close to his.

"I can't hear you," I said, my voice sounding muffled in my own ears, like I was underwater.

I tried to move again, feeling disoriented. My head pounded like a bitch, but I think the rest of me was in one piece.

Physically, at least.

Then it hit me. What happened. Why I was lying on the concrete with Gabriel leaning over me, panic on his face.

I struggled to get up, my ears still ringing.

Gabriel stopped my motion, his mouth moving again.

I kept struggling, gazing past his face. There was black smoke and flames rising from the remains of Rosie's car. People were running around everywhere; it was like watching a silent movie, the chaos on mute. I couldn't see past the smoke and debris. Couldn't see Rosie. Or Lucy.

They had been right beside me. Or where I was seconds before. Now it looked like I was a good five feet away from my previous spot.

"Let me up," I snapped, my voice not sounding right in my head.

Then in a soft pop, sound came back in, more grating and painful than the ringing. People were yelling, one in particular.

"Stay the fuck down, Becky," Gabriel growled. "I don't know what other injuries you've got, and I'm not lettin' you hurt yourself."

I kept struggling. "Other injuries?" I repeated, my ears still ringing. "I don't have any. I'm fine. Where's Rosie and Lucy? Are they okay?"

"Stop," he commanded, taking my neck in his hands. "Babe. You are injured. Stop movin' so I can put some pressure on that."

I stared at him. He wasn't looking into my eyes, but at my forehead. "What?"

I answered my own question as warm liquid trickled down the side of my face and I put my hand up to my cheek. It came back red.

"Oh," I said, vacantly.

"Yeah," he clipped. "Now tell me, you hurt anywhere else? You can feel all your toes?" His gaze flickered down my body.

I followed it, taking stock with my mind. My cropped white shirt was no longer white and it was streaked with black marks. There was a rip in my jeans and one of my sneakers was missing.

"These are my favorite jeans," I moaned. "Where's my shoe?"

He frowned at me.

Before he could say anything, Gage crouched beside him, his usually emotionless face showing a twinge of something.

Concern, maybe.

Or, more unsettling, fear.

"She okay?" he clipped, his eyes running over my body much in the same way Gabriel's had.

"I lost my shoe," I answered before Gabriel could.

His jaw was hard as he turned to Gage. "I think she's got a concussion," he said, gathering me gently in his arms.

Everything spun as I was lifted and could view the carnage. "Rosie," I said, my voice panicked. "Lucy, are they okay?"

Gage nodded. "Banged up, but Cade's got Rosie and Keltan tore away with Lucy to the hospital before we could fuckin' blink."

My heart dropped. "Hospital?" I repeated, my mouth full of ash.

He nodded again, his face grim. "She'll be fine. Broken wrist, most likely."

He moved with us as men ran with guns out and sirens sounded in the distance.

Gage regarded me. "Could have been worse. Much worse. If it weren't for you."

Gabriel's arms tightened around me.

"How'd you know?" Gage continued, his voice flat, not accusing, not curious, not anything.

Gabriel's head whipped to his friend. "Jesus, brother. You save the interrogation for when my woman isn't fuckin' bleeding from a head wound," he growled.

Gage didn't react to the rage, just nodded. "Not blamin' her," he clarified.

We made it into the club room which was full of people. There was no party in sight. It was a strange mix of chaos and stillness. Gwen and Amy's eyes bulged at the sight of me, and Lily jumped from Asher's side.

"Oh my God, oh my God," she chanted. "Bex? Are you okay? Please tell me you're okay."

I nodded, still confused and unable to properly grasp the thoughts bouncing around in my brain. The motion hurt, a lot. "I'm fine," I said slowly, slurring my words slightly. "My jeans aren't." I wiggled my toe. "And I don't know where my shoe is."

"Jesus," Gabriel gritted through clenched teeth. "Someone find Becky's fuckin' shoe," he ordered to no one in particular.

Then he set me down on the sofa, which a few people were crowded around.

A dazed-looking Rosie was sitting in a chair, Cade crouched in front of her, his jaw hard and his hand on her neck.

Her eyes focused on me, and then they widened. "Bex," she said, trying to get up. Cade stopped her and she glared at him. "You're bleeding. That is not cool, dude. Not cool."

"I know," I agreed. "And I ripped my jeans."

"Bummer." She frowned down at her feet. "I think I may have

ruined your boots."

I shrugged. "No big. I needed a new pair anyway."

"Can we stop talkin' about fuckin' clothes and let me fuckin' look at your *head wound?*" Gabriel roared, making me jump.

"Ouch," I muttered, putting my hand to my head.

His face softened immediately. "Shit, sorry, baby. Just let me look, okay?"

I met his eyes, saw what a tenuous hold he had on his rage. "Okay," I agreed.

A hard-faced Brock handed Gabriel what looked like a first aid box.

"You okay, darlin'?" he asked, his voice soft.

"I—"

Gabriel's head snapped up. "If you say anythin' about your fuckin' shoe or jeans again, I'll lose it," he growled.

I scowled at him, then smiled at Brock. "I'm fine."

He leaned in and squeezed my arm. "Happy to hear. Though that head makes me think otherwise."

His hand was gone as quickly as it was there, but I still shivered at the contact. Gabriel didn't miss it and he glared at Brock.

"Sorry, bro," Brock muttered. "We're gonna have cops crawling this place...." he trailed off as the sound of sirens intensified and flashing lights illuminated the windows. "Right about now."

"Yeah, well, let them come. We've got nothin' to hide and as much as I loathe Crawford's little visits, maybe we can make the boys in blue work for our taxes and fuck around while we find who did this," Cade muttered from his spot in front of Rosie.

She blanched at his words. One in particular, I thought.

She tried to get up again. "I've got to go," she exclaimed suddenly.

Cade stopped her once more. "Are you fuckin' insane?" He paused. "No, wait, I already know the answer to that question. But you were almost just fuckin' blown up, kid. You're not goin' anywhere."

Her eyes flared in panic, flickering to the windows. "I'm fine. My eyebrows bore the brunt of it, but nothing a spa day can't fix. Now I've really got to go. I think I left my straightener on." She struggled against her brother.

There was a commotion at the door and the hunky cop stepped

through, his eyes scanning the room until they settled on Rosie.

She stopped struggling.

His government-issue boots pointed in her direction and didn't stop until he reached our little huddle. Cade immediately stood in front of his sister, going toe to toe with the hot cop I knew as Luke.

"The flaming and smoking remains of the bomb that almost killed my sister are outside, deputy," Cade said, his voice even. "I would assume that's where you should be doing your job." His stare was scary, even from my position on the sofa.

I winced at the dabbing against my head.

"Sorry, baby," Gabriel.

"Shh." I waved my hand at him, my eyes on the stare off.

"Did you just shush me?" he asked.

I ignored him.

"I'm right where I need to be, Fletcher," Luke gritted out, though he didn't return the death stare. His eyes were focused on Rosie, the look similar to the one in Gabriel's eyes. "Are you okay?" he asked her, as if he didn't have a six-foot biker all up in his face.

She nodded.

Luke didn't seem satisfied but gave Cade his attention anyway, his expression changing in an instant. "I see the story of you going 'legit' was a total pack of fuckin' lies. What did you do now to put your own flesh and blood in danger?" he spat. "That's low, even for you."

You could taste the change to the air. "Careful, Deputy," Cade warned. "You're getting very fuckin' close to sayin' somethin' you might regret."

"You threatening me?"

Cade's stare was even. "Yeah. If you keep talkin' shit 'bout my family, my club, lookin' at my sister in a way that isn't professional, you bet your ass I am."

Luke moved his glare to Rosie once more. "She's comin' with me," he declared.

Cade's jaw went granite, and Brock and the one everyone called Dwayne stepped forward.

"No, she's fuckin' not," Cade replied.

"She needs a hospital," Luke argued. His eyes went to me. "So does

Bex."

Gabriel and I stiffened at the same time. I put my hand on his to make sure he didn't bite the cop's leg or something.

"I don't do hospitals, Captain America," I informed him. "They mess with my complexion. Plus, the nurses here are way hotter." I moved my eyes to Gabriel, whose eyes were granite.

Luke's jaw went hard as he realized he was not going to win this one. "None of you go anywhere," he growled. "I'm gonna want statements from fuckin' all of you." He gave Rosie one more stare and turned on his heel.

My mind was so focused on what was going on between the two of them that the memory took me by surprise, it having taken a while for me to get all my thought processes back.

"This is my fault," I whispered.

Gabriel froze. "No, it's fuckin' not."

"Yes, it is. I knew about what was going to happen because I was warned. Or threatened," I said, my voice low. "It was Dylan. He called me and said this was payback. This. So it's my fault."

The air, which had already been bitter, turned rancid at my words. Cade and Brock both focused on me.

"That fucker called you," Gabriel bit out, the hand at my forehead shaking with rage.

Cade put his hand on his shoulder. "Easy, brother. How about you take care of your bleeding woman. Then we work on the other shit."

Gabriel was still for a moment, his eyes on me but not really seeing me. Not the me in front of me, anyway. I had a feeling he was seeing the me in that room. He shook himself and he was back here, nodding once and setting to work. Not before clasping my chin in his hands and bringing our foreheads together. "This is not your fuckin' fault, Becky. None of it," he promised.

He waited for my nod before he continued his first aid in silence.

TWENTY-FIVE

*"She who walks the floors of Hell finds the key to the gates
of her own Heaven, buried there like a seed."*
-"Underworld", Segovia Amil

Gabriel patched me up.

Then I was questioned relentlessly by Luke and the sheriff about the explosion. I'd grown up with a distrust of law enforcement, even the hot ones, so I lied my effing ass off.

"I don't know what to tell you, Captain," I said sweetly. "I was walking, minding my own business, and then the car went boom." I shrugged.

I knew the men approved of my story since the corner of Cade's mouth turned up and Brock full-on grinned. Gabriel's granite expression didn't move, nor did his grip on my hand which was bordering on painful. The sheriff, a balding, older, and very tired-looking man, had eventually put his hand on Cade's shoulder talked in hushed tones and then literally dragged Luke off the premises. I was guessing Cade had the older one on payroll.

That was totally dope.

I wondered if we could figure out a way to get me off my parking tickets.

I didn't get to ask because I was spirited away to biker church, which had no crucifixes in sight, only a grim reaper etched into the long table. Very apt.

Then I recounted my phone call, word for word, to the room of grim-faced bikers. They'd all stared at me in varying degrees of fury.

I considered myself a strong woman. Only recently had I come to believe that was true after the events in that room, but I was getting there. The weight of their stares proved too much, as was the memory of my two newest friends almost dying.

I looked at my hands. "I'm sorry. I know I brought all this shit here, almost got Rosie and Lucy killed—"

"Stop," a male voice growled.

I glanced up to Gabriel. He was hard-faced, but wasn't the one who spoke.

It was Bull, the scary large one with a lot of tattoos who barely spoke but had a crazy wife who spoke enough for the both of them.

"None of this shit is on you," he told me, his voice excruciatingly gentle for someone I thought would have been on a watch list somewhere. "This is on them. The fuckers who made the bomb, placed the bomb, and pressed the button. No one else. We clear?"

I nodded. "We're clear, Rambo."

Gage shook his head and grinned at me. That weirdo grinned whenever everyone else was grimacing, and grimaced whenever everyone else was grinning.

After that, I'd been kicked out of the war room so men could talk battle plans, I guessed. The women and their delicate ears were obviously placed outside.

Gabriel set me on the sofa beside Lily, who reached out to squeeze my hand. "You feel sleepy, nauseous, or get dizzy, you fuckin' tell someone. None of this staunch woman, crap. It's hot as fuck everywhere else, but not here," he ordered.

I nodded, though the motion hurt. I didn't tell him that, I was a staunch woman after all.

He leaned forward to press a hard kiss on my mouth before disappearing into the war room.

I looked around the room.

Evie locked eyes with me, smoking. "Well, babe. You know how to make a fuckin' entrance," she stated mildly.

Maybe I was concussed, but I grinned. I had the biker queen's approval.

All it took was a car bomb.

••••

The men appeared not long after Amy had sucked down her third cocktail. I was totally jonesing for one, but I resisted.

Rosie and Lucy were mysteriously absent. I had an inkling that their non-biker significant others had spirited them away somewhere.

I'd so like to see how they'd managed that.

Cade stood at the front of our strange little crowd, his face grim. "We're on lockdown," he declared.

All women groaned, and Amy let out a string of curses that so didn't go with the while Upper East Side princess thing she had going on.

"Lockdown?" I asked Lily. "Please tell me that isn't what it sounds like."

Instead of Lily answering, Gabriel pulled me closer to his side. "That's exactly what it sounds like," he murmured. "You not leaving and going somewhere where you're in danger."

I swallowed and tried to ignore the panic at being locked anywhere. Unable to leave.

Nope. Not happening.

"We've got some major shit going down," Cade continued, oblivious to my incoming freak-out. His gray eyes touched his wife. "Shit that will not come anywhere near our women. Or our kids. But shit that is dangerous. Players who won't hesitate to hit our hearts. Which is you." He hadn't stopped looking at his wife. "As evidenced by today's events. Luckily, we got warned." His gaze flickered to me. I barely noticed it.

I had one word replaying on my mind.

Lockdown.

"So we're going to make sure these players are wiped from the face of the earth. We just need to make sure you stay safe while we're doing that."

"Nope," I blurted out.

Gabriel's hands tightened around me. "Becky," he warned.

I yanked out of his arms. "Don't 'Becky' me," I snapped. "I'm not getting stuck here while you all run off and save the day. Leaving us here in some biker version of an ivory castle. I don't know what acid trip you're on, but this place got *blown up* not three hours ago. I'm thinking it's not the best place to serve as a fortress." I paused. "In fact, nowhere is going to serve as a fortress, at least not for me. Welcome to the twenty-first century. Men no longer ride steeds, and women no longer are confined to palace walls having to wear corsets—outside the bedroom, anyway."

Gwen choked out a giggle at that.

"In light of these developments, I think I'll have to use my not-so-recently

liberated voice and say you are not fucking locking me down. Anywhere."

Amy grinned at me. "Amen to that, sister." Brock glared me, then her. She blew him a kiss.

The weight of every single alpha male's stare was heavy, but I managed to shoulder the load.

I looked around the room, running my eyes over the attractive, grim-faced stares. All were grim-faced, apart from Gage, of course, the crazy fuck he was. I purposely didn't stare at the man behind me.

"You men, you're all so desperate for validation for your manliness that you seek out women you think need saving. Fashion them into damsels who need their dragons slayed. Have you ever thought for a moment we could slay our own fucking dragons?"

I pointed to Gwen. "This bitch shot a fucking psychopath *three times*, and then gave birth moments after doing so. With no anesthesia. That's not even mentioning all the shit she survived before that."

I pointed to Amy. "She managed to somehow come out with a soul and a sense of humor when it sounds like her parents did the best to suck both out. Then she survives not one but *two* kidnappings, *and* a punctured artery."

My eyes went to Mia. "She got knocked up at fifteen, by another psychopath drug dealer kingpin maniac. Gets beaten within an inch of her life, while nine months pregnant, but manages to survive that and deliver the baby. Then escapes said psychopath to raise her daughter, give her a home and love when she had nothing. Sixteen years on, she faces him again and manages to make it through the other side. Now her kid is a fucking famous rock star who will support her in her old age."

My eyes rested on Lily. They got a little misty but I managed to keep my steam. "This one," I whispered. "She struggles with a demon more ferocious than any of you have ever seen. One you'll never see because it only exists inside the mind. She conquers that on her own. Then finds her way to untie herself and drag my bleeding old man out of a *burning fucking building* and saves his life."

I tore my gaze away to focus on Gabriel, who was regarding me intently.

"Something I'll be forever indebted to her for." With effort, I looked around the room. "Sure, you muscled brutes may have had a small"—I held my thumb and forefinger inches apart—"hand in that, but it was mostly the chicks who bore the brunt of the horrors. And are still standing. Laughing. And wearing fucking heels. You'll never know that pain either." I paused. "So how about you stop treating us like we're made of glass, because here you've got living, breathing, glittering proof that we're not glass. We're diamonds, and we're fucking unbreakable."

All the men were glaring at me by the end of my speech, and all the women were grinning. Wide.

I ignored all of it. "Now, if you'll excuse me, I'm going home to watch *Women Who Kill* and eat frozen pizza." I glanced around the room. "I'd advise you to free up some time in your weightlifting, steel-eating schedule to give it a watch. It'd prove educational so you can see what might happen if you do something like, I don't know, try to 'lock down' a woman who spent three fucking weeks in chains and isn't looking to spend two more fucking seconds in them."

On that, I turned on my heel and walked out. I realized mid-storm out that I'd come on Gabriel's bike and didn't actually have a ride.

"Shit," I muttered under my breath. Asking for a ride would seriously mess with the badass vibe I had going. Maybe I could hotwire a motorcycle. I hadn't driven one before, but I was guessing it couldn't be that hard.

"Okay, I'm going with her," I heard Amy's declaration from behind me.

"Fuck, Sparky," Brock growled.

"I'm totally going too. She had me at frozen pizza," Mia's voice chimed in.

"Jesus, Mia, don't you fuckin' dare," Bull warned.

"Love you too, honey," she called.

I grinned and stopped.

Amy caught up with me. "Movie night?"

"Sounds good."

So that's how we ended up crowding Rosie's living room watching serial killer documentaries while Rosie was noticeably absent.

LUCKY

"Jesus, brother, your woman...." Brock shook his head, rubbing his hand against his mouth. "Fuck, I thought I had the one with the most fire, but she's givin' Sparky a run for her money," he exclaimed.

Lucky didn't smile. "I fuckin' know," he muttered. All that shit Becky had said? In front of his brothers? Pissed him right the fuck off. And turned him right the fuck on. And made him proud as punch all at once. All the while fighting that shit that lurked in her eyes as she spoke of dragons and diamonds. Because he saw it. She was fighting the pull of that fuckin' room, and she was winning. He was proud, but he also hated that she even had to fight.

Cade leaned forward. "We owe your woman a lot. I owe her a lot. My sister...." He visibly flinched. "Shit would have gone fuckin' dark if she hadn't stepped in."

"Stepped in?" Gage repeated. "The bitch fuckin' ran into the fire to save Rosie."

The thought chilled Lucky. To the core. His woman, so fucking fearless. Dauntless. He was terrified it'd be the end of her. And him.

On that poisonous thought, Cade spoke.

"We need to up our efforts to find and exterminate these swine. This was close to home. Far too fuckin' close. No one hits us where our families walk and lives to tell about it." He looked to Bull. "We got any more on Devlin?"

Bull shook his head. "Nothing from our end. Info Tucker gave us? Old and useless. This Devlin fuck was smart enough to cut off everything the Tuckers had on him. Must have known about our meet."

"Fuck," Cade bit out. He looked to Jagger, who was there temporarily until they fought this shit. "Your charter got anything on him?"

Jagger shook his head. "All smoke and mirrors. Sorry, brother."

The lack of info had Lucky set to explode when Wire entered the room.

"You better have some fuckin' good news, kid," Cade gritted out.

Wire looked up from the laptop. "Does the location of Dylan Tucker count as good news?"

The whole table stilled.

Simultaneously, Lucky and Gage grinned.

••••

His screams of pain were like a lullaby. Music to his fucking ears. The blood on his hands was exquisite.

"Brother," Gage brought him out of his happy place. That being slowly killing Dylan Tucker.

Cade had a turn, obviously. And they'd tried to get info on Devlin or Carlos. He had none. They were sure of that.

So now it was just the killing to be done.

He glanced up, his eyes unseeing. "What?" he hissed.

Gage nodded to the door. "She's here."

Lucky immediately found his lucidity. His brothers hadn't exactly been on board with him bringing Becky to this little party—he was sure the words 'fucking insane' had been used—but he'd persuaded them.

Gage had volunteered to get her.

Lucky's jaw had stiffened slightly at that, but he let him. Namely because he had a dragon to feed and he begrudgingly knew the connection the two of them had. He didn't have to like it, which he didn't, but he understood it. He was a selfish fuck, wanting to share every connection possible with her. Fuck, he'd even shoot up just so he could have that, know what she was craving. But then that was a little crazy, even for him.

So he indulged in his drug of choice, blood and revenge.

He'd known Becky would need it, to see it being done. His brothers couldn't understand it because their women were different. They were strong, fuckin' strong. They'd danced with the darkness but they hadn't become it, not like Becky.

So she needed this.

"Hold this." He handed Gage his bloody knife, wiped his hands, and went to the door to the warehouse, rented for that purpose. Though it hadn't gotten much use since they'd gone legit. It hadn't been desolate—they were still fuckin' Sons—but the stains on the floor weren't as fresh as they used to be.

The bitter air swarmed him as he opened the door, as did the smell of smoke. He frowned at the light in the darkness and snatched the smoke from Becky's mouth, stubbing it under his boot.

"Hey," she protested.

He stood in front of her. "Those kill you, you know."

She jutted her chin out. He could see her fire, even in the darkness. Fuck, it shone the brightest in the darkness. "So does breathing," she countered.

He shook his head. "Well, I'm not too hot on anything that opens up the prospect of me losing you prematurely. I'm kind of fond of you," he said, his face close to hers.

He heard her breathing quicken. "Ditto," she whispered. Then she pulled her head back, squinting at the building. "You said you're fond of me, but is that all just a ruse to get me here and murder me? I promise I won't tell anyone about the Brony thing."

He shoved his hand over her mouth, forgetting what was on it for a second. "Be quiet, would you?" he snapped.

As soon as he realized where his hand had been, he ripped it from her beautiful skin.

She rubbed her face. "Is that blood?" she asked evenly.

"Fuck," he cursed, reaching into his pocket to retrieve a bandana to wipe her face. When he was done, he clasped her neck. "I've only got you here because I know your monsters are fuckin' ferocious, babe. Because I know they can't be fought with happy thoughts and rainbows. They need to be fought with monsters." He paused. "I know you think they don't exist, but I disagree. The one in there?" He nodded to the building. "He ain't human and he ain't going to die like one. You got a choice. You can go in there, step further into the black, and I'll follow you without hesitation." He tightened his grasp on her neck. "Or you can get on the back of my bike and we'll leave it, monsters and all. Your call."

There was no hesitation. She stepped out of his grasp and into the dark.

BECKY

Blood had a smell. People who'd seen a lot of it would tell you. Their descriptions may differ, but it was unmistakable. As soon as I stepped into the warehouse, I was assaulted with the metallic, bitter twang.

I welcomed it.

It was the smell of justice. Probably not the kind sanctioned by the state, or even conventional society, but whatever.

Gabriel's hand was firm in mine as we walked over to where the big men in cuts were standing.

They turned, all regarding me with expressionless faces. Apart from Gage, who grinned.

My attention didn't stay on him for long, instead going to the bloodied, battered lump that was tied to a chair.

Dylan.

I thought I'd be a vengeful cold bitch when I saw him, but in those first few seconds, I struggled to breathe. He may have been touching death right then, but his mere presence had me hurtling back into that room.

Gabriel's squeeze on my hand brought me back out.

"Becky," he asked, his voice taut.

I met his eyes. "I'm fine."

I was reluctant to do it, but I stepped out of his grasp. He tightened his hand in mine once more before he let me go. I held my hand out to Gage.

He didn't even hesitate in handing me the stained blade. Brock raised an eyebrow but said nothing.

DAUNTLESS

I silently walked over to the lump in the chair, my boots echoing on the concrete. I didn't even pause as I brought the knife down right between his legs, leaving it there for a second then yanking it back out.

I barely acknowledged the animal scream before I turned my back on him.

All of the men were gaping at me. Well, apart from Gage, who was still grinning. Gabriel's eyes were shimmering with a lot of things. Things not to inspect in the blood-filled warehouse.

I walked past them, handing the blade back to Gage. "As you were, boys."

I clutched Gabriel's red-stained hand. "Take me home," I whispered.

He didn't say a word, just squeezed my hand and nodded.

And then I left it behind.

What I could, at least.

••••

We didn't speak until we got home. That's what this was—my home. Not the four walls, though they were comforting. No, it was him. The biker in the middle of the room, staring at me with concern and pride and most likely struggling to fight his own monsters now that I'd quieted mine.

Not that he said anything—that guy was a fucking fortress—but I could sense it.

I stepped close to him, my body brushing his. "I almost died today," I whispered.

He held himself rigid. "Don't fuckin' remind me." His hand was featherlight on my forehead, which barely even throbbed. Mostly because my heart was pounding and drowning everything else out.

"I'm addicted to you," I whispered. "And it's worse than any drug I've craved because that was a choice. Not the addiction and everything that came with it, but I knew what it meant and what the consequences could be. And I still chose." I paused. "With you, it wasn't even a choice. It was addiction before I even knew you were another substance I could abuse. And I'm scared. I'm fucking terrified because it hurts worse than any chemical and the high is so much higher. I'm scared of the overdose, the crash back down to earth. But mostly I'm scared of the withdrawal if I ever lose you. Because I survived heroin, but I couldn't survive a life without you." My admission had me arguably more terrified than I had been in a long time. Maybe not more terrified than I had been *then*, but it was a different kind of fear.

Gabriel's eyes were glittering with depth I could drown in. "Fuck, Becky," he murmured, holding my body close. "You're never going to lose me. Fuckin' never," he promised.

I moved my hand to trail his jaw. "I don't want to think about it. Any of it. Death, monsters. I want to forget and just *live*."

His eyes flared with hunger and unease as he immediately understood my words, the suggestion in my tone. "Fuck, babe. You sure?"

I tried to swallow the glass of his words. "If you don't want to...." I started to bring my hand down, shame filling me.

He captured my wrist. "I fuckin' want to," he growled, his voice rough with desire. He brought my hand to his mouth. "I wake up wanting you, Becky. I go to sleep wanting you and everything in between. I want you." He paused. "But I want *you*. Not for your body or for what you can do with it. Just you. And when you're ready, I'll take your body."

"I'm ready," I whispered through the roar of my pounding heart. "Maybe not for everything we did before." My mind panicked at the image of cuffs, at being helpless as someone owned my body, even him, the one I'd given my soul to willingly. I couldn't do that. Not yet. "I just need to be in control."

He searched my face. "Yeah, you do," he agreed. He laid his mouth against my hand once more before dropping it. "Stay there," he ordered.

I did as he asked, mainly because I couldn't move. A rabbit stuck in the headlights. Frozen with the prospect of what I was about to do. With fear—there was a lot of that. And excitement, arousal, something I didn't think I'd ever feel again.

It was like I was a teenager on the brink of her first time. Or how they were supposed to feel on their first time.

He came back and every ounce of excitement left as I saw what was in Gabriel's hands, the ones still stained with the faded pinkness of blood. Ice rushed over my body.

His jaw was hard as he immediately gauged my reaction. "Easy," he murmured, cupping my face. "Look at me," he ordered.

Through labored breaths, I did.

"You're safe with me. Always," he promised.

I let the warmth in those hazel eyes chase the cold away.

"You need to have control? I'm giving you that. Complete control over this, over me. Though you don't need these for that." He pressed the cuffs into my shaking hands. "It's to show you I'm at your mercy, baby, though I've been there since the moment you took the stage." His mouth brushed against mine as he spoke.

Then he kissed me. Long and slow and gentle. Nothing like before. He let me lead. Let me get my feet back.

And before I knew it, I was so hot I could barely remember the ice anymore.

Through my haze, a thought came to me. I reluctantly pulled back from his lips and I saw he felt the same about the loss as I did. But he didn't move. He held himself tight, the veins in his neck pulsing.

"I've got an idea," I murmured.

"Please don't say Scrabble," he rasped.

I choked out a laugh, then nodded to his dining room chair. "Sit," I ordered.

Without hesitation, he did so, though his gaze stayed locked on me. It ate me up. Consumed me. And it was so full of heat and hunger it didn't tarnish me. It gave me power.

I wanted more. More of that foreign yet familiar feeling of power. What I'd been searching for when I tried to take the stage again.

I moved to his stereo system and plugged my phone in. Scrolling through, I found the perfect tune. Led Zeppelin's "I Can't Quit You Baby" started to play through the speakers.

Dangling the cuffs in my hands, I sauntered over to him, leisurely and unhurried, finding it. My strength.

"I think I had the right idea," I purred, leaning over to clasp

Gabriel's muscled arms behind the chair. He sucked in a breath as I rubbed my chest against his face, my nipples standing to attention the second they made contact. "Trying to find my control by doing what I used to do." There was a metallic click as I fastened his hands and stepped back from him.

He groaned in frustration, his expression cloaked in desire.

I started to move, unbuttoning the top of my shirt. "The stripping, I mean," I continued. "Reclaiming ownership of what was mine in front of an audience." I kept unbuttoning until I reached the bottom, letting the shirt fall to the floor so I was in the lacey bra and my jeans and combat boots.

Gabriel's hiss penetrated the air.

I grinned slyly. "But I think I had the wrong audience. The wrong stage." Instead of taking off any more, I stopped moving and slid my boots off, kicking them to the corner of the room.

The bass thumped and I moved with it, finding rhythm with my body once more, finding the tune when it had been so out of sync.

"The only audience I need, the only person I need to show the ownership of this?" I trailed my finger down my chest, between my boobs and down to the button of my jeans, undoing them. I glanced up, playing with the waistband of my jeans. "He's sitting in that chair." I stepped forward and touched my finger to his shoulder, trailing my hand over the letters on his cut as I circled the chair. I stopped behind him, circling my hands down his arms, tracing the ink and touching where the cold steel met his blazing skin. I bent down, past the skull on his neck so my mouth brushed his ear. "You know who owns this body?" I whispered, pressing my breasts to his back. "Me," I answered, biting his earlobe.

He let out an incomprehensible grunt as I pushed away and circled back to his front.

I stood in front of him, my hands going to my waistband. His eyes were brands, glued to my body. Slowly, I pulled the jeans down my legs until they were gone and I was standing in front of him in my bra and panties.

I lost it there, a little of my bravado.

Okay, a lot of my bravado. This was the most I'd shown to anyone since *then*. The skin that was now becoming foreign thanks to the ink I was covering it with was still the same underneath, and I felt a terrible sense of panic at exposing it once more.

Gabriel didn't look at my body, his eyes on mine. "You're beautiful," he grunted out.

With those two words, so simple, yet containing so much, I found it again. I leaned forward, my face going to his, and he hissed through pursed lips, his restraint. "This is mine. And it's yours." I pressed my lips to his, tasting the nirvana of our kiss. "Whatever there is left to give, to own, you have," I murmured as I pulled back.

"Everything," he rasped. "You've got everything left to give."

I leaned back, my eyes not leaving his. I didn't say anything to that; instead, I showed him what I had. My hands went to my bra, letting it fall to the floor. Then it was time for my panties. I sucked in a breath and stepped out of them.

There I was.

Naked.

In every way I could be.

And I was terrified.

My eyes met his. I was terrified, but I was safe.

I padded forward, my thighs on either side of the chair.

"Fuck, Becky," Gabriel hissed.

I leaned down to his jeans to unbutton them, my hand shaking as arousal pulsed through my body.

He grunted when I freed him, when I stroked my hand down his smooth skin.

All the while I was looking at him, into the gaze that had turned feral with desire. I had to stay anchored with his eyes in order not to wander from that room. Get taken back into the past. So I kept his gaze as I lowered down.

"Becky," he hissed. "Are you ready for me?" His voice was almost unrecognizable with desire, but the concern was evident.

He was worried. Because it had been a while and there had been no foreplay. But there had. I was primed.

"I'm ready."

Then I lowered myself onto his lap, guided him inside. We both sucked in breath at the same time. My body both rejoiced and revolted at the intrusion. The feeling of fullness.

It was a battle between the pleasure and the pain. The wrong and the right. Because the corners of my mind danced with demons, with the feeling of filth that came with his intrusion.

"Becky?"

I blinked the demons away.

And I won.

Just like that.

I still felt filthy at the edges, but I could handle it. It mingled with the pleasure and gave me something new, something that was so good it was bad. So evil it was good.

"I'm good," I whispered.

Then I moved.

And it was beyond anything.

Because I had control. I found it. I owned my body.

But Gabriel owned my soul.

The good, the bad, and the ugly.

TWENTY-SIX

"Revenge is never stupid, darlin'. It's the single most satisfying thing in the world."
-JR Ewing

THREE WEEKS LATER

I was driving, so I didn't pay attention to the number on the screen until I answered it.

"Don't hang up" was the first thing Nat pleaded.

I was tempted, sorely tempted. One of the rules of the meetings Gage and I went to every week was not to associate with people from your old life. The toxic people. It was safe to say I hated rules, but this one kind of made sense. Hanging with the girl who introduced me to sex, drugs, and destruction wasn't high on my to-do list. But I hesitated because, despite that, Nat was a friend. A kindred soul. She had her own shit she was running from. She wasn't a bad person. Most drug addicts weren't *bad* people. Mostly they were normal people who made a lot of bad decisions.

"Give me one reason why I shouldn't," I said.

"Because I know where Carlos is."

I slammed on my brakes so hard I almost smacked my head on the steering wheel. Luckily there was no one immediately behind me or my shitty car most likely would have fallen apart around me.

I guessed that was why it was against the law to talk on the phone and drive. Made sense now.

I pulled to the shoulder and didn't miss that my constant shadow did the same. I was surprised he didn't rear-end me.

"What?" I hissed, once I was safely stationary.

"I know what he did to you and that your boyfriend's club has pretty much scorched everyone who had a hand in taking you right off the face of the earth."

She was right. I'd seen some of their handiwork up close and personal. Got my own hands dirty. With the good kind of dirt.

Things had calmed down a little since the whole car bombing thing, but everyone was on high alert. Gabriel called me about a thousand times a day, plus visited the club multiple times, despite the fact he had someone 'on me' whenever he wasn't 'on me.' Which was, since that night, a lot.

I wasn't entirely back to myself sexually, and the prospect of the cuffs still sickened me, but that didn't mean I didn't indulge in my addiction daily. Multiple times every day.

The cuffs were still used. It seemed my dominator sure liked me rendering him helpless.

I kind of liked it too.

I didn't like being followed everywhere and having my whereabouts known every second, but Gabriel was concrete on that score.

Carlos and that Devlin guy were still on the loose, which pissed Gabriel right off. Understatement of the century. I wasn't too hot on it either, but I was trying to live my life. The one I was just getting back. And actually liking.

So obviously this had to happen.

"And I hate him for what he did to you," Nat continued on a whisper. "And for what he's doing to everyone else."

I didn't miss how her voice shook. "Everyone else?"

"Yeah. He's making sure all his girls are soliciting and hooked on drugs." I heard a sniff on the other side of the phone. "He owns us, Bex. And I don't want anyone to own me anymore. So I thought if I told you where he was, your boyfriend and his club...."

I didn't miss her meaning.

"Where is he?" I snapped.

"Aimless," she whispered, referring to the bar which had been my old haunt. "He's only with one other guy. Tyson, I think."

"Okay." I was about to hang up when I stopped. "Nat, he doesn't own you. Neither does that shit you put in your body. *You* own you."

And then I hung up.

I checked my bag for my gun.

Satisfied, I pulled back onto the road.

In the direction of Aimless.

LUCKY

He glanced down at his phone and shook his head. "No, Skid, you do not have to drink a gallon of Gatorade if Becky tries to make you. You have to wait until I'm there to watch."

Gage grinned.

Since Skid had been tailing Becky and she'd been very vocal about how she felt about it, she made it her personal mission to torture the poor guy enough to run from her.

The opposite was happening. Lucky reasoned the fuck would still follow her around even if he stopped ordering him to. She had that about her.

That spirit. It was coming back. Coming back stronger than ever.

The fact his wrists were slightly sore was testament to that. His dick hardened at the memory.

It took three words to chase that hard-on away.

"We've got trouble," Skid yelled, obviously on his bike.

His blood ran cold and he burst up from his chair, spilling his beer in the process. "Where is she?" he demanded.

"Currently? She's driving, and we seem to be going in the direction of Aimless."

"Are you fucking kidding me?" he roared. "Stop her."

"Unless you want me to make her crash her car, I kind of can't."

"Fuck!" he yelled, swiping a glass so it shattered on the ground. "We'll be there in twenty. Do not let her set foot in Aimless."

He put the phone down and both Asher and Gage stood in front of him.

"We got trouble," he declared.

Gage rubbed his hands together. "Good."

BECKY

The second I pulled into the parking lot, a bike roared in beside me. Skid was up in my face as soon as I climbed out of my car.

I gripped the gun inside my bag. "Get out of my way, Jason," I gritted out.

He didn't move. "I can't let you go in there."

"You don't *let* me go in anywhere. I'm a grown woman. I go where I please."

"Yeah, but you going in there?" He nodded to the abandoned-looking bar. "It's not smart."

"I'm not smart. I'm angry. And an angry woman is dangerous. I don't want you to bear the brunt of that, but I will shoot you in the kneecap if you don't move," I threatened, unearthing my gun.

He must have gauged my threat because he stepped back. "Fuck," he muttered, pulling out his own gun.

I raised a brow. "I didn't ask you to come in."

He stared at me. "If I don't, your old man is gonna shoot me, and not in the kneecap."

I squinted at him. He was serious, and I didn't doubt Gabriel might do it. "Well, I'm kind of fond of you, so alrighty then, let's go."

I didn't think much as I was walking through the desolate gravel parking lot. In fact, I didn't think at all.

It was empty apart from my car, Skid's bike, and a black town car I recognized.

So I knew what to expect when I burst through the open door. Carlos, leaning against the bar, drinking from a glass and chatting with Tyson.

They both turned as we walked in and I didn't even falter, just kept walking even as Tyson raised his gun.

There was a loud boom from beside me that had my ears ringing. Tyson crumbled to the ground.

I stepped over him with little effort, and, like I'd practiced it, lifted the gun and squeezed.

The glass in his hand smashed to the floor.

In the movies, revenge came to a big crescendo, a climactic moment full of the action and drama you'd been waiting for since it all started.

In real life, unsurprisingly, it's a little different.

It was over quickly with little to no drama. Or action. I guessed it depended on the situation. It lasted twenty seconds. Less.

Shit, Carlos was still holding his glass when I shot him.

My shaking hand dropped the gun so it landed next to his body. The one missing half its head.

I shot him.

The sound still rang in my ears.

"Shit," Skid whistled as he came to stand beside me.

"Yeah," I agreed.

He stared at the slightly headless body I'd created.

"You ever shot anyone before?"

"Nope," I said, making a soft popping sound on the *p*.

"Me neither." His voice didn't shake or anything, but there was an edge to it. The same edge I had to mine.

"I have killed someone before," I continued casually.

"Oh yeah?"

I nodded. "But he deserved it."

"So did he." He nodded to the body.

"Yeah. He did."

A heavy silence cloaked the room, not just the silence of death but of being the dealer of that death.

It didn't feel nice. Or good. But I felt less... dirty. Cleansed, somehow. Which was ironic, considering murder wasn't cleansing. It was a sin. And against the law. Though murder was concerning humans. I put down an animal. A feral one at that.

"Scott," he said, the word harsh on the soft silence.

I turned my head to regard his profile.

He met my eyes. "That's my name," he clarified. "I figure it's time you knew it, since we, you know, just killed people together."

"Scott," I repeated. "Are you fucking kidding me? I got it the first time. You nutcase, why didn't you tell me?

He shrugged. "Was kind of funny. Hearing you come up with stupid names." He paused. "And then after what *they* did." He nodded to the body. "It seemed to distract you, kind of bring that part of you back, remind you of yourself. Couldn't exactly take that away."

Wow.

His name was Scott and he was awesome.

I reached out and grasped his hand, squeezing it. He squeezed back.

And... nothing. Nothing apart from his warm, slightly clammy grip.

No dirt. No ice. Just peace.

Then the doors burst open and the peace was shattered.

"Becky!" Gabriel growled, his voice low and dangerous.

Both of us whirled around and watched Gabriel, Gage, and Asher survey the room.

Only Gage smiled. Obviously.

Asher's eyes went to the bodies, then me. "Oh fuck," he muttered.

Gabriel's eyes did the same thing, though that was while he stormed over to us. His eyes were so feral, his body so tight, that Scott stepped in front of me as if to protect me.

He crumpled to the ground about two-point-five seconds later when Gabriel put his fist through his face.

I gaped at Scott's unconscious body. "That was so not cool," I shouted at him.

He grabbed my shoulders and shook me. Roughly. Enough so my teeth chattered together. "Are you fucking insane?" he roared.

I waited for the shaking to stop. I wasn't scared, though his fury was something to behold. I knew he wouldn't go further than that. And he didn't, stopping almost as soon as he started.

"I'm not insane," I answered slowly. My gaze flickered to Gage, then back to him. "Especially not when compared to current company."

Gabriel gritted his teeth. "You think this is a fuckin' joke?"

Ironic that the man who used to laugh about everything, failed to find the humor in this situation. Granted, there wasn't much.

I didn't lower my gaze. "No, I don't think it's a fuckin' joke. I think this is life. Which is really the biggest joke of all, but I'm not in the mood to talk philosophy." I sucked in a breath. "I'm in the mood for revenge, and a taco. But the former was better."

Gabriel gaped at me. "And you thought comin' here, without fuckin' telling me, or anyone else, not letting us take care of it, was a suitable form of fuckin' revenge?" His grip tightened on my shoulders.

I jutted my chin up, not caring about the audience of Gage, who was kicking at a body with his boot, or Asher, who was talking on his phone, using the word 'cleanup.' "I'm not going to sit here like a little lady while the 'men' do the 'man's work' of exacting revenge. I'm not entrusting *my* revenge in someone else's hands, no matter how muscular the arms attached to them are." I regarded him evenly. "It happened to *me*. They took everything from *me*. Whatever shreds of my soul I had left, they tattered. I'm not letting someone else take care of the punishment for that theft. I'm going to be doing that myself. I'm going to make sure I take everything from them too, and I'm going to make sure I leave nothing." I looked around. "Maybe the way you're used to doing things is letting the man take the gun and do the shooting. I'll tell you now, that's not what's going to happen here. I may have a kick-ass manicure, but that doesn't mean I'm not afraid to get my hands dirty, to get them bloody. To squeeze some triggers."

He stared at me a long time, then down to the body at our feet.

"You got this?" he asked Gage and Asher.

Gage nodded.

"Good. Take care of Becky's car." His eyes went back to me. "We're leavin' now."

He didn't really give me a chance to say anything before he just dragged me out. I didn't protest because the smell of blood was starting to get more than a little sickening. That and the fact I'd spilled that blood.

Twice. I'd done that twice.

I chewed over that thought the entire ride home, wondering what that made me. I'd killed two people. Evil people, yes. But two wrongs didn't make a right, or whatever. But they wouldn't hurt another girl or woman now, and I was pretty sure that was right.

As soon as we pulled up at our place, Gabriel yanked me off the bike and pulled me inside.

He slammed the door and started pacing. Then he stopped. "How did you know? Where he was?"

"Nat called me," I said.

His eyes were dark. "And it didn't occur to you that it could've been a fuckin' trap? That they weren't waiting for you to get there so they could take you away? Away from me, from everything, for fuckin' good?" he asked.

I scrunched up my nose. "Not at the time."

He did make a good point. I guessed I was lucky.

"I didn't think of anything, really. Apart from the fact he was still breathing. Polluting the earth with his presence. Hurting people. Then all I thought was how good it would be if he weren't breathing. That maybe it might make me breathe a little easier."

Gabriel stepped forward and yanked me into his arms, all brutality gone. "You're fearless, babe. So fuckin' fearless that it scares the absolute shit outta me. You lay your life on the line for your friends in an instant. Without hesitation. Run in front of fuckin' bombs for them. I need you to have that hesitation, Becky. I'm proud as fuck that my girl's so fearless. But I need you to feel fear at the possibility of leaving this world. Leaving me."

I blinked away my tears, everything that had happened hitting me in one fell swoop. "Don't you see? Up until recently, death was the one thing I didn't fear. It was *life* that scared the shit out of me. No one would care whether I lived or died. Only me. That's Darwinian, ingrained into our psyches, as a survival instinct. I didn't want to die. But I wasn't afraid of it. If it came, it came. I don't think about the future."

His hands circled my neck. "Firefly, there's so much wrong with that it breaks my heart to hear those words. If I could find fuckin' *Doctor Who* I'd steal that fucker's Tardis so I could be by your side the moment life started dealing you those blows. I'd take them myself without hesitation." His hands tightened and his eyes twinkled. "But as much as it pains me to admit, *Doctor Who* is trapped in the world of TV and I've only got the future with you. The past, I can't change. The future, this present moment, is mine. *You're* mine. So I need you to hesitate. To think about the future. 'Cause someone cares if you live or die. A lot of someones, actually. But right now it's just me, pleading with you to have some self-preservation. Still be fearless, babe. Still be you. But be mindful of the fact that, if your light goes out, mine does too."

"I've got to be fearless," I explained. "If I'm not, it's surrender. It's weakness. They'll get me. Consume me."

"Who, baby?" he asked gently, stroking my spiky hair.

I met his eyes. "The demons. The ones I live with every day."

His entire body jolted as if I'd struck him, and he was silent for a long while. Then he grinned. It was small, but it was there. "Good thing you've got a scary-as-fuck biker as your old man, then," he told me. "I'm bigger, tougher, and a hell of a lot more attractive than any demon you can conjure up. I'll conquer them all, babe. If it takes the rest of my life, I'll do it. So you don't have to be fearless. I'll protect you, from everything. Even yourself. A little fear's good, firefly. Means you've got something to lose. If you've got something to lose, you've got something to live for. To fight for."

"I'll fight," I promised.

His nose brushed against mine. "Good," he murmured.

My eyes went hooded. "But right now, I don't feel like fight. I feel like surrender."

His body stiffened. "You mean what I think you mean?"

I nodded slowly.

He kissed me, slow and rough. "You scared?"

I nodded. "Terrified."

"One thing in this world you get to be dauntless with, baby, is me. This. Us."

He led me into the bedroom as he spoke, his eyes darkening as he did so.

His mouth captured mine once more. "Clothes off, now," he ordered.

The tone of his voice had me instantly wet, his eyes almost black as I stripped and stood naked in front of him. He didn't touch me, but the weight of his gaze was a thousand hands on my body. In a good way.

"On the bed." I did as he asked, watching as he shrugged off his cut and yanked off his tee. I drank in his body hungrily.

He rounded the bed slowly, lithely, like a panther. Opening the drawers beside his bed, he unearthed two sets of cuffs. Unease tainted the desire in his eyes. "You sure, Becky?"

"I'm sure."

I was, like eighty percent. But this was Gabriel. I was safe with him.

He nodded and bent down, but he didn't cuff me immediately. Instead, he kissed me, rough and brutal. Then he moved down, past my neck and aching nipples to my shoulder. He trailed kisses all down my arms until it was white-hot with his touch. That was when the icy steel encircled my wrist. I flinched at the click but managed to chase the ice away.

Gabriel's gaze burned into me as he climbed over my body to reach my other hand. He repeated the same process, trailing his other hand past my bellybutton to my magic spot. I cried out in pleasure as he clicked the second set of cuffs on.

He kept working me while he moved his mouth to my nipples, giving them the attention they yearned for.

On the edge of release, he stopped.

I wanted to scream in frustration at his wicked grin.

"You don't come on my hand," he growled. "You'll come in my mouth, and then around my dick."

He lowered his head and moved down. Slowly, to torture me. Then his lips fastened around my clit, working it relentlessly until reality become fluid and soft and I exploded into a million pieces.

My hands rattled against my cuffs as I struggled to touch him. Realizing they were bound, the ice came back.

Gabriel's body was on mine before it could settle and corrupt the moment. He clasped my neck. "Becky?" he rasped.

"I'm okay," I whispered.

His eyes searched mine. "Gonna fuck you now. Hard. Can you take me?"

My entire body twitched at the sex in his tone. "Yes," I breathed.

The word was barely out before he surged into me, his hands curling up with mine.

"Fuck," he growled.

Then he fucked me. Hard.

And it was brilliant.

Magnificent.

I never feared cuffs again.

TWENTY-SEVEN

"The enemy doesn't stand a chance when the victim decides to survive."
-Rae Smith

You'd think after committing murder life wouldn't start looking up. But since my life was upside down since the moment I was born, it did.

Every day wasn't better. Some days were worse, and I had to literally battle through the air like it was made of jelly. Had to constantly fight the temptation to find nothingness.

Not because my somethingness was bad.

Because it was good.

So good I couldn't understand it.

Couldn't breathe around it.

The good wasn't pure and white and sunshine. It was clouds, murky gray and polluted by the demons of before and memories of yesterday.

But I think that was better than any kind of pure goodness.

Because it was real.

Too real.

Which was how I found myself blowing off work in the middle of the day and searching for nothingness.

"A glass of your crappiest red, please," I said to Laura Maye, flopping myself on the barstool. I resisted the urge to lay my head on the bar and smack at it repeatedly.

Laura Maye was the woman from that day at the supermarket, the one who had grinned like a kid on Christmas as Gabriel dragging me away.

Rosie had introduced us.

Which should have said it all.

The woman, like Rosie, was insane.

Completely and utterly. Like Rosie, in the best way.

I could only do well around women who only flirted with sanity, never embraced it completely.

She raised a perfectly groomed eyebrow, though her face was kind. Even underneath all that totally amazing makeup, she managed to relay a variety of emotions. I dug that. If I had that much makeup on, I think my face would crack if I tried to mimic her look of concern and hesitation. Though, maybe that's exactly what I needed. The only thing I had was a heavy-handed kohl liner, my trademark. I'd been experimenting with toning down my mask, trying to let my real face peek out and not be shocked by it. It had been going well, until that day. It was a day when I was caught by surprise by the demons I thought I'd tamed. They'd shown up just to let me know how feral they were. So I needed more than winged eyeliner. I'd asked her to borrow her hot pink lipstick. You know, just to shake things up a bit.

"You sure about that, sweetheart? Considering your situation?" she asked, not unkindly.

I gave her a look. She obviously knew about my... situation. Nice euphemism for it. It was a small town, plus the biker circle was even smaller, and my kidnapping, rape, and rescue were not small news. Laura Maye may not have had an alpha biker claiming her and growling in monosyllables like the rest of the women did, she still had a weird place in it all.

"Oh it's not the wine I have a problem with. More so the heroin," I said, waving my hand dismissively.

The side of her face jerked as if a smile were growing there. She reached up for a glass and starting pouring. "Well, we don't sell that here, so you're safe," she deadpanned.

I gave her a jaunty smile, or what I hoped passed for one. Safe? Yeah right. I could be ten thousand miles from a needle and still sense its pull. I'd never be 'safe' from it. Never be free. I just had to learn to live with the chains. Accessorize around them.

"Plus, I think after what you've been through, not having something to salve the burn might just be cruel." She pushed the glass towards me and leaned forward. "We all need a little something to get us through the hardships that life throws at us, and babe, you've had a lot more than many."

I gulped my wine, needing it to anesthetize against the kindness.

"I'm sure there are many people out there who've had it worse. I'm still here." I shrugged.

Laura Maye didn't buy my nonchalance. I wasn't exactly convincing. "It's okay to not be okay, you know. To scream at the world and curse whatever may control us all for putting you in this situation. To fall apart."

I barely knew this woman, and the bitch part of me urged me to tell her to mind her own business and leave me to my own shit, but I didn't. Such naked kindness shouldn't be treated with vulnerability disguised as cruelness. I met her eyes.

"I'm already apart," I confessed. "A thousand little pieces rattling inside an obviously hot package." I grinned slyly. "I've already fallen apart. That was the easy part. It's putting myself back together that's the bitch."

Laura Maye blinked at me a couple times and then nodded, pouring herself a drink. "Don't I know it," she murmured, her tone hinting at the fact demons lurked behind the long mascara laden lashes. She clinked her glass to mine. "To putting ourselves back together."

"May we figure it out before we're fifty," I added.

She grinned and sipped her drink.

"There a reason why you're sittin' in here alone when you've got a very delicious biker sharing your bed?" she asked, her eyes going to the rest of the bar. It was pretty much empty since it was the lull between afternoon and evening. And it was a Wednesday afternoon. The place was still dope, and I had the feeling the people of the small town would filter in, plus the numerous tourists who headed for coastal towns this time of year.

I sighed, running my fingers up the stem of the glass. "I just needed a minute. A vacation from it all." I glanced up. "A vacation from a life that is actually just starting to get good again. Because I can't take all the good in one go, I have to escape and inject some of my bad into it, just to dilute it, so I don't overdose." I sipped the wine, for something

ANNE MALCOM

to do more than anything. "Am I completely fucked-up?" I asked.

She put her bedazzled hand on top of my chipped black nails. Something as simple as a touch from a stranger was something I could handle now. "Yes," she said. "Completely fucked-up," she clarified. "But aren't we all?"

I grinned at her.

Yeah, I liked her.

Spent the whole afternoon talking about everything and nothing, taking my little vacation. I left and my first glass of wine remained, unfinished and half full. I didn't need a substance to chase nothingness.

I needed my latest addiction.

One I didn't plan on kicking any time soon.

So I went home.

To Gabriel.

•••

"Shit, firefly, it's freezing. What are you doing out here when you should be in bed with me?" Lucky asked, rubbing my arms before yanking me into his warm embrace.

I keep my gaze upwards, smiling. "You weak-blooded Californians," I scoffed. "It's barely cold."

"I'm far from weak. Let's go inside right now. Arm wrestle," he challenged.

"Because challenging a woman who can't even do a push-up counts as a display of strength?" I asked in a serious tone.

The arms around me tightened. "How about I use my considerable strength in the way which God intended," he murmured.

I let out a chuckle and warmth pulled at my stomach as his hands delved into the front of my panties. I felt him harden at my back.

"First," he mumbled, kissing my neck, "you need to tell me why we're out here freezing our balls off."

I sucked in a breath as his hand pushed all the way in, cupping me. "Only one of us out here has balls," I whispered. "You're feeling the evidence of that right now."

Lucky chuckle and it vibrated in my ear. "Sounds like you're evading the question, firefly."

I sighed as he caressed me. "Sometimes I just need to look at the sky," I choked out. "See how big it all is. How small I am."

Lucky's hand stopped, his body stilling for a moment before he whirled me around, pulling our bodies flush together. "You're not small, Becky," he declared. "You take up my entire soul. You're far from small."

His words made my trampled heart flutter. "Small's good," I told him softly. "'Cause all of that up there"—I gazed up again—"that's all big, beautiful, magnificent. Infinite for all we know. It makes me realize how small I am. How small my problems are. My pain." I paused as his hands flexed. "Sometimes I need reminding. Sometimes I need to feel small."

My words hung in the night air and tumbled up to those very stars.

"I wish I could take that away," Lucky rasped finally, his voice tortured. "All that pain, all that shit that makes you need to feel small."

I reached up and stroked his head. "No you don't. Don't wish for that. Pain is who I am. It's who I've always been. Without it I wouldn't know who I'd be," I whispered.

Lucky leaned forward. "Mine," he murmured against my mouth.

I smiled a sad smile, even though he couldn't see it. "Don't you see? Loving you is the most exquisite pain of all."

His entire body stilled the moment the words left my mouth. That infinite silence stretched out once more, but it was charged with intensity that rivaled even the star's magnificence.

"You love me," he said, the softness of his voice seemed to boom through the open air.

Instead of running from the fear that came with that statement, letting it out into the world instead of holding it captive in my heart, I surrendered to it. To him. And the fear of loving him. "Yeah," I whispered. "I love you."

He yanked me close so our foreheads touched. "You love me," he repeated.

I swallowed. "Do I need to hit you on the side of the head? You're playing on a loop," I joked.

His thumb brushed my lips, silencing me. "No. I think I'm done." He paused. "Those words make everything we've been through a little softer at the edges. It'll never be okay, what happened to you, but at least something's okay. You and me, babe. The world may be fucked-up—shit, we may be more fucked-up than that twisted world—but that's okay 'cause you love me. And I love you. Fuck the rest of it."

I smiled through my tears. "Yeah. Fuck the rest of it."

He claimed my mouth in the moonlight, brutally and exquisitely. And I didn't feel so small anymore. In fact, the two of us felt larger than the entire universe.

He pulled back. "Now it's time for me to fuck you," he rasped.

And he did. And everything else melted away.

••••

In fairy tales, when the couple exchange the 'I love yous,' it's usually the signal for the world to become all bright and everything be okay.

We've established this isn't a fairy tale.

So it was only right for the world to turn darker, almost completely black after the 'I love yous'. One day after, to be exact.

We were lulled into a false sense of security, I guessed. Thinking that I'd put a bullet in Carlos's head and they'd scared off all but one mysterious player in the game that had almost beat me.

Almost.

I'd gotten all smug thinking I'd won. Or at least wasn't about to be beaten anytime soon.

Then it turned out that one mysterious player could indeed fuck it all up.

"You don't have to keep trailing me, you know," I informed Scott as we walked across the parking lot of the clubhouse. It was pretty deserted considering it was a Sunday and most of the big bad bikers were all whipped, having Sunday brunches or whatever.

"I do, and not just because Lucky tells me to and threatens my manhood if I don't," he replied. "And not just because I kind of enjoy the perks of hanging out at a strip club." He grinned and I rolled my eyes. "But 'cause Devlin's still out there. We might have eliminated all of his partners, and since you snipped our last loose end"—he grinned at me—"he's most likely crawled back into his cave by now, but there's still a risk. So I'm here."

I shrugged. "Your funeral when you die of boredom now that I'm not a junkie or stripper. My life is dangerously monotonous now."

He barked out a laugh. "Yeah. I doubt you'll be living anything close to a monotonous life when you're eighty."

He may just be right.

I was meeting Gabriel after work, as we planned on heading up to the cottage and escaping all the chaos on the outside to embrace our own.

Peace, for us, was a fantasy.

Who needed peace? It was far too boring.

On that note, there was a weird popping sound followed by a splattering of warm liquid on my cheek.

I turned, frowning.

"Scott, if you just—" I sucked in my words when my eyes landed on the air where Scott used to be. It was empty.

Because at my feet was Scott's body. Half of his head was gone.

I blinked down at it, frozen as I watched the blood spread from his skull to the edges of my boots.

These are new, I thought distractedly.

After a blinding white pain in my temple, I didn't think anything.

•••

I didn't wake slowly, or groggily. It was a snap, and then I was conscious. With a really bad headache.

My head lolled around a bit before I could make it stay in one place.

"Becky."

The voice snapped me back into the land of reality. The urgency in it. The panic.

I blinked. I was on a chair in the clubhouse, my hands bound behind my back uncomfortably.

That didn't matter.

What mattered was that Gabriel was in front of me, blood running down his head and gushing from a hole in shoulder. Yeah, a hole. A big one. The leather of his cut had been ripped through and the black was now maroon.

"Someone shot you," I exclaimed, my voice shaking. I glanced down at my boots. "Someone shot Scott too," I added, my voice small. My stomach roiled. "He's dead, though." I said the words, but I didn't believe them. He wasn't dead. Couldn't be. I just got hit on the head too hard. He'd be fine.

Gabriel's eyes hardened. "Becky," he clipped urgently. "Are you okay?"

I gaped at him. "You're shot, and you're asking me if I'm okay? Are you fucking insane? Wait, I know you are, and you're a tough man, but that"—I nodded to the wound—"is a bullet hole. You can't just rub some dirt on it."

He smiled weakly. "Yeah, you're okay."

"Why are we tied up?" I asked, slightly delayed.

His face went hard.

"I can answer that," a smooth voice exclaimed as a very expensive-looking loafer stepped in front of me. I gazed up at its owner, wearing an equally expensive-looking suit. A white suit.

"Let me guess: John Travolta, *Saturday Night Fever*?" I asked.

An alligator grin, all teeth and no humor. And promises to rip me apart. "I see the little three-week stay you had with my boys didn't do much good shutting that mouth." He shook his head. "You can't hire good goons these days. Can't even break a white-trash junkie."

"I'm going to fuckin' kill you," Gabriel roared, struggling against his bounds like a wild thing.

The man in front of me with the small beady eyes and a slick comb-over grinned but didn't look his way. "Oh no, I think I'm going to be the one to do that, considering I'm the one holding this." He waved a gun. "But first I'll make you watch while I kill this one." He lifted the gun to stroke my cheek. I flinched away from the cold steel but didn't lower my gaze. No way was I going to give in to the terror creeping up my throat. That's exactly what he wanted.

"I thought it would be poetic, to start with the couple I began this whole campaign with," he drawled, glancing to Gabriel, whose eyes were wild as he continued to struggle against his binds despite the fact blood was flowing freely from his shoulder. "I had wanted to start with the biker scum and his slut who killed my father, but I thought that'd be much too obvious. I needed you to think it was because of this particular junkie." He nodded at me.

"*Ex*-junkie," I corrected on a hiss.

He smiled at me. "My mistake." He tilted his head at me. "I didn't expect you to manage to get clean. To not overdose in some tragic end. That had been the plan." He reached into his pocket and before I even saw it, I knew what it was. It was like I could fucking smell it.

He regarded the syringe, twisting it between his fingers. "I guess I don't have to abandon the plan completely, even though you and your *brothers*"—he spat the word at Gabriel—"have retired all of my business partners." His gaze went back to me. "I'm a reasonable man. I like my plans. And it vexed me when you didn't go to plan. See, of everything that I thought could go wrong, all the chaos, I thought the junkie with childhood issues would be the surest thing. You'd be the biggest distraction so the entire club would be focusing on their bleeding limb and wouldn't notice when I came in and chopped the head off." He stepped forward, and the allure of what he held in his hand did the same. "But you were the thread that unraveled it all."

I sneered at him. "Well, I'm sorry I fucked up your little plan. I'll send a card to your funeral."

He smiled. "Still so sure, what, that your man will come and save you?" He glanced to Gabriel. The cords in his neck were almost exploding with the effort of his struggle, his helpless eyes on me. "Sorry, that's not going to happen. You're not getting saved."

I felt the ties at my hands give and I grinned. "No, I'm not," I agreed. "Because I'm saving myself." In one swift move, I lifted my arms. I had two options, snatching the gun or the syringe.

I took the syringe. And without hesitation, I plunged it into his neck.

He was taken by surprise, obviously not expecting a helpless woman, a junkie at that, to make such a move. He stumbled back, lifting his gun sluggishly.

ANNE MALCOM

"Becky, get out of the fuckin' way!" Gabriel roared.

Instead, I stepped forward and snatched the gun from his hand, unworried. It came easily as his eyes glazed over with the telltale effect of the high.

I lifted the gun and instead of holding it to his head, I moved downwards and pulled the trigger.

He crumpled to the ground, screaming soundlessly.

Happy that he wouldn't be causing trouble, I rushed to Gabriel.

"Stop moving," I snapped. "You're shot and bleeding."

I reached around to untie his binds, but they were zip-ties. He got the legit stuff; obviously the dickless dick hadn't worried about me getting out of mine.

"Knife, in my belt," he grunted.

I grabbed the dangerous-looking knife and moved to his back.

"Don't cut yourself," he warned.

I yanked it through the plastic, freeing his hands. "Yes, because I just overpowered a man who got the best of you but I'll cut myself on a knife," I snapped.

The second he was free he surged up, yanking me into his arms. "You okay, baby? You hurt anywhere?" His eyes went up and down my body.

I quirked a brow. "You're bleeding from a bullet wound. Take that question, flip it, and reverse it."

His jaw hardened. "I'm fine. It's a flesh wound."

"Yes, of course it is."

"You stole my part," he said, his eyes light.

"What part was that?"

He clutched my face. "The saving you part," he murmured.

I smiled against his mouth. "Yeah, well, maybe I can save myself."

"You can save us both, baby. But before I show you how fuckin' hot that is, we've got business."

His eyes went hard, granite, and he stepped back, taking the gun from my hands. He turned to the bleeding lump on the floor and started to circle him.

"You're going to die. But not yet. Not even in the near future," he told him. I doubted he could fathom his words as he was not only high but bleeding from a crotch bullet wound. "But it'll happen. I've got a brother who's so very anxious to meet you."

"Step away from him and put down the gun, Lucky," a voice said from the doorway.

Gabriel's gaze snapped up and he held the gun at the owner of the voice, lowering it immediately when he saw Luke. Or maybe when he saw Rosie standing beside him.

She gave me a grim smile. There was blood staining her white dress.

Not hers.

I paled.

She'd found Scott.

"Can't do that, Luke," Gabriel replied easily. "This swine"—he kicked who I deduced was Devlin—"is the reason Skid is dead. The reason Becky almost fuckin' *died*." His gaze flickered to Rosie, who was reaching into her purse. "Why Rosie was almost blown into a thousand pieces. So I suggest you leave, pretend you didn't see a thing."

Luke's jaw was hard. "My father may do that shit but not me. I can't turn a blind eye to this." His gaze flickered, like he was faltering in his resolve, but he didn't lower his gun. "Don't make me shoot you."

I glared at him. "Dude, in case you hadn't noticed, he's already been fucking shot," I snapped.

Rosie tugged on his shoulder. "Luke, don't do this. You know what he did. You know he deserves this. Just leave. Let us handle this," she said in a small voice.

Luke's gaze didn't lower, nor did his gun. "I can't do that, Rosie." His voice was losing some of its earlier iron, though. "I don't want to, but I'll shoot him if I have to. Arrest him."

Rosie nodded gravely. "Yeah I know," her voice was sad, resigned.

The she stepped into the line of fire. "But you won't shoot me." Her heels clicked as she moved forward, calmly retrieved her gun from her bag, and put a bullet in the man's head.

It was just like the anticlimactic moment at Aimless. 'Blink and you miss it' kind of action.

He stopped moving.

The silence that echoed through the room was deafening.

Rosie and Luke engaged in a stare-off, his horrified face locked on hers.

"Holy fuck," Gabriel muttered, eyes darting from Rosie to the body.

"You got that right," I muttered.

"You going to arrest me?" she asked, her voice even.

He shook his head, lowering his gun. Then he turned and walked out the door.

Rosie's glistening eyes followed his exit.

I had to get the skinny on that, but not with my man shot and a dead body on the floor.

"Rosie, you need to call the doctor and your brother," I ordered.

Rosie jerked out of her trance and nodded. "Yep. Got it." She unearthed her phone, stepped over the man she'd just killed like he was a downed log, and went to the corner of the room.

I turned to Gabriel, my hand on his shoulder. "Please don't die," I requested, my voice starting to shake. "I'm really fond of you."

He lifted his bloodied hand to cup my face. "Ain't going fuckin' nowhere, baby. Holding a very convincing reason to live right here."

"Fucking Hollywood," I muttered. "It tricked us. Before that it was books. But not real books. Shakespeare, Emily Brönte, they were all trying to tell us what a fucking tragedy love was, but somehow the Hallmark people made a miracle out of tragedy. Convinced us this love thing was something to strive for, to exist for. Told us it was beautiful thing that enriched your life, set your soul on fire. You know what? Your soul is the house your sanity lives in. So when love sets your soul on fire, it's burning your fucking house down. Hollywood doesn't tell you that. That the moment you love, your sanity goes up in flames."

"Baby, if I got you, I'm happy with insanity."

I rolled my eyes at him. "What are you talking about? You've always been insane. This isn't a change for you. It's *me* I'm worried about."

He gave me a warm look, one that hit my toes. Like we weren't standing in front of a body and he wasn't bleeding from a bullet wound. "You're trying to convince me of your sanity?" He chuckled, yanking me to his side so he could kiss my head. "Well, that's the beauty of insanity, firefly. No worries. We can just be happy in our padded cells with each other for company."

EPILOGUE

"That's the lesson of life, isn't it? It gives us one person who both shows us that true love exists and fairy tales don't."
-Leo Christopher

SIX MONTHS LATER

"I'm coming."

I folded my arms. "You're not."

His hazel eyes narrowed. "I thought we'd established the mutual need for hand-holding in these situations, and my required presence when a man has his hands all over my woman."

I cocked a hip. "Seriously? You're gonna play that card?"

He went for innocent. "What card?"

"The one that is guaranteed to piss me off because the notion of getting jealous over my *gay* tattoo artist is batty, even for you."

"Even for me? What's that supposed to mean?"

I rolled my eyes. "I'm going. You're not. End of."

"Try and go without me, see what happens," he challenged, an erotic glint in his eyes.

Despite my irritation, my downstairs area responded to that glint. I ignored it and grinned wickedly at him. "Oh, I'll see what happens when I go to the club party tonight and inform your brothers about your affinity for rainbow magic."

He gasped, putting his muscled, tattooed hand on his chest. "You wouldn't."

I cocked a brow. "Try me."

"You're meant to love me," he argued.

"All's fair in love and war," I responded, hitching my bag on my shoulder. I tried to go around him but he didn't move.

"You're evil."

"You love it," I shot back.

His eyes flickered. "Yeah, baby, I fuckin' do. And you'll get punished for using that against me," he promised, his voice velvet.

My stomach dipped. "I look forward to it."

Then I scuttled past him before I could forget the whole tattoo and let him cuff me to the bed and punish me right then and there.

Which was tempting.

Very tempting.

But I had plans.

A lot of them.

Finishing my sleeve was top of the list, and later in the week I had three assignments due. I was a procrastinator of the ninth degree so I was yet to start them.

Gabriel always scolded me for doing that and got all pissed and worried for my well-being when I didn't sleep for forty-eight hours and drank six coffees a day.

He was weird like that.

I was studying to be a social worker, planning on putting my experience to use. Instead of forgetting my dark past, I was going to utilize it to help little girls and boys who had the same start as me.

I would make sure they didn't have the same end.

Though, arguably, my end was not bad.

After that day in the club, it was. Bad, that is. Burying Scott was hard. Horrible. I'd never had many friends, so it hit me hard having to watch one be put in the ground. I had nightmares for months after that.

Gabriel was always there to chase them away, the ones that could be, at least. The ones that couldn't, he showed me how to live with them.

Rosie disappeared.

The day of Scott's death. Right after she'd called in the cavalry, she just slipped off. Gabriel and I had been kind of busy and hadn't noticed.

Cade flew off the handle, until he got a call that she was okay, just 'on vacation,' whatever that meant.

I thought it might have a lot to do with the look she'd shared with Luke and the shit that went down.

He didn't bother the club for the four months he stayed in town, not even a parking ticket.

Then he left.

L.A. was the rumor. I reckoned he was on the hunt. For Rosie. At least I hoped. I missed my friend. I wanted that insane chick to have her very own fucked-up happy ever after. And if it was with Luke, you could guarantee it'd be fucked-up.

I missed my friend but I had a lot more that were equally as crazy, in different ways. I found my place with them.

And two weeks ago, Gabriel slid a glittering black diamond on my finger. "You're not arguing with me on this or I swear to God I'll pay off a judge and let him marry us while I have you cuffed to the bed."

So I was engaged. We weren't married yet but Gabriel already had a black band tattooed on his left finger.

"You're meant to wait until it's legal for that," I pointed out, my voice shaky after he'd had it done.

He yanked me to his chest. "I'm an outlaw, baby. We spit in the face of laws."

So apparently, in outlaw world, we were already married.

Though Gwen, Lily, and Amy would have heart attacks if we didn't have the wedding. They were already planning it.

I had no input in anything, apart from the dress.

"Black?" Gwen had cried. "A black wedding dress?"

I nodded.

"But it's traditional to wear white."

I quirked my brow at her. "Babe, anything about me look traditional?"

She gave me a once-over and grinned. "You're right. Black is perfect."

So there was that.

I wasn't cured, or free. I still struggled every day. Had a standing date with Gage every single week to go to meetings.

I was seeing a shrink too. Lily had to half drag me to the office, but even someone as stubborn as me knew that having a panic attack at the sight of a stuffed fucking bunny meant I needed to subject myself to serious therapy.

I couldn't be afraid of fucking *bunnies.* So I went. And hated the first session. Hated that I spent half of it sobbing like an idiot, while Jonathan got his hands dirty reaching into my head. But I was getting used to it. Jonathan wasn't a bad dude either, as far as shrinks went.

I still had nightmares. Half of me was still cloaked in black. But I was learning to live with it. Embrace it.

Which was what I was doing at the tattoo parlor—embracing the last of it.

••••

"Finally," Gabriel bellowed as soon as I closed the door.

He almost pounced on me before I'd even put my bag down.

"Down, tiger. Did you get into the sugar while I was away?"

He ignored me. "Show me," he demanded.

Apparently I wasn't quick enough because he snatched my hand. Though his touch didn't match his impatience. It was gentle, unhurried, reverent.

He turned my arm over to reveal the last piece in my sleeve covering my forearm.

Gently, he pulled off the plastic wrap protecting the fresh tattoo.

Then he froze.

The last piece of my fairy tale was my prince charming. Of course, that's how they all ended, didn't they? The man coming in to save the day.

Though Rosie and I had kind of turned that one on its head.

Half of my tattoo was the chiseled jaw, floaty-haired, Abercrombie prince, riding his steed and brandishing a sword. The other half was a sharp-jawed, tattooed biker with no hair in sight. He wasn't riding a steed but a Harley, and his hands gripped a semiautomatic weapon instead of a sword. And no finery like the other guy. His leather cut was clearly visible thanks to the fact that Lex was a fucking magician.

He stared at it for five full minutes without saying anything.

"Does it hurt?" he asked finally, his voice thick.

I met his eyes. "Always," I whispered. "But it's the best kind of pain."

"That…. Am I the hero or the villain?"

"You're both," I replied. "And neither. You're my damnation and salvation. Because you didn't save me. I wasn't looking to be saved. But you gave me life. A home in the darkness. And in my opinion, that's better than any happy ever after anyone could ever get."

He pulled me into a savage kiss, proving for hours, and years, to come that he was in no way a hero. And that he was. My hero and my villain. My damnation and salvation.

And I was totally down with that.

THE END

They didn't live happily ever after because this isn't a fairy tale.
But they lived. With pain, suffering, and darkness.
And happiness, love, and laughter.
And, most importantly, each other.

ACKNOWLEDGEMENTS

Every book I write is only possible with the help and support from some truly special people I'm lucky enough to have in my life. Great solitude is needed to write a book, but love from family and friends is needed to finish it. To make it the best it can be.

This list will always begin with one of the most special people in my life. **Mum**, how lucky I am to have you. You've always been my biggest cheerleader and have believed in me even when I couldn't believe in myself. None of this would have been possible without you. You're my hero.

This book wouldn't be what it is without my wonderful team of betas. These special ladies helped to make this book what it is. **Ginny, Caro, Amy, Sarah**, and **Judy**... you are amazing. Thank you.

Andrea. Your strength amazes me, as does the utter depth of your kindness. You are a wonderful person and I treasure our friendship.

Amo Jones. The woman who supports me through everything and who totally gets my crazy. You're my soul sister and a truly talented human being.

And to **you, the reader**. Thank you. Thank you for reading my books. Thanks for every e-mail, comment, and review you give me. None of this would be possible without you.

Anne

Xxx

ABOUT THE AUTHOR

ANNE MALCOM has been an avid reader since before she can remember, her mother responsible for her love of reading. It started with magical journeys into the world of Hogwarts and Middle Earth, then as she grew up her reading tastes grew with her. Her love of reading doesn't discriminate, she reads across many genres, although classics like Little Women and Gone with the Wind will hold special places in her heart. She also can't get enough romance, especially when some possessive alpha males throw their weight around.

One day, in a reading slump, Cade and Gwen's story came to her and started taking up space in her head until she put their story into words. Now that she has started, it doesn't look like she's going to stop anytime soon, with many more characters demanding their story be told as well.

Raised in small town New Zealand, Anne had a truly special childhood, growing up in one of the most beautiful countries in the world. She has backpacked across Europe, ridden camels in the Sahara and eaten her way through Italy, loving every moment. For now, she's back at home in New Zealand and quite happy. But who knows when the travel bug will bite her again.

Made in the USA
Coppell, TX
23 December 2020